EYE BLEACH

PAUL E. CREASY

Book layout by www.ebooklaunch.com

ISBN-13: 978-0692103050
ISBN-10: 0692103058

"Be sober-minded; be watchful. Your adversary the devil prowls around like a roaring lion, seeking someone to devour." - 1 Peter 5:8

For S.O.L.O.M.L.

Preface

Sometimes the strangest seeds find a home in the most exotic soil and yield the most unexpected crops. Such is the case of this book, *Eye Bleach*.

In the summer of 2017, I read a fascinating article in the *Atlantic Monthly* about the daily life of Content Moderators at YouTube. The psychological toll inflicted on those who must sort through the daily barrage of uploaded filth, just to make the internet palatable to civilized society, is simply incredible. I had no idea. I thought, incorrectly it turns out, algorithms handled these things. They don't. Thousands of people are employed, to view unimaginable depravity, at no small cost to their psyche, just so we can be entertained by cat videos and other such diversions. We owe them all a great debt.

Another seed of inspiration for this story, completely unrelated to the trials of Content Moderators on the internet, comes from my late Uncle Ralph. He was a hilarious man, and, a Great Uncle, both literally (he was my Grandmother's baby brother) and figuratively (he was pretty great). Growing up, I spent every summer with he and his wife, my Aunt Gladys, in their Washington DC apartment. I have many fond memories of those times. Uncle Ralph and Aunt Gladys never had any children, so, I think I was sort of a surrogate grandchild to them. We all had a blast!

Uncle Ralph was a member of the 'Greatest' generation. Sadly, their kind is almost extinct now, and that generation's final passing will make our nation weaker. Like many of his generation, he was not particularly a 'man of his feelings'. Leo Buscaglia had not yet donned his trademark sweater and started hugging everyone. I, as a small boy, with an intense interest in history, of course asked him about his military service in World War II.

I knew from my Grandmother, Uncle Ralph fought in the 'Battle of the Bulge', so I was pretty relentless in trying to pry any information from him any chance I could get. It was not a subject he wished to discuss. As an aside, he once told me there are two types of veterans — those who never talk about the war and those who won't ever shut up about it. My Great Uncle was firmly in the first camp.

Uncle Ralph did talk about his army service in generalities, though, but every story he told was a funny one. He told tales of getting lost in France, losing his jeep and having to sleep in a barn. He told lots of stories about various poker games he won as well as his first taste of TRUE vermouth when he passed through Amiens. This led to him becoming a lifelong fan of the apertif. I have never known anyone with such a violent passion about the sublties of a cocktail mixer as him. As my wife can attest, this trait was passed on to me.

But he never told any combat stories. Those were the ones I really wanted to hear. No doubt, the stories of his time in France and Germany, which grew more ribald as I grew older, were all great, but I wanted some real G.I. Joe material. I wanted machine guns and Tiger tanks. I wanted flame throwers and live grenades tossed back into enemy lines. I wanted to hear about him bayonetting some crazed Nazi charging his trench. Whenever I would try and pry out some John Waynesque tale from him, he always just looked bemused and then would tell another joke.

Finally, after years of relentless, but subtle, badgering, I asked Uncle Ralph flat out what it was like during the Battle of the Bulge — no hedging or jokes, just the straight facts. I remember the afternoon vividly. I was seventeen years old. We were sitting in Poor Roberts bar in the Cleveland Park district of DC, a favorite hangout of his. He sighed, put down his scotch (a rare event) and looked me cold in the eye. He said it was so horrific, so terrible and awful, he had chosen to forget about it. He said his rational mind knew he was terrified during the battle, but, beg though I may, he had no more details to provide. He had scrubbed them all from his mind. When I asked him how he could purposefully forget such a traumatic event, he shrugged, picked up his drink, took a long sip and said, "Sometimes, you gotta do what you gotta do". He then winked and proceeded to tell me about the time he received some R&R in Paris for a whole weekend, and his buddy gave him fifty cartons of stolen Winstons from the commisary. That tale, X-rated in the extreme, could be the inspiration for an entire library of books!

Years later, and now sadly, several decades after his passing, I have often wondered two things. One, just how is someone capable of willing such a bad memory away? How is it possible? Obviously, the brain can be controlled, and as any trip to your local bookstore will show you, oceans of ink have been spilled detailing strategies for programming your own mind for success. Many books by Tony Robbins come to mind here. But, no doubt, those dark memories still lurk in the subconscious somewhere. For my Uncle Ralph, I am sure the effect of his suppression manifested itself elsewhere. After all, who considers beer a breakfast drink, and has the ironclad rule that all your beverages should darken as the sun goes down? Vodka at noon, brandy at three, scotch at five and, of course, bourbon at nine, right? Doesn't everyone's family have such a tradition?

The second thing I have always wondered is this: just what exactly happened to my Uncle Ralph during the war that was so horrible, so terrible, so soul-crushingly awful it would enforce a code of silence on him for fifty years and require a sea of booze to drown? I really would have liked to have known. Now that he has passed, I guess I will just have to wait and ask him when we meet again in the next world.

I hope you enjoy reading this novel as much as I did writing it. It is a strange tale and takes quite a few unexpected and dark twists; but I think you will find the journey interesting and worthwhile.

Chapter 1

April 13, 2017 - UVid corporate headquarters - Mountain View, California. - 10:30 AM

"SNICKERDOODLE?" PHIL BARTLETT asked as he cocked his head to the side. He was persistent at least, and especially pleading this time.

"No thanks, really," Sylvia Marstens answered as she gently shook her head. This little game had gone on for a while now. In fact, this Turret-syndrome-like request kept popping out of Phil's mouth at various points throughout the whole job interview which was fast approaching two hours now. It was still cute, in a boyish charm sort of way, but it still seemed a bit too much "on the spectrum" for her taste. *Computer people*, she thought, always the same story. Luckily, she was being interviewed by Phil and not the other way around. Interviewers can afford to be odd. Interviewees always must be on their best behavior.

This allusion to an endless "on-demand" candy benefit was intriguing, though, and just one of the myriad of fantastic perks in her potential new career. Several times during her interview she heard dogs barking from down the hall, an oddity to be sure. Knowing that UVid allows its employees to bring their pets to their office caused her to wonder how Snowy, her white Pomeranian, might react to joining Mommy at work. Knowing her dog's tendency for intense vocalization (e.g., barking), it might be on her shoulders that this policy gets scrapped. But…, perhaps not. Silicon Valley really is different than the rest of the world. And it is especially different from her very familiar East Coast world of Academia. No shower of Zagnuts or avalanche of M&Ms offered there; only burnt coffee and stale donuts on Fridays in the faculty lounge. Would her recently toned and slimmed thighs survive the allure of an endless cornucopia of chocolate on demand? She doubted they would, but, at least she would be able to work off any new layer of flubber in the world-class gym, complete with several paid full-time yoga instructors, UVid provided their staff. And they even had excellent dental coverage — amazing.

"I know," Phil said. "Clark Bar! That must be the ticket. You look like a Clark Bar kind of gal."

Sylvia smiled and shook her head. "I really am quite full from breakfast. The hotel you arranged for me has been just fabulous. They put out quite the buffet this morning. I can't remember ever seeing so many croissants."

"Rosewood Sand Hill is fantastic, isn't it?" Phil said as he smiled and leaned back in his chair. "We have our annual Christmas party there every year, and I have always loved the place. It is top shelf all the way. On a clear day, if you are standing at the ninth hole, and stretch your neck a bit, you can just catch sight of San Francisco Bay off in the distance. Beautiful."

"It is all so glorious," Sylvia said. "As is this whole UVid campus. I have been most impressed with the facilities. As a hopeless fan-girl of modern architecture, I have been blown away by this place." She smiled as she added, "It definitely has that *Logan's Run* look about it, but in a good way, not a bad one."

"*Logan's Run?*" Phil asked.

"Ah…," Sylvia said. "I guess that reference is a bit before your time, isn't it?" She knew it was almost as soon as she said it. What was Phil, 25, 26 at the most? And at such a young age he was already a major executive in a multi-billion-dollar tech company. Things certainly were different in her day. The long slog up the corporate ladder of her generation was over. Another big deposit on the dustbin of history. The future, it appears, belongs to the tech-savvy young.

Her eyes again scanned Phil's office, drinking in all the crystal-clear glass and shiny chrome everywhere. It was pristine — almost to the point of sterility, but still achingly pleasant. It was almost like she had accidentally wandered into some BBC documentary about the world of the distant future. A world she was completely unfamiliar with yet held much intrigue. Where else but in this techno-paradise could some T-shirted, high-top red tennis shoes and jean-clad twenty-something run an HR department for a company employing tens of thousands? Brave new world indeed.

"Wait a minute, *Logan's Run*," Phil said as he scratched his soul-patched chin. "Was that the old TV show where all of the inhabitants are sent to 'sanctuary' on their thirtieth birthday?"

"That's the one," Sylvia said.

"When the crystals in their palm started flashing, right?"

"Yes."

"I remember my Mom saying she used to watch that show when she was in grade school. She said it scared the crap out of her as a kid."

"Thanks, Phil," Sylvia said with a laugh. "Now I feel even older than I did. That was my favorite show — in *Junior* High School!"

"Oops!" Phil said with a laugh.

Sylvia chuckled. "Don't worry, though. My crystals flashed out a long, long time ago."

"Well...," Phil said as he cleared his throat, his tone suddenly becoming more serious. "Getting back on topic, I hope you are considering our offer."

Sylvia glanced down at the folder in front of her on Phil's desk. It was her proposed salary package and contract. It was a doozy. Two hundred thousand per year, travel expenses, company car, housing allowance — it was a dream. And even stranger, it was an unsolicited dream. There had to be a catch.

"I am quite interested, Phil," Sylvia said. "But...,"

"But?" Phil said. "Look, if we need to tweak the salary a bit, I can see what we can do. To be honest with you, though, we may be maxing out the budget, but it's possible we could make some adjustments. Give me some time."

"No, it's not that," Sylvia said. "Although, more money is always better," she added with a wink. "It is, well..., I really don't know anything about what you want me to do here? I certainly am impressed with the company, and the money and benefit package are quite nice."

"And the weather, Sylvia, don't forget that," Phil said. "You don't even have to pay taxes for this benefit."

He pointed out his large picture window to the beautiful spring morning bursting into life outside his office. It looked like an orange juice commercial — clear blue sky, the ocean just on the horizon, fruit trees dotting the immaculately manicured grounds, a gentle breeze swaying the palms. Pure loveliness on an exponential scale. At any minute it seemed as if the Beach Boys might start singing *California Dreaming..., on a winter's day. On a winter's day....*

Sylvia laughed. "Well..., I can't say I would miss New York winters."

"Good God, no," Phil said. "I remember them well. They suck."

"But how exactly did my name come to your attention?" Sylvia asked. "I mean, I am never one to look a gift horse in the mouth, but..."

Phil smiled and paused before saying. "You don't remember me, do you?"

Sylvia confessed, "I—, I am sorry, but..., uh, should I?"

"It's not surprising, actually," Phil said. "I was one of about two hundred in your Psych 101 class back in 2007."

"You were a student of mine?"

"Yep! Class of 2011, computer science major."

Sylvia swept her hand out into his office and said, "Good choice, apparently."

"It was. But..., of all my non-IT classes, I really enjoyed yours the most. It was incredibly insightful."

"Well, I am quite honored," Sylvia said. She laughed and added, "And if I had known I had a future internet mogul in my midst, I would have paid more attention when I taught that class. Frankly, most of those mongo intro classes, with the mob of freshmen in attendance, I just phone in."

Phil laughed, and said, "And who could blame you? We were all a snotty, motley bunch I am sure. But..., I liked your teaching style, and, most of all, I really enjoyed your book. Fascinating. In fact, I have read all your books. They are cutting edge."

"Thank you," Sylvia said. "I am glad you like them. Unfortunately, you are in the minority. My department head, as well as the rest of the psych department, are not big fans of my writing."

"No, I would not think they would be," Phil said.

"Yeah, people tend to get a bit defensive when you start poking holes in their idols, like Sigmund Freud."

Phil laughed. "Yes, and that is why I knew you were the perfect person for this job. UVid is a revolutionary company, and we love rebels. Your first book, *Reprogram your mind, Reprogram your life,* was really mind-blowing. You had me at the chapter entitled *Freud - 100 Years of Fraud and Counting.* Hilarious and dead on accurate. Your book threw the whole field of psychology on its head. I am sure you have helped so many people and deserve more credit than you get."

Sylvia beamed. This was unexpected but very welcome. "Thank you. I put a lot of research into that book. Sadly, research still sorely needed."

"And the theories you espouse fit in perfectly with not only my own thinking but also, the rest of the management team here at UVid. Your analogy of the human mind as being as programmable as a computer, with algorithms and subroutines and code. Genius! Why, if I didn't know any better, I would have sworn you were a coder."

"Too much math," Sylvia said with a grin.

"And having the power to scrub the negative experiences of life from your memory and then rewire positive ones instead is fantastic. What a beacon of hope this must be to those suffering from traumatic memories."

"Yes. In the few private counseling patients I had, my methods worked wonders. I was very encouraged. But..., alas, the Human Subjects Committee at the university objected. I was forced to give it up, and without a grant, I was out of the research business. So, it was back to teaching."

"But you see, Sylvia, this is why this new position is the perfect fit for you," Phil said. "You apparently enjoyed helping people. Well..., you will be doing that full-time now."

Sylvia paused and inhaled deeply. It was tempting. No more threats of denied tenure. No more derisive comments from her colleagues. The ability to put her theories into full practice. It was very tantalizing.

"You are making a compelling case, Phil," Sylvia said. "But…, let me be straight with you here. I certainly do not want to mess up such an outstanding offer, but, I have to be honest. Above all, I am a woman of integrity."

"Of course."

"And since you read my books you must know that my treatment was for Post-Traumatic Stress Disorder, nothing else. Now…, no offense intended, and I know that programming work is stressful, but I don't think it necessarily rises to a PTSD level."

Phil threw back his head and laughed. "No offense taken. And you are entirely correct, of course. Let me assure you, most of the stress our programmers deal with around here can usually be solved with ample application of Red Bull and Pizza. Plus, I don't think to have your character die on the latest Halo 5 Mod counts as warranting treatment for PTSD." He winked as he added, "thrilling and as lifelike as those graphics are."

"So, if I am not going to work with your programmers, who will I be working with?"

"Our Quality Assurance Rating Team, or Quarts, as they like to call themselves."

"Excuse my ignorance here, Phil, but, exactly what do the Quarts do?"

"They act as sort of janitors for our website," Phil said. "They take out the trash. They pull down the filth and flush out the scum that floods into UVid every second of every day."

"Wow, I learned something new today," Sylvia said. "I am embarrassed to admit this, but, I always assumed algorithms took care of all that."

Phil sighed. "We tried that. By God have we tried, but, contrary to what the artificial intelligence apocalyptists say, there are some things only people can do. And filth removal is one of those tasks that cannot be automated. We had some major egg on our face a few years ago that caused us to give up on AI being able to handle the problem."

"Oh? How so?"

"Our AI was unable to distinguish between porn and legitimate historical videos. It was humiliating. For a company like ours, committed to being a beacon of free speech and a major public force opposed to censorship, the mistake was almost our Death knell."

"Ah," Sylvia said. "I do think I remember something about that. This was about the blocking of that famous picture of the poor little naked Vietnamese girl whose village had been napalmed, right?"

"Yes. That was it," Phil said as he closed his eyes and shuddered. "That documentary is entirely legit, of course, but, all of our algorithms flagged it for removal. The AI just could not distinguish that video from old run of the mill porn. This was, and remains, a huge problem."

"I suppose that former Supreme Court Justice Potter Stewart was correct when he said he could not define obscenity, but he knew it when he saw it."

"Exactly our problem. How can you tell between filth and art? It is largely undefinable but somehow instinctive. The week after that incident happened our user base dropped 10% and our stock 15%! The average internet user, and especially the 'so-called' thought leaders in cyberspace, were very quick to cry, George Orwell. It almost sunk the company." Phil grinned and added, "So, until we are able to program the Potter Stewart 3000, we have to do it manually. This is a huge expense and a constant problem."

"Well..., if you don't mind me asking, but, why do you bother?" Sylvia asked. "I mean, it's not like you are producing this vile content. It is not illegal, is it?"

"No, it is not," Phil said. "But here is the ugly little secret." He pointed over to the glass wall in his office overlooking a vast open floor below filled with hundreds of programmers typing away at their computers, their enormous supercharged screens filled with thousands and thousands of lines of code whizzing by in a blur. "We may look like a technology company, and a tremendous amount of our resources go into expanding technology, but it is not really true. At our core, we are primarily an advertising business. And we have the same pressures as all advertisers have always had — do not upset your customers. And the guys who pay the bills around here do not want to be associated with filth."

"Yeah," Sylvia said. "I see your point."

Phil said, "The sheer volume of content uploaded each day is breathtaking. The job of monitoring is almost impossible." He added, "You may not know this, but, since we have been talking this morning, over 36,000 hours of videos have been uploaded to UVid!"

"Good Lord," Sylvia said.

"And most are monetized to serve up the automatic ads in our revenue sharing program. Now..., you can see the problem that may arise if say some huge international cosmetics company, drops a couple of million on UVid ads, only to be accidentally coupled with some heinous porn video playing on their name. This actually happened, by the way, and we lost millions when they pulled their ads."

"But weren't you able to go after the original poster of the video? I have seen your terms of agreement, and they are pretty extensive."

"Yes, but you see, the scammers get paid for the click, so by the time we find them they have their money and have evaporated into the ether. You can't sue a ghost. It is a real problem."

"I see," Sylvia said. "So..., I am curious, but given the volume of uploads you have, how many people do you have working in the Quart program?"

Phil paused and glanced up at the ceiling for a few seconds before saying, "At this campus, right around 3,000, give or take. There are thousands more located at our various other locations. Our turnover rate is very high, so we are always having to hire and train more in a constant churn."

"3,000! Wow!" Sylvia exclaimed. "But..., if you don't mind me asking, I still don't know how this relates to my unique skills? I mean, I understand that porn scares off advertisers, but I would doubt a little T&A would cause such deep psychological scarring." She grinned and added, "And, I know for a fact, I have a friend who has a nephew who would willingly come here and watch porn for you all day — for free."

Phil laughed but paused before his expression grew somber and his tone serious. "Well..., the problem is, Rule 34 has run amok; and even the most jaded among us can become quite disturbed by what they have to watch."

"Rule 34?" Sylvia said.

"Oh," Phil said. "A little 'inside baseball' jargon, sorry. Rule 34 is an old internet meme that states that any scenario, no matter how bizarre or disgusting you can imagine, somewhere, someone has made porn of it and uploaded it onto the internet. Godzilla porn is a thing, apparently. If you doubt me, look it up."

Sylvia shook her head and said, "No thanks. I will take your word for it."

"And as I stated, our burnout rate is very high for our Quart team. Very high. This not only costs us millions of dollars in retraining expenses, but it opens us up for potentially costly labor lawsuits. It also severely hampers our ability to stay ahead of this problem. There are millions of coders and shady producers in the Ukraine right now, coming up with new and inventive ways to trick our systems. The Tsunami of filth uploaded every minute is nearly unstoppable. And when you finally get a Quart team member up to speed, and they quit after only a month or two, it cripples us. Fixing this problem is a top priority for us, and…, well…., we would be honored for you to join our team. At the end of the day, we need to take care of our employees, and I can think of no one more qualified to see this get done than you."

"So, I would be in charge of counseling for the entire Quart team?" Sylvia asked. "That is a huge staff to contend with. I don't know if I am —"

"—Yes, it is a big staff," Phil interrupted, "but you will not be dealing with everyone at once, of course. We want to try it out as a pilot program first. If your methods achieve the results I expect them to, well…, your position, along with your salary, will expand dramatically. I would fully expect that you would then hire dozens of therapists, all working for and trained by you, of course, to help manage the load."

Sylvia smiled. It was the ultimate offer. Not only would she be making more money than she ever had in her life, but she would also finally be able to put her methods into real life practice.

"Well, Phil, I have made my decision. You convinced me. I will take it."

"Wonderful!" Phil exclaimed.

"But only on one small additional condition," Sylvia said.

"Condition? What condition?" Phil asked.

"I want to work as one of the Quarts, for a week or two," Sylvia said.

"Interesting…., kind of see how the system works, I suppose?"

Sylvia nodded and said, "exactly."

"Sounds like a good idea to me, agreed," Phil said. "I will introduce you to the team leader and get you all—,"

"—Wait. I think it best if I go in and work entirely undercover, and without any special treatment or filtering. I want to see exactly what these employees have had to contend with. I want to experience their lives for a while. Walk a mile in their shoes, so to speak. It has always been my experience the best therapists are ones who understand what their patients have been through as thoroughly as possible, first hand."

Phil smiled broadly as he nodded. "I think this is a fantastic idea, Sylvia." He thrust his hand into hers and shook it. "I knew contacting you was a stroke of genius. Welcome aboard."

"So, can I see where the Quarts work?" Sylvia said. "I am anxious to check this out."

"Absolutely," Phil said as he got up from his desk and opened his office door.

Sylvia nodded and followed Phil down the main hall and onto one of the five glass elevators on the third floor. It was evident UVid was designed by an architect with a flair for the dramatic. Phil pushed the letter B, for the basement, and they began to descend. As they passed by the second floor, Sylvia observed the bright sunlight room, numerous plants, and rows of desks filled with coders pass by before they descended another floor and the expansive lobby of UVid came into view. It was especially breathtaking from this vantage point, high in the ceiling. It was like some sort of Sci-Fi - Willy Wonka mashup, with fifty-foot palm trees, a freefalling waterfall and several, very expensive Henry Moore bronze sculptures dotting the faux tropical rainforest enclosure.

"This is really magnificent, Phil," Sylvia said as they continued their journey past the lobby into the basement.

"It should be," Phil said. "It takes a lot of money to get investors to cough up the dough — especially back in the early days when we were just cat videos and not making any money."

Sylvia laughed as the car noticeably darkened and they continued their descent.

"I suppose the darkness down here doesn't help people struggling to get over their upsetting memories?"

"Just wait until you see," Phil said. "The facilities are quite nice."

When the doors opened, Sylvia audibly gasped. Phil was right. It was gorgeous. Everything was painted in bright colors and was fully lit. Multiple windows were spaced along the walls opening into a lush and green atrium connected to the lobby above. The reality of being underground was completely obscured. Soft murmuring earth sounds were played over the internal sound system, and tons of tropical plants and trees were arrayed throughout the cavernous space. Rather than looking like a dungeon, as she expected, it looked like some sort of island paradise.

"This is lovely…, simply lovely," Sylvia said as she glanced around the room. The space was immense, at least the size of a football field, and despite being staffed by hundreds of people, it was deathly quiet. All of the employees were glued to their screens, earbuds firmly planted into their ears. Along the walls, and on the many pylons holding up the ceiling, dozens of "feel good" paintings had been placed. Knockoff Monets, fake Renoirs, and various other impressionists artists were well represented.

Everything in the area was calibrated to keep the mood light, airy, and most important of all, upbeat. When Sylvia stepped forward to look at one of the workstations nearby and she adjusted her focus, she caught sight of something on the screen. It was a flash of …, something. Red, or brown, she could not tell, but, she did get a tingly sensation in the back of her throat that told her it was unpleasant. The worker at the computer paid no attention to his visitor, the earbuds successfully blocking out any noise.

"We keep a privacy screen over all of the monitors. These prevent anyone seeing what is being viewed," Phil said. "Trust me, I learned that lesson the hard way with a particularly horrified group of Japanese investors who wanted the grand tour and insisted on seeing the entire operation."

"Yes," Sylvia said. "I can see that would be a problem."

"So, now that you are officially going to be an employee, do you mind if I ask you a personal question?" Phil asked.

"No problem."

"Any issue with your family moving out here to the West Coast? I know some New Yorkers, and my Aunt was one of those types, think no civilization exists west of the Hudson."

Sylvia shook her head and paused before saying, "No.... I am completely solo on this journey. No family at all."

"Well, that makes it easy then," Phil said. "And you will note, as a good HR manager, I did not ask that question as part of the interview."

Sylvia glanced over at Phil and teased, "I think I may remember you now from my class. You were that very bright boy in the back, right?"

"Yeah...," Phil laughed. "Right."

"Oh...," Sylvia said as she pointed to a lone, homemade poster on one of the columns. "It appears that one of the Quarts decided to add their own decoration to this whole Walt Disney / Renoir motif you have going on down here."

Phil followed the point of her finger to the poster, and his face dropped. It said, in big, bold red letters "Abandon all Hope ye who enter here!"

"Well..., as you can see," Phil said. "The gallows humor gets a bit thick down here, sometimes."

"Phil," Nancy asked as she pushed the candy cart towards the center of the room. "Slumming down here today?"

"Not quite," Phil said as he stepped forward and quickly glanced over her selection. "But, since you are here—"

Nancy smiled, reached down into her cart and pulled out a To-blerone candy bar. As she handed it to Phil, his eyes brightened, and he snatched it from her hand, quickly unwrapping it. "Nancy, you are the best. You always remember to stock my favorite." He glanced over at Sylvia and said, "I suppose there is no point asking you again, is there?"

"Well now," Sylvia said as she leaned forward and surveyed the array of snacks. It was impressive, literally every possible candy bar, potato chip or snack her mind could conceive of. "Let's not be hasty." Seeing her favorite treat on the rack at her fingertips, she glanced over at Nancy as she reached for it.

"It's OK, you can take whatever you want," Nancy said as she stifled a giggle. She looked over at Phil and said, "She must be new."

"She is," Phil said. "She is a new member of our Quart team."

Sylvia finished her selection and lifted the package up to her face, smiling as she turned towards Phil. Holding up the bar like a trophy, she whispered, "this seems appropriate today."

Phil laughed. It was a Payday bar. "Yes, Sylvia. It is very appropriate. And of course, you know what this means don't you?"

"No, what?" Sylvia said as she took a large bite into the caramel peanut cluster goodness.

"We have you now! You can never leave," he said as he mocked a sinister tone in his voice. "Resistance is futile. You have been absorbed by the Borg."

Chapter 2

April 20th, 1996 - Central Park, New York City - 1:45 PM

"CAN YOU BELIEVE THIS weather?" John said as he wiped away the fresh river of sweat from his brow. It was a steady stream flowing into his eye now, and the tiny creek rolling down his face had multiplied into a raging flood. "Already in the upper 80s and expected to only get hotter next week. Such a change from this past winter. New York seems to be going through some crazy swings lately."

"Maybe the scientists are right," Sylvia said. "They say the earth is getting warmer, you know. Still...," she added as she stretched out her bare legs and wriggled her toes in the grass. "It's nice to be outside today. I have been cooped up in my dark office all week grading papers, so I need a bit of sunshine. I don't care if it is hot. It is a beautiful day for a picnic, even if global warming will burn us all to a crisp in twenty years."

"Oh, I heard about that," John said. "I think I read an article in Newsweek about it last week. Frankly, it all sounds like a bunch of alarmist crap to me."

"I don't think so," Sylvia said. "The scientists I know at NYU are always talking about this now."

"Well..., it wasn't that long ago they said it was getting colder. This past winter when we were socked in with three feet of snow I didn't hear too much about global warming then," John said as he shook his head. "Who knows? But as for me, today, I would rather be sitting home in the A/C."

"Or out at the club, finishing up the back nine," Sylvia teased.

"True," John said as he smiled. "So…, I guess you got all of your grades posted?"

"Yep. Just a few more weeks and I will be all done for the summer. And then…, three glorious months before the students return in the fall," Sylvia said. As she spoke, she felt a bead of perspiration run down her neck and pool on the top of her back. John was right. It was a much warmer day than she had anticipated. She turned to him and said, "You know, it may be a bit too hot today after all." She then glanced over at their son playing at the foot of their picnic blanket and added, "And Billy, I think it is too hot for you to wear your costume today. You need to change."

"Mommy, that's not fair," Billy said. Their rambunctious seven-year-old son was dressed head to toe in a red and blue Spiderman costume. It was made of thin latex, and obviously meant for Halloween, but Billy would have none of her request for him to wear something else. He loved it and wore it every day. Keeping all the bad guys from ravaging the upper west side was a full-time job, after all. And despite his blond hair now dark and wet with sweat, and his young chubby cheeks red from the heat, it was evident he was having a ball.

"And why is that, dear?" Sylvia asked.

"You signed a contract!" Billy cried as he pulled out a crumpled sheet of paper from his pocket and waved it in the air. It was a white piece of construction paper the boy had written on in crayon. At the bottom, Billy and Sylvia's signatures were evident. The letters were large and shaky. It had taken him over an hour to write. He was just learning to make all his letters, so he was extra careful. A frown formed on the boy's face as he pointed at the paper. "See, right here it says, *If Billy eats all of his peas without complaining, and picks up his toys all week, he can wear his costume to the park on Saturday.*"

"I know, Billy, but…, it really is too hot today. I don't want you getting sick."

"Spiderman doesn't get sick, Mommy. He has super spidey powers."

Sylvia grinned, and said, "Yes, of course. But…," she added as she pointed at his 'contract.' "The contract doesn't say for how long you would get to wear your costume today. I think it has been long enough now."

"Ah!" Billy exclaimed. He glanced over at his Dad and nodded. "There are terms in the agreement that are implied. And, since both parties acted in good faith, and it is not ex…, uh, expli…, uh, *explicitly* stated, it is reasonable to assume it was for the entire day."

"That's my boy!" John said as he leaned forward and gave his son a high five. "See Sylvia, he's a natural."

Sylvia shook her head. She turned to John and said, "I see your influence here." She sighed and added, "and now I am going to have to contend with two lawyers in the family!"

"Our son here is going to make a fine attorney one day," John said. "Just like his dear old dad."

"I bet he makes partner by the time he is twelve," Sylvia said as she smiled at John. Turning back to Billy she said, "OK, dear, you win. I cannot possibly compete with your superior litigator skills. You can keep it on. But…, promise me that if you start to feel woozy, you will tell me. It is hot today. You can easily get overheated in that getup."

"Superheroes don't have to worry about getting overheated, Mommy," Billy said. "They have superpowers."

"He's got you there, Sylvia," John said. He grinned and added, "He is a *super* hero, after all."

"Well, even Superheroes have to worry about getting ill. Especially when they are wearing such a thick, hot costume."

"Didn't you like Superheroes when you were growing up?" Billy said. "Didn't you want to dress up when you were little?"

"Well…, yes. I wanted to be Wonder Woman when I was a little girl."

"Why don't you dress up too, Mommy? We could fight crime together," Billy said.

"Oh, I *like* this idea," John said. He looked Sylvia up and down and smiled. "Yeah…, those latex red boots, and of course, the golden lariat. I am all in."

"Shut up, John," Sylvia playfully snapped.

"Come on, Mommy!" Billy squealed. "You can buy one at a department store, and we can go and play tomorrow. Please!"

"I think me being Wonder Woman would end up being more fun for your Dad than you," Sylvia said as she winked over at John.

"You got that right," John whispered.

"Plus," Sylvia said as she pointed back at the contract. "This deal was for today only, Billy. We will need to make another deal if you want to wear your costume to the park again. You are going to have to pick up your toys all week to earn—"

"—You know, Grandma lets me wear my costume every day when I am at her house," Billy said. His eyes lighted up as he added, "and she said when I come to see her this summer, like last, she will even let me wear it when she takes me to the beach!"

Sylvia sat up straight on the blanket as she tightened her jaw. Like a spring being wound inside a clock, you could almost hear the creaking, snap snap snap as her fingers curled into two tight fists. She jerked her head sharply to the right and glared at John.

"Uh…, Buddy," John said as he turned to Billy. He pulled a ten-dollar bill out of his wallet and held it up in the air. "You see that ice cream vendor over there?"

"Yes," Billy said. "Are you going to buy me some ice cream?"

"Well, you are a big boy now, and a superhero to boot," John said. "I am going to have you go buy us all some ice cream. Do you think you can do that?"

Billy jumped up to his feet and squealed. "Oh boy! Yes! I want a Nutty Buddy."

"Perfect," John said.

"That is what Spiderman likes to eat," Billy said. "I saw it on TV."

"I always saw Spiderman as more of a Dreamsicle kind of guy."

"Ewwww, yuck," Billy said as he pinched up his face in disgust. "Spiderman hates orange. Just like me."

"Fair enough," John said. "And I will have an ice cream sandwich. You remember what those are, right?"

"Yes, Daddy," Billy said with a sigh. "I am not a baby. I know what ice cream sandwiches are!"

"Of course," John said.

"And Mommy gets some ice cream too, right?" Billy said.

"Absolutely," John said. He turned to Sylvia and said, "what do you want our son to buy you?"

Sylvia said nothing, her icy stare continuing to bore into John's face. Billy saw his mother's irritated look and said, "Don't you want any ice cream, Mommy? I don't understand. You love ice cream! I have seen you take a quart out of the freezer sometimes and eat the whole thing in the —"

John quickly reached forward and pulled his son over to stand in front of him. "I don't think Mommy wants anything to eat right now. She is…, she is not hungry."

"More for us then, right Daddy?"

John suppressed a smile, nodded and said, "yes…, now be a big boy and go get our ice cream. This is your first special mission as a Superhero."

Billy laughed and turned, ready to bolt across the short expanse of lawn to the ice cream truck. "And remember, Billy," John said. "Don't eat any until you bring it all back."

"I won't, Daddy," Billy said as he took the bill from his father's hand and scampered across the lawn.

Once he was out of earshot, Sylvia, her lips pursed and her tone terse, turned to John and said, "And just when were you going to tell me about this?"

"It…, it just came up yesterday when Mom called," John said. "I had no idea she was going to invite him. I certainly did not agree to anything, and I told her we had—"

"—Look," Sylvia snapped. "I know your mother means well, and I am grateful she wants to be so involved in her grandson's life."

"Mom loves being a Grandma, there is no doubt about that."

"She does…," Sylvia said. "But after the stunt she pulled last summer, she should be grateful I allow her to see Billy at all! I have held my tongue so far, but I swear to God, John. I have my limit, and it is fast approaching."

John dropped his head and sighed, the air going out of his lungs like an old tire that had just been gashed by a rusty nail. "Sylvia…," he said after a long pause. "We have been over this and over this. I don't like what happened any more than you do. But, you know she meant no harm."

"Yeah," Sylvia said. "They never do, do they?"

"Who?"

"People who mean no harm," Sylvia said.

"I know it was not right, what happened and all," John said, "but I think we need to move past it now. What is done is done, and you cannot unring a bell. And after all, she is Billy's only living grandparent, and—"

"—John!" Sylvia interrupted. "I can't believe you just brought that up!"

"Sylvia, I…," John said as he reached out for her arm.

When he touched her skin, she flinched, as if she had been scalded by a pot of boiling water. She crossed her arms tightly, locking her fingers down in the crook of her arms. She said, "I just wanted to have a nice day today. I really did. Just a beautiful, pleasant day in the park with my husband and son. Why did you have to bring that—"

"—I didn't mean it like that. I didn't mean to dredge up any…, look…," John said. "It is just that — you have to understand. My mother is very old-fashioned. You know, that kind of thing is…, well, it is just very important to her. It happened to me, and I was much younger than Billy. I am sure she is just concerned and overly involved with her only grandson. I am sure in her world, she did the right thing."

"I do not doubt her sincerity, John," Sylvia said. "And you are probably right. In her world, it was the most natural thing on earth to do. But I swore I would raise my children differently when I became a parent. I don't live in her world, and I don't want her filling Billy's head up with a bunch of superstitious crap."

"I know, I know," John said.

"And if your mother wants to keep on seeing Billy, she is going to have to adjust her thinking — big time! She can't just do whatever the hell she wants to — to our Son!"

"I know, I know. Look, I will talk to Mom, OK?" John said.

"You need to. I won't have it, John. I swear to God, I won't have it!"

"Understood," John said as he affected his most soothing tone. "But, let's not let this spoil today. I will talk to Mom, next week, I promise. It will all be straightened out, trust me. Plus...," he added as he put on his most convincing smile. He could always make Sylvia smile. "It was just a few splashes of water, after all. It's not like it meant anything, right? We both know that. Mom can think whatever she wants. What she believes has no effect on us, or more importantly, Billy."

"It's the principle of the thing," Sylvia said. "And it is so disrespectful! She didn't even ask first — but purposefully did it behind our back when she kept Billy last summer. I don't mind her coming over to our house, Billy loves seeing her and all, but as for him going over there, unsupervised, never again! It will be a cold day in hell before I —"

John grinned slightly, and said, "—Don't worry. I promise this summer will be different. Very different indeed. And..., in keeping with the water theme, maybe instead of Billy going to see Mom, she can join us at the beach house. And there we can splash all the water over Billy that we want — no strings attached."

"Beach house?" Sylvia said, her frown suddenly disappearing. "What beach house?"

"Remember the weekend we stayed at my boss' vacation house out in East Hampton a couple years back?"

"John, no, are you kidding?" she said as her smile grew wider. "You mean that big gorgeous house with the huge pool and the private access to the beach?"

"The very one. Frank and his family are going to Florence for the summer, and he asked me if I would be interested in using their beach house while he was gone." John smiled and said, "he certainly remembered how much you and Billy enjoyed yourself, and he said it would be a shame for it just to sit empty during the high season."

"Incredible," Sylvia said. "The place is like a dream."

"Amazing, isn't it? And to make matters even more spectacular, when I agreed, he acted like I was doing him a favor."

"I love that place," Sylvia said. "We had such a good time that weekend. I can't believe it — all summer? Are you sure? The house was magnificent."

"It was that, and, yes, we have the use of it for the whole summer. I figured you and Billy would enjoy getting out of the city for a while and really live it up like one of the Jet Set."

"You know, I think JFK, Jr. has a place out there," Sylvia said.

"He sure does. In fact, he will be our neighbor for the summer."

"Incredible. But...," Sylvia said. "But what about you? You will be stuck here in the city for work still, right? If I know you, you certainly aren't taking off the whole summer."

"No, my sweet," John said as he ran his finger down Sylvia's nose. "I don't keep academic hours, like you. I have several M&A deals coming to a head, so, I will be quite busy for the next few months."

"Well, I don't know. It is going to be hard being separated as a family all week. Are you sure this is OK with you?"

"Eh..., it'll be tough, but I am certain I'll be fine. As you know, during the week, especially when I have several deals in the pipeline like now, I'm usually up to my eyeballs in due diligence requests. I am at the office late most weeknights anyway, or at least until well after Billy has gone to bed."

"True enough," Sylvia said with a sigh.

"But with you and Billy at the beach, I can fully concentrate on work during the week with extra late hours and then come out to the Hamptons for the weekends, full and clear. And who knows, I might even knock off a bit early on Fridays to beat the traffic. And you know, a little Vitamin Sea will do us both good."

"I love the beach," Sylvia said.

"And anyway, won't you love having the next few months off free, and in the clear? The house has a staff, you know."

"Oh my God, really?"

"Really. And this will be the perfect time for you to finally finish your book. And what better place to finish it than relaxing by the sea in a luxury beach house?"

"You sure are a sneaky little jerk sometimes," Sylvia said as she shook her head and laughed, her smile impossible to hide.

"Like all great corporate lawyers, of course," John said.

"So, I suppose you had this delightful surprise in reserve, didn't you? You are always good at wriggling out of a fight with some kind of spectacular diversion." She smiled and added, "not that I mind, of course."

John grinned. "Of course. I always believe it is good to have an emergency backup plan." He raised his right hand to his forehead and made the boy scout three-fingered salute. "You know, be prepared."

"You can be such a charming bastard, you know," Sylvia said as she leaned over and kissed his nose. "And just out of curiosity…, exactly when were you going to tell me this fantastic news?"

"In June," John said. "Specifically, on the 10th."

"Billy's birthday," Sylvia said. "Of course."

"Yes," John said. "It was going to be part of his big surprise. It is not every day our little boy turns eight, after all."

"Well, let's not say anything about the beach house yet. Let it still be a birthday surprise." Her smile dissolved a bit when she added, "and let's hold off on inviting your mother. Let things cool down a bit first."

"Agreed," John said.

"Daddy, is this right?" Billy said as he rushed forward with the ice cream. In his right hand was a half-eaten Nutty Buddy, a thin trail of melted vanilla ice cream dripping down his latex clad arm. In his left was a dripping, mushy, mess that appeared to have once been an ice cream sandwich. It was soft and bent in the middle, and it seemed to be on the verge of collapsing any second. It was a hot day, and not the ideal conditions for frozen treats. But most unappetizing of all, clumps of grass and leaves adhered to the sides of the package. It was apparent the trip from the vendor's stand had not been uneventful.

"Yes…, I think so," John said as he took the mushy envelope of melted milk from Billy's hand. He held it gently with the tips of his fingers so as not to get it all over him. He chuckled as he brushed several leaves and a large clump of dirt off the white foil. "It appears you had a bit of trouble here, Buddy."

"Sorry Daddy, I…, I dropped it."

"Yes, I can tell," John said as he glanced over at Sylvia and grinned. "Well, I suppose even Superman has his off day."

"Spiderman, Daddy!" Billy exclaimed. "Remember, Superman has a cape."

"I stand corrected," John said as he turned back to his wife and smiled.

"You know, John," Sylvia said. "I think I may have changed my mind about that ice cream after all."

"I knew you would," John said. "You are never hungry until you see someone else eat." He flicked his fingers clean of the melted ice cream and added, "I think I might need to go back and replace this anyway, so, what do you want?"

"I think a Dove Bar," Sylvia said. "I had one the other day, and it was fantastic."

"A Dove bar it is, then," John said as he stood up.

"Do you want me to go get it, Daddy?" Billy said. "I promise not to drop it this time."

"Tell you what, Buddy," John said. "Why don't we both go, even Spiderman needs a side-kick. I will be Robin, what do you say?"

"Daddy, you are so silly," Billy said as he laughed. "Robin works for Batman! Everyone knows that."

John reached out and mussed up Billy's hair. "You really have this whole Superhero thing down pat, don't you? So, who is Spiderman's sidekick?"

"I dunno," Billy said. "I don't think he has one."

"Well…, he needs one. Every superhero needs a sidekick," John said. "I know. I can be IPO boy!" This comment immediately triggered a muffled snicker from Sylvia.

"IPO boy," she said under her breath as she shook her head.

"That's great!" Billy cried. "So…, what are your superpowers?"

"Oh, they are very super," John said. "They are the most terrifying and powerful weapon on earth?"

"Oh, what's that?"

"Billable hours!"

Sylvia laughed again.

"So, come on IPO boy," Billy said. "We have our mission."

John bent down to Billy's ear and said, "Yes sir! And maybe, once we complete this mission, we can convince Mommy here to be Wonder

Woman for our next adventure." He turned to Sylvia and added, "You know, I bet she will be able to fight all sorts of crime in those red leather shorts."

"John!" Sylvia exclaimed.

"You are so silly, Daddy," Billy said. "Everyone knows that Wonder Woman has stars on her shorts."

"Not the way I imagine her," John said.

Sylvia smiled as she watched John and Billy walk across the lawn to the ice cream vendor. It wasn't far, maybe 60 feet, but there was a crowd now. As the first sweltering day of the season, it seemed like all of Manhattan had decided to come to the park for ice cream. She knew John and Billy would be gone a while.

Lying back on the blanket, she kicked off her sandals and stretched out her bare feet onto the lawn. She sighed. It was wonderful feeling the warm, freshly mown grass between her toes. Living in the city does make one out of touch with nature. And soon, instead of grass, it would be sand. Nothing is better than that. Amazing. She could not wait until June. With a big yawn, she reached over and dug out her paperback romance novel out of her purse. On the cover, Fabio was in his full, chiseled jaw, bare-chested, long hair flowing, glory and appeared to just be about to whisk Lady Catherfield onto his pirate ship. Many bodices would be ripped for sure. It was a guilty pleasure she knew, and completely mindless, but hey, why not? As a working Mom, alone time was erratic, and she needed to take advantage of this rare, albeit brief, opportunity.

*****

"John? John Delaney! Imagine seeing you here today," Stuart Noel said.

"Stuart," John said. "What are the odds? I guess everyone in New York is out enjoying the great weather today." He paused before adding, "You know, I called you a couple of times last week, but your secretary said you were out."

"Sorry, Nicole was sick at home with the flu and, well…, you know how that is. With the kids and all."

"I do," John said.

"And is this your son?" Stuart said.

"It sure is," John said.

"Wow, he is getting so big."

"Growing like a weed."

Stuart, glancing down at Billy, said, "And what is your name?"

"Today, I am Spiderman," Billy said. "But Billy is my real name. Spiderman is only my alter ego."

"That's great," Stuart said with a chuckle. "You know, my son loves Spiderman too."

"What would you like, sir?" the ice cream vendor interrupted.

"Oh, right…, sorry Stuart, give me a second," John said. He grinned as he pointed to Billy and added, "we are on a secret mission."

"No problem," Stuart said as he held up his own ice cream cone. "I had a similar mission for my own son. Except mine required a twenty-minute wait."

"I would like a Dove Bar and an ice cream sandwich," John said to the vendor.

"Dove bar? I hope we aren't out. They have been very popular today," the vendor said. After bending over into the freezer, and rearranging some of the other selections, he said, "You are in luck. We have one left."

John turned to Stuart and said, "Thank God for that. The Dove bar was a special request from my wife."

"You certainly don't want to mess that up," Stuart said with a chuckle.

"Don't forget the Nutty Buddy," Billy interrupted.

"Now, now, Billy," John said. "You had your ice cream already."

"It's not fair," Billy said as he stomped his foot. "You and Mommy are getting ice cream."

"Yes, but we haven't eaten ours yet. You can get another one, maybe later," John said as Billy crossed his arms, huffed out a big gasp of air and frowned.

The vendor passed John the ice cream. John paid, stepped out of the line, and turned back to Stuart.

"Are you going to be in the office next week?" John asked.

"Actually, no," Stuart said. "I have to fly out to California on Monday."

"This is a problem," John said. "We really need to get together on those projections your team sent over to my office — and soon. I went over some of the numbers on your prospectus, and there is no way they are going to pass muster with the Dog & Pony show we are planning for the big institutional guys."

"Oh?" Stuart asked. "You don't think this will screw up our rollout, do you?"

"Daddy," Billy said as he pulled on John's pants leg. "Don't forget our mission."

John turned to Billy and then looked up the hill to the beach blanket where they had been sitting. There was Sylvia, stretched out reading her book. It wasn't that far, and for the moment, it was relatively quiet. The large mob choking the park earlier appeared to have temporarily dissipated. "Tell you what, Buddy. I have a special mission here with my friend, so, why don't you go take Mommy her ice cream for me. Can you do that?"

"Sure thing, Daddy," Billy said. "And I promise not to drop it this time."

"That's great, Buddy," John said. "And if you go right there, and don't drop it, I will buy you another Nutty Buddy before we leave today."

"Yay!" Billy squealed as he started to walk up the hill. His steps were plodding and cautious; the prospect of another Nutty Buddy hanging in the balance is a tremendous incentive. IPO boy was an expertise at performance-based compensation packages.

"Cute kid," Stuart said.

"Thanks."

"Now...," Stuart said, "about these projections, exactly what do you think is wrong with them?"

John smiled, turned back to Stuart, and began to speak.

*****

"Well now, you sure look relaxed," John said as he stood over Sylvia. She was deep asleep, the trashy novel placed squarely on her chest.

"What the—" Sylvia said as she sputtered awake. "Oh. Sorry. I must have dozed off."

"I guess old Fabio there just isn't as exciting as he used to be, eh?" John said as he pointed at the cover of her book. "So, did the Dove bar meet up with your expectations? You got the last one, I think."

"What? I haven't—"

"—And where did Billy run off to?" John said as he scanned the perimeter.

"What?" Sylvia exclaimed as she quickly sat up. "I thought he was with you!"

Click... *Click... Click...*

Chapter 3

April 17th, 2017 - UVid headquarters - Mountain View, California - 9:15 AM

"YOU ARE GOING TO really love our dental insurance, Sylvia," Gloria said. "No co-pay, no deductible, 100% coverage all the way — for everything."

"Wow, impressive," Sylvia said. "And you would think, with all of the candy you folks push around here, that extensive of coverage would be cost prohibitive."

"You are a funny lady, Sylvia," Gloria said. "You are going to fit in around here just fine."

"Well, I noticed there was a certain high level of dry humor running strong in the Quarts department. I thought I might as well get on board early."

Gloria's expression darkened a bit, and she nodded. "Yes…, they are a…, well…, I suppose one must maintain a healthy sense of humor. Especially given the sort of…, you know, work they do."

"Yes," Sylvia said. "Humor, and especially gallows humor, is very prevalent in certain high-stress occupations. You should hear what policemen, EMTs and firemen say during their off times. It can get very dark — very dark indeed."

"Yes, I am sure it does…," Gloria said. "Which, uh, brings me to the last topic. I know you are moving here from New York."

"Yes."

"Do you have any locals we can use for an emergency contact?"

28

"Sadly, no. I am all alone out here on the west coast. I am sure eventually I will make some acquaintances, but for now, it is just Snowy and me."

"Snowy?"

"My white Pomeranian," Sylvia said as she smiled. "I am not moving everything from New York until June, but I wanted to get started on my new job as soon as possible. Snowy and I are living in a fully furnished apartment down on Camino Real. It is…, well…, you know, I have the name of the place here somewhere but…"

"Avalon Terrace?"

"Yeah, that's the one."

"Oh, that's a beautiful place," Gloria said. "And very pet-friendly."

"Like here," Sylvia said. "It was one of the reasons I picked it."

"Absolutely. I would bring my cat Mittens to work if I could. But cats are known for possessing many admirable traits but traveling well is not one of them."

"No," Sylvia said with a chuckle. "And I am sure I will bring Snowy into work, eventually. It may be a while, though. She is still recovering from the plane ride."

"Yikes," Gloria said. "I am sure that was traumatic. I have never flown my little Mittens anywhere, and I can only imagine. All that noise in the cargo hold, the poor baby. I am sure it was most upsetting for her. But maybe not. Dogs are different."

"They are, but, Snowy can be quite the drama queen. Mittens, I am sure, could do no worse than my white princess. She sulked up a storm the first day we were here, but, she soon recovered. Now she loves our new place. It is so much bigger than our old apartment back in New York, and it has a patio and access to a yard — dog heaven."

"Avalon Terrace is a very nice place. We have quite a few of our employees living there. Who knows, there may even be a carpool you can join?"

"Well, that would be convenient. Having lived in New York for years, I never bought a car. No need to, and certainly not worth the hassle, and expense, of parking."

"I bet," Gloria said. "You know, I should have noticed your Avalon Terrace address from the Employee Data Form. God knows I have typed it in enough times. But anyway…, given that Pommes, although a bright breed, are probably not the most reliable of Emergency Contacts, who should I list instead?"

"Do I have to list anyone?"

"Well…, hmmm, that is an interesting question," Gloria said. "I can honestly say, I don't think anyone has ever asked that before."

"I am a very private person," Sylvia said. "You understand."

"I do," Gloria said flatly. "I don't know whether it is possible to skip that section, but, I will try." She focused her eyes tightly onto the computer screen and tried to advance her cursor to the next question. It was no use. It would not move. "Sorry. It appears our system requires an emergency contact."

"I see," Sylvia said as she glanced down at the desk.

"But…, don't worry about it," Gloria said. "You have to remember, we have the best internet security systems in the world here. I mean, we are UVid, after all. You don't have to worry about any of your personal information getting out. It will be safer here than anywhere else on earth."

"I am sure it will be," Sylvia said.

"And if you cannot come up with anyone local to use as a contact, surely you have some family back East you can list?"

"No. No family."

"I see…," Gloria said as her eyes darted back over to the screen. The cursor continued to blink, the flashing green signal appearing impatient for the final input to complete the setup procedure. She squinted and said, "How about a close friend then? It doesn't have to be family."

"That I have," Sylvia said. "OK, list Gayle Nussbaum. Her address is 232 West 34th street…"

*****

Another thirty minutes passed before the new employee survey input was finally completed. After the standard W4s and 401K paperwork were finished, and a full tour of the facilities was had, Gloria took Sylvia down to the Quality Assurance Ratings Team (Quart) in the basement. As the elevator door opened onto the bottom floor, a tall, heavily tattooed man approached. His broad, friendly smile was a stark contrast to his overall appearance. He, like almost everyone Sylvia had met so far, appeared to be in his early to mid-twenties, although after a closer look at his face, she thought he might be older. There was a hint of a few grey streaks in the man bun he wore. By UVid metrics, he was 'old', possibly 35, which of course meant she was ancient.

Extremely tall, he was dressed all in black. Thick silver rivets ran up his pants legs, which were tucked tightly into a rather imposing set of black leather hiking boots. His T-Shirt, which fully exposed his elaborately tattooed arms, said it all. It was a cartoon picture of a unicorn, reared back on its haunches with its mouth open wide in a primal scream. The words over the image were ironic, of course, and spelled out, in loud bubblegum pink lettering, the slogan —"The Rainbow Brite Fisters - 2015 World Tour — Sausalito, Burbank, and Fresno". Sylvia could not help but stare. Which, she suspected, was the whole point.

"So, here is where I am going to turn you over to one of the top team leaders at UVid, Steve Rickshaw," Gloria said as she pointed to the man approaching. "He is one of the chief supervisors in this department and will fill you in on all of the technical aspects of the job, as well as being the leader of your section." She paused before adding, "and you will soon discover that Steve is the absolute best in this field. He has been with us for nearly ten years now, so there is no greater expert around here."

"Yep," Steve said as he looked over at Gloria. "A full decade on sewer patrol — where on earth does the time go?"

Gloria winced.

"But, it has been a productive time trudging around in the septic tank of the world, and we always need new recruits," Steve said. Turning back to Sylvia, he shook her hand and said, "Glad to have you onboard." He glanced down at Sylvia's employee file and said, "I assume Gloria got you up to speed on all of the benefits and what not."

"I did," Gloria said.

"It is an impressive facility," Sylvia said.

"Yeah, but the best benefits are not listed in the manual," Steve said. "Snacks on demand has been my own personal golden handcuff to this place. After all, who can resist an endless supply of Baby Ruths?"

Sylvia laughed, and said, "I will admit, it is a most unusual, but fantastic perk. I am sure I am going to take full advantage, and no doubt ultimately balloon up into a whale."

Gloria patted Sylvia on the shoulder, glanced nervously around the room at the various workers silently working at their desks, and said, "Well…, you are in good hands here. I will be off." She then quickly turned and rushed back onto the elevator.

"Gloria doesn't like to hang around down here too long if she can help it," Steve whispered into Sylvia's ear as they both watched the elevator doors close behind her. "She much prefers her upper world, all glass and chrome and nice and neat. So sad. Some people just are afraid of hanging out in the garbage, you know. It is like she has some sort of condition."

"Purgamentophobia," Sylvia said.

"The what now?" Steve said.

"The irrational fear of garbage," Heather, one of the Quarts walking by, interrupted.

"Excellent! I am impressed," Sylvia said as she turned to view the unexpected visitor. She turned back to Steve and added, "You have a bright team it seems. This is not a term most would understand."

"Oh, Heather is real bright," Steve said, his tone dripping with sarcasm, as he pointed to Heather. "I guess she finally found a reason to show off something she learned from that Psychology Degree she got from UCLA. You two should have a lot in common."

"Oh?" Heather said.

"I have a Ph.D. in Psychology," Sylvia said. "In fact, for the past 25 years, I was a professor in the field at NYU." She extended her hand to Heather and shook it. "Pleasure to meet you, Heather."

"Same here," Heather said. "Well, this is truly amazing. A Ph.D. in Psychology! I never got that far, but I wanted to. Life seemed to get in the way."

"It has a tendency to do that sometimes," Sylvia said.

"So, Doctor, I hope you are prepared to see everything you ever read about in the DSM acted out daily, and on screen, in full living gruesome technicolor," Heather warned.

"What the hell is a DSM?" Steve asked.

"DSM stands for Diagnostic and Statistical Manual of Mental disorders," Heather said. She winked over at Sylvia and added, "And it won't take long for you to discover that Steve here is a perfect example of *puer aeturnus*. In fact, he is such a classic case, he could probably have his own page in the manual." She pointed at his shirt, shook her head, and said, "for a man his age to wear his band's t-shirt to work is a sure giveaway."

Sylvia suppressed a giggle and stared down at the floor. She didn't correct Heather, as she did not want to embarrass her. Nothing was more offensive than being corrected in public, especially by a stranger. And she didn't want to be a know-it-all, either. God, she hated know-it-alls, and it was always a temptation to be one herself. *Puer Aeternus*, AKA 'Peter Pan' syndrome, was not in the DSM, but, if it were, Heather would probably be right. Thirty-five-year-old men still chasing their teenage-boy fantasies of achieving Rock-God status made up a huge number of Peter Pan Syndrome sufferers. To avoid getting off on the wrong foot with her new boss, Sylvia quickly changed the subject. "So, Steve, exactly how does this whole video review system work?"

Steve shook his head and laughed, instantly putting Sylvia more at ease. "Oh, I can see it is going to get very fun around here, especially now that my assistant Heather has a new playmate. God help me! Now that I have two headshrinkers in the department, I am going to be completely outnumbered."

Sylvia grinned.

"But, before we get you started," Steve said, "a few preliminaries. Are there any particular issues you are more sensitive about, or, are there certain subjects you would most like to avoid?"

"I don't understand," Sylvia said. "I thought the videos would just come in — raw."

"No, it doesn't work that way," Heather interrupted. "And thank God for that!"

"Yeah, we would be quickly swamped in a deluge of depravity," Steve said. "No…, although the AI routines have not been perfected," he winked as he added, "and that is why we all still have jobs, they are at least capable of sorting out the videos into certain categories."

"Yeah, we don't review everything. It would be impossible," Heather said. "Just the troublesome ones."

"Oh," Sylvia said. "I was told that—"

"—No," Steve said. "The HR department barely knows what we do. Which is just as well. If we reviewed everything, we would spend most of our day looking at cat videos."

"And we save those for the Eye Bleach Lounge," Heather said.

"You got that right," Steve said.

"Eye Bleach Lounge?" Sylvia asked. "What is that?"

"You will love it, I am sure," Steve said. "It is one of the most popular areas down here. And hey, with your background, you might even be able to make some suggestions on how we can improve it."

"But what is it?" Sylvia said. "I don't understand."

"The Eye Bleach Lounge is an exclusive area we set up for members of our Quart team to decompress," Heather said. "Especially after they watch something particularly disturbing. Inside it is all pastel-colored walls, soothing music, fresh cut flowers delivered daily, and of course hours and hours of cat videos." She smiled and added, "We even have real live animals brought in there for cuddle time. Kittens especially — since everyone knows they make even the most heinous events palatable."

Sylvia said, "well, I am more of a dog person."

"Yeah, so am I," Steve said. "And that's why we bring in puppies occasionally, too. Every Thursday. But, hopefully, you won't have to visit too often. You strike me as a resilient person. I have a sense of these things."

"Thanks," Sylvia said.

"But, despite that, I still like to find out where all of my people's pressure points are in advance. It helps me to funnel the right videos to the right person. Everyone has something they can't handle."

"Do they? I have my own theory on that…" Sylvia said. "But, now I am curious. What is yours?"

"For me," Steve said, "it is bodily fluids. I can't take it. Snot, piss, shit..., ugh. It's all too much."

"Not such a tough guy, are you, Steve?" Heather said as her grin turned into a smirk. She glanced over at Sylvia and said, "Don't let the rough Biker Garb fool you. Inside, Steve is nothing but a big leather-clad pussycat."

"Well, I especially draw the line at vomit. But hey, I have seen you retreat into the Eye Wash Lounge over much less, Heather," Steve said as he laughed. "She can be such a prude, you know," he added as he looked over at Sylvia.

Heather turned to Sylvia and said, "I am no prude, despite what Steve is insinuating. But..., I am also not warped — like he is. Certain private functions between consenting adults are best left..., private. I have not fully joined the ranks of Perve City."

"Her line of thinking is in a distinct minority down here," Steve said as he turned to Sylvia and smiled. "You would be surprised what she finds offensive." He wrinkled his nose and said, "So uptight, really — quite sad. It's a wonder she is able to review *any* videos."

Heather, pointing at Steve, said, "Uptight, says the man wearing the 'Fisting Rainbow Bright' T-Shirt." She rolled her eyes, looked at Sylvia and added, "Like I said, Perve City! But, despite what he says, my main issue is with seeing anything happen to animals. That is where my line is drawn. Disgusting!"

"So, Sylvia," Steve said. "We came clean to you, now you need to confess to us. What sets your teeth on edge?"

"I don't know," Sylvia said. "But..., I have a feeling, I am going to find out."

Steve's smile widened, and his eyes glinted as he said, "Yeah, you probably are." He turned to Heather and said, "So, where should we put her? Any empty desks nearby? The churn has seemed to settle down a bit lately."

"Alyssa's desk is open," Heather said.

"Alyssa? Are you sure?" Steve said.

"I should be," Heather said. "She has not been in for a while now, and no one has heard from her."

"Maybe she is on vacation, I will check the—"

"—I don't think so. I am pretty confident Alyssa is never coming back."

Steve shook his head and said, "Such a shame. Alyssa was really coming along, too. Well...," he added as he turned to Sylvia, "We are always short on desks so we can start you in her spot. If she does come back, we may have to move you. I hope you don't mind."

"No, no problem," Sylvia said.

Heather smiled at Sylvia and mouthed, "She is not coming back."

As Steve and Heather guided Sylvia through the caverns of repetitive cubicles, Steve ran down the basics. Sylvia learned she would be working through a queue of videos that Steve would assign at the end of each day for the next day's work. At the end of each video, she would answer a series of questions. He claimed it was for proper categorization, but, it was evident what the true object was. UVid was no fool. They were trying to 'teach' the AI. Well..., perhaps she could help. Her analytical researcher instincts began to tingle at the prospect of tapping into the collective ID of the entire world. Some habits were hard to break — the academic urge always dominates. Who knows, this might even be fun?

Each video she watched needed to be categorized into various slots, from gratuitous violence on one end of the spectrum, through hate speech and criminal activity in the middle all the way to standard, run-of-the-mill porn at the other end. There were categories for offenses related to religious sensitivities, animal cruelty, child abuse, simulated rape and murder, and other crimes as well. And of course, nudity and explicit adult content was its own category with an incredible myriad of subcategories. Shockingly, in addition to subcategorizing each video into its proper slot, she was also to rate the level of offense on a ten-point scale, with ten requiring an instant ban of the video and the account that posted it. She shuddered to think what an Animal Cruelty or Child Abuse rating of 10 would entail.

Sylvia was pleased to learn that anything illegal she discovered was to be reported immediately. This point was emphasized several times, so she knew it was sincere. UVid has a vigorous policy to cooperate with the justice department on anything that may be linked to a crime.

This is a top priority. This cooperation is no doubt one of the many reasons the Feds kept a hands-off attitude to the internet giant.

When Steve explained that at least ten or twelve times a week an actual suicide is filmed and uploaded to UVid, Sylvia felt her throat grow dry. He also told her of a host of other horrific real-life criminal acts they routinely receive, too awful to detail. Was it not enough to commit the crime, she wondered? Was the level of perversion of these individuals so deep they were compelled to film it, too, and then broadcast it to the world?

People, despite her years of study of the human mind, remained ultimately mysterious — especially when exploring the depths and degree of their total depravity. The trick, Steve said, was determining real crimes from fake, but, in time, he assured her she would learn how to distinguish. He said it was more of an art than a science, but, he was confident she would catch on quickly. She hoped he was right. When they reached the end of the row of cubicles, Sylvia saw an empty desk.

"And here we are, your new home," Steve said. "At least, assuming Alyssa doesn't return."

"I told you, Steve. She's not coming back," Heather said.

"She might, you never know," Steve said as he pointed to the desk. "After all, she left all of her stuff. Who leaves all their stuff behind?"

"Obviously, Alyssa. But, Sylvia is going to be a lot more fun as a neighbor. See," Heather said as she pointed to the adjacent cubicle. It was hers and she added, "you are right beside me."

"I wonder if this is going to be a problem?" Steve said as he smiled. "Having you two together is going to lead to all sorts of trouble. I can just sense it."

"Don't worry, Boss," Heather said. "We will go easy on you."

"OK," Steve said as he shook Sylvia's hand. "Once again, welcome aboard." He leaned over the keyboard and typed in a Username and Password on the computer. "I hope you don't mind, but, I am going to have you work through Alyssa's queue today. I got it all set up already, and…"

"And he is too lazy to set up a new one for you right now," Heather said.

"Bingo," Steve said. After a few more keystrokes, the UVid welcome screen filled the monitor. "There we go. All good to go. If you need to take a break, just click on pause. Otherwise, the videos will just advance automatically."

"OK, Steve, got it."

"Good luck," he said as he turned and left for his office. He called back, "and if you have any questions, your neighbor there will be sure to provide a good answer."

After Steve left and Heather returned to her cubicle, Sylvia sat down at her new desk and breathed in deeply. It was just as she hoped; in fact, it was much better. These next few weeks would be a full immersion into a world she wanted to understand, and what better way to help people in this world than to live in it herself. Steve seemed great and Heather was a hoot. She didn't like most people, generally, but she liked them. That certainly was an unexpected bonus.

She leaned back into her surprisingly comfortable chair and glanced over her workspace. She smiled. It would do. Despite its small size, it was, in reality, not that much smaller than her 'private' office back at NYU. Sylvia examined her surroundings and took inventory of what Alyssa had left behind. It wasn't much of value, really. A lone picture frame sat on the desk along with an array of other personal items: a personalized coffee mug, a Star Wars mini-poster, various animal and or motivational stickers and other bric-a-brac common in most office settings. Sylvia turned her attention back to the frame and studied the picture carefully. It was a photo of a young woman that looked to be in her late 20s, maybe 30 at the oldest. She was a fairly non-descript, typical California girl: long blonde hair, bright shining face, blue eyes. The picture was a stereotypical beach snap — something you would see on thousands of desks around the country. There was something, though…, something familiar. *What made you leave, Alyssa? What was the final straw?*

"Did you know Alyssa?" Sylvia asked.

"A little," Heather called out from the other side of the divider. "But honestly, I did not get to know her that well. She was a bit standoffish."

"Oh? How so?"

"Well…, we didn't have much in common, actually," Heather said. "She was more of a…, how can I say this politely? I guess I can't. She was more of a reality TV type of gal if you get my drift."

"Ah, yes. I see," Sylvia said.

"Not to be mean, or anything," Heather said. "But, the girl wasn't that bright. I doubt she had a single deep thought in that bleach-bottled blonde head of hers."

Sylvia glanced back down at the photo and focused on Alyssa's face. It is hard to draw conclusions from just a picture. Years of her graduate training, along with having dealt with thousands of students, did come in handy in rendering some snap judgments. Alyssa certainly didn't look stupid, that was too harsh, but, she did have a certain innocent quality about her face. As she looked back at Heather, poking her head over the divider, Sylvia grinned. It was no secret why the two women didn't get along. The contrast between them could not have been greater. Where Alyssa was a sun-kissed, bright and friendly blonde, Heather was far darker, bordering on Goth. Her long black hair, stark white makeup and the prominent nose ring glimmering on her face shouted that Heather was a blend of world-weariness mixed with cynicism and a healthy dose of snark thrown in. Interesting flavor, but no doubt a bit bitter. *Yeah, I bet poor old Alyssa didn't get along too well here.* The bright hopeful young face gazing up at her from the picture didn't look like it had a cynical or dark thought under those blonde tresses.

Sylvia said, "It is odd she would just leave everything behind like this, though. Especially this picture. The frame is silver and engraved, so it was obviously very important to her. It makes one wonder."

"It is not *that* odd, really. I don't want to be unkind, but, Alyssa was an airhead and…, a bit too squeamish for this job. Trust me, she was a frequent visitor to the Eye Bleach lounge. I knew the first day she got here she would not last."

"Well," Sylvia said. "I shudder to know what you think about me, then?"

"Oh, I have a good feeling about you, girl," Heather said. "You strike me as someone with a soul of pure steel."

"I guess I will take that as a compliment," Sylvia said. After a pause, she turned back to her monitor and moved her cursor over to the play button. Putting in her earbuds, she settled in. This, she thought, ought to be interesting.

Three hours later, and Sylvia was anything but interested. Surprisingly, she found the job to be strangely dull. Filth and degradation can get terribly repetitive after a while. Perhaps it was her iron-like constitution that prevented her from being offended, or the years of working with some seriously disturbed individuals? She really had heard most everything.

The videos she reviewed had been a relatively routine mashup of what she had expected. Fools faking their own deaths, which made her wonder how many hundreds of gallons of Karo Syrup she had just watched being splattered all over the place making these cheap fake horror "masterpieces"? Also, lots of very inappropriate, highly sexualized videos were in the queue. It seems that in the race between Porn and Art, Porn was winning — hands down. She sighed as she watched yet another highly flexible, and apparently quite open-minded girl, insert something somewhere that should not be filmed. She yawned when the next video started and she watched a guy in an Elmer Fudd-like hunting outfit wander out into a large open field.

"Well…, this should be entertaining. At least it is creative," Sylvia thought as she watched the "hunter" crouch down and aim his gun into the woods. After the shot was fired, and she determined a large black bear had been killed, she wondered exactly why the UVid algorithm had flagged this video for review. The internet has thousands of hours of hunting videos that were perfectly fine. What made this one questionable? When a rather top heavy, and quite naked, young woman entered the frame and started disrobing the hunter, she had her answer. As they approached the poor dead animal, both naked, and then proceeded to…, to…, she quickly reached out and turned off her screen.

As she took off her headphones, the hunter's loud taunting frat boyish shouts could be clearly heard. "Shake that bear! Yeah! Shake that bear!"

"Oh no," Heather said as she overheard the audio, and she arose from her chair and leaned over the cubicle wall. "I see you got the infamous 'Bear Lovers' video in your queue."

"Uh…, yeah…," Sylvia said as she swallowed hard. She turned the monitor back on and paused the video. It was horrific, but, try as she might, she could not look away from the screen. Even paused, it was about the worst thing she had ever seen, and all she could focus on were the cold dead eyes of the animal shown in closeup.

"Do you need to….," Heather said as she gestured down the hall towards the Eye Bleach Lounge.

"No…," Sylvia said. "I…, I will be all right. I just need a second to…, regroup."

"Candy time!" Nancy called out as she turned into Sylvia's row and ferried her cart through the maze of cubicles. One by one the other employees nearby spun around and began making their snack selections, swarming over the shelves of her cart like a school of sharks attacking a fresh dump of chum in the water.

"Well, that could not have been timed better," Heather said as a smile formed on her face. "Girl, you know what you need?"

"No. What?" Sylvia asked.

"You need chocolate," Heather said. "I know I happened upon that horrid video a few months ago, and it led to my scarfing down at least a quart of ice cream when I got home to my apartment. It was disgusting! I am sure it was under another name then, no doubt. Those perves keep reposting this garbage under different titles, but, I watched it, and it messed me up pretty bad. Some people are just really — twisted, you know?"

"Yeah," Sylvia said as she waved to Nancy. When the candy cart rolled over, she asked, "Any Reeses?"

"Any Reeses she asks?" Nancy said as she glanced knowingly over at Heather. "Of course, we have Reeses! We aren't Barbarians, you know."

Sylvia took her Reeses cups from the cart while Heather grabbed a Zagnut. Once Nancy was onto the next row, Heather said, "You can take a break, Sylvia. Really. It is not a bad reflection on you to take a mental health pause. Steve is super cool about it."

"No, I am all right," Sylvia said. "And you know what," she added as she popped the second cup in her mouth. "You are right. Chocolate does help."

"Works every time," Heather said. "And, it helps me get through many a day. In time, you will find this is a pretty cool place to work…, assuming you don't develop diabetes."

Sylvia laughed. "But…, I wonder. I wonder if Alyssa watched this video? It was in her queue, after all."

"Nah," Heather said. "The system always serves up new videos only. Once you view and evaluate it, it won't come back again. At least, not the exact video."

"Hmm," Sylvia said. "It does make me curious. I wonder what video set Alyssa off? I wish there was a way to find out what was the last video she watched before she quit."

"Assuming it was primarily one video, of course," Heather said.

"Of course."

"My money is on her getting hooked up with some doofus, and that's why she left. She seems that type, too. I thought I noticed her plumping up a bit. I think she might be pregnant."

"Heather!" Sylvia said.

"I'm just kidding," Heather said. "But, it 's not really that hard to figure out what Alyssa watched last if you really want to find out." She came around the divider and stood beside Sylvia, and added, "Since Steve signed you in under his administrator account, you can still see all of her history on this machine."

"Really?"

"Really," Heather said as she leaned over Sylvia's keyboard and typed in a few commands. She pointed at the screen, "See, there is the last video she watched. Something called…, Homecoming, back on…, wow, March 29th!" She grinned and said, "I guess Alyssa has been gone a lot longer than I thought. Like I said, we weren't close."

Sylvia said, "yes, that seems obvious."

"Now you have me curious," Heather said. "I want to watch the video. Maybe it was some taped reminder of how her empty, vacuous life was coming to nothing and she decided to run off and join a cult or something."

"Heather!"

"I'm sorry, that was a bit bitchy," Heather said. "Even for me. I can't help it. The snark runs hard in my veins."

Sylvia smiled and said, "Mine too."

"But, you have kindled the flames of curiosity in me now," Heather said. "I have to know. You can't really tell anything by the title."

"Homecoming seems like a pretty innocuous title," Sylvia said.

"Oh, don't be fooled by that," Heather said. "In fact, it has been my experience that the more wholesome, warm and fuzzy the title is, the darker and more twisted the content. Trust me on this. I watched a video a couple of months ago entitled 'Brandon's First Christmas' and…, well…., let's just say, I spent the rest of the day in the Eye Bleach Lounge. It was like the first time I ordered sweetbreads in a French restaurant. They were neither sweet or bread — yuck!"

"I assume it was not about Christmas, then," Sylvia said.

"Not exactly…," Heather said. "Although…, there was a pine tree involved." Heather shuddered, and said, "honestly, where do people come up with this stuff?"

"Well, I'm game," Sylvia said. "Let 'er roll."

"OK," Heather said. "But…, be prepared to lose whatever flickering flame of hope you might still have for the dignity of the human condition." She added, "I'm immune. That fire got put out years ago. I am fully reconciled to the reality people are absolute pigs."

"True enough," Sylvia said.

Heather reached over and pulled up the video, clicking the box to show it full screen. The two women shared earbuds and stared at the screen as the video began to play.

After the first few seconds, Heather cocked her head. She was confused. This was not an ordinary video. First of all, the film was yellowed and had a brownish sepia tone. It was also silent, so the earbuds were superfluous. It looked to her like an old home movie that had been converted to video and uploaded to UVid. It was still in color, though, so it wasn't that old, maybe from the late 60's or early 70's. It had that look. Something about it, though, seemed unreal, ethereal, almost like you were watching the scene play out through a thin haze.

Two minutes into the video Heather was growing bored. The whole film consisted of just a long shot of a field of tall grass with rolling hills in the background. It was relaxing, in its own way, and off in the distance was an old white farmhouse, complete with green shutters and one of those old-timey aluminum screen doors on the front of the house. She could almost imagine hearing the creak of the springs as it opened. After another dull minute or so, a small figure opened the door and emerged onto the porch. The camera was quite a distance from the house, so nothing was clear, but, it looked to her to be a small boy. She squinted as she tried to focus, but details were hard to make out. The deterioration of the original film, along with the distance from the camera made everything out of focus. It looked like the kid was wearing some sort of costume. He started to walk down the stairs toward the field. The costume was blue and red. Suddenly, the film stopped.

"Well, I don't mind telling you, Sylvia," Heather said. "That was possibly the most boring video I have ever seen. Why on earth the algorithms flagged it, I will never know." She glanced over at Sylvia and paused. Sylvia was staring straight ahead at the screen, her eyes unnaturally opened wide. Her pupils were fully dilated. A single bead of sweat was running down her forehead and, most odd of all, although her mouth was open as if to scream, she was stone silent.

"Sylvia? Sylvia?" Heather said as she shook her shoulder. "Are you OK? Sylvia!"

Click... *Click... Click...*

Chapter 4

April 30th, 1976 - 15 miles east of Pikeville, Kentucky - 5:15 PM

THE LITTLE GIRL SMILED AS she ran her toes through the thick grass, her giggles echoing through the spring air. The grass, lying like a living carpet beneath her bare feet, felt so smooth and cool against her skin. It had been such a long winter — all heavy socks and rubber boots with endless grey days and lots of snow. Kentucky was like that. She loved snow, of course, and especially snow days when school was canceled. Mom would make hot chocolate and they both would build snowmen in the front yard. It was all such fun. But feeling the warm spring breeze on her bare arms and the bright rays of the April sun on her face, she knew she liked Spring, too. Because ultimately, that led to summer and no school.

She rolled over onto her back, looked up at the sky and sighed. The clouds were so beautiful — especially at this time of day. She squinted her eyes as she studied the shapes. She could just spend hours and hours doing this. Today with the sun just starting to set behind Black Mountain, they were spectacular — a never-ending parade of big, fluffy pink clumps of cotton candy floating across a bright blue sky. Her mouth watered as her mind wandered. *Cotton Candy, just like the kind Daddy bought her at the County Fair last fall. What a fun day. I wonder if we will go again this fall? Mommy thinks she will be too big for the Tilt-a-Whirl by then.*

A cool breeze brushed across her cheek and she sat up. She needed to be alert. The afternoon was ending and she knew any minute, Mommy would ring the bell. The rule was once Mommy rang the bell, she had to come inside. If she had to ring it twice, there would be no

TV the next day. She couldn't risk it. Tomorrow was Saturday, and Bugs Bunny would be on! So, she kept her ears open as she continued to play. Only time for one more adventure before Mommy called so she raised up on her knees and got ready. Fluffing out her doll's long dark hair and straightening out its blue cape, she lifted the tiny doll's arms up over its head and began twirling it on one of its red-booted feet.

"Wonder Woman! Wonder Woman! Kee...Rack!" she sang as she tried to imitate the sound of thunder and lightning.

"Sylvia! Sylvia!" Darlene shouted as she rang the bell. With a farm of at least thirty acres, this old-timey dinner bell was the best way to call her daughter in for dinner. Ironically, it worked on the dogs too. "Time to come in Baby!"

"Coming Mommy," Sylvia shouted as she jumped to her feet and began running up the long hill towards the house.

It was a charming white clapboard, two-story house with green shutters and a matching green tin roof — desperately in need of a fresh coat of paint. It had a full wide-open porch on the front, complete with an aluminum-framed screen door and several hanging baskets of petunias. Pink ones to the south, purple ones to the north, just like Maw Maw always says. It was nothing unusual, just the standard, run-of-the-mill, farmhouse. God knows Pike County was full of them, but, to Darlene and her husband Joe, it was home. With four bedrooms, there was plenty of room, and, with a new baby on the way, Darlene was glad that little Sylvia wouldn't have to share a bedroom like she did growing up in a house with five sisters and three brothers.

Darlene shook her head as she watched her daughter rush up the lawn and clamber onto the porch. All legs and knees, just like she was at her age. Glancing over her shoulder to the large brass bell bolted into the side of the house, she had to admit, this was a good system. She never did have to ring it twice. The threat of TV revocation is such a good motivator, especially to a ten-year-old.

"I made it in two minutes this time, Mommy," Sylvia said as she panted and leaned over to grab her knees. "I think this was my best time yet."

"You are a born runner," Darlene said.

"Just like Wonder Woman, right? You saw how fast she can run on the TV show, right?" Sylvia said. She spun around and sang, "Ker-Pow! Wonder Woman!"

As Sylvia twirled, Darlene grabbed her shoulder and stopped her in mid-spin. "Sylvia, just look at your pants. Were you rolling around in the grass down near the creek again?"

"Uh…, maybe," Sylvia said.

Darlene bent down and lightly brushed Sylvia's bottom. "Honestly…, just look at this mess. You are as dirty as one of Daddy's stinky old hogs. What were you doing out there, rooting in the mud? You are filthy!"

"Sorry Mommy, but…, you did say I could play until you called me in."

"Yes, I did," Darlene said. "But I also said to keep yourself clean, too, right? Remember, we have everyone over tonight. I have been cooking all day, and now I have to deal with all of this."

"Is Maw Maw coming?"

"She is," Darlene said. "In fact, she should be here any minute. So, you need to go upstairs and—"

"—Wheeee! Is she bringing ham biscuits? I love Maw Maw's ham biscuits. She is bringing biscuits, isn't she?" Sylvia said.

"Of course," Darlene said, "she always does. And a whole bunch of other stuff too…, but…, don't you like my biscuits?"

"Well, they're OK…, but, they're not the same as Maw Maw's."

Darlene laughed as she shook her head. "You sure do know how to hurt a woman's feelings, Sylvia."

"That's OK, Mommy," Sylvia said. "I still think your potato salad is the best! And, of course, everyone loves your pies better than anyone else's."

"Well, that is good to know," Darlene said. She wiped her forehead with the back of her hand and said, "And it's a good thing, too — I have about a dozen of them out cooling on the counter."

"Oh boy, let me have a—" Sylvia said as she lurched for the screen door. She was yanked back when Darlene clutched her shoulder.

"Oh no you don't," Darlene said. "As I was trying to say, you need to march yourself right upstairs and get in the tub. I don't want you getting mud everywhere. It's a special occasion, you know."

"It is? What is the—"

The screen door opened, and Joe walked out onto the porch. "Damn, Darlene, how much food did you cook? There is enough in there to feed Cox's army."

As he spoke, Darlene smirked as she spied a spot of merengue stuck on the end of Joe's beard. "You didn't eat any of those pies, did you? You know those are for company."

"What?" Joe said as his face brightened into a grin. "Me? Never!"

Darlene knew that grin so well. And that devious, up to no good, devilish smile got her to do most anything. *Hell, that is how we ended up with Sylvia*, she sighed as she thought to herself. *That and quite a few Jack n Cokes.* She leaned forward and kissed his lower lip. "I think you are busted, Mister."

"Well…," Joe whispered back. "What are you going to do about it?" As he spoke, he reached around her waist and ran the palm of his hand down the small of her back. She always looked sexy to him, but even more when she wore this thin cotton purple sundress. It was her favorite and showed off her womanly charms so well. Even now, six months pregnant, it still fit — although some of the flowers were starting to stretch.

"Daddy," Sylvia said as she yanked on his pants leg, quickly dousing the romantic moment.

"Yes, Pumpkin?" Joe said.

"Will you watch Gilligan's Island with me?"

"You bet," Joe said. He looked down at his watch and saw the time. It was nearly 5:30. "You know, Pumpkin, I think today they finally get off the island."

"Really?" Sylvia said.

"Yep, I read about it in TV Guide."

"Joe," Darlene said as she shook her head. "You are being played."

"What?" Joe asked.

"Slippery Sylvia is just as bad as you," Darlene said. Glancing down at her daughter, she added, "she knows what she is supposed to do first. Don't you, Sylvia? She always plays her Daddy like a fiddle."

"Yes Ma'am," Sylvia said as she lowered her head. "But..., can't I watch Gilligan's Island first? I mean..., this might be the day they get off the island!"

"See what you did," Darlene said as she turned to Joe.

"Please Mommy, I promise I won't get dirt on the couch. I will stay on the slipcovers this time. I promise..., please..., please!"

"Pumpkin," Joe said as he squatted down on the porch and held her arm. "I think it is a safe bet that you aren't going to miss anything big on Gilligan's Island today. I think I misread that. You won't miss them getting rescu—"

"—But you said—"

"—Take my word for it," Joe said. "They aren't going anywhere. At least not today. Now, go and take your bath like Mommy said."

"Yes, Sir," Sylvia said as she dropped her chin to her chest and went inside. As the screen door creaked and slammed behind her, Darlene sighed.

"Is it really 5:30? It is much later than I thought," Darlene said. "This isn't good."

"Yes, it is just now half past," Joe said as he glanced down at his watch. "Do you have a cake in the oven or something?"

"I should have started earlier!" Darlene said. "There is so much to do, and I am running out of time. Why do I always wait until the last minute?"

"It's what you do," Joe said.

"And everyone is going to be here soon! I am not going to make it. It's all going to be ruined."

"You'll make it," Joe said. "You always do. The house looks great and the food smells delicious. I know everyone is going to have a great time."

Darlene said, "and this is the first time we have hosted Circle in ages. I certainly don't want to embarrass myself, not with Father Ted coming and all. I don't think we are going to have anywhere near enough to eat. I am such a fool, I wish I had—"

Joe reached out his hands, cupped them behind his wife's back and pulled her into his chest. He leaned forward and kissed her forehead. "You have gotten yourself all worked up into a stew. It is going to be all right. We have more than enough food. You forgot I got a big old pork barbeque simmering out in the pit."

"You picked a nice one, didn't you?"

"I did, ended up sacrificing two of the best we had today. One for eating and one for—" Joe said.

"—Cornbread! Damn it, I forgot about the—"

"You didn't forget," Joe said as he smiled. "Emma Jean told me she was bringing the cornbread. And besides, everyone is bringing a dish. You know it is potluck. And with all of your sisters and mine, coming — If anything, we are going to have too much food."

"Maybe, but we still need to set up the tables and get the—"

"Shhh," he said as he ran his hands down her back. He lowered his voice and added, "Why don't you let me worry about all of that? Your mother is going to be here soon, and she can help finish off the entrees. God knows, she will have this house filled with fried chicken before you know it. I will take care of setting up the yard. Maybe you should go lay down for a bit? You know, with your condition and all."

"OK, Joe, maybe you are right," Darlene said. "I must have a case of baby brain right now. You always did know how to calm me down."

*****

Much later, Sylvia lifted her toes out of the water and wriggled them against the cool tiles above the tub. She was all wrinkly and pruned and starting to get cold, but she didn't care. Mommy told her to go take a bath, and so she did. It wasn't her fault she didn't specify for how long.

It was better in here anyway. Mommy always got kind of worked up when company was due, and today, with so many people coming to the house, she was in rare form. Sylvia was no fool. She knew best when to lie low. And what better place to do it but in the tub? She loved just lazing away the hours in the bath, splashing and playing, all the while daydreaming. Below her, she heard the house fill up with a horde of relatives and friends as her nostrils filled with the smells of all sorts of delicious goodies. There was the distinctly warm and cinnamony smell of apple pie, along with the unmistakable perfume of fried chicken wafting up the stairs.

Still, even the siren call of Maw Maw's fried chicken was not enough to force her to budge. It was so many people in the house — aunts and uncles and a whole bunch of cousins she never even knew she had. It was all too much. But soon, they would all be gone, and tomorrow Daddy promised to make her pancakes and watch Bugs Bunny with her on TV. Then, all would be back to normal.

"Sylvia! Aren't you out of that tub yet?" Darlene shouted from the bottom of the stairs.

"I'm getting out now, Mommy," Sylvia shouted. She frowned. Fun time was over.

"Well hop to it," Darlene ordered. "I laid out the dress I want you to wear on your bed. Now hurry up, get dressed and come down. Maw Maw has been looking for you."

"Yes, Mommy," Sylvia said. She got out of the tub and dried herself off with a big fluffy towel, before wrapping herself up like a terrycloth burrito and padding down the hall to her room. Upstairs was empty — everyone was either outside or down in the kitchen. She could hear her Mommy and her sisters cackling up a storm in the kitchen. That was good. She would be in a better mood.

On her bed she saw a fine linen white dress waiting for her. It was beautiful, with a big blue bow around the neck and everything. She giggled as she put it on. *I bet Diana Prince would wear this. If only I had some glasses.*

She glanced out the window and saw her Daddy and a couple of his brothers standing around a fire in the backyard. She squinted her eyes and then broke out into a broad grin when she saw what they were looking at. *Barbeque! I can't wait! I hope I don't get any sauce on my dress.*

She slipped on her shoes and walked to the top of the stairs. She stopped when a loud voice boomed from below.

"Now there is my Sweet Pea! Just look at you, pretty as a Princess."

"Maw Maw!" Sylvia cried as she rushed down the stairs.

"Slow down there, Sylvia," Maw Maw said. "I don't want to spoil the big night by having you fall down and bust your head open, or something."

"Maw Maw, I am so glad you're here," Sylvia said as she rushed into the plump woman's arms. Maw Maw smelled of biscuits and gravy and was all squish and plump, just like those delicious pots of mashed potatoes she always made. "Did you bring ham biscuits, Maw Maw?"

"You hear that Momma?" Darlene said as she turned the corner and entered the hall. Turning to her mother, she said, "My little girl is just nuts over your ham biscuits. She says mine are 'OK,' but, need a little work."

Maw Maw threw her head back and laughed. "Well, dear, serves you right."

"What?" Darlene said.

"Oh, how you have forgotten," Maw Maw said. "You loved Granny's deviled eggs and said I should try and get her recipe." She turned back to Sylvia and said, "it appears the apple did not fall far from the tree."

Darlene nodded and said, "yeah, I guess I forgot about that." She touched Maw Maw's arm and added, "but Momma, I do think your deviled eggs are the best."

"Can I help you make deviled eggs, Maw Maw?" Sylvia said.

"I have a better idea," Maw Maw said. She glanced over at Darlene and said, "I think your Mommy has more than enough helpers in the kitchen, with all of her sisters here. So, I think you need to help me set up for Circle tonight. Would you like that?"

"Would I!" Sylvia said.

"Momma," Darlene cautioned, "are you sure? Isn't she a bit too young for that?"

"I'm not too young, Mommy," Sylvia said. "I will be eleven in July!"

"See, Darlene," Maw Maw said. "Sylvia says she is not too young. And you know what? She isn't. Don't you remember when you helped Granny set up for Circle the first time? How old were you then?"

"Well...," Darlene said. "I don't know..., it seems a bit—"

"—You were eight!" Maw Maw said. "And…, I then, like you now, said you were too young. It is hard, I know."

"I guess you are right, Momma," Darlene said. "I guess Sylvia is growing up."

"She is," Maw Maw said. "Growing up like a weed, too. Just look at how tall she's getting."

"Daddy said I should try out for basketball," Sylvia said.

"So, how about it, Sweet Pea?" Maw Maw said. "Are you ready to go help me prepare for Circle?"

"You bet!"

Maw Maw looked down at her watch and said, "We need to hurry, though. Father Ted will be here soon, and we need to have everything all set up nice and pretty for him before he arrives."

"OK!"

Sylvia and Maw Maw walked out the back door and into the yard. It was bustling with activity, a full-on celebration. On the left side of the yard, Joe and several of the other men (mostly his brothers) were standing around the barbeque pit laughing. Who knows what about, but it was probably some tale that ended with the line - "and that's what she said." As always, the joke wasn't that funny, but a quick glance at the growing pile of crushed Pabst Blue Ribbon cans at their feet helped explain the level of hilarity. Warm cheap beer makes everything more amusing.

To their right, Sylvia spied an army of her aunts and cousins busily preparing the tables in the yard. Thick checkered plastic tablecloths were spread out on each and in the center of every table was a mason jar filled with water and containing a flowered Rhododendron branch. *Spring in the mountains is a thing of pure beauty.*

"Mmmm, the barbeque smells delicious, Joe," Maw Maw said as they walked past the pit.

"Thanks, Maw Maw. I picked out the best of the litter myself."

Maw Maw paused as she leaned over the fire pit and took in a deep breath. The thin grey smoke poured over her like one of the early morning fogs that crept over Black Mountain every dawn. She closed her eyes in delight and bathed in the aroma. "I see you selected the fattest one," she said as she patted Joe's cheek. "Good boy... Good boy..."

"Only the best for tonight," Joe said.

Maw Maw asked, "Did you bring the—"

"—Got it right here," Joe said as he smiled. He reached down by his feet, lifted up a weathered old leather bag and handed it to Maw Maw. "I stopped by Johnson Memorial Gardens myself last Friday and picked it up. I made sure everything was done just like you said."

"And they had a fresh one?"

"Yup," Joe said. "I saw it in the paper that morning. I had to wait in the woods, though. They had the service late, and there were a few stragglers that stayed behind."

"There always are," Maw Maw said as she shook her head. "But..., you came through, just like I knew you would. I always knew Darlene was the smartest of my daughters when she married you," she said as she patted his cheek again.

"Hey!" Randy, one of Joe's many brother-in-laws, said as he stepped forward and laughed. "You know, I'm standing right here."

Maw Maw winked and said, "Well, your wife, Brandine, always was the pretty one, but, that girl never was that bright. I suppose I shouldn't have dropped her on her head when she was a baby."

"Maw Maw's got your number, Randy," one of the other men called out from behind as the whole group broke into laughter.

Maw Maw turned back to Sylvia and said, "you know, your Daddy here is a good man. A very good man. He always delivers in a pinch. So..., are you ready to get things set up?"

"I am," Sylvia said.

"Randy," Maw Maw said as she pointed over into the crowd of men. "Rustle me up a couple dozen of those Tiki Torches, will you?"

"Will do, Maw Maw."

Sylvia followed her grandmother across the broad lawn of the backyard to the edge of the woods. At least fifty yards from the house, three card tables were set up adjacent to one another, forming an extended surface — like a banquet table. Over the top, a beautiful silk tablecloth had been spread, all purple and green, like the colors of a peacock.

"Isn't it beautiful, Sylvia?" Maw Maw asked.

"It is," Sylvia said. "It is the most beautiful tablecloth I have ever seen. What is it made of?"

"Silk and gold and all sorts of goodies," Maw Maw said. "It has been in our family for many, many years. Each generation adding their own embellishment before handing it to the next." She pointed at the edge to the silver tassels hanging down onto the grass. "See those?"

"Yes."

"I made those myself when Granny gave it to me before she died. And no doubt, one day, your mother will make her own addition to this heirloom. Eventually, you too will make one."

"Me?"

"Yep," Maw Maw said. "Each generation stands on the shoulders of the one that proceeded it."

"But I don't know how to."

"Don't worry about it," Maw Maw said. "Your mother will teach you, as I taught her. And speaking of teaching, let's get one of your lessons started right now." She passed the leather bag to Sylvia and said, "Now…, I want you to sprinkle this in a wide circle on the ground around the table. Make it big, though."

Sylvia opened the bag and looked inside. She wrinkled her brow. She did not understand. It was just a bag of dirt — damp, black soil.

"Begin the circle near the woods. Start about six paces from the table."

Sylvia paused and then said, "OK, Maw Maw." She walked to the edge of the forest, dug her hand down into the bag and took out a fistful of soil. Methodically, she began sprinkling it onto the ground, leaving a thick trail of black on the bright green grass.

"Wonderful, Sylvia, wonderful!" Maw Maw said. "Now…," she added as she pointed to the table, "keep it wide. And don't dump so much at once. You gotta make it last."

"OK, Maw Maw," Sylvia said as she continued, arcing around the table as she faithfully deposited the entire contents of the bag onto the ground. When she was finished, she went back to stand by her grandmother. "Did I do OK?"

Maw Maw leaned down and kissed her forehead. "You did perfect-ly! I am so proud of you. It is a perfect circle."

Randy walked up to them with the Tiki torches and said, "where do you want them, Maw Maw?"

"I need you to lay them out in two intersecting triangles, inside the circle. It needs to form a perfect, five-pointed star."

"You got it," he replied as he walked behind the table.

"Start at the top of the circle, OK?"

"OK."

After a few minutes, and a couple of adjusting directions from Maw Maw, the torches were on the ground in their assigned spots.

"I bet it is going to be real pretty when they are lit," Sylvia said.

"Oh, they are," Maw Maw said. "Real pretty."

Click... *Click... Click...*

Chapter 5

April 18th, 2017 - UVid Headquarters - Mountain View, California - 4:45 PM

"TAKE DEEP BREATHS," Sylvia instructed. "Dig down deep into the pit of your stomach as you feel your lungs expand and the oxygen flows into your body."

"Shew…., OK…, OK…," Heather said as she gulped air into her throat. She was flat on her back, sprawled out on the floor in the Eye Bleach Lounge, the thick, soft carpeting surprisingly comfortable beneath her back. She was remarkably relaxed, and that was amazing, all things considered.

"Not too quickly, Heather," Sylvia said. "You don't want to hyperventilate. Slow your breathing and take long, deep breaths. One…, Two…, Three…"

"OK, but…," Heather said. "I'm sorry. It's just that I can't stop seeing those—"

"—No, don't think about them. Don't get sidetracked. Don't think about those kittens from the video. They are fine now, I'm sure of it. Just focus on your breathing," Sylvia said. She watched as Heather, her face glistening with sweat and her brow twisted, finally slipped into the deepest end of her relaxing sequence. She was getting it now. Everything was registering, and her chest slowly rose and dropped as she exhaled long deep sighs.

"Yes, Heather, that is good…, just long deep breaths. In…., and out…."

"In…., out….," Heather repeated as the words rolled off her tongue like velvet, her consciousness drip drip, dripping away.

"Good, good, you are doing just fine," Sylvia said. "Now, you need to go back. Open your mind wide, go through the door and go back..., deep...., down...."

"Yessssss," Heather said as she elongated the last letter into a sighing, yawning hiss. "I am going deep now. Deep..., Deep..., uh..., where am I now? I don't recognize anything. Where are you sending —
"

"—Now, as I count backward," Sylvia interrupted, "you will feel the years flake away, one by one, just like peeling an onion. As each layer is removed, you go down..., down..., down.... and back in time. Ready?"

"Ready," Heather said.

Sylvia began counting backward. "10..., 9..., 8..., 7..."

Heather's breathing grew slower as the muscles in her face, arms, and legs released like a drawn bow slowly retracted. Her mascara stained cheeks were dry now, and as Sylvia counted down, Heather felt herself grow lighter, each digit called seemingly lifting her up off the floor. As Sylvia reached the number one, Heather's stomach fluttered. It was both exhilarating and disconcerting, like the feeling you get at the top of a roller coaster and the car pauses, right on the precipice.

"Now Heather, open your mind's eye and tell me what you see," Sylvia said.

Heather complied, and a smile crept onto her lips. She was six years old again and standing in her Grandmother's kitchen. She glanced around the room and nearly burst into an uncontrollable giggle fit. It was all so amazing. Directly in front of her was the old white gas stove she remembered her Grandmother using, the dials rusted and broken from years of cooking. To her right there was a high set of shelves. The bottom was stocked with spices and the middle contained knick-knacks, but on the very top, she saw her favorite thing of all — the forbidden blue and white cookie jar.

But better than all of this, on her left, sitting in a low-backed kitchen chair, was Nonny — her grandmother. A cup of coffee was in one hand and a lit Virginia Slim in the other, her green, threadbare housecoat wrapped tightly around her thick body. It had been so many years..., so many years.

"It…, I can't believe it, it…," Heather stuttered.

"Who is it, Heather?"

"It is Nonny! I haven't seen her since I was a little girl. But…, she is—"

"—Don't worry about that now, Heather," Sylvia said. "Nonny is alive and well in your subconscious."

"Incredible…, simply incredible!"

"Heather," Nonny said. "Are you OK, baby? Do you want a cookie?"

"I do, Nonny!" Heather squealed. Her six-year-old-self emerging as easy as putting on an old, well-worn pair of slippers.

"Wonderful, baby, I thought you looked hungry," Nonny said as she stood up and crushed her cigarette out in the tiny plaid beanbag ashtray sitting in her lap. "But first, I have to ask you a question."

"Yes, Nonny?"

Nonny walked across the kitchen floor and stood in front of Heather. Reaching down with her soft, yet weathered and wrinkled right hand, she carefully brushed Heather's bangs out of her eyes. "Have you been crying, girl?"

"I…, I have Nonny. I'm sorry."

"Don't be sorry. But why? What has gotten you so upset?"

"I…, oh Nonny," Heather said, her lower lip quivering as she burst into tears. "Those kittens. Those precious little kittens. Who would do such a terrible thing? Why? Why would someone set those little babies on—"

"—Shh…," Nonny said as she pulled Heather forward and hugged her tight.

Heather sighed as she felt her Grandmother's arms enfold her, and the sweet smell of her Jean Nate cologne, cheap bourbon, and cigarette smoke engulfed her. It was a scent she knew so well. It was the smell of Nonny and it instantly calmed her.

"There are some messed up people in this world, and they do some bad things," Nonny said. "But…, that does not mean you have to worry about it."

"But, I can't stop—"

"—Or even think about it ever again! I am going to fix it up nice."

"But how, Nonny?" Heather said. "I..., I can't stop seeing them. I can't stop hearing their pitiful little mews. They were clawing on the box, trying to get out, as the flames..., oh Nonny!" More tears flowed as Heather began sobbing uncontrollably.

"Heather," Nonny said, "reach into your back pocket."

Heather complied and felt something in her jeans pocket. She said, "What? What is—"

Nonny said, "Now, give it to me."

Heather pulled her hand out and opened it. In her palm was a folded-up sheet of paper. She held it up and Nonny reached down, took it from her hand, unfolded it, and examined it.

"Disgusting! Absolutely disgusting! What monsters! Monsters!" Nonny exclaimed. She quickly refolded the paper and slid it into the side pocket of her housecoat. "But..., now we will make sure it doesn't bother you anymore." She asked, "Do you remember where Grandpa used to keep his coin collection?"

"Oh yes!" Heather said. "He never let me play with those."

"No," Nonny said with a laugh. "I am sure he did not."

"He always kept them locked up tight and put away. Down in that big box in the basement, right?"

"Yes, it was," Nonny said. "He used to call it his strong box, remember?"

"Yes, just like Captain Kidd."

"Right," Nonny said. "And, like Captain Kidd, he kept all his special valuables, things he didn't ever want anyone to find, locked up inside that strong box down in the basement, behind the washer. And now...," she added as she took the paper out and waved it in the air, "that is exactly where this is going to go. Locked up and put away, forever and ever and ever. Would you like that? Would you want to seal this away for good?"

"Oh, Nonny," Heather said as tears began to stream down her cheeks again. "More than anything. I just cannot stop seeing... or hearing...."

"Enough of that, now," Nonny said. She smiled, and added, "Nonny is going to make it all better. Follow me."

Heather followed as Nonny walked to the far side of the kitchen and opened the door to the basement. The two walked down the rickety wooden steps, the sides littered with empty glass soda bottles waiting for the trip to the grocery store for the nickel deposit, grandpa's work boots, stacks of old Life magazines and other debris. Once in the basement, Heather was overwhelmed by the memories flooding into her mind. There was the old family Christmas tree. Artificial and made entirely of plastic, it looked like a series of bright green bottle brushes jammed into a painted brown metal pole. It was still decorated and covered in a translucent plastic bag, awaiting its seasonal debut. Nonny always liked to be efficient. Christmas decorating for her took no more than ten minutes every year, right after Thanksgiving dinner. Just a short haul up the stairs and with one pull on the bag — whoosh, Merry Christmas!

Heather glanced around the basement until she spied what she was looking for. There on the right side of the long narrow room was the washer and dryer placed against an unpainted brick wall. She watched intensely as Nonny walked over and carefully removed two loose bricks above the washer, reached inside the hole and pulled out a grey metal box.

"Here we go," Nonny said as she opened the box and placed the folded-up paper inside beside the coins. "Exactly where Grandpa left it. Now, go and fetch me that chain," she said as she pointed over to the other side of the basement. There, on top of some old newspapers and a large stack of McCall's magazines, was a long rope of chain and three bicycle locks, all belonging to a bike that had long since been taken to the town dump. Heather brought them back and handed it to her grandmother.

Nonny took the chain and wrapped the metal box several times over, crisscrossing the chain over the box like a decorative ribbon tied on a carefully wrapped birthday present. Pulling the chain tight, she lined up the links on the chain and took the locks from Heather's hand.

"I think three will do, don't you?"

"Yes! It will stay nice and locked away now."

Nonny nodded and winked as she closed the locks over the chains. Click… Click… Click…

"There we go," Nonny said. "All safe and secure. So, how about we go back up to the kitchen and have that cookie?"

"Yay!" Heather exclaimed. "Oatmeal raisin?"

"Of course, and I even have some Mallomars."

"Wheeee, my favorite."

Back in the kitchen, Heather greedily devoured the cookie as Nonny watched on with a broad grin on her face. "Heather…," she said.

"Yes, Nonny?"

"Close your eyes and start counting. One…, two…, three…"

*****

"Holy crap, that was the most amazing thing I have ever seen!" Steve said. He and Sylvia stood on either side of Heather lying prone on the floor of the Eye Bleach Lounge. Her face was in a full grin, her eyes were closed, and she was chewing. Chewing and grinning. Most surprisingly, though, the wrinkle in her brow was gone.

"Heather, are you awake?" Sylvia asked.

"Wh… what?" Heather said as she sat up and wiped her mouth, the feel of the dream cookie crumbs still on her lips. "What happened?"

"That was effing crazy!" Steve said. "Just incredible." He paused and added, "do you think it worked?"

"What worked?" Heather said. "I…, what is going on?"

"Heather, do you want to talk about the kittens?" Sylvia asked.

"Kittens?" Heather asked. "What about kittens?"

"Damn…, it really worked," Steve said as he shook his head. He turned to Sylvia and said, "I am very impressed. I thought you were just talking a bunch of bullshit before, but…, I stand corrected. This shit works!"

Heather stood up and brushed her pants off. "Well…, I am not exactly sure what happened here…., but," she said as she glanced around the room, closed her eyes and took in a deep breath, "I know I have never felt better. It is like everything is now…, clear, you know? Like a great burden has been lifted."

"You just got your brain washed, Sylvia," Steve said.

"Steve! This is not brainwashing," Sylvia snapped.

"Sorry," he said as he grinned. "How about brain dry cleaned, then."

Sylvia shook her head and sighed.

Heather walked over to Sylvia and touched her forearm. "Thank you. I have never felt better."

"You are welcome, but, you really did it all yourself."

"I really need to get your book," Heather said.

"I will get you a copy," Sylvia said.

"Say…," Steve said. "Can you show me how to do this?"

"Sure," Sylvia said. "If you have time, we can start right—"

"—No…," he interrupted. "It's not for me. It is for…, well…"

"I bet it is for his fiancé," Heather said as her lips turned up into a smirk. "No doubt old Stevie here wants her to forget something."

"Oh, I bet he does," Sylvia said as she grinned and nodded knowingly.

"Hey, it's not like that. It would be better off if she just…, misremembered a few things."

"Yeah, I bet — like that skank from Opal's you tried to hook up with last month."

"How was I supposed to know it was her sister?" Steve said.

"Steve, Steve, Steve," Sylvia said as she shook her head.

"Such a pig," Heather added as she cast a sideways glance at Sylvia.

"It doesn't work that way, anyway," Sylvia said. "Those morons out there in the magic clubs with those hypnosis acts have done a real disservice to the public. They have given out a lot of faulty information and created an entirely erroneous narrative about how the brain works."

"But, I thought—," Steve said.

"—The subject has to do the work themselves, Steve. Unless your fiancé wants to blot out the memory of your indiscretion…, with her sister, I might add," she added as she frowned, "you are out of luck. You cannot force this technique on anyone. It really has to be done by the person who wants to do the rewiring of their own memories."

"I doubt she is going to be open to that," Steve said. He smiled and said, "So, can you help me blot out the memory of her constant bitching about it then?"

"That…, I can help with," Sylvia said.

"You know, this would have saved me a butt load of money in therapy," Heather said. "God, the money I spent trying to get over Dave. Where were you three years ago?"

Sylvia smiled and said, "I was back in New York making lots of enemies in my department."

"Oh, I bet," Heather said. "Dr. Saferstein got a lot of money out of me with his Freudian techniques."

"Oh, my dear," Sylvia said as she reached over and touched Heather's arm. "You had a Freudian as a therapist?"

"Yeah," Heather said as she looked down at the ground. "Stupid, wasn't it?"

"Well…, I wouldn't be that harsh, but, I assume you wanted to get better, right?"

"Of course," Heather said.

"Well then, having endless therapy sessions with a Freudian is literally the least effective way to achieve wellness. They tend to create far more issues than they ever solve."

"Yeah," Heather said. "I can see how you were real popular back in the Psychology department at NYU."

Sylvia laughed.

"But…, this certainly worked wonders," Heather said. "Whatever it was that bothered-"

"—Oh, it was about that big box of kittens that idiot set on—" Steve said.

"—No, no, no!" Heather barked. "Please, Steve, I just got over that. I don't want to get re-traumatized by whatever it was I saw. Plus, I don't know how long this will stay…, you know, fixed."

"Well," Sylvia said. "I wouldn't watch the video again; but, you should be good for a long time, probably forever."

"You should do this procedure for the guys in the military, Sylvia," Steve said. "I know I have some buddies that saw some pretty messed up shit over in Iraq. This could actually help them, and, it is so fast. I will say it again, I am just blown away."

"I had quite a few clients from the military, but, my technique is controversial, and so the Defense Department stopped allowing any active duty clients from seeing me." Sylvia shrugged and added, "I think it embarrassed quite a few of the Military Psychologists they have on staff. Politics, you know. Politics."

"That is horrible!" Heather said.

"Typical bureaucratic bullshit," Steve said.

"It is," Sylvia said with a heavy sigh. "But, I had quite a few retirees and other servicemen that left the service come and see me. And of course, my book was moderately successful."

"Oh yes," Heather said, "You wrote, *Reprogram your Mind, Reprogram your Life*, right?"

"Yes," Sylvia said. "You did your homework!"

"I did," Heather said. "I looked up your name and got the title. I meant to pick up a copy from Amazon. Now I know I will."

"I just had it formatted into eBook form," Sylvia said.

"But, don't you have to be a therapist or something to use this technique?" Steve said.

"Not really," Sylvia said. She smiled as she lowered her voice into a conspiratorial tone, "I will let you in on a little industry secret. Most of the healing done by psychologists is done by the patients themselves. We psychologists, are, at best, only guides. I wrote my book specifically for the layperson who wanted to rewire some troubling memories out of their own mind. You do not need a "professional" to facilitate, but, of course, it doesn't hurt."

"So, not to pry, but, have you done this procedure on yourself?" Heather asked.

"No," Sylvia admitted, "but, of course, if I had, how would I know? The bad memory would be gone, as would the memory of the therapy itself."

"Incredible," Heather said. "Just incredible. And…, no side effects or anything?"

Steve turned to Sylvia and said, "Didn't you say something about Turrets Syndrome occasionally flaring up, or sudden homicidal urges?

And of course, when Heather took off all her clothes during the trance and started writhing around on the floor, it was quite a show." He grinned as he turned to Heather and said, "I always wondered whether you were a natural brunette. Now I have my answer."

"What?" Heather cried.

"Don't listen to him," Sylvia said as she laughed. "I said no such thing, and you did nothing like that! This is all done only with your own mind, and without drugs—"

"—Nothing wrong with drugs, you know," Steve interrupted.

"Drugs," Sylvia continued as she glared back at Steve. "It is all natural. No side effects at all."

Heather smacked her lips and said, "I was wondering if an increase in appetite was a side effect. Suddenly, I have this overwhelming urge to eat an entire box of oatmeal raisin cookies, or even better, Mallomars."

"Last call, guys," Nancy said as she opened the door and entered the lounge, her cart rattling before her as she walked. "I saw the light on and thought I should check. So…, any snacks for the road?"

"Well, you couldn't have stage managed that better," Steve said as he glanced over at Sylvia.

"What time is it?" Heather said.

"It is coming up on 5:30," Nancy said. "Everyone has left for the day, and I was just about to pack up myself."

"I think I will have a Kit Kat," Steve said.

"Do you have any oatmeal raisin cookies?" Heather asked.

"I do," Nancy said as she handed the Kit Kat bar to Steve. After digging through the shelf for a few seconds, she lifted out a bag of Archway Soft Oatmeal Raisin cookies and said, "Will these do?"

"Perfect!" Heather said as she took the bag from Nancy's hand and ripped it open. After jamming one in her mouth, she added, "I am starving."

"You going to get anything, Sylvia?" Steve said.

"No thanks. I think I will pass on the sweets today," Sylvia said. "I need to watch my blood sugar. I had a little episode the other day and went kind of — funny, for a minute or two." She smiled and added, "This infinite candy supply is starting to have an adverse effect. God knows, if I don't end up with diabetes working here, it will be a miracle."

"An occupational hazard," Heather mumbled with a full mouth of cookie.

"Don't let her fool you, guys," Nancy said. "I just wheeled my cart past Sylvia's desk and noticed she brought in ice cream for herself." She turned to Sylvia and in a joking tone said, "And I don't think she means to share. You know, if everyone sees you eating ice cream at your desk, I will have to stock it."

"Ice Cream?" Sylvia asked. "What are you talking about? I didn't bring in any ice cream."

"Well…, you have some waiting for you on your desk," Nancy said. "Assuming it hasn't melted already."

"Well now, this is mysterious," Heather said.

"Hey, who knows," Nancy said. "Maybe you have a secret admirer or something?"

Heather said, "I would be in heaven if the company started handing out Rocky Road, you know."

"Yeah," Steve said. "Probably means our dental insurance is getting ready to be downgraded again. Make up the difference in Eskimo Pies."

Sylvia laughed and said, "Well, now I am curious." She headed out the door and towards her desk. The others followed, and when they turned the corner to enter the row where Sylvia's desk was located, Heather pointed and said, "Look Sylvia, all of Alyssa's stuff is gone."

"Well, that explains it," Sylvia said. "She must have left the ice cream as a…, gift? It is odd, but, nice."

"Alyssa was odd, and nice, if I remember correctly," Steve said.

"A Dove Bar!" Sylvia said. "My absolute favorite! How could she possibly have known?"

"Look," Heather said as she picked up a folded-up piece of paper from the desk. "It looks like she left a note."

"What does it say?" Sylvia asked as she greedily bit into the Dove Bar, her eyes half closed in pleasure.

Heather read the note and cocked her head. "It doesn't make much sense. Did you know Alyssa or something?"

"No, I never met the girl. You know that. She was gone before I got here."

"Why do you ask?" Steve said. "What does the note say?"

Heather said, "It says... *'Sorry it took so long, Mommy. At least I didn't drop it this time.'*"

Chapter 6

April 20th, 1996 - Central Park, New York City - 2:30 PM

SYLVIA TRIED TO FOCUS HER eyes on the page of her book but it was no use. The letters seemed to jump around on the page, leaping and dancing about like a troupe of black clad ballerinas twirling across a stark white backdrop. In her rational mind, she knew it made sense. In the logical side of her brain, she knew John was right. She knew she should stay put so when Billy returns, he will see her and not wander off again. It was not easy, though. Her mind boiled like an overflowing pot of spaghetti as one horrific scenario after another flashed before her mind's eye. The logical side of her brain was not in control now. The irrational side, the one full of fear, dread and terror was firmly in charge.

He is just playing hide-n-seek, that's all. He always does that. He will be here any second, Sylvia thought to herself as she tried hard to resume reading her book. She tried to will herself calm. John is always so calm in these situations. "*Oh, you know Billy, he loves to play jokes,*" John had said as he headed back down the hill to find their son. Well..., if this was a joke, it was a joke that had gone on far too long.

"Mommy!" a voice cried out behind her.

Sylvia exhaled an explosive burst of air out of her lungs. She spun around towards the voice, half delirious with relief but also with her jaws itching to scream. *First, I am going to kiss and squeeze him tight,* Sylvia thought. *And then I am going to spank his ass!*

"Billy!" she cried. "You had me worried to—" Her words froze in her throat. It wasn't Billy. The crying child, unaware of the drama he had been an unknowing participant in, ran past Sylvia and across the lawn to his waiting mother. The temporary euphoria in her gut transformed into a solid iron ball in the pit of her stomach.

Sylvia looked down at her watch. *Has it only been ten minutes? It feels like ten hours! John is right. I always worry too much. I just need to think about something else and get my mind off of it,* she thought. *Billy has pulled this hiding game many times before. I am sure this is no different. He will be back any second…, any second now, I just know it.*

A few agonizingly slow minutes passed, and Sylvia looked up from her book again. The muscles in her calves were throbbing, as if they, separate from the rest of her body, wanted to leap to her feet and run off hunting for Billy. She knew better, of course, but the body often wants what the head does not. She glanced out over the people in the park and her brow furrowed. The sights of such happy families — eating their hot dogs, playing cards, chatting and lounging on the grass in the warm spring air only angered her. *How can this day be so ruined? Why can't we just have one day out in the park as a happy family? Just one! I swear to God, when Billy gets back I am never letting him out of my sight again! He will be under my thumb, and on a very short leash until high school.*

Her anger turned to panic as new images, terrible and gut-wrenching visions, flooded into her mind in a torrential mudslide. She thought about the nearby rock climbers, just a few yards away out of her sight. Had Billy gone down there to hide? Was he, right now, dangling from the top of that stony manmade hill, ready to fall? Or worse, had he already fallen and busted his head open, blood pooling all over his tiny Spiderman suit, unnoticed and injured?

She could almost see it happening in her mind's eye. It wasn't hard to imagine, especially for a bright and energetic kid like Billy. Seven-year-old boyish logic didn't always make sense to her, but, it does to the boys. She could just see him, his tiny arm outstretched as he spun his imaginary web onto an adjacent rock. He steps off, attempting to jump and then — She shut her eyes tight.

No! No! You have got to stop this, she thought to herself. *This is not helping anything!*

I just need to read, Sylvia decided. *Working myself up into a half-crazed nervous breakdown is not helping the situation. A watched pot never boils. He is coming back, right now, any second. I just need to calm down and finish reading my book.*

With all of the willpower she could muster, Sylvia forced her eyes back onto her book. She gritted her teeth with a steely determination and ground her molars together. She was going to do this. This is supposed to be a relaxing day. This day in the park is meant to be fun. So far, it has been neither, but by God, she is going to force it. Billy is going to be back any second, and there was no use fretting about it! She turns the page to continue reading of Lady Catherfield's exploits with her perpetually shirtless pirate pursuer. Such mindless trash almost always works its charms on her nerves. Whisked away to another world, another time. She begins to read.

Lady Catherfield felt Captain Scarantino's hot breath on her neck. It smelled of rum... and lust. Lust for her. Lust for her treasure, but more than anything, lust for the sea. The swirling waves that rolled over the bow of her...

"Jesus!" Sylvia exclaimed. *How far is that duck pond from here?* She wondered to herself. *We just started Billy in swim class last year. He doesn't know how to swim that well, yet. He barely has even learned to keep himself afloat. Did he try and swim out to see the ducks? He loves feeding the ducks. Did he try and swim out to catch one? Is he, right now, lying lifeless on the bottom of the pond, his tiny face blue, his lungs exploding as he runs out of air?*

"Billy! Billy where are you!" Sylvia screamed as she leaped to her feet. "Billy! Billyeeee!"

"Are you OK, lady?" a woman's voice from behind her asked.

"It's my little boy, he is missing. He went with his father to get ice cream, and...," Sylvia said as she pointed at the ice cream stand. She turned around to the woman and added, "He was supposed to come right back, but he didn't."

"Where did your husband go? Wasn't he right here?"

"He went looking for him. He was only gone a...," she turned and yelled, "Billy! Billy come back here, now!"

"I think everything is going to be all right, dear," the woman said. "I have been sitting right here for the last hour. I couldn't help but notice you all. Your little boy is the one in the Spiderman costume, right?"

Sylvia felt the knot in her stomach begin to unravel. The woman was older, plumpish and had kind blue eyes that seemed to match her silver hair perfectly. Normally, she would be unnerved by a total stranger confessing to having been watching her family, but now, it seemed oddly calming. One look at the woman told her that she too was a mother, probably a grandmother now, and she did not seem nervous. Perhaps she was overreacting after all.

"Yes! Did you see him leave?" Sylvia asked.

"Of course," the woman said. "He was hard to miss. Simply adorable. I apologize for watching you and your family, but, it really took me back. My late husband and I used to bring our sons here to the park to play when we were your age. How old is your son?"

"He will be eight in June," Sylvia said.

"Oy! Such a rambunctious age. I remember when my two boys were that young. Like a moron, I had them close together," the woman said. She pointed at her hair and laughed. "I can tell you one thing, I earned every gray strand you see on my head right now. If you think one seven-year-old is tough, try having a seven-year-old and a six-year-old at the same time! Madness!"

"Did they run off all the time, too?"

"Good God, yes!" the woman said. "All the time! Boys are like that, you know. Always running, hiding, climbing — it was a never-ending carnival. I'll tell you this, if I had a dollar for every time I said 'Sammy, stop biting your brother,' I would be living over there on Park Avenue right now."

Sylvia laughed. "I guess I should be thankful Billy isn't a biter, then."

"Oh, you should be," the woman said. "Both my boys were always fighting with each other. It was like we were raising two wolverines, sometimes. Jesus, it is a wonder I didn't end up in Bellevue, let me tell you."

"So, you think I should calm down, I suppose?" Sylvia asked.

"Yeah," the woman said as she nodded. "But I get it. Momma instincts are hard to control. You just want to fix everything and keep them safe, but, you have to let them go be boys, too."

"Yes, but it is hard," Sylvia said.

"It is, but, trust me on this, it gets better." The woman smiled and added, "And now my two sons are grown, and each have two boys of their own to deal with. I am getting the last laugh. Those little boys keep my sons, and their wives, in a constant state of turmoil while I get the best job of all."

"Oh?" Sylvia asked. "What is that?"

"Grandma!"

Sylvia smiled. "I guess it is all worth it, in the end. They will worry you to death, though."

"They will that," the woman said. "Say…, you don't mind me asking you a question, do you?"

"No, go ahead."

The woman reached over into her purse and pulled out a paperback book. When she lifted it up, and Sylvia saw the cover, she smiled. It was very familiar. It was the same type of overflowing bodice-ripping story that she was reading, complete with a buxom lady being swept away by yet another Fabio stylized hero. Only this time, Fabio was not a pirate but was wearing a Kilt.

"I was just about finished with *Lady Catherfield and the Highwayman*, and I could not help but notice that you were reading *Lady Catherfield and the Pirate*. Is it any good? I was thinking of switching to another author, but, who knows. I may stick with the series for a bit longer."

"It's not bad," Sylvia said. "But I think her books are getting a bit repetitive."

"True," the woman said.

"I mean," Sylvia continued. "Lady Catherfield so far has fallen prey to the Lusty Lord, the Pensive Pirate and the Horny Highwayman…, I think she needs to switch it up a bit. The formula is getting a bit stale for my tastes at least."

"Well," the woman said as she pointed to the cover. "I don't disagree, but…, I know I would let old Fabio here rescue me whenever he wanted, especially if I was the beautiful Lady Catherfield from Oxfordshire Hall. Sadly, I'm only Gladys Bernstein from the Bronx. I think my young, damsel in distress days are in the rear-view mirror!"

"You are a hoot!" Sylvia said.

"So…, do you feel a little better now?" Gladys asked.

"You know…, I think I do," Sylvia said. "I had gotten myself worked up into a complete lather there for a moment."

"It is easy to do," the woman said. "But, the best thing to do is to keep your mind off the time. When your kids are hiding from you, a minute can seem like an hour."

"Isn't that the truth."

"But, all's well that ends well," the woman said as she pointed down the hill. "I think I see your husband and son returning."

Sylvia quickly turned her head to look. She sighed as she saw them. They were still a little way off, and she could not see them clearly, but, she recognized John and saw a child was walking beside him. It was hard to tell for certain, as they were both in a crowd, but, it appeared her self-inflicted drama was ending. She exhaled loudly as her whole body relaxed.

"Thank you," Sylvia said as she turned back towards the woman. "You really helped calm my nerves."

"I will consider it my good deed for the day," the woman said. "I could tell you were upset, and little ones grow up so fast. You will miss the frenzy they generate when it is gone. Before you know it, you'll be joining the Grandma club with me."

"I can't think about that yet," Sylvia said.

"It will happen before you know it," the woman said. "Time tends to sneak up on you."

"Let me get Billy through high school first. Thank you again. I appreciate your help."

Sylvia picked her book up and resumed reading. She did not want to appear overly concerned. She had had enough razzing from John already about her overprotective parenting style. He always said she was a smothering mom. If he could have seen her for the past fifteen minutes, he would have had ample evidence to build his case. Knowing he was getting close, she glanced out of the corner of her eye, over the cover of her book, to see him approach. He was only twenty feet away now, but the look on his face instantly caused the bottom to fall out of her gut. Her eyes immediately darted down beside him, towards Billy— but there was a problem. She felt her arms tingle and the hairs on the back of her neck start to rise. It wasn't Billy. It was some other child, and…, another woman walking alongside them both — accompanied by a police officer.

"John!" she shouted as she jumped to her feet. "What is going on?"

"Sylvia…, we…, we need to go to the police station," John said, his voice soft and strained.

"What! What do you mean — police station? What is happening?"

"Billy…, he…," John said.

"Where is Billy? My baby! Oh my God! Where is my baby? What has happened to my baby?" Sylvia screamed. Her gut-wrenching cry of despair echoed through the park, all the way to the rock climbers near the duck pond and caused every head in earshot to turn.

Chapter 7

April 18th, 2017 - Fred's Bar & Grille, Mountain View, California - 7:30 PM

"WHAT IF I WERE to ask my girlfriend Donna to come and see you for something else?" Steve asked. "Say…, for example, to quit smoking." He smiled as he added, "Yeah…, that would work. She has been trying to kick the habit for years. So…, say she wanted to quit smoking, could you then, when she is already under, and you are already in there, so to speak, you know, do your magic?"

"We have been over this already, Steve," Sylvia said. "Anyone who wants to undergo my technique must do it of their own free will. You can't pull a bait and switch. The secret of their recovery lies within the person themselves wanting to lock away the unfortunate memory. It is really all up to them. And from your description, it sounds like Donna is quite determined to remember your piggish behavior with her sister for quite some time."

"Amazing, isn't he?" Heather said after taking a long gulp of her margarita and placing it on the table. "He is like a dog with a bone with this harebrained scheme of his." She turned back to Steve, and said, "Boy, you sure must be enduring a never-ending shitstorm from Donna to keep bringing this plan of yours up."

After taking a swig of his beer, Steve rolls his eyes and said, "You have no idea. There was always bad blood between Donna and her sister before, and…, well…, this didn't help. Again, how was I supposed to know? I wasn't doing anything bad, really. I am just naturally a very…, gregarious person."

"Is that what they call it these days?" Sylvia said with a laugh. "I always knew it by another name."

"What? Being a pig?" Heather said with a snort.

Sylvia nodded, pointed her finger at Heather like a pistol and pretend fired as she said, "Bingo!"

"Man," Heather said as she shook her head and turned back to Steve. "You went to college, right?"

"Sure did," Steve said. "Got my undergraduate in Computer Science with a minor in Electrical Engineering from Caltech before I got my masters from—"

"—As I figured," Heather said. "It all fits. Your balloon is all bunched up on one side. Totally out of balance, just like all the rest of you tech guys."

"What in the hell are you talking about?" Steve asked.

"Balloon?" Sylvia said. "Out of balance? Now you have me curious. What are you talking about?"

"Well, you especially will be able to appreciate my theory, Sylvia," Heather said. "Having your doctorate in Psychology and all."

"Perhaps," Sylvia said. "But…, balloons? An interesting metaphor, I am sure. I am dying to hear what it means."

Heather pointed to Steve and snickered, "Oh yes, it fits perfectly. Steve here could be exhibit A of my theory in practice. It is more accurate to call this syndrome the lopsided balloon theory."

"OK," Steve said. "I'll bite. First, you call me an example of the Peter Pan principle, and now you refer to me as a lopsided balloon. You are definitely not holding your punches lately." His lips curled into a devilish smile as he shifted in his chair. "I can assure you, Babe. There ain't nothing balloonish going on down here. It is all 100%, grade-A, Steve."

Heather rolled her eyes and sighed before she said, "Don't be such a perverted child, for once."

"Well, we are off the clock," Steve said.

"Yes, we are. And you should take this after work time as a learning opportunity. You need to listen to me. It might do you some good."

"OK, I'm game. What are you getting on about?"

"You are obviously brilliant," Heather said.

"Damn straight," Steve said as he took another swig of his beer. After putting the bottle down, he added, "you don't graduate from Caltech as a moron, you know."

"No," Heather said. "But, like many intelligent people I know, all of your smarts are bunched up in one area. Your intellectual resources are not spread out very efficiently. You may know everything there is to know about computers, circuit boards, routers, and whatnot; however, when it comes to women, you are a stark raving idiot. Intelligence is fairly consistent in the general population and does not deviate greatly from one individual to another. The distribution of those smarts individually, however, is very erratic."

"So," Sylvia said. "I assume what you are saying is, everyone is about as intelligent as everyone else, but some people just have all of their..., air, so to speak, all pushed up against one side of their balloon."

"Yes!" Heather said. "Think about it. How many highly intelligent people do you know that are masters in one or two subjects, but complete idiots in everything else? You know the type, they can rewire your whole network in an hour but cannot carry on a simple conversation."

"I know quite a few people like that," Sylvia said.

"Yeah, me too," Heather said. "In fact, I have dated quite a few guys like that, some of them bordering into *Rain Man* territory. So, our subject Steve here is not a natural pig, but, he is just handicapped. It really isn't his fault. There has been a malfunction in his brain. He needs to have his intellect spread out a little more over the rest of his decision-making processes." She smirked as she turned to Steve and added, "Such as knowing it's a bad idea to hit on your fiancées' sister."

"Yes," Sylvia said as she squelched a laugh. "That would be a good move."

"OK, OK, Heather," Steve said. "Duly noted."

"And maybe," Heather said, "instead of trying to get Sylvia to treat Donna, you should have her put you under instead. Who knows, she might be able to get you all fixed up nice and straight."

Steve threw his head back as he bellowed out a deep laugh. "Oh no, I think not." He raised his eyebrow and added, "I much prefer all my squiggles and curvy lines. I earned every deviation. But..., you know who might have benefitted from Sylvia's drip-dry brainwashing routine?"

"It is not brainwashing, Steve," Sylvia said as she shook her head.

"If you say so," Steve said with a grin.

"Who would benefit?" Heather asked.

"Alyssa, of course," Steve said. "I always knew she was a bit flakey, but..., obviously she had some real problems."

"Yeah," Heather said. "That weird note about the ice cream was bizarre. I always thought she was just an airhead before, but now, oddly, I am more intrigued by her."

"Yes, it was a strange message," Sylvia said.

Steve asked, "Heather, your desk was right beside hers. Did she ever show any..., you know, wacky tendencies before?"

"It is hard to judge wacky tendencies when you are working in an insane asylum," Heather said. "Everyone in the department is a bit off. Hazards of the job, I suppose."

"Well, you seem stable enough," Sylvia said as she turned to Heather. She grinned as she added, "You are definitely better adjusted than most of the others I have met here."

"Thanks," Heather said. "But, that is sort of like being named the thinnest kid at fat camp. Not really much of an award, now is it?"

"No, I suppose not," Sylvia said. "Still..., I would have liked to meet this Alyssa, especially after the phantom ice cream gift and all."

"Did the Dove bar taste all right, Sylvia?" Heather said. "You never know..., that psycho might have put something in it."

"Yeah, Sylvia," Steve said. "You did get all spacey there for a minute. I hope the chocolate coating didn't have arsenic sprinkles."

"It was fine," Sylvia said. "Jesus, you guys are dark."

Heather and Steve exchanged a knowing glance. Steve said, "Who us?"

"We are nothing but a warm bundle of sweetness and light," Heather said. "See, aren't you glad you joined us for our weekly tradition? Fred's does have the best food."

"And a two-for-one drink special on Tightwad Tuesdays," Steve said as he raised his beer into the air. "Don't forget that."

"It has been great," Sylvia said. "I thank you both for inviting me. You really have made me feel at home since I moved to California."

"Oh, we come here every week after work," Heather said. "You are welcome to join us anytime."

"Well then, I may have to make this a regular stop," Sylvia said. Turning to Heather, she added, "And you were dead on right about those tacos. Pure heaven!"

"And since you are a doctor and able to wriggle inside people's psyches, it is best to keep on your good side," Steve said as he winked. "It is always good to have your type close at hand."

Heather laughed and said, "Yes, it is going to be fantastic to have an actual Psychologist in our group. God knows, we have had so many neurotics in our merry band in the past, I bet we could keep you quite busy for years to come."

"Or decades," Steve said. "And now it appears we even had some psychotics on staff, like Alyssa."

Sylvia chuckled and said, "Hardly. Back in my old practice, it was my experience that any psychotic break usually has a long-term cause. If Alyssa did have some sort of mental breakdown, it was likely a while in forming. Probably due to some unresolved traumatic event. Ironically, she could probably have benefited from my technique."

"Maybe," Heather said. "But she was such a New Age nitwit she probably would have wanted to try out her healing crystals first."

"Oh?"

"Yeah," Heather said. "Like I said earlier, we weren't friends, so to speak, but, we did talk occasionally. She was way out there, always dabbling on the fringes. There was no insane, bizarro-theory she did not entertain — healing crystals, Reiki, mystical yoga weekend retreats, past life regression, you name it."

"I think she told me once her parents were big Hippies back in the 60s," Steve said.

"That figures. Those horrendous peasant skirts she used to wear were a big giveaway, too," Heather said.

"And no doubt helped hide her pregnancy," Steve said.

"Pregnant?" Sylvia said. "So, she was pregnant?"

"I didn't know that! I only said it to Sylvia to be, you know, bitchy," Heather said.

Steve rolled his eyes and said, "And women say we guys are unobservant." Smiling as glanced over at Heather, he asked, "Didn't you notice her growing baby bump? Or the fact that she was sick every morning? Or that she was getting a little bustier than usual?"

"It figures you would notice that," Heather said. "I thought she was just getting fat." Glancing at Sylvia, she said, "the endless supply of free snacks does have its downside."

"Maybe your balloon is a bit lopsided too, Heather," Steve said. "I thought it was obvious she was knocked up."

"Well…, pregnancy can wreak havoc on a woman's hormones," Sylvia said. "That might explain things."

"Do you have kids, Sylvia?" Heather asked. "I…, I hope that isn't too personal a question to ask. I apologize if it was."

"Oh…, no, it isn't," Sylvia said as she closed her eyes and shook her head. She reached up and rubbed her temples and said, "I think I might need to switch to tea now. These margaritas are making me dizzy."

"That is the point of margaritas, is it not?" Steve said as he glanced over his shoulder. He snapped his fingers at the waitress and indicated it was time for another round of drinks.

After the fresh round of drinks were delivered, including tea for Sylvia, Steve turned to Sylvia and said, "I am curious about something, something about your technique."

"Oh?" Sylvia said.

"Are there any side effects to your technique? I mean, it just doesn't seem natural. Memories don't ever really go away, they just get suppressed. What are the long-term effects of consciously suppressing your memories?"

"I take issue with your statement that my technique is not natural," Sylvia said. "Frankly, it is the most natural thing in the world."

"Oh?" Steve said. "How so?"

"Well…, do you remember being born?"

"No, of course not," Steve said. "Nobody does."

"Which is my point," Sylvia said. "Or, consider the fact that so many women forget how painful childbirth is; that is perfectly natural and happens all the time. Our minds evolved over millions of years specifically to selectively forget things, and the thing we forget first is the horror of birth, both mother and child."

"Yes, but, those memories are still in your mind, right?" Steve said. "They don't disappear."

"No," Sylvia said. "They don't disappear. Memories don't really fade, they just get..., misfiled, either intentionally or automatically..., like memories of your own birth. My technique is nothing but purposefully controlling this natural process for our own benefit."

"Yes, but, such repressed memories do resurface, don't they?" Steve said.

"Not if you lock them down properly," Sylvia said.

"I don't know, Sylvia," Steve said. "Although I am impressed with what you can do, I cannot help but think there is a potential downside to your treatment. Human beings are not machines. Are we not the total sum of our experiences, both good and bad? If there were no sour, how would we know something is sweet?"

"It is an interesting philosophical question you pose there, Steve," Sylvia said. "But, there are some things, and some experiences, that need to be eradicated root and branch. Some things need to be forgotten forever."

"But how do you know what needs to be forgotten and what needs to be remembered?" Steve asked. "I am no Psychologist, like you, but I do know the human mind is incredibly complicated. As much as Artificial Intelligence is all the rave now, and scientists keep saying we are on the verge of creating the singularity, I have my doubts. That which makes us human is far more than just algorithms."

"Well now," Heather said. "This is a side I have never seen of you, Steve. I would never have guessed you at being the soft and feely type."

"I'm not, really," Steve said. "Perhaps it is because I have worked with computers all my career that I recognize the fallacy here. Computers aren't any smarter than your kitchen toaster, really."

"I don't understand, Steve," Sylvia said. "What does my technique have to do with computers?"

"Oh, it is reminiscent of the great debate raging through the tech community right now. Many computer scientists believe eventually, the computer will achieve the same level of intelligence and even consciousness people have. They have a similar theory of the human brain that you have."

"Well, on a practical level, isn't the mind essentially a giant database of memories and feelings?" Sylvia asked. "And if we can reprogram those memories, we can—"

"—Maybe," Steve interrupted. "But, I have my doubts about whether machines can truly be perfected into something as wondrously complex as the human mind. And that which separates us from our iPads or iPhones, or even the kitchen toaster, is not just the sophistication of our programming. It is something else…, something intangible. Call me a skeptic but, I always think we should worry when people try to monkey around with a system they truly don't understand. And who, really, can fully understand the human mind?"

"You are correct, Steve," Sylvia said. "The human brain is incredibly complex, and we cannot, and probably will not, ever actually understand all of it. But…, we still have the power to take control of our own minds, especially when it comes to destructive memories, and to remake our past into what we wish. Maybe you have just been fortunate and have not had any trauma occur to you that has sucked away your life into a cycle of endless darkness, but many have, and those people need to be helped. You seriously underestimate the benefits obtained by jettisoning old, useless, and painful memories. Trust me…, there are some things that are best left dead and buried."

"Perhaps," Steve said. "But, be careful about playing God, Sylvia. Every action we take creates consequences we can scarcely imagine."

"God?" Sylvia said with a dismissive shrug. "That mythological concept has nothing to do with my work. We are our own Gods, and it is in our power to create the life we wish to live."

*****

Several hours later, and after a few more rounds of Margaritas, Steve, Heather, and Sylvia ended their pleasant evening. Sylvia wisely decided to take an Uber back to her apartment. There is no sense getting a DUI the first month she lived in California.

As she inserted her key into the lock of her apartment, she smiled when she heard the click click click of Snowy's nails on the tile floor in the foyer. The clicks were soon drowned out by a storm of yips and barks.

"Hey there, Baby Girl," Sylvia said as she stepped inside the apartment. After placing one foot in the door her leg was assaulted by her Pomeranian. She reached down and scooped the little dog up into her arms, her face immediately covered in tiny canine kisses.

"Well, I am glad to see you, too," Sylvia said. "Were you a good girl today? Were you a good girl?"

Excited yaps and the flicking of her tail indicated Snowy's good behavior that day.

"Now, let's let you out," Sylvia said.

The apartment was huge — much bigger than her tiny apartment back in New York. Sylvia decided it was much cheaper, and far quicker, to store her old things back East and take a furnished apartment out here and she was glad she had. Although the décor was a bit bland, all beige on taupe colors, tan wall-to-wall carpeting and unremarkable art on the walls, she did not regret it. Everything was fresh, new and clean. Brand new furniture, in a brand-new apartment, for a brand-new life on a brand-new coast. She breathed in deeply and sniffed that oddly sweet, fresh-paint smell. It was wonderful. It had been at least ten years since her old apartment had been renovated and nothing ever seems as immaculate as a freshly-painted home.

The living room was spacious with a widescreen TV on the right and a beige wrap around couch along the wall. To the right of the entrance was the kitchen, which was almost the size of her New York apartment. Adjacent to the kitchen was the dining room, and beyond the living room was a glass sliding door leading out to a patio that emptied into a large common backyard. She glanced down at Snowy and grinned. "Now Girl, let's keep these carpets nice."

Snowy wagged her tail and continued her loving assault on Sylvia's face all the way down to the floor as Sylvia lowered her. They both walked to the sliding door and when Sylvia placed her hand on the door handle, Snowy began to bark excitedly.

"Settle down! Isn't this nice?" Sylvia said. "See…, we don't have to take the elevator down to the street here."

For about twenty minutes Sylvia and Snowy walked together outside. The common area was a large oblong lawn, decorated with numerous flowering bushes and small trees, and on this warm April evening, it was simply beautiful. It was late, though, coming on 11 PM and Sylvia watched the lights of the other apartments start winking out one by one. She yawned as she glanced down at Snowy, wildly sniffing at everything in sight, and said, "OK, Girl, let's wrap this up so we can go to bed."

Snowy finally squatted and her business for the night was done. Sylvia reached down and scooped up the dog in her arms and walked back inside. "I think we are going to like it here," Sylvia said. Snowy barked her agreement.

Around midnight, Sylvia fell asleep, her latest Lady Catherfield romance novel laying open beside her, Snowy curled up into a little powder puff ball at the end of the bed.

At 3:00 AM, Snowy's ears perked up, and a tiny growl rumbled in her throat. She sensed something. She stood up at the end of the bed, sniffing the air. Something was not right. Something… Her growl turned into a whimper as she watched the bathroom door slowly open. She scooted back up the bed towards Sylvia, her fur bristling and body shaking.

"Go to sleep, Snowy," Sylvia said as she reflexively reached out and petted her dog. She wasn't fully awake, but, her sleeping mind still knew how to calm her pooch.

Snowy was not comforted. She leapt to her feet and began to quiver as she saw something in the bathroom mirror. She couldn't see it clearly, and her nose told her there were no strangers in the house, but it was definitely something. A reflection in the mirror, or…, no, it was something else. It wasn't right. It was a form, a blue mass slowly congealing into a human figure. The stranger was tiny and was just peeking out of the corner of the mirror. A child perhaps, but a child watching…, waiting…. The dog could stand no more, an explosion of barks erupting from her mouth at once.

"Jesus, Snowy!" Sylvia cried as she sat up straight in the bed. "It is the middle of the…" Sylvia paused as she felt the hairs on her arm stand straight on end. A chill crawled up her spine, and her hearing suddenly became highly tuned, like when one's ears clear after descending a steep mountain. Out of the corner of her eye, she saw a sudden movement, and her head jerked to see. In front of her, the bathroom door was open, and in the darkness, in the bathroom mirror she saw…, what? *What is that?* Her heart fluttered, and she scrambled to flip on the side table light. She exhaled out a long sigh. Her bathrobe was hanging on the back of the bathroom door and a blue sleeve could be seen reflected in the mirror.

"Bad dream, Girl?" Sylvia cooed as she ran her fingers across Snowy's head. Snowy did not respond, her eyes remained glued to the mirror in the bathroom as she shivered and growled.

Sylvia got up, closed the door, and returned to bed. Pulling her dog up onto the pillow, she playfully scratched Snowy's stomach. The growls disappeared, replaced by yips of joy. Within a few minutes, both were fast asleep.

Chapter 8

April 30th, 1976 - Pikeville, Kentucky - 6:00 PM

TRAFFIC WAS LIGHT OUT ON route 119. The occasional coal truck, monstrous in size and weighted down with its two-ton cargo of black gold, would barrel around a bend, scaring any wayward driver half to death; but otherwise, the road was empty. Rhododendrons, clinging to the side of Black Mountain, were just starting to bloom. A scattering of freshly fallen cherry blossoms continuously blew across the dark pavement like a pink snowdrift. Spring had definitely sprung.

A lone car burst through the swirling floral shower dancing over the road that late afternoon. It was a pea green, 1972 Lincoln Continental. From the blinding shine on its freshly polished hood, to the glinting sunlight reflected off its gleaming chrome bumpers, it was apparent the car was well tended. And equally well tended was the driver — Father Ted.

He was a painfully handsome young man, his longish black hair slicked back with a good quart of Vitalis, his body was bathed in copious amounts of Hai-Karate. From the grey snakeskin boots on his feet to the black, silk short-sleeved shirt wrapping his muscular chest, Father Ted had spent all afternoon getting ready. He was looking good. It was a big night. The biggest of the year and he knew he needed to put on his best.

He squinted as he peered down the country road, searching for the turnoff. These backroads were always murder to navigate, and with the trees all fully in bloom, it was easy to miss the road sign. He opened his eyes wide when he finally spied the road marker, almost entirely camouflaged by a thick blanket of Kudzu slowly devouring it. It was not what he expected to see. Perhaps he made a wrong turn? He pulled his car over to the side of the road and parked. After popping open the glove compartment, he pulled out his Exxon gas station map.

The map unfurled out like an accordion and he studied the criss-crossing blue lines on the grid for a few minutes. In all of Kentucky there were, at best, twenty miles of good road. Sadly, he was not on one of them. A quick glance back up to the road sign, and then back to the map confirmed the good news. He had not missed his turn, after all. This was it. After refolding the map and depositing it back into his glove compartment he adjusted the rear-view mirror down and stared at his reflection. The right side of his mouth was curled up into a half sneer. His facial expression, coupled with the thick, black and oh so shiny hair-tonic-soaked sideburns hugging the side of his face, completed his youthful Elvis-like appearance. He dug out his Roman collar from his shirt pocket and put it around his neck, straightening it as he glanced back at his reflection in the mirror. Once it was on just right, he grinned at the handsome, chiseled face staring back at him. Father Ted was ready for service.

He started the car up and turned right onto the unpaved road. It would be just a few miles more. He was used to navigating rough roads over the years on the circuit, and he had gotten quite good at finding his way through the endless mire of backwoods roads. Circle was always turning, though, always rolling; forever roll roll rolling along, but it always found a home. This was a new location for Circle this month, and although it was a bit tricky to find, it seemed to be just right — blissfully remote and perfect for the high holiday.

He rolled down the window fully open and breathed the fresh country air deeply into his lungs. He was far off the beaten path now, and the smell of the moist dark earth bursting into life flooded into the car. A low rustle came from his right and his eyes darted over to a wooden crate sitting on the passenger seat. He smiled and gently patted the top of the box.

"Almost there, girl," Father Ted said. "Almost there. Save your charms for later."

He reached down to the floorboard and pulled out an 8-Track tape from a small black leather case. "Some nice tunes will set the mood for us all," he said. He shoved the tape through the retractable door on the dashboard player and before pressing play, he pushed his screwdriver into the drive with his free hand. Damn thing always skips. He turned the volume up and began to sing along.

"*I..., am a man, of constant sorrow. I've seen trouble, all my days...*"

*****

"Momma, did you remember to bring the ambrosia salad?" Darlene asked as she brought out a fresh tray of deviled eggs and placed them down on the picnic table. "You know how everyone always raves about it."

"You are too kind," Maw Maw said as she deposited an aluminum foil pan filled with freshly fried chicken right beside it. "But, I didn't. I asked Helen to make it this month."

"Helen? Are you sure?" Darlene said. She pointed across the lawn at a group of young women giggling and gossiping together. "I hope she remembered to bring it. Cooking for Circle is a big responsibility, you know."

"It is," Maw Maw said. "But so is obtaining her second-degree athame, and Helen is receiving hers next month."

"What?" Darlene said. "She is a bit young for that, don't you think?"

Maw Maw said, "Nonsense, she is almost eighteen now. She can handle it."

"Yeah, but, this is my first-time hosting Circle, and I want everything to be perfect. I can't have Helen..., well..., messing up the night by screwing up the ambrosia salad."

"You need to calm down, Darlene," Maw Maw said. "You are more nervous than a cat sleeping on a porch full of rocking chairs. Everything is going to go off fine tonight, without a hitch, so relax."

"I know, I know," Darlene said. "But it is just—"

Maw Maw gently touched Darlene's arm and said, "—Tonight, will be perfect, trust me. And plus..., you know your sister is no fool. She certainly should be able to handle mixing up a can of sliced coconut and mandarin oranges into a bowl. How hard is that?" She grinned and added, "I even had your Dad make it for me a couple of times when I hosted Circle, and that man could burn Jell-O!"

Darlene laughed, and said, "You are right. I know you are right." She pointed over to the group of young women at the end of the lawn, and added, "But it is just…, well, she doesn't seem to take things very seriously, you know? She still seems very young to me."

Maw Maw glanced over at Helen, standing with several of her cousins chatting away on the lawn. They were laughing and giggling, and all looking so lovely in their thin cotton sundresses — pure perfection and the living embodiment of spring.

"You have such a short memory, Darlene," Maw Maw said. "You know, when you were her age, you were already engaged to be married."

"Yeah, but, that was different," Darlene said. "And, you forget. I was older when I got engaged. I was nineteen, and that extra year makes a difference."

"Well…, you were not that much older," Maw Maw said. "And…, if I remember correctly," she added. "You weren't taking things too seriously at Helen's age, yourself."

"I don't know what you are talking about?" Darlene said. "I was a lot more responsible than Helen is. I mean, just look at her carrying on with her friends. I know I might have been a bit rambunctious, but, I know I wasn't out carrying on with every boy who looked my way."

"You have a very selective memory," Maw Maw said. "In fact, when you were Helen's age, I know Joe had already been plowing up your garden like a greedy hog for quite a while, and that little Sylvia was already on her way. I haven't had that problem with Helen."

"Momma!" Darlene said.

"You think I didn't know?" Maw Maw said. "Honestly, Darlene. You must think I was born yesterday."

"Well…, I don't believe that, Momma," Darlene said.

"And as for taking things seriously, need I remind you of all your other antics at her age? Hmmm?"

"Like what?" Darlene said. "I know I wasn't perfect, but compared to—"

"—Compared to Helen? Frankly, you pulled far more wild stunts than she ever has. Remember breaking into your Daddy's bourbon? Remember that? I certainly do."

"Well…"

"Or when I caught you and your friends all smoking those funny cigarettes up on the roof?" Maw Maw said. "You know, people can see you up there, and they do have phones, and they do know my number at the diner," she added with a twinkle in her eye. "Or…, best of all, how about the time when I came home early from the market and found you and Joe on the couch and—"

"—OK, OK," Darlene said. "Perhaps I am too harsh about Helen."

"You are," Maw Maw said. "Helen has matured into a fine young woman now." Pointing over at Sylvia, standing next to Joe by the barbeque, she added, "and soon enough, much sooner than you will like, that youngster over there will be all grown up and giving you grey hairs." She ran her fingers over her head as she added, "just like all the ones you gave me."

"Oh, I'm not sure I'll be ready for that!" Darlene said.

"Well, you will need to be. It'll be here in no time, mark my word," Maw Maw said. "And then, before you can catch your breath, it'll be her turn to Altar Serve."

"Yes," Darlene said with a sigh. "It all goes so fast. I remember when I was first called for altar service. I was so nervous, but also excited."

"Remember that lovely little white dress you wore?"

"Oh, I certainly do," Darlene said. She shook her head and added, "What I wouldn't give to be able to fit into that again."

Maw Maw reached out, touched Darlene's stomach and laughed. "Yeah, well…, spitting out these babies do take a toll. I should know, I had twelve! This is only your second." She laughed and said, "And, believe it or not, before I had all you kids, I was quite fetching in my little size two yellow sundress. Your father always did like it when I wore that." She looked over at Darlene and said, "but you have a nice figure. You should be proud of your curves."

"Well, thanks," Darlene said. "But looking at my baby sister over there makes me pine for my old days. I must say, I was quite a doll in that little white sundress that night. After Circle, Joe couldn't wait to sneak me off into the woods."

"I declare, the things that went on in my own house," Maw Maw said as she grinned and shook her head. "But, I must admit, you sure were pretty as a postcard. Glorious as a warm spring night." She nodded, pointed down the hill and added, "just like Helen is tonight."

"What..., Helen, tonight?" Darlene said. "Do you think so?"

"Well..., it is not my call, of course, but, at last month's Circle, I swore I caught Father Ted studying her real careful-like. He has a keen eye for these things, he does," Maw Maw said as she paused and turned to watch Helen and her friends. "And just look at her, she is ready. She sure has filled out quite nicely. And..., lucky for her, she got Granny's hips."

"She sure did. It makes me wonder, what did I get, Momma?" Darlene asked.

"You got your Daddy's eyes," Maw Maw said as she reached out and stroked Darlene's cheek. "Your precious Daddy always had such beautiful eyes."

"That's sweet, Momma."

"Yes..., but just be thankful you didn't get my ass!"

"Momma!" Darlene said before bursting out a loud snort.

*****

"Helen, you sure dressed extra slutty today, even for you," Angie said. She grinned and added, "I guess it's true. I guess tonight you're finally going to let old Jimmy-boy go all the way, aren't you?"

"Shut up, Angie," Helen snapped. "You know I'm not seeing him tonight. You know Jimmy doesn't come to Circle; and besides, you have things all wrong. He has been a perfect gentleman on all our dates."

"Oh, I bet he has," Angie said. "You know, I heard he told all his friends that he was already parked on second base, and by summer he would be rounding home, banging you six ways from Sunday. So, I don't think he is quite the gentleman you think he is."

Helen furrowed her brow and said, "Look, Angie, it's not my fault you only have mosquito bites for boobs, and nobody even wants to get to your second base. Hell, they probably couldn't even find it if they tried. But, you are wrong about Jimmy. Dead wrong."

"I don't think so," Angie said. "But, if it isn't Jimmy you got all gussied up for, perhaps it is Father Ted."

"What?" Helen said as her face dropped, and her eyes lowered.

"Bingo," Doris said. "I think you struck pay dirt on that one, Angie."

"You girls don't know nothing," Helen said.

"Oh, I think we know plenty," Angie said. "I've seen how you traipse around like a two-bit whore when he is around." She clucked her tongue and added, "quite pathetic."

"Well," Doris said. "Who could blame her?" She bit her lower lip and added, "That Father Ted is a hottie. Have you seen him in those tight black jeans he wears? Damn! You could eat a plate of baked beans off those buns."

"You are terrible," Helen said as she laughed. "But still...," she continued as she twirled her long hair around her index finger. "I must admit. He is a looker."

"So," Angie said. "Who do you think he will pick for Altar Serve this month? Is that why you are so tramped up today then? Do you think he'll pick you?"

"Who knows, Angie?" Helen said. "Maybe Father Ted is going to take pity on you and lower his standards and call you to serve."

"Listen here—" Angie barked.

"—Hey!" Doris said as she pointed down the driveway. "No sense arguing about all that now. I think that is him coming up the road." They all turned to look.

Just turning onto the gravel drive was Father Ted's Lincoln Continental. The wheels of his great green tank crunched across the pebbles and kicked up a thick cloud of dust. Joe and several of the other men walked down the front yard to meet him.

"Welcome, Father Ted," Joe said as he walked up to the open driver's side window. "I hope you didn't have too much trouble finding the place."

Father Ted smiled, opened the door, and stepped out. He gripped Joe's hand in a firm handshake and said, "No trouble at all." Seeing Darlene and Maw Maw approach, he added, "all I had to do is roll down my window and sniff my way here. Between the smell of Maw Maw's famous fried chicken, and of course, your lovely wife's cheese pennies, it was easy to find."

"You like my cheese pennies?" Darlene said.

"Like 'em," Father Ted said as he patted his toned stomach. "I must've put on five pounds from eating so many of them at last Circle. Delicious! They are my favorite."

"You know, Father Ted," Maw Maw said. "You are going to make me very jealous." With her tone light and flirty she added, "you told me it was my fried chicken you loved best."

Father Ted winked and said, "what can I say, Maw Maw. I just have so much love in me. I can love her cheese pennies and your chicken, too, both equally." Turning back to Darlene, he smiled as his eyes dropped down and he studied her body. He lightly touched her stomach and said, "You are full of life and the spirit flows abundantly in you!" He turned to Joe and said, "you should be so proud."

"Oh, we are," Joe said.

Father Ted closed his eyes and placed both hands on Darlene's belly. Half singing and half chanting, he said, "Oh glorious woman who life bestows, who calms the reaper from ceaseless mow. Like a sprig of pine or babbling brook, from the darkest green verdant nook, Spirit come forth and shine upon, this blessed daughter of your golden dawn!"

"Glory! Glory Hallelujah!" Maw Maw cried.

He glanced up and saw a crowd had gathered around him. All stood still, hands outstretched above their heads as they watched him pray. He called out, "Glory Hallelujah! The spirit flows with great abundance tonight!"

After the loud chorus of Glories sputtered out from the crowd and dissolved into a collective whimper, he turned to Joe and said, "Hey, can you give me a hand with a few things for Circle? I need a couple of strong backs to lift this box I brought."

"Sure thing, Father Ted," Joe said. "Anything you want." Joe turned and looked back into the crowd. Spying a couple of his brother-in-laws standing in the back he motioned them forward.

"Great," Father Ted said. He walked around to the passenger side of his car and opened the door. There, sitting on the passenger seat, was a large wooden crate. It was painted white, and an iron bar lid on top was closed with a rather imposing looking padlock. Maw Maw saw the box and her face brightened.

"Is that what I think it is?" she asked.

"It sure is, Maw Maw," Father Ted said. "And, of course, you, of all people, immediately recognized it. The gifts of the spirit are strong in you."

"Glory Glory!" Maw Maw cried as she threw her hands up in the air. "It has been so long, Father Ted. So long since we—"

"—Well, it is a very special day," Father Ted interrupted.

"That it is. That it is," Maw Maw said. She turned to her right and saw Helen walking forward. "Oh…, you remember my—"

Father Ted reached out, took Helen's hand into his and lifted it to his mouth. After lightly kissing it he said, "of course I remember your daughter. So lovely. So very, very lovely."

Helen blushed and could not help but giggle. No one had ever kissed her hand before. It was just like what she saw in the movies and she loved it.

"And who is this young lady?" Father Ted asked as he glanced over at Sylvia, hiding behind her mother.

"Oh, this is my daughter, Sylvia," Darlene said. She looked down at Sylvia and said, "go say hello to Father Ted."

Sylvia said nothing. She clung tightly to her mother's leg, her tiny fingers gripping Darlene's calf like a drowning sailor clutching a life preserver in a stormy sea.

"She is such a pretty little girl," Father Ted said. He looked down at Sylvia and said, "and what is that you are holding in your hand, darling?"

Sylvia still said nothing, but her grip on her mother's leg grew tighter.

"Tell him, Sylvia," Darlene said. "Go on, don't be so shy." She turned back to Father Ted and said, "I am so sorry. She normally isn't so bashful."

"Oh, that's OK," Father Ted said. "It can be overwhelming making new friends, what with all of the people here and what not." He smiled as he squatted down and got eye to eye with Sylvia. When he reached her level, he softened his voice and said, "but it sure is a pretty little dolly you have there, Sylvia." Cocking his head to the right, he asked, "Is that Wonder Woman by any chance?"

"It is!" Sylvia exclaimed. "You know about Wonder Woman?"

"Of course, I do," Father Ted said. "I used to read all those comic books back when I was your age. And, of course, I watched the TV show the other night. Very exciting." His mouth melted into a soft smile as he added, "She is so much cooler than that stuffy old Superman."

"She is!" Sylvia said.

"And I bet you would be a good Wonder Woman, too. I can tell." He lowered his voice to a conspiratorial whisper as he added, "You have a secret power, don't you, Sylvia? Just like Diana Prince."

"What? Do you think I—"

"—Of course, you do," Father Ted said. "I can tell." He pointed to his collar and grinned. "This collar lets me know things, you see, and it told me all about you and your special powers. I am very impressed. You are an exceptional little girl. Very special."

"Wow!" Sylvia cried. "Do you really think so?"

"Oh, I certainly do," Father Ted said. "So..., would you like to help me today?"

Sylvia looked up at her Mom, who smiled and nodded. "Yes, I would like that," she said.

"Wonderful," Father Ted said, "just wonderful. Now..., I have something in my trunk that I need help with, and...," he paused as he reached out and ran his finger down her nose, "I need a special little girl, especially one with secret powers like you, to help me get her ready for Circle. Do you think you can be a help?"

"Oh yes, Father Ted," Sylvia squealed. "I want to help. You know, Maw Maw had me help her draw the circle out in the backyard earlier!"

Father Ted's face beamed. He winked at Maw Maw and said, "I knew it! I knew you were a special little girl. Yes...., a very, very special little girl. It isn't just anyone who can help draw the sacred circle, you know."

"Really?"

"Yes, really," Father Ted said. "It is a great honor, and your grandmother is a wise, wise woman. Now, I know you will be able to help me."

Sylvia felt as is if she was walking on air. Every hesitation and worry evaporated from her body like the early morning fog on a sweltering August day. Her shyness melted away too, and she skipped behind Father Ted as they both walked to the back of his car. She could not help but run her hands over the doors as she passed, her fingertips luxuriating over the soft curve of metal. It was the fanciest car she had ever seen, and she wondered if the President drove a car like this. When they got to the rear of the car, Father Ted opened the trunk, and she peered inside.

She felt a shiver go up her spine and she stepped back. Her eyes grew wide and tears filled them as she stared into the open trunk.

"Now, don't be scared, Sylvia," Father Ted said. "I need you to help me dress her for Circle tonight. You want her to look pretty, don't you?" On the right side of the trunk was a small blue suitcase. Father Ted lifted the lid, revealing several silk gowns inside. Pointing to the dresses, he said, "Our Lady needs help to put on her best clothes for tonight. I know you will be able to tell me which one she should wear."

"I..., I don't understand," Sylvia said. "Who..., who is she? Is she..., dead?"

Father Ted reached down and cupped Sylvia's chin. He smiled as he shook his head. "No, child. She is very much alive. Very alive!"

Sylvia continued to stare, her skin growing clammy as she could not look away. A flash of bright light, those hollowed out eye sockets..., a glimpse of..., Sylvia looked away as her stomach turned. The setting sun was so bright, it made everything glare. It was so white..., blindingly white. She turned back to Father Ted and said, "but why is she..., she looks like one of those decorations they put up at Grants at Halloween."

"I know, but don't mind that, Sylvia," Father Ted said. "She is just the skinny girl right now. But soon, with your help, she will be all decked out proper as our Lady; all fixed up nice and beautiful. Now, you are going to help me, right? You want our Lady to look all nice and fancy, don't you?"

Sylvia shivered, but finally nodded as she forced herself to look back down into the trunk. She opened her eyes wide and said, "Yes, Father Ted..., yes."

Click... *Click... Click...*

Chapter 9

April 19th, 2017 - Avalon Terrace Apartment 102, Mountain View, California - 5:45 AM

SYLVIA, STILL SLEEPING, murmured as Snowy continued to stand on her chest and lick her face. When this failed to wake her, Snowy began to bark — small yips at first but getting louder by the second. Eventually, this two-prong canine assault worked, and Sylvia's eyes began to flutter open.

"What the...," Sylvia said, her voice thick and groggy as she spoke. She opened her eyes fully, and after they adjusted to the dim early light, she gently lifted the dog off her chest and set her down on a side pillow. Sylvia smiled, looked at her dog, and said, "That is a rather sloppy way to greet the day."

Snowy whined and leaped forward, digging her paws at the rumpled sheets like she was trying to bury one of her bones.

"You know, Snowy," Sylvia said as she sat up and leaned forward to scratch the dog behind the ears. "Back in New York, you used to hold it a whole lot longer. This California lifestyle is making you soft!"

Snowy was unmoved. The light yips now quickly escalated into a full bark. When Sylvia pulled back the covers and got out of bed, Snowy bolted down to the floor and began spinning.

"All right, already," Sylvia said. Under her breath she muttered, "Thank God we live on the first floor."

After letting the dog out to quickly relieve herself, Sylvia drank a cup of coffee before walking back into the bedroom to get ready to take her shower. Snowy, now back inside, stood pensively on the bed, her fur ruffling as a low constant growl emitted from her throat.

"What is it, girl?" Sylvia said. "Is that mirror freaking you out again?"

Snowy lay down on the bed, her tiny brown eyes glued to the mirror in the bathroom. "I will keep the door closed," Sylvia said. "But honestly, you can be so weird sometimes, Snowy."

Sylvia showered, washed her hair and shaved her legs. It was nice to take a long, luxurious, hot shower and she enjoyed every hot and foamy moment. Her bathroom back in New York always ran out of hot water, and usually right after she had soaped up. This was one of the many things she was not going to miss about back east.

She lingered in the shower, but, knew she had to get to work. As enjoyable as her private sauna was, it was time for it to end. When she pulled back the shower curtain, her eyes struggled to adjust in the fog. The bathroom was entirely filled with steam, looking more like a Turkish Bath than a California apartment bathroom. She reached over to the wall and turned on the fan. After the air cleared a bit, she gasped. There, in the mirror, letters had been written in the condensation.

"What the hell?" she cried. She quickly grabbed a towel off the rack and covered herself before glancing around the room. A quick look showed she was apparently alone; and Snowy, for once, was quiet. Sylvia's heart raced as a chill flowed over her like a cold drizzling rain.

She turned back to the mirror and read the writing in the condensation but couldn't understand what was written. It made no sense. If it was indeed a message, it was a garbled one, and besides, how could anyone have written it while she was in the shower? She shuddered as another chill ran down her spine. The letters appeared to spell out MAERC ECI EHT EKIL UOY DID. She opened the door, ran to her nightstand, and returned with her iPhone. She needed to take a picture before the image melted away. A quick click and she took the photo. She returned to her bedroom and looked down at Snowy. Now, oddly, the dog was calm.

"Was anyone in here, girl?"

Snowy just wagged her tail in response but then peeked around Sylvia and growled at the mirror.

"OK, this is too creepy," Sylvia said as she got dressed faster than she ever had in her life. She double checked the locks, and even went through the security log on her ADT system. Nothing. No one had entered since she had last night.

"There must be some logical explanation for this," Sylvia said as she filled Snowy's dog dish. Looking down at her dog, she added, "OK, girl, you need to be on extra guard duty today. OK?"

As if to answer, Snowy wagged her tail and sat down.

*****

"You OK, Sylvia?" Heather asked.

"Yeah, I'm good," Sylvia said as she pushed the chair back from her desk and rubbed her eyes. "I just think I am just a bit done for today — way too many videos in my queue. The things people think of! It truly boggles the mind." She smiled as she added, "You know, I think I would have been better off not knowing what a Furry was."

"You, too?" Heather said as she suppressed a snicker. "It is amazing how things like this come in waves. Lots of copycat perves, I guess. My feed has been filled with nothing but a frothy filthy furry-fest all day, too."

"Yes," Sylvia said. "I think I could have happily lived the rest of my life not having been forced to see people explore the romantic possibilities between Oscar and Grover." She shuddered as she added, "another precious childhood memory ruined!"

"Were you a big Sesame Street fan as a kid?"

"Oh, big time," Sylvia said. "And back then, it was still new. That's how old I am."

Heather asked, "what were you like as a kid?"

"You really want to know this?"

"Oh, if it is too personal, forget I asked. I didn't mean to offend."

"You didn't offend me," Sylvia said.

"That's good," Heather said. "You have been the first person around here worth talking to. I bet you have an interesting story."

"Everyone has an interesting story," Sylvia said.

"You are too generous," Heather said. "But…, I am curious about *your* story. Did you grow up in New York?"

"Yeah, born and bred," Sylvia said.

"You still see your folks? God knows, every year mine come out here to have Thanksgiving with me, and it turns into one scary weekend. I suppose they think it's the 'family' thing to do."

Sylvia laughed and said, "I don't have that problem, thank God."

"No scary holidays with your parents?"

"Well…," Sylvia said as her lips curled into a smirk. "If mine were to show up for the holidays, it certainly would be scary. They have been dead for quite some time now."

"Oh!" Heather said as her hand jerked up to her mouth. "I'm so sorry. I am such an idiot. My old boyfriend always told I run my mouth too much."

"Hardly," Sylvia said. "Your natural curiosity will make you a good psychologist one day. It's a good skill to have. One I never did acquire."

"Oh? I wouldn't say that," Heather said. "You seem quite curious about people."

"A little," Sylvia said. "But, I am more interested in how the human brain works. As for people…, well…, I have found that most of the time, the less you know about someone the better." She grinned as she added, "hence the reason I spent most of my career either teaching or writing."

"I don't follow," Heather said.

"Didn't you know? All great writers or teachers are usually really accomplished misanthropes."

Heather threw her head back and laughed. "I knew I liked you the first time I set my eyes on you. And now, you just confirmed the wisdom of my first impression."

"I like you too, Heather," Sylvia said. "And that takes some doing."

"So, since I have already outed myself as a perpetual nosy busybody, can I ask you another personal question?"

"Fire away," Sylvia said. "You are on a roll."

"Well…, all morning I have watched you moving little pieces of paper around on your desk. I guess it isn't too revealing of me to admit, I already checked them out when you went to get a cup of coffee and saw they were letters."

"Like you said, you are curious," Sylvia said.

"And since you don't strike me as a crossword puzzle type of gal—
"

"—You are correct," Sylvia said.

"So…, what is it all about?"

"Well…," Sylvia said. "It's kind of embarrassing."

"Oh? Well, now I am even more intrigued," Heather said. "So, are you running numbers on the side? Or are you a secret agent of Putin's?"

"No, none of those things," Sylvia said as she grinned. "I am afraid I am just a middle-aged woman with an overactive imagination."

"OK, Sylvia," Heather said. "Now you have to tell me. You know I not only have a serious issue with personal boundaries, and I am a horrible snoop, but you may not know that I also have an impulse control problem."

Sylvia smiled. "You know, it isn't a stretch to see that. I already had you pegged on the DSM."

"Touché," Heather said. "So, go ahead. You know you are going to tell me anyway, so you might as well not wait."

"OK," Sylvia said with a sigh. "But…, I don't want you to think I am a nut."

"Oh boy," Heather said. "This must be good, then." She grinned and added, "and you of all people should know — psychologists don't use the word 'nut' lightly."

"True…," Sylvia said. "OK. Well, what I am about to say sounds kind of spooky—"

"—I love spooky!"

"Well, this morning, after my shower there appeared to be some kind of message written in my mirror," Sylvia said.

"Written? How do you mean…, written?" Heather asked.

Sylvia said, "The letters were formed in the condensation on the mirror." Drawing in the air, she added, "like someone wrote it out with their finger."

"That is spooky…, and kind of cool, actually," Heather said, her smile growing wider as she spoke. "But, it isn't that much of a mystery, really."

"Oh?" Sylvia asked.

"You are living in a new apartment, right?"

"Yeah."

"Well…, without getting too personal, I would bet you haven't cleaned your mirror yet."

"Well…, no," Sylvia said. "But what does that—"

"—Here, come with me. I'll show you," Heather said as she stood up and led Sylvia down the hall to the women's bathroom. Once inside, she walked up to one of the mirrors above the sink. "Now, what were the letters you saw written in your bathroom this morning?"

"It didn't make much sense," Sylvia said. "It was just a bunch of letters."

"Well, it doesn't matter," Heather said. "Just spell out what was written."

"MAERC ECI EHT EKIL UOY DID," Sylvia said. "All in caps."

"OK," Heather said as she traced the letters with her finger over the glass. "That should do it. Now, watch," she added as she turned the knob on the faucet to hot. Within a few seconds steam rose from the sink and as if by magic, the letters Heather had traced with her finger appeared on the mirror.

"Well, will you look at that," Sylvia said.

"Your finger leaves a trail of oils on the glass, and when the steam hits, it doesn't fog up. Don't ask me how I know this," Heather said.

"I guess the former tenant was writing something out," Sylvia said. "Well…, thank you. Mystery solved." She smiled and added, "I was in full Nancy Drew-mode this morning."

"Nancy who?"

Sylvia shook her head, "Never mind." She grinned as she added, "you sure know how to make me feel old."

After Heather turned off the faucet, the two women walked out of the bathroom and back toward their cubicles.

"I feel like such a fool," Sylvia said as they walked. "You should have seen me this morning as I wandered around my apartment checking and rechecking all the doors and windows. I was a complete wreck. I was totally convinced someone had broken in."

"Mountain View is pretty safe," Heather said. "Plus, what did you think these robbers did? Break into your house to write on your mirror and then leave without taking anything?"

"When you put it that way, it does seem kind of silly," Sylvia said. "I guess if they broke in, they would have taken *something*."

"Yeah. Like I said, Mountain View is very safe, unless, of course, you are operating a computer network. Then all bets are off." She grinned and added, "the only actual crime I see being committed in this town are crimes against fashion. For example, did you see Susie's shoes yesterday? Honestly, someone needs to talk to that gal."

"You are so harsh," Sylvia said as she stifled a giggle. "I can only imagine what you have to say about my espadrilles behind my back."

Heather raised her eyebrow and said, "Well…, I was going to talk to you about that."

Sylvia and Heather both returned to their desks, and Sylvia sat down and turned her monitor back on. "Time to return to the Furry-a-palooza! Sheesh…, watching this perverted nonsense makes me feel dirty."

"You can always shower in the gym before you go home," Heather said.

Sylvia's office phone rang and she answered it. "Hello. Sylvia Marstens speak—"

"Listen up, bitch!" the voice on the other end snarled. It was a woman's voice and the rage coming through the line was palpable. The accent was Southern, and the caller was obviously agitated.

"Excuse me?" Sylvia said. "I'm sorry, but you must have a wrong—"

"—Oh no, it's no wrong number. I have been trying to track your moldy ass down for weeks. Obviously that moron man of yours forgot that I pay his phone bill!"

"I am sorry, Miss, but you really do have—"

"—Stop with the games, Alyssa! We are past all that now. Daryl made a lot of calls to this number. I guess you, and he, thought you were being cute by not using your home or cell number. But damn, you two are dumb. Maybe you are perfect for each other after all."

"Ah…," Sylvia said as she nodded her head. "Now it makes sense. You have the right number, but the wrong person. Alyssa doesn't work here anymore."

"Don't try to fool me, Alyssa. I know it's you. And I also know that if you think he is going to let you keep that baby, you need to have your head examined! Typical. Typical dumbass, redneck bitch."

"I really am not Alyssa, she is—, wait…, what was this about the baby?"

"Oh, I see you are still trying to hide things, Alyssa. Pretending you are someone else," the caller said. "I gotta hand it to you. You always were a sneaky bitch. You haven't changed a bit."

"I hate to tell you this, but you really do have the wrong number. And despite this being such a pleasant and exhilarating chat, I am going to hang up now."

"I should have known something was up when I first met you and that punk ass, bitch, Goth friend of yours," the voice said. "I knew you two were trouble. Well, you think you can fool me, but you can't. Your Kentucky accent is still seeping out of your throat like pine tar, baby. I can hear it. I can hear it in your voice, buried under those layers of respectability you have piled up on top of your coal dust-covered roots. Yeah…, you may have duped Darryl, and snowed his Momma, but you sure as shit didn't con me. You ain't nothing but white trash, and you know it."

Sylvia felt the hairs rise on the back of her neck, and despite her instinct to immediately hang up, she kept on the line and listened in silence.

"Well now…, that shut your cracker, pie-hole up, didn't it? I must've hit the bullseye with that one. Truth hurts, don't it? Now listen to me carefully, cause I'm not going to be long."

"Go on," Sylvia said.

"I don't care about you, or Darryl, or any of you crazy loons anymore. I just want my money! Darryl cleaned out the account— twenty thousand dollars, and I want it back. You can keep him, the lying bastard. But you can tell him he has exactly forty-eight hours to get me my money, or I am going to call the police. And I tell you what, you and he won't like that one bit…, no sir."

"The police? Listen, if Darryl stole your money, then, go ahead. What do I care if you call the—"

"—Oh…, you are good, ain't ya?" the voice said. "Playing it up real slick, like you don't know nothing about it. Well, I'm not going to the police about the money, you dumb bitch. It was Darryl's account anyway, but it was *my* money in it. Damn, what a fool I was. No, this is about something much worse than stealing money. Much, much, much worse, and it will end up with you two going away for a long time."

"Well, I know I am going to regret asking, but, what are you talking about?"

"Ah…, now you're interested. See…, I know all about what you and Darryl and the rest of you freaks been up to. I know all about that whacko Circle shit, or whatever you call it. And I am quite sure the California State Police might take a dim view of your activities. Lots of farmers up in the valley been complaining. Disgusting! I got enough pictures to put you, Darryl and that witchy friend of yours away for a long time."

"Farmers?"

Heather, watching from over the cubicle divider, motioned to Sylvia to hand her the phone. "Let me talk to this nut job," she whispered.

"OK, but try and find out what she is talking about," Sylvia whispered back as she covered the receiver with her hand.

Heather nodded, took the phone, and spoke. "Now listen here you toothless redneck bitch, you don't know who you are dealing with."

Sylvia sat back as she watched Heather take command of the conversation. It was quite impressive. If this job at UVid didn't work out, or if Heather never pursued her counseling license, it was clear that she could have a lucrative career in credit collections.

After an initial shouting match where Sylvia heard some of the most poetic and forceful obscenities she had ever heard uttered, the conversation became subdued. Hearing only one side of the call, it was hard to gauge what was being said, but it was apparent, the caller had calmed down.

"So, we have an understanding then, don't we?" Heather said. "Yes…, Good…., OK then…., And don't ever call here again!"

After Heather hung up the phone, Sylvia and Heather turned towards the sound of applause coming from over their shoulders. It was Steve.

"Holy crap that was the most impressive thing I have ever seen," Steve said. "Very Alpha. Man…, you are one badass beeyotch, Heather. So sexy."

"Perve," Heather said as she rolled her eyes.

"Guilty as charged," Steve said as he raised his hand. "But, in the interest of at least pretending to be a manager around here, just exactly what was this all about? You were very loud." He grinned as he added, "even for you."

"Some psycho called here for Alyssa," Heather said. "But I am confident she won't call back."

"Alyssa must still be listed in the dial by name," Steve said. "I guess I need to let HR know to update the phone directory."

"I wonder if someone needs to get in contact with Alyssa and warn her about this woman?" Sylvia asked. "She sounds kind of dangerous."

"That mental case?" Heather said after emitting a dismissive huff and pointing to the phone. "I wouldn't worry about her anymore. Someone just needed to stand up to her. I know the type, all bluster and no follow through."

"Yeah, but, all that talk about the baby, and then that weird stuff she was saying about the police and—"

"—Alyssa was into some weird shit," Heather said. "That mama had way too much drama going on in her life. Frankly, I am not surprised she was involved in some sort of ménage-a-trois redneck love triangle. Typical."

"Still…, I think she needs to be told," Sylvia said.

"Well," Steve said. "You could tell her yourself. She is your neighbor, you know."

"What?" Sylvia said.

"You live at Avalon Terrace, right?" Steve said.

"Yes."

"Apartment 102?"

"Yes! How do you know this?"

Steve smiled and tapped his right temple. "The curse of photographic memory. I saw your address when I filled out your new employee paperwork. Alyssa lives in apartment 103." He shrugged and added, "what are the odds?"

"Holy crap!" Sylvia said. "This is too freaky."

"It is weird," Heather said. She turned to Sylvia and said, "and this might just change my theory about your message. It just seems so…, crazy."

Sylvia sat back hard in her chair and exhaled. "I don't like this. I don't like this one bit!"

"What are you two talking about? What message?" Steve said.

"Sylvia saw something written in her mirror this morning," Heather said as she pointed to the pieces of paper on Sylvia's desk. "We were just talking about it when she got that call."

Steve hummed, "Doo doo doo do, doo doo doo do."

"It's not funny, Steve," Sylvia said.

"I know," he said. "I didn't mean to make light of it. But…, you must admit, it does seem like an episode of the *Twilight Zone.*" He then leaned over and saw the letters written on the paper. A knowing look fell over his face as he quickly stood up straight. "Well now…, this is freaky. You do know what this says, right?"

"No! What? I thought it was just a bunch of mixed up letters," Sylvia said.

"No. See, it's written backward," he said as he pointed to the paper.

"How do you know this?" Heather said.

Steve tapped his temple again before saying, "Here, I will show you. Do either of you have a mirror?"

"I do," Heather said as she reached into her purse and pulled out her compact. She held it over the paper. When she saw the letters reflected in the mirror, she stepped back. "What the hell?"

There, reflected in the mirror, was the phrase '*DID YOU LIKE THE ICE CREAM.'*

Steve turned to Sylvia, cleared his throat, and said, "well…, maybe you should pay a visit to your neighbor after all."

Chapter 10

April 20th, 1996 - 1 Police Plaza - NYPD Missing Persons Division - New York City - 4:45 PM

"MA'AM, WOULD YOU like a cup of coffee?" the officer asked.

"What…?" Sylvia asked, her voice trailing off into a whisper. She could barely hear what the officer was saying, and she shook her head back and forth, trying to clear her thoughts. Her mind was foggy like she had just woken from a deep dreamless sleep. Her ears rang constantly. Everything sounded as if her head was inside an empty fishbowl — all echoes and hollowed out sounds. The voices she could make out, like the officer's, were unclear — everything muffled by a constant pound-pound-pounding of her heartbeat thumping in her head.

The fog lifted. Her mind cleared, and she emerged from her stupor. She took in her surroundings. Her vision was still blurred and everything seemed to move at half speed, but it was improving. In the cavernous room, dozens of desks were all around her. She saw numerous other distraught individuals like herself. Each were busy pouring out their lives to earnest and yet apparently jaded men in blue. The officers took notes, and all had the same world-weary look on their faces — attentive, efficient, and numb. Each had seen this tragic movie before and they knew the ending. Blaring over the sea of chattering voices, in a constant patter, was the continuous sound of sprat zip sprat. The incessant noise came from countless printers, all pounding out the missing person reports, potential suspects, physical descriptions, and last known addresses of New York's lost and missing. She was surprised there were so many and frowned as a brief splash of clarity spilled into her brain. She was now one of them, too. *How on earth did it come to this?*

She raised her hands and studied her palms. Those hands — the ones that had brushed Billy's hair this morning, the ones that had bathed him last night, the ones that had made his favorite breakfast this morning — Captain Crunch, now looked foreign to her. They resembled lifeless chunks of meat clinging to her body.

"Sylvia...? Sylvia...? Are you OK?" John asked.

"What? Oh..., yes..., I'm sorry," Sylvia said as she shook her head. "I just got a little ... It is just all too...," she paused as a sob caught in her throat.

"I understand," Sergeant McIntyre said. "It is difficult, very difficult." He was an enormous man — like a vast amorphous blob of pink flesh poured into a tight blue polyester suit. Twenty years of RC cola, ho-hos and pork rinds had taken their toll, and the buttons on his shirt were buckling as if at any moment they might break free of their synthetic bindings and shoot across the room. His eyes were kind, though, and Sylvia could see his genuine concern.

"It is a very difficult time," he repeated. "But, know this, Ma'am; we are going to do everything humanly possible to get your son back. You can take that to the bank." He glanced over at a large institutional style clock on the wall, and added, "and any minute, I am sure the sketch artist will be finished with the Sampson boy's description. Mark my word — once we have the sketch, I wouldn't be surprised if this doesn't turn out to be just a big misunderstanding. It usually does."

"Do you think..., I mean, how good are these sketch artists?" Sylvia asked.

"Oh, Ma'am, you are in good hands. We have the absolute top professionals working in our forensic art department." He smiled as he added, "one of the many advantages of living here in New York, I suppose. You can't swing a dead cat and not hit an artist, you know. Why, I bet we probably have more artists in Manhattan than anywhere on earth — and many of them work for us. They will help us find your boy in no time. Do you have a picture of your son?"

Sylvia lifted her purse to her lap. Because they were spending the day in the park that day, it was her big one and was bulging full.

Opening it up, she saw the suntan lotion, her romance novel, and the bag of gumballs she was going to save for later as a surprise for Billy. Her gut dropped. It was just the detritus of a simple fun day in the park, but now it seemed coated in sadness. Who knew that a day spent in joy could turn tragic so quickly? In the briefest flicker of a moment, everything she knew and loved was turned upside down. She felt tears begin to well up in her eyes again, but she ground her teeth together and steeled her nerves. She had to be strong. Crying would not help find her son.

She found her wallet and fished out Billy's school picture from last year. He looked so small in the photograph, much smaller than she remembered. Her hand shook as she gave the Sergeant the picture. The thought of her tiny child, just a baby, really, out there in New York, all alone, made her stomach churn.

Sergeant McIntyre took the picture in his hands, looked at it, and smiled. "Cute kid," he said. "How old is he?"

"Seven," Sylvia said. "He will be eight in June."

"I got a daughter that age," he said. "And my twin boys are ten. They keep me and my wife hopping, let me tell you."

"Yes," Sylvia said, her voice blank and lifeless. She struggled to form words on her lips, all small talk now was a herculean effort to pull off.

"And boys, especially at that age, will worry you to death," Sergeant McIntyre said. "What was he wearing today?"

Sylvia glanced over at John and frowned.

"Is there something unusual about what he was wearing today?" Sergeant McIntyre asked after noticing Sylvia's withering look at her husband.

"He was wearing a Spiderman costume," John said.

"Spiderman?" Sergeant McIntyre asked as he wrote something down in his notepad.

"Yes…," Sylvia said. "It was his favorite, and he wanted to—"

"—Oh, I understand, Ma'am," Sergeant McIntyre said. "It's funny, but my two boys are big fans of Spiderman too." He smiled as he added, "You know, last Halloween, they both gave my wife and me a big scare. Similar to the one your Billy is giving you now, I bet."

"Oh?" Sylvia said. "What happened?"

"It's embarrassing," Sergeant McIntyre said, "but, you will appreciate it. My wife and I sent our boys out trick or treating in our building. We do it every year, and all of our neighbors are good eggs, so we let them run free. Just like we all did when we were kids."

"Yes, times are different now," John said.

"They are," Sergeant McIntyre said. "But, my two boys wandered into one of my neighbor's flats when they were trick or treating and joined into a Halloween party. They were gone for hours and, being in costume, our neighbors didn't know they didn't belong. I thought I would have to take Shelia..., my wife, to Bellevue she was so upset. And in fact, I figured I was going to have to go there myself."

"Oh," Sylvia said, the tension on her face visibly releasing a bit, if only a small degree.

"Like I said, kids will worry you to death. But..., just like your Billy, I am sure, my boys were just fine."

"But this isn't Halloween, Sergeant," John snapped. "And Billy was seen talking to—"

"—Billy..., oh God! This is such a nightmare — a nightmare!" Sylvia said as she put her face in her hands and began sobbing.

"Please, Ma'am," Sergeant McIntyre said. "Let me get you that cup of coffee. I am sure it will help."

Sylvia looked up, her eyes brimming with tears, her mascara running down her face in long dark streaks and nodded weakly. She said, "OK, perhaps you are right. It might help clear my head."

"Trust me, it will," Sergeant McIntyre nodded as he turned and lifted a small glass pot from the hotplate on the table behind him. He poured the coffee into a Styrofoam cup and slid it across the desk to Sylvia. "Too bad I can't Irish it up for you." He added, "Everything is going to be just fine..., just fine."

Sylvia took the cup, lifted it to her lips and took a long sip.

Sergeant McIntyre said, "Feeling better?"

"A little."

"Good. You know, in the vast majority of these cases we find the missing child within twenty-four hours. Typically it turns out to be—"

"—Yes, but…, I…, oh Billy!" she said before her voice cracked into a sob.

Sergeant McIntyre turned to John while pushing a box of tissues across his desk to Sylvia. "It is true what I say, Mr.—"

"—Delaney," John said. "John Delaney."

"Right," Sergeant McIntyre said as he looked down at his notes for confirmation. "I know this is very upsetting for both you and your wife, but, you really should take my word on this. I see cases like this all of the time, and in 97% of the cases, everything turns out to be a big misunderstanding."

Sylvia wiped her nose as she sniffled out, "and in that other 3 %?"

"Let's concentrate on the likely scenarios," Sergeant McIntyre said. "Now, most of the times a child goes missing it turns out to be a disgruntled, divorced parent at the root of the issue. Is Billy both of—"

"—Billy is *our* son!" John snapped. "Neither one of us have been married before, and we do not have any other children."

"I'm sorry, Mr. Delaney," Sergeant McIntyre said. "I know these are difficult questions, but…, I had to ask."

"Yes…, I understand," John said.

"Do either of your parents live locally?"

"Why do you want to know that?" John said.

"Well…, it is well known that grandparents, and occasionally aunts or uncles, will sometimes take a child without the consent of the parents. Especially if there has been any kind of…, trouble."

"What kind of trouble?" Sylvia asked.

"Oh, you know. Some families are well adjusted and get along better than others. Sometimes it's a relative who doesn't agree with how the child is being raised and so…, they sort of take matters into their own hands. Has there been any trouble in this area?"

"No!" John said. "My mother lives in New Jersey, and she simply adores Billy. She would never —"

"—I did not mean to insinuate anything, Sir," Sergeant McIntyre said. "But, it's just that, in my experience, I have to explore the avenues where I have seen this sort of thing happen before. It is not personal, you understand."

"I do," John said as he sighed. He wiped his forehead, now red and perspiring with his handkerchief. "It is just very stressful. I just want to get Billy back."

"As do I, Sir. And it is because I do, plus the witness' testimony, that led me into this area," Sergeant McIntyre said.

"Witness testimony? What do you mean?" Sylvia said. "What did that Sampson boy say? I haven't even gotten to talk to him yet!"

"He is still with the sketch artist, but, he seemed to indicate it appeared Billy knew the person he spoke with."

"What? I didn't know that he saw Billy being *kidnapped*," Sylvia cried.

"No…, the Sampson boy did not see any abduction. In fact, we cannot even say he was kidnapped yet, that is too preliminary. But…, he did say he saw Billy talking to someone, and, it appeared Billy knew the person. That is why I asked the question about the extended family. Perhaps it was an uncle he was talking to? Or even a grandfather?"

"My father is dead, and my brother lives in California," John said.

"And you Ma'am?" Sergeant McIntyre said as he turned to Sylvia. "Any family nearby?"

"No," she said quietly, her voice trailing as she dropped her chin to her chest.

"So, are you new to New York? Perhaps it is someone from where you—"

"—No," Sylvia said. "I grew up here. I don't know why you are focusing on this! It is like you are accusing us of knowing who kidnapped our son!"

"OK…," Sergeant McIntyre said, his voice dropping. "Look, I am not accusing anyone of anything, but…, it really would be helpful if you—"

"—Sergeant, my parents are dead," Sylvia said. "They have been dead for quite some time."

"Ah…, sorry."

"But, they lived here. Actually, we had a three-bedroom up on Amsterdam."

"Well, I live not far from there," Sergeant McIntyre said. "Any brothers or sisters?"

"No," Sylvia said. "Only child."

"How about uncles?"

"Listen, Sergeant," John interrupted. "Perhaps once we see the sketch something will click. But I am telling you, you are going in the wrong direction here, and we are wasting precious time. Sylvia has no family in the city, and neither do I. I do not know why you seem so confident it is a family member involved in this. I think you should concentrate on—"

"—It usually is a family member involved in these kind of cases," Sergeant McIntyre said. "Or a family friend. Stranger..., abductions," he added as he winced, preparing himself for an outburst from Sylvia, "are very rare."

Sylvia suppressed a sob.

"Well, you are the expert," John said.

"Are either of you — religious people by any chance?"

"Religious?" John asked as he rose from his chair. "What is this? Why are you asking about that?"

"—Sit down, Mr. Delaney, it is a standard question," Sergeant McIntyre said. "And..., I have a hunch about this."

"Well, my mother is religious, but there is no way she would take Billy without our knowledge. No way in hell!"

"No, of course not," Sergeant McIntyre said. "But, the more background information we can gather, the easier it will be to track down the appropriate leads." He turned to Sylvia and said, "how about you, Mrs. Delaney? I take it you and your husband are not religious."

"You can say that again," Sylvia snapped. "And I don't see how this is helping anything."

"How about your late parents, though?"

"What? Why would you be asking about them? They have been dead for many years."

"Yes, but, you aren't answering the question. The more I know about your families' backgrounds, the better results we are going to have in this search." Sergeant McIntyre placed his hands on his desk and added, "I am just trying to do the right thing to help find your son. I am only trying to help. I have dealt with many cases like this over the years, and I do know what I am doing."

"Of course, of course," Sylvia said as she lifted a tissue up to her eye and wiped away a tear. "And, if you must know, my parents were quite religious; bordering on zealots, frankly. No doubt this is the main reason I am not."

"And we certainly did not raise Billy that way," John said. "My wife and I are committed to raising our son in a loving and nonjudgmental environment. Neither of us goes in for all of this hocus pocus nonsense."

"I see," Sergeant McIntyre said as he scribbled more notes in his book. "Are any of your close friends religiously oriented?"

"I really do not see what this has to do with—" John said. "Look, we don't hang out with that sort! This is getting old, and we are wasting—"

"—Do you know if Billy had any religious inclinations on his own, then?" Sergeant McIntyre asked.

"What? A seven-year-old boy developing religious inclinations on his own?" Sylvia asked. "What is going on here? What did that Sampson boy say?" She jumped to her feet from her chair, clutching her hands together as she cried, "this is not right. I must know what was said! I must know!"

"Sergeant McIntyre," a police clerk interrupted as he approached the desk. In his hand, he carried a manila envelope. "The forensic art department told me to bring this up to you right away."

Sergeant McIntyre opened the envelope and looked at the picture inside. He glanced back at the clerk and said, "have you checked this against the 428 file?"

"Yes, and we are still reviewing, but so far, the results are negative. Nothing hit," the clerk said.

"Well, that's a good sign," Sergeant McIntyre said.

"Let me see it!" Sylvia said as she reached forward for the sketch. "I must see the face of the person who kidnapped my son."

"We don't know that he was abducted, yet, Ma'am," Sergeant McIntyre said. "But, at least now we have a picture to review." He glanced at the drawing, raised his eyebrow and asked, "are you sure neither of you have any religious relatives or friends? Look carefully at this picture and see if you recognize this man."

*****

"My, my, my," JoAnne Tucker said as she grinned and nodded her head. "You seemed to really enjoy those."

"I did," the stranger said as he wiped the dribbling syrup off his chin. "I am positive they were the best pancakes I have ever had..., ever!"

"Well, that's what we are famous for. That, and our raisin pie, of course," JoAnne said as she refilled the stranger's cup of coffee. "Can I get you anything else?"

The stranger looked deeply into her eyes. His cool, steely blues cut through her like a knife. A smile slid easily across the stranger's face as he said, "Well, I could use a little company before I have to head out." He glanced around the restaurant and said, "I hope that is ok, but, it appears you are a bit slow right now."

It was true. It was slow, and that was unusual. Big Joe's All-Day Breakfast Diner, located off exit 18B on US-71 in Allentown Pennsylvania was typically packed with customers. Being so close to the interstate, and only a two-hour drive from New York, it was a popular diner, especially with truckers. Before the endless hassles of the toll roads loomed, it was always best to stop at Big Joe's and load up on scrambled eggs, pancakes, gallons of coffee and of course, their world-famous raisin pie.

"Yeah, it has been a bit slow tonight," she said. "It should pick up soon, though. We get a lot of overnight long-haul truckers stopping here on their way to—" She jolted as she felt him reach out and gently touch her stomach.

"I'm sorry, darling," the stranger said. "I don't mean to be so forward, but, life flows so abundantly in you, I just couldn't help myself. Your glow is simply radiant. They always say pregnant women glow, but darling, you are blazing like a diamond! Again, I am sorry," he said as he started to pull his hand away.

JoAnne blushed. She looked down at her stomach, unconsciously twirling her long brown hair on her finger. She bit her lip and held his hand flush against her belly. "Don't be sorry. I liked it."

"Wonderful," the stranger said. "Now, before I have to leave, I was wondering if you would mind if I prayed a blessing over your baby?"

"Oh..., ah..., of course not. I would be honored," JoAnne said. As she felt his strong hands caress and stroke her pregnant belly, an electric jolt ran down her spine and out her toes. It was warm and inviting, like a great bath of delicious sweet honey poured all over her body. It had been so long since she had been touched by a man, especially one as handsome as this one. So very, very, very long.

The stranger closed his eyes and said, "Oh glorious woman who life bestows, who calms the reaper from ceaseless mow. Like sprigs of pine or babbling brook, from the darkest green verdant nook, Spirit come forth and shine upon, this blessed daughter of your golden dawn!"

"Oh, that is pretty," JoAnne said. "Thank you. What does it mean?"

The stranger took her hands in his and brought them to his mouth. She gushed as she felt his breath wash over her palms before kissing them both. "So lovely, JoAnne. So very beautiful. As it says in the good book, 'How beautiful are your sandaled feet, princess! The curves of your thighs are like jewelry, the handiwork of a master. Your navel is a rounded bowl; it never lacks mixed wine. Your waist is a mound of wheat surrounded by lilies. Your breasts are like two fawns, twins of a gazelle'."

"Oh..., oh...., well..., that ain't like any Bible reading I ever heard before," JoAnne said as she blushed.

The stranger looked up, winked and said, "Song of Solomon, chapter 7, verses 1 to 3. You can look it up." After a knowing smirk crawled over his face, he added, "thanks be to the Spirit."

JoAnne reflexively gasped out, "Amen!"

They both turned to the right as they were interrupted by the sound of tiny running feet clacking against the tile floor. "I got the top score! I got the top score!" a boy exclaimed as he bounded around the corner into the restaurant like a bull running wild through the cobbled streets of Pamplona.

The stranger spun around on his counter stool and clapped as the little boy entered. "That's wonderful, Sport! Just wonderful." He pointed at the boy, and then back to JoAnne, and said, "I think that t-shirt just looks great on him, don't you? Thanks for helping us pick it out."

It was a slightly oversized blue T-Shirt, emblazoned with a picture of a piece of pie and lettered with the words *Big Joe's All-Day Breakfast Diner - Home of the world-famous Raisin Pie - Allentown Pennsylvania.*

"You are welcome. And you are right about the t-shirt, it sure does look mighty fine," JoAnne said. Looking down at the little boy, she added, "I bet that is a lot more comfortable than that hot costume you were wearing when you came in here, isn't it, Sweetie?"

"Yes Ma'am," the little boy said. "I was getting kind of sweaty."

"I bet," she said. "But, I must say, you do look handsome in that t-shirt. I'm glad those shorts fit, too."

"I have to thank you for helping me out," the stranger said. "I could tell he was getting overheated. You all sell quite an amazing collection of things here, other than just your delicious food."

"Well..., we do like to supplement our food sales with souvenirs. Big Joe was always the best marketer in the business. And like I said, despite the look of the place, it is kind of famous," JoAnne said. "Just like our giant billboard says out there on the highway."

"Hence the reason we stopped. You can tell old Big Joe his billboard worked," the stranger said. Turning back to the boy he said, "so, Sport, all out of quarters, I suppose?"

The boy grinned sheepishly and looked down at his feet. "Yeah... Sorry, I tried to make them last."

"You did great," the stranger said. He turned to JoAnne and added, "how far away are we from I-81? We still have quite a ways to go tonight."

"Oh, maybe an hour," JoAnne said. "It isn't that far. Traffic's not too bad today."

"That's good," the stranger said. "I would like to get to Kentucky before midnight."

"That might be a challenge," JoAnne said. "Sometimes 81 south gets very backed up."

"Well then," the stranger said as he turned to look at the little boy. "I think we need to hit the road now, Sport. What do you say? To the Spidey-mobile?"

"Spiderman doesn't have a car, silly," the little boy said as he laughed.

"Oh? Well…, I think he should, and since you are Spiderman, in your clever civilian disguise, we need to hit the road in the Spidey-mobile." The stranger grinned as he added, "But, I am going to get one of those big raisin pies to go. We can eat one of them on the road."

"Pie? Yay!" the little boy cheered.

After JoAnne retrieved the pie and placed it in a to-go box, the stranger slapped down a crisp hundred-dollar bill on the counter. "Will this cover it?"

"Oh, my!" JoAnne said. "I can't possibly accept—"

"—Darling," the stranger said as he took her hand and placed it on the bill. "I insist. With a little one on the way, I have no doubt you can find a home for some extra cash."

"Bless you, Father," JoAnne said.

"Oh, don't be so formal, Love," the stranger said. "I thought we were on a first name basis by now."

"Oh, of course," JoAnne said.

He lifted her hand to his lips. After lightly kissing it, he said, "it was a beautiful time together, JoAnne."

She blushed, as she fidgeted with her nametag. "That's not fair. You know my name, and I don't know yours."

"Oh? It must have slipped my mind. My name is Theodore, but…, my friends call me Ted," the stranger said. "Sorry to eat and run, but, we have a lot of miles to cover tonight."

JoAnne waved goodbye to the pair. After they left, the door to the kitchen swung open and a cigarette-ravaged, older female voice said, "So, is Reverend Hottie gone?"

"Myrtle! You shouldn't say such things. He is a man of God, you know," JoAnne said.

Myrtle smirked and shook her head. "Yeah…, I saw the collar, so I know the drill. But, I sure know you weren't praying while he was in here. I don't think your mind was filled with holy thoughts, now was it?"

"I don't know what you are talking about," JoAnne said.

"Puh-leeze," Myrtle said as she tossed her kitchen towel over her shoulder and leaned against the counter. "Damn girl, I just popped my head in here to make sure you hadn't jumped that boy's bones. You weren't very subtle, you know?"

"I really don't know what you are—"

Myrtle laughed and in a melodramatic manner batted her eyes and leaned over the counter. She imitated JoAnne and said, "Oh Father, can I offer you some of our world-famous raisin pie? Yes? How wonderful," she added as she swayed her chest back and forth and said, "and maybe you would like two scoops?"

"Myrtle, you are terrible, you know that?" JoAnne said as she snickered. "I think you have the wrong idea about him."

"Oh no," Myrtle said. "I had his number the moment he and his..., who was that little boy with him anyway?"

"He said it was his nephew," JoAnne said.

"OK, he and his nephew came in here. And look, I may be nearly 70, but I can still appreciate a fine ass in a tight pair of jeans. And he filled out his spectacularly."

"He sure did," JoAnne said as she sighed. "And he was nice, too. Real polite."

"Oh, I bet he was," Myrtle said. "He wanted to..., ahem, lay his hands on you, as they say. Yeah, I know his type well. Trouble. T-R-O-U-B-L-E, trouble."

"You are such a cynic," JoAnne said.

"Well, when you get to be my age, it comes with the territory," Myrtle said.

JoAnne sighed. "I think you are wrong about him, though. But, what does it matter? He was just passing through anyway." She laughed before adding, "And doesn't it just figure though that the first guy to pay any attention to me in months would end up being a priest? That just seems to be how my luck goes these days."

"Oh, let me tell you something, girlie; Reverend Hottie there was no priest," Myrtle said. "I don't know what he is, but I know this. He ain't no priest."

*****

John squinted as he stared intensely at the drawing in his hands. He felt his heart race as his retinas traced over every line, every bump, every patch of skin on the face in the sketch, searching for some flicker of recognition. There was none.

The person depicted was handsome and looked to be in his early thirties, perhaps forty at the latest. With a chiseled movie star face, and thick, dark wavy black hair he could easily have passed as a soap opera star. In an odd twist, the man was wearing a Roman collar of a priest. The effect was off-putting, like a joke with the punchline not yet known. A priest, a rabbi and an elephant walk into a bar... He put the drawing down.

"I cannot place his face," John said. "He is a stranger to me." He turned to Sylvia and said, "why don't you take a look, Sylvia? Maybe you can recognize who it is."

Sylvia nodded and reached out for the picture. Her hand shook slightly as her fingers stretched for the paper. She closed her eyes, took a deep breath, and felt it placed in her hands.

As her eyes opened and the drawing came into focus, all of the air shot out of her lungs in one loud gasp. Her pupils grew wide and she began to shake, spittle foaming in the corner of her mouth.

"Sylvia? Are you all right?" John said as his brow crinkled in concern. "Sylvia!"

"No. No! No! No!" Sylvia screamed, each no progressively louder than the one before. Her eyes started to roll back into her head.

"Mr. Delaney, we need to call a doctor, your wife is having a seizure!" the Sergeant said. He got up from behind his desk and ran over to Sylvia, grabbing her face and saying, "Try and stay conscious and do not swallow your tongue, Mrs. Delaney. Do not swallow your tongue!"

"No! No! No!" Sylvia continued to shriek with the words now forming into one long continuous wail. She tried to stand but collapsed as her knees buckled. Now writhing on the floor, she continued to scream, "No! No! No!"

The Sergeant picked up the phone and yelled, "Code 26, third floor! Code 26!"

Click... *Click... Click...*

Chapter 11

April 19th, 2017 - Avalon Terrace Apartments, Mountain View California - 7:00 PM

SYLVIA GLANCED DOWN AT SNOWY squatting on the grass and shook her head. "Are we done, yet?" she asked.

The tiny dog stared back up at her blankly and then sat down. The answer was clear. Snowy was not done yet.

Gently pulling on the leash, Sylvia began to amble across the lawn, the dog reluctantly following. "Well, all right then, get on with it. We don't have all night," Sylvia said. "You kicked up such a fuss in the apartment, I thought you had urgent business. I hadn't planned on taking a *fun* walk."

This little game had gone on since Sylvia had come home from work thirty minutes earlier. It was fast becoming tiresome. She usually enjoyed the normal routine of being greeted at the door with a nightly show of enthusiastic barks, desperate pawing at the air and canine dancing. Snowy was always so excited when Sylvia came home. After being cooped up all day, she was desperate for petting, and dog treats, and most of all, desperate to find a patch of grass to water.

Tonight's welcome home was different, however. Snowy was not at her usual post by the front door, but in the back bedroom. The dog was staring and growling into the darkened bathroom, the fur on her back standing up straight. Even when Sylvia opened the back door, something that usually was irresistible, Snowy was not coaxed from her vigil. In fact, nothing would tempt the dog to move. Eventually, Sylvia placed the leash around the dog's neck, picked her up and carried her out the front door. Once out in the commons the old Snowy returned, complete with many happy barks and yips.

"Well, at least it's a lovely evening," Sylvia said as she and Snowy sauntered across the lawn. It was a slow walk, with the dog wildly sniffing everything in sight, and still refusing to do her business. Sylvia guessed that being in a new place, and with so much to explore, Snowy had forgotten the purpose of the stroll.

"You are right, Snowy. The air sure is clean here, isn't it, girl?" Sylvia said as she watched her dog frantically shoving her nose into the air. "It sure beats that noxious stew of bus exhaust and falafel stands back in New York, eh?"

As if to answer, Snowy yipped her agreement. The dog then paused, pulling the leash tight in Sylvia's hand, before spinning three times and squatting on the bright green grass. Business, thankfully, was done.

"Finally!" Sylvia said. "You know, girl, you are getting spoiled going on fresh grass. When we were back in New York, you didn't make such a production of business time. It was drop, squat and go every night."

Snowy responded the way she usually did, by standing on her back legs and pawing the air.

Sylvia scooped her dog up in her arms and started walking back to her apartment. "Well, we need to hurry this evening up," she said. "*Real Housewives* is on soon, and we don't want to miss it, do we?" As she turned the corner of the hall, leading to her apartment, the dog began growling as she passed the closed door of Apartment 103. It was Alyssa's apartment.

Sylvia felt a slight tingle on her neck and shuddered. Snowy felt it too and began trembling.

"Well…., I guess I have been putting this off too long. I just need to bite the bullet and do it," Sylvia explained to Snowy as she scratched the dog behind the ear. "I owe it to Alyssa to warn her about that crazy caller. And, I also want to know just how in the hell she got into my apartment and wrote that weird message in my mirror." She glanced down at her dog and added, "now, you are going to be no help with this, so…, off you go." With that, she opened her own apartment door and guided Snowy inside.

After the door closed, she could hear her dog's crying and scratching from the other side. Snowy hated being left out. It was quite dramatic, but, Sylvia was not moved. She turned and walked over to Alyssa's apartment and prepared to knock on the door.

Sylvia heard the TV playing inside through the closed door. This probably indicated Alyssa was home. She couldn't be sure, though, so she screwed together her courage, squashed down the riot of butterflies wrestling in her stomach and gently rapped on the door. To her surprise, the moment her knuckles hit the wood, the door creaked open. The latch was not engaged. After waiting a full minute, with a healthy sense of trepidation, she stuck her head inside and called out, "Hello, anyone home?"

There was no answer, only the muffled sounds of the *Entertainment Tonight* theme song coming from the back bedroom.

"Helloooo," Sylvia called again. "Anyone here?"

Again, nothing. Sylvia started to leave before something caught her attention. It was just a flash in her peripheral vision, but it instantly registered in her mind. It told her something was off —very, very off. Through the open door to Alyssa's bedroom, she saw a chair. Nothing special, really, just an everyday ordinary chair to a vanity, not unlike the one that she had back in her own apartment. This chair was on its side, however, and that caught Sylvia's attention.

That fact alone would not be remarkable. Lots of people leave furniture scattered about. Not all homes are immaculate. God knew hers wasn't, but this seemed strangely out of place. Something seemed sinister about this chair laying on its side. It felt like a warning, like a flashing yellow caution traffic light or a do not enter sign. It wasn't quite right.

A low bubbling began rumbling in her gut that set her nervous system flashing. She leaned further in and glanced around the apartment again, making mental notes of what she saw. The place was spotless. Everything was neat as a pin with nothing out of place. From the bookshelves to her left to the coffee table in the center of the living room, everything was free from any clutter. The kitchen was visible to her right, and from what she could see, it was sparkling. She could see the sink and noticed it was clean and clear of dirty dishes. This Alyssa was obviously a neat freak, so unlike herself.

Sylvia dropped her eyes and glanced at the pristine floors. The wood was still shining with that new apartment high gloss, and the carpet in the living room still had vacuum tracks across the fabric. Oddly, despite the obsessive fastidiousness of the surroundings, a thin layer of dust coated all the surfaces. It was as if time had stopped, and, from the thickness of the dust that had flurried onto the dining room table, it halted a while ago.

"Hello? Alyssa? Are you in here?" Sylvia said as she edged her neck further into the room. Again, silence greeted her. "OK, I am going to leave now," she said as she began to back up to leave. As her eyes dropped to pull the door shut behind her, she spied the latch bolt on the frame. It was stuck open, with clear packing tape pressed over the tumbler.

"What the hell?" she whispered. A chill ran up her spine. What was merely strange before now was far more menacing. "Why would she..." Sylvia paused as her mind reeled with the possibilities. *Has Alyssa been taken against her will? Should I call the police?*

Sylvia, despite the surge of adrenaline rushing through her veins, and a cool bead of sweat now traveling down her back, stepped inside and closed the door behind her. *What if Alyssa is unconscious in the bathroom? What if she fell and hit her head?*

She crept across the floor, her ears ringing as she tried to pick up any sound other than the *Entertainment Tonight* show playing in the bedroom. Somehow, the chirpy, overly friendly, voice of the host, Nancy O'Dell, made the still and otherwise quiet room seem even creepier. When Sylvia reached the bedroom, she knocked on the open door before she leaned inside.

"Alyssa? It's your neighbor. Are you—"

She froze. Alyssa's bedroom, like the rest of her apartment, was pristine. The bed was made with the bedspread tucked tight as a drum against the mattress. And here, like in the rest of the house, everything was both painfully neat while also covered lightly with dust. The vanity chair was overturned in the center of the room and three feet from it, on the threshold of the door leading to the bathroom, a crumpled white bath towel lay on the floor. *Maybe she has fallen in the tub?* Sylvia thought. Steeling herself for some gruesome discovery, she walked through the room to the open bathroom door and peered inside.

She exhaled in relief. Mercifully, the tub, as well as the rest of the bathroom, was empty. Alyssa was not home. She turned to leave, realizing full well she had crossed the line separating concerned neighbor and criminal trespasser. Sylvia halted when she turned around and saw Alyssa's closet door on the opposite wall. It was closed, but, unlike the rest of the apartment, which was decorated in a neat minimalistic chic, this was a shrine to gaudy excess. Thousands of beads covered the surface of the door.

The look was completely out of place with the rest of the apartment. It was as if someone had propped up a boozy, bead-strewn, Mardi Gras float right in the middle of a Quaker meeting house. Curiosity roared in her gut as Sylvia walked over to the closet. Once she got close to the doorknob, she gasped.

"What kind of crazy shit is this?" she whispered to herself.

The door was not covered with Mardi Gras beads, as she first thought. They were rosaries. Hundreds of rosaries of all sizes and styles; from the cheap plastic kind found in cathedral gift shops, to some rather expensive gold and silver ones dangling down the center of the door. Sylvia ran her hand across the beads and listened to them clack and jingle against one another. *What in the hell is this all about?* She moved in closer, and her eyes grew wide when she realized that it was not just one layer of beads covering the door, but multiple overlapping layers hanging thick like a rope. *This is too freaky.*

She placed her hand on the doorknob and started to turn. Metal scraped metal with a loud click. The closet, of course, was locked. Everything else in this apartment was unsecured, including the front door, but this was locked. Typical. She turned and headed to the kitchen to hopefully find a key. As she passed the front door it suddenly swung open wide. A dark figure stepped inside. She couldn't see the person clearly. All was a blur as it was so quick, but it appeared to be a man. Her vision did lock clearly on one thing, though, the Roman collar around the man's neck. As this image sunk in, her mind reeled, and everything went black.

Chapter 12

April 30th, 1976 - Pikeville, Kentucky - 7:00 PM

SYLVIA'S HEARTBEAT THUMPED IN HER neck as the air around her grew thick — like hot, suffocating tar pouring down her throat. Her feet were rooted to the ground, and her gaze was transfixed into the open trunk of Father Ted's Lincoln Continental. Everything was deathly still, not even a light breeze stirring the nearby trees. A swirl of terrifying emotions washed over her body like a chilly rain — fear, revulsion, horror; but somewhere buried deep in that downpour was something else, something strangely warm, and inviting. Curiosity rose in her chest.

With her hands shaking, she reached down and pressed her small fingers against the tiny, fleshless hands stretched upward out of the trunk before retracting her arm back like a spring. The skeletal hands were nearly the same size as her own, and their bony fingers were curled upwards in an almost pleading gesture. Sylvia swallowed hard, reached inside again and closed her eyes. She ran her palms over the chalky, cool tips of the bony fingers. They tickled her flesh, and a smile curled onto her mouth. Suddenly the horror of her actions slapped her cold in the face, and she jumped back from the trunk as if burnt by a stove. She popped her eyes open and looked up at Father Ted.

"Good girl, Sylvia," Father Ted said. "I knew you were a brave girl — just like Diana Prince."

"Y-you think so?" Sylvia said, her cheeks flushing as she struggled to control her shivers. "It is very hard. I am so scared."

"Absolutely," Father Ted said as he nodded. "And I knew you were a brave girl the moment I saw you. I know it is scary. New things

PAUL E. CREASY

often are. But, I knew that you, more than any of the others, were the one to be called for this special duty today. I am very proud of you."

Sylvia, fortified by his words of encouragement, crept back to the open trunk. Her eyes squinted as she braced herself to look at the ghastly figure again. It was a struggle, but she forced her lids open, if only a little bit.

She slowly and deliberately ran her eyes up from the skeleton's feet, along its femurs and pelvic bone, across its stark white exposed rib cage, to end her gaze at its skull. She flinched as the two hollow eye sockets glared back at her.

"Can..., can she see me?"

"Oh yes," Father Ted said. "Our Lady sees all."

"But..., I don't understand. S-she doesn't have eyes," Sylvia said as her teeth chattered.

"You are most perceptive, my child," Father Ted said. "Our Lady is using her spirit eyes now. But..., that isn't good enough for tonight." He shook his head and added, "not at all proper." He reached down into the side of the trunk and lifted out a small red velvet bag. Holding it up to his right ear he shook it, the contents rattling inside like a sack full of marbles. He lowered the bag down to Sylvia and pulled the drawstring, opening the bag. "I want *you* to pick out our Lady's earthly eyes for tonight."

"What?" Sylvia gasped as she stepped back.

Father Ted smiled as he poured the contents of the bag out into the palm of his hand. Sylvia timidly stepped forward again to peek.

In Father Ted's hand were several round gems, all glittering in the late afternoon sun. There were all sorts of stones in his palm: red rubies, green jade, yellow citrine, blue topaz and, the most alluring of all, a sparkling pair of black onyx stones resembling two shiny dark pearls. Sylvia was mesmerized as the fear in her gut melted away.

"They are *so* pretty," Sylvia squealed. "I don't think I have ever seen anything so pretty in my life."

"They *are* pretty," Father Ted said. "After all, our Lady deserves the best. So..., what shall it be today? It is up to you, Sylvia. The choice is yours."

130

"Are you sure you want me to choose?" Sylvia asked. "I am too little."

"Who better than a special little girl to give our Lady sight?" Father Ted asked. "You have proven your worth, Sylvia, and our Lady wants you to choose her eyes for this glorious night."

"There are so many..., I...," Sylvia stuttered.

"Now, don't get overwhelmed, darling," Father Ted said, his voice dropping into a treacly syrupy tone. "They are all for our Lady's glory."

"But..., what do the colors mean?" Sylvia asked. "Maybe..., maybe I am supposed to pick a particular color for tonight."

"You are a smart one, aren't you?"

"Momma says I am," Sylvia said.

"Your Momma is right," Father Ted replied. "The colors do have meaning. See, the red ones here are for romance. Our Lady loves to help the lovelorn."

"Like my Aunt Helen?"

Father Ted laughed. "Yes..., she could probably use the help."

"And how about those," Sylvia said as she pointed to the green stones.

"Oh, these pretty ones, they are jade. They are for justice."

"You mean to help out with the police?"

"Yes!" Father Ted said. "You are a quick study. Do these call to you?"

"Well..., Daddy did get a speeding ticket a few weeks ago, but, I think it all was taken care of already."

"Well then," Father Ted said. "Maybe you should pick another. The stones will call you."

"What are these pretty black ones for?" Sylvia said as she pointed. "They are so beautiful. See how they glimmer? The others don't shine like they do."

"Those are the best of all! They are extra special," Father Ted said.

Sylvia nodded.

"Would you like to hold them?"

"Really?"

"Yes, really," Father Ted said.

Sylvia cupped her hands together and held them out in front of her. Father Ted picked the two black spheres out of his hand and placed them in the center of her palms.

"Wow, they are cold," Sylvia said. "Like two ice cubes."

"Look at them closely," Father Ted. "Tell me what you see."

Sylvia lifted one up to her eye and squinted. The surface was smooth, and although they looked solidly black from a distance, up close, she observed swirling currents of purple and red snaking their way across the surface.

"Cool! This is super cool! The colors are so…, so pretty. So pretty!"

"I thought you would like them," Father Ted said. "Our Lady will be most pleased with your choice. Very pleased indeed. So…, Sylvia, it is time. It is time for you to give our Lady sight."

"Wh-what do you mean," Sylvia said.

Father Ted pointed at the two eye sockets on the skull and said, "place the gems in there, one for each eye. Then all will be in place, and we can start the ceremony."

Sylvia felt queasy. She couldn't do that. *No. No please, not that.*

A few seconds passed, and she remained motionless. Father Ted's smile dissolved into a frown. Sylvia was just standing ramrod still in the yard like an old fencepost in a windswept field — neither moving or fleeing, just standing. The dappled sunlight shining through the nearby trees traced strange designs over her face. Occasionally the rays reflected into her eyes, but even then, she did not blink. Not once.

"Well…," Father Ted said. "Our Lady is waiting. Don't make our Lady wait too long."

"Do…, do I have to, Father Ted?" Sylvia said. She lifted the two jewels up towards him and added, "maybe you should do it. I really am too little."

"No," Father Ted replied. "Our Lady has spoken. The stones called you!"

Sylvia swallowed hard again and leaned over the open trunk. She held one of the gems in her fingers and started to slowly lower it into the eye socket. When she was just inches away from the skull, she pulled her hand back. Tears filled her eyes as her voice shook. "I can't do it! Please don't make me! Please don't!"

Father Ted's frown returned, and his tone grew sharp. He said, "well..., I guess I was wrong about you, Sylvia. I thought you were like Diana Prince, but, I guess I was mistaken." He glanced up the hill towards the house and saw the rest of the party was in progress. People were milling about, other children were laughing and playing, and the smell of fried chicken was just starting to waft its way down to them in the breeze. "I guess I should go ask Sally to help me instead. She is a big girl and seems quite brave, too. I guess she is more like Diana Prince than you, so, let me go ask—"

"—No! Not her!" Sylvia said. "I... I'll do it. I'll be brave."

Sylvia bit her lower lip, closed her eyes, and lowered the gem into the empty eye socket. As her knuckle passed over the bone, she felt something slimy brush against her skin. She gagged but continued to push down until the gem came to rest at the back of the skull.

Her voice quivered as she asked, "Won't it fall out?"

"No. But, you need to move it around in there, Sylvia," Father Ted said, his grin now returned and growing wider with each downward descent of Sylvia's fingers into the eye socket. "You should feel it just start to—"

Click... Click... Click...

Father Ted sighed and said, "Ah, there we go!"

Sylvia shuddered and said, "That was yucky. I thought I might throw up!"

"I am very proud of you, Sylvia. You were very brave," Father Ted said, his tone sweet again as he squatted down next to her. "You know, sometimes we need to do yucky things. Sometimes, out of the vilest and most disgusting acts imaginable, horrors and terrors beyond anything mere human minds can comprehend, something beautiful will emerge. Only something horrible can create something truly beautiful. You understand that, right?"

"You mean like a butterfly? How it's a gross, disgusting worm and then—"

Father Ted's face lit up, and he ran his hand over the top of Sylvia's head and down the back of her neck. "—Absolutely! You understand perfectly! Diana Prince would be proud." He glanced down at the skeleton, now with one black onyx pupil and said, "and you are sure you felt it lock-in?"

"Yes," Sylvia said. "It made a sound like my bike chain does when I pedal backward."

He pointed to the other gem in her hand and said, "Wonderful. Now…, go ahead and put in the other eye." He winked as he said, "we don't want our Lady looking like some silly pirate, now do we?" Closing his left eye, he added, "Arrgh!"

Sylvia laughed. "No, that would be silly. We don't want that." She closed her eyes again and began to lower the black gem into the other socket.

As she lowered the onyx into the skull, Father Ted said, "Our Lady was very wise when she chose you for this high honor, Sylvia."

Click… Click… Click…

Chapter 13

April 19th, 2017 - Avalon Terrace Apartments, Apartment 102 - Mountain View California - 9:00 PM

"ARE YOU SURE I can't get you any coffee, or at least some water, Father?" Sylvia said as she handed the priest another wet towel for his head. This was his fourth one, and Sylvia was glad she had just done laundry. Three bloody hand towels already were laying in a pile at his feet. Snowy, as if to participate in the impromptu nursing session, desperately jumped and pawed at the stranger's black polyester pants.

"No, thank you, I think I am going to be all right now. The bleeding appears to have stopped," Father Hector Morales said. He grinned as he added, "Although, as to your offer for a drink, I think a shot of tequila right now might help things heal up faster."

"Damn, I am sure it would. Trust me, if I had any, I would be taking a shot myself. Several, in fact," Sylvia said. "I again want to apologize. I…, I just don't know what came over me. I have never done anything like this before in my life. I promise you, I'm really not a violent person by nature."

"Well…, I should have knocked before I barged into Alyssa's apartment. I am sure I startled you," the aging priest said. He laughed and added, "I don't know what you do for a living, Ma'am, but, if you ever want to take up boxing, I have connections. I coach the boy's boxing team part-time at St. Sebastian's."

"You are being a very good sport about this, Father," Sylvia said. "I am so sorry; and here I slugged you and I didn't even get your name first. Quite a way to make a first impression in my new home!"

"Father Hector Morales," he said. "And you?"

"Sylvia Marstens," she said.

"Are you new to Mountain View?" Father Morales said. "I hope you are finding the natives friendly," he added with a smile.

"Yes, I am new," Sylvia said. "I just moved here from New York, and everyone seems nice so far." She grinned as she added, "Even the ones I haven't punched in the head. It is funny you asked about the 'natives'. I don't think anyone is actually a native here. Everyone I have met so far seems to be from somewhere else, just like me — but it is a lovely place."

"It is lovely. This is the real California dream here, isn't it? Everyone comes here to the land of milk and honey from somewhere else — me included. Originally, I am from Mexico City." He reached out and shook her hand. His wrinkled face grew even more creased as he smiled. "Well, it is a pleasure to meet you, Sylvia Marstens," he said as he rubbed his head and added, "and hey, if boxing isn't your thing, maybe you should put in for border guard. You know, I hear once that wall goes up there will be lots of openings for people with your martial arts skills."

Sylvia laughed. "Ugh, let's not talk about that! Last year was more than enough talk about that stupid wall."

"Agreed," Father Morales said. "So..., now that we have been properly introduced, I have to ask. How long has it been since you have seen Alyssa? I must tell you, I am getting very worried about her."

"Well...," Sylvia said as she blushed. "The thing is..., you see..., I have never actually met her."

"Oh?" Father Morales said. "I don't understand. I mean, I see you are her neighbor, and...," he said before he paused and began laughing. Snowy, who could wait no longer for an official invitation, leaped into his arms and was now crawling up Hector's chest and coating his face with a shower of tiny dog kisses.

"Snowy, no! Bad girl! Get down, right now," Sylvia said.

"Bueno! Bueno perro," Father Morales said. He ran his tired weathered hands down her fluffy back. Snowy was spellbound, panting and grinning as her tail wagged ferociously.

"Here, I will take her from you. Sorry for my crazy dog's terrible manners," Sylvia said.

Father Morales said, "Please Ma'am, I don't mind at all."

"Call me, Sylvia," she said. She blushed as she added, "after all, since I punched you in the face, you should at least get to use my first name."

"OK, Sylvia. It is always nice to be on a first name basis with those that wallop you in the head," Father Morales said with a chuckle. He shook his head and sighed as he felt the scab on the side of his face. "I may have to fib a bit about this incident to my boys back at St. Sebastian's." He squinted and held his hands up in front of his face, framing Sylvia between his fingers like a camera. "Yeah…, you might end up being a drunken biker I was trying to win for the church in the final version of my story."

Sylvia laughed and said, "Now, let me get this dog off you. I have shamed myself enough for one day. There is no reason for you to be mauled by my dog too."

"No, it is OK, really," Father Morales said as he started to lightly scratch behind Snowy's ears. "I love dogs, and this one here reminds me so much of my little Juanita back at the parish."

"Well, I can tell you love dogs," Sylvia said.

"I always have," Father Morales said. "And who could resist this little fuzzball?" he asked as he began tickling Snowball's stomach.

"And, it appears they love you right back," Sylvia said. "Honestly, I have never seen Snowy behave so shamelessly. You have a new fan."

"She is a cutie. But…, back to Alyssa for a moment. I am curious," Father Morales said. "If you have never met her, why were you in her apartment?"

"It is a long story," Sylvia said. "And, I will say, it is an odd one. But…, you first. What is your connection to Alyssa? Have you known her long?"

"Not very," he said. "Just a few months. She seems like a very intelligent and wonderful young woman. I do hope she is all right. We had an appointment a few weeks back that she missed. I tried calling her multiple times only to get her voicemail. I feared she might be avoiding me, so, I thought I would just show up uninvited."

"What, if you don't mind me asking, brought you over tonight, though?" Sylvia asked.

"Ladies first," he replied. He crooked his mouth into a wry grin as he added, "After all, I did ask you first, and, I do love a long story — especially if it is odd, as you say."

Sylvia said, "well…, OK, here goes. Through a set of circumstances, I still cannot fathom, not only am I Alyssa's neighbor but, I am sitting at her old desk at work."

"Oh," Father Morales said. "You work at UVid?"

"Sure do," Sylvia said. "I just started."

"Well…," Father Morales said, "I hope this isn't offensive, but…"

"—But, how can I work for such a purveyor of filth?" Sylvia responded, anticipating his question.

"I would have been more polite about the phrasing, but, yes," Father Morales said. "Alyssa really hated that job. The stuff she told me people post online! Sick!"

"Yes, very much so," Sylvia said. "And hence the reason the burn-out rate for the video reviewing staff is so high."

"So I heard," Father Morales said. "And from what Alyssa told me, I can certainly see why."

"Yes, and that is why I took the job," Sylvia said. "I am actually a psychologist by training."

"A psychologist? Well…, no doubt you will have plenty of material to work with. Some of those videos had to have been created by the mentally ill. But…, I don't understand. I thought the videos were uploaded from the general public."

"They are. I work with the employees reviewing the videos, like Alyssa," Sylvia said. "My specialty is treating patients suffering from PTSD, and it appears quite a few UVid employees are disturbed by what they have to view."

"Ah, I see," Father Morales said. "That makes sense."

"So, did Alyssa come to you for guidance over something she saw in one of the videos?" Sylvia asked.

"Well…," Father Morales said. "Take this the right way, but, you know I can't answer that."

"Oh?" Sylvia asked. "Confidentiality of confession, right?"

"The sacrament of reconciliation is absolute," Father Morales said. "And even if I were inclined to violate it, which I'm not, I would be defrocked if I did."

"I figured as much," Sylvia said.

Father Morales said, "But, now that I have that out of the way, I *can* tell you this. She did not come to me because of any videos. It was something else entirely." He paused before pointing at Sylvia and saying, "But *you* aren't constrained by any rule of confidentiality. Why don't you say what brought you here tonight?"

"Among the many other things I can't quite wrap my head around, the final straw bringing me to Alyssa's apartment tonight was the call I received at work. It was meant for Alyssa," Sylvia said. "It was so threatening and bizarre, I thought I should warn her about it."

"Warn her? What was the call about?" Father Morales asked. "Did someone threaten Alyssa?"

Sylvia paused and then asked, "Did you know that Alyssa was pregnant?"

"I did," Father Morales nodded. "And I also know she is keeping the baby."

"Maybe," Sylvia said.

"Maybe?" Father Morales said, his brow furrowing as his voice dropped. "What do you mean, maybe? I was helping to arrange an open adoption. It was all set up."

"Well, she may have told you that was her intention, but the caller indicated her boyfriend, Darryl, might have quite a different opinion on the baby," Sylvia said. "I don't know exactly what Alyssa and her boyfriend were involved in, but it appears one of those things was a twisted love triangle that apparently went sour. The caller appeared to be a crazy Ex of Darryl's. Anyway, the conversation was kind of spooky, so, I thought I owed it to Alyssa to give her a head's up."

"Spooky? How so?"

"The caller made some allusions to some money Daryl owed her."

"That doesn't sound particularly spooky," Father Morales said.

"No," Sylvia said. "But, it was her weird references to some sort of Circle ritual that set my teeth on edge. It had a bizarre cultish feel to it."

"Alyssa, like many young people, has made some poor choices in her past," Father Morales said. "She dabbled in the darkness for far too long, but, I know she is turning her life around now. I will not let her slide back into that pit again."

"Dabbled in darkness?" Sylvia said. She reflexively rolled her eyes.

"Ah…," Father Morales said as he spied her skeptical glance. "I see you are not a person of faith. Well…, believe me, darkness exists. Alyssa danced with the devil a bit too cozily. Thank God she saw the light before it was too late."

"I don't know about all of that sort of thing," Sylvia said, "but I do know her office mate said she was into all kinds of new age crap. Frankly, it astonishes me that people still fall for all this mumbo jumbo nonsense. It is the twenty first century, after all."

"They do. And one should always be careful about what doors they open," Father Morales said. "Because once some doors are opened they cannot be so easily closed. What comes through is not always what was invited."

"Yeah…, OK," Sylvia said as she struggled to remain polite and not have some snide remark slip out. "Well, Father, on the bright side, it appears that whatever you said to her took. You should get a load of that crazy closet of hers. No doubt that was your influence. I was just about to open it when you came in."

"Closet?"

"Oh," Sylvia said. "I guess you didn't see it."

"No," Father Morales said as he lightly rubbed the side of his head. "Things took a sudden and dramatic turn when I first arrived, and then, of course, we came over here to your apartment."

Sylvia blushed, looked down and said, "yeah, again, I am sorry about that."

"Really, it is no problem," Father Morales said. "But…, about this closet—"

"—Well, Alyssa's door is still open," Sylvia said. "Let's go take a peek. It is better to see it for yourself. I can't really explain it."

"I wonder if we should call the police first?" Father Morales said. "The call you described sounded pretty threatening and it is not like

Alyssa to just go missing like this. Maybe the caller did something to her?"

"Well, first of all, we don't even know whether or not she is missing," Sylvia said.

"No, but it sure seems like a crime was possibly committed here," Father Morales said.

"Yes," Sylvia said. "By us. Technically, we broke into her apartment, even though the door was unlocked. And even if we did call the police, what would we say? We walked into some woman's apartment that I don't know, and you *barely* know, and found she wasn't there. Whoop-de-doo! I doubt they are going to put out a dragnet for a young woman not meeting up with her priest as promised. No offense, Father, but I doubt you are the first man of the cloth to be stood up."

"Yes, I suppose you are right," Father Morales said. "When you put it that way, I am sure the police would just tell us to mind our own business."

"Or arrest us for breaking and entering," Sylvia said. She laughed as she added, "and they could book me on assault and battery, too, as icing on the cake!"

"Still, we can't just sit here," Father Morales said. "I feel something is wrong — terribly, terribly wrong."

"Let's go back to her apartment," Sylvia said. "Maybe we can find something that will clear all of this up. Who knows, maybe she ran off with Daryl and went back home to Kentucky."

"Kentucky?" Father Morales said. "Was Alyssa from Kentucky? She never said."

"I guess she is," Sylvia said. "The caller said so. It was crazy. The woman thought I was Alyssa when I was on the phone with her. She said she could tell from my accent. It's weird. I always thought I didn't have an accent."

"Frankly, I wouldn't know," Father Morales said as he grinned. "All you Anglos sound the same to me."

After coaxing a very reluctant Snowy out of Father Morales' arms, Sylvia and the priest returned to Alyssa's apartment next door. Everything was just as it was when they left a half hour ago. Sylvia glanced down at the floor and exhaled. "Shew, I am glad we didn't get blood on the carpet. That sure would be hard to explain."

Father Morales glanced around the apartment and said, "Alyssa sure keeps a tidy place." He ran his finger over the dining room table and added, "but it is strange. This layer of dust everywhere worries me."

"Yeah, me too," Sylvia said. "It is like the apartment has been empty for quite a while. It is very odd. It is almost like…, hey…., wait a minute—" Her words stopped in her throat as her eyes narrowed. Across the living room on the floor she spied a small, blinking, red light. Sylvia walked across the room as her feet made fresh tracks in the perfectly vacuumed carpet.

"What is it? What do you see?" Father Morales said.

"I don't know yet, but I have a hunch." She bent down and said, "Ah…, just as I thought." Sylvia lifted an object off the floor, held it out in front of her, and said, "it's Alyssa's cell phone."

"That's not good," Father Morales said.

"No. It isn't," Sylvia said. Something else caught her attention. Reaching over to the chair in front of the desk, she retrieved a red purse off the back. After opening it, she peered inside and saw a wallet, keys, makeup, and various other items. "And this is a very, very bad sign. There is no way Alyssa willingly left the apartment without her cellphone, keys, and purse. No way! Something has happened to her! When I think about the knocked over chair and her towel laying on the bedroom floor, completely out of place with the rest of the apartment, I think something really terrible has happened to her. I think we are going to have to call the police."

"You are right," Father Morales said. "But before we call the police, I want to see this closet you mentioned. I too have a hunch, and God, I hope I am wrong."

"Right through here," Sylvia said as she led him into the back bedroom.

When they entered, Father Morales gasped and crossed himself when he saw the rosary covered door. "I see she took my advice, but I never thought she would go this far."

Sylvia flinched and took a step back as a small bubble of dread started percolating in her spine. She reflexively glanced back at the front door, looking for a quick exit, just in case. "You *told* her to do this?" she said as she pointed at the closet door. "Why? I just thought it was something she did on her own."

"Like I said earlier," Father Morales said. "Alyssa was into some very dark things. Playing around with forces she should never have engaged. Evil must be disposed of properly. I told her to rid her apartment of all the remnants of her old life and seal it away with something holy before I was able to come over. One of the things I was going to do when we met again was to dispose of everything properly."

"Evil things, I suppose?" Sylvia said as she smirked.

"Yes, evil things," Father Morales said. "Evil exists, Sylvia, whether you believe it or not."

"Evil is a social construct, Father," Sylvia said, her eyes closing as she spoke. She lightly bit her lip. She had said too much. Her words had flown out of her mouth before she could stop them. Sighing, she forced her tone to lighten as she added, "But..., I too am curious as to what is inside."

"Look, Sylvia," he said. "I know you do not believe in these things, but, your belief or disbelief makes no difference. Evil exists, and it is dangerous. Now, you are going to have to trust me on this. We need to do this correctly before we call the police."

"OK, OK," Sylvia said as she put her hands up in the air and backed away.

He pulled a leather pouch from his coat pocket and opened it. In it was a small vile of water, similar in size to a flask, but clear with a gold cross etched into the crystal. Sylvia immediately guessed what it was. *Of course, how cliché. What Priest doesn't carry holy water?*

Father Morales crossed himself and said something under his breath. Sylvia guessed it was a prayer. She then watched him dribble a small stream of the water onto the floor. Swinging his hand in a semi-circle, he traced an arc of holy water in front of the door. He reached for the door and turned the knob. Click... Click... Click...

"I tried earlier. It is locked," Sylvia said.

Father Morales said nothing but nodded. He reached up to the doorsill and ran his fingers along the edge. He smiled as he brought his hand down and held up a small key. "Bingo! I thought it was worth a shot."

"That was one hell of a good guess, Father," Sylvia said.

"Before we pop open the champagne and celebrate," Father Morales said, "let's make sure it fits the lock." He slid the key into the tumbler and turned. Click. The door opened.

Sylvia leaned forward to look inside. She was unimpressed. There were a dozen black candles, a couple of golden pentagrams, a silver chalice and a rather elaborate looking dagger. Nothing she had not seen in abundance at the local Spencer's Gifts store. It was all too Black Sabbath, 1970s Heavy Metal rock-ish for her taste, and it all seemed so juvenile.

In the back of the closet, however, something was left behind. It was covered by a blue tarp. She turned and watched Father Morales mouthing more prayers as he made the sign of the cross over the contents of the closet. If Alyssa wasn't missing, and there wasn't the distinct possibility of foul play, this whole ritual would have seemed silly. Under normal circumstances, she was sure she would have been laughing by now. After a few minutes of more prayers, and a couple more dousings of holy water, Father Morales pulled off the tarp with a sharp jerk.

Sylvia felt her knees buckle and she grew dizzy as the contents were revealed. There, leaning up against the back wall of the closet was a small statue, approximately three feet tall. It was a skeleton. Instead of looking sinister, like some sort of Halloween decoration all in orange or black, it was bright white. The statue was wearing a wedding dress. Its eyes were red, but not a demon fiery red from some cartoonish decoration. The red came from the two rubies inserted into the skeleton's empty eye sockets. The smile leering out at her from the skull - full, stark, and uncanny, was broad, and oddly, cheerful.

Father Morales sighed, crossed himself and said, "not this again. Dear sweet Jesus in heaven, not this again." From behind him, he heard a loud thud. When he spun around, he saw Sylvia sprawled out flat on the floor. She had fainted.

Chapter 14

April 21st, 1996 - New York Presbyterian Hospital - Room 312 - New York City - 8:30 AM

SYLVIA OPENED HER EYES AND blinked as she awoke. Everything around her was blurry and fuzzy, like she was looking at the world through a mason jar of olive oil. Her sense of hearing was normal, though, as was her sense of smell. In fact, it was her sense of smell that woke her. A crisp, antiseptic stench ripped through her nostrils and shook her into consciousness. As she struggled to focus her vision, she heard low murmurs in the background. Charts were being reviewed, diagnoses were being discussed, and these sounds caused a tide of panic to rise in her chest. *Where the hell am I?* Then, like the morning fog dissipating under a hot August sun, her vision cleared, and she could see unimpaired. Now her suspicion was confirmed. She was in a hospital room.

"Billy!" she cried as she sat up in bed, "where is Billy?"

"Someone needs to get her husband in here, now," the nurse said to one of the orderlies who promptly charged out of the room.

"Who..., who are you?" Sylvia said as she continued to rise. "And where the hell am I?"

"It's OK, Mrs. Delaney," the nurse said. "Your husband will be here in just a moment. He had to excuse himself for a—"

"—Where is my son? What is happening here? Why am I in the hospital?"

"You had a bit of an attack, Mrs. Delaney."

"Attack? What kind of an attack? Where is Billy? Where is John? I demand to know what you have done with them."

"It was a panic attack, Mrs. Delaney," the nurse said. "But, it is nothing to worry about. I am happy to report your MRI results were negative. There has been no brain damage, and you should make a full recovery."

"I…, I don't understand," Sylvia said, her mind confused as a torrent of fresh and terrifying images flooded through her brain. Everything swirled about in her thoughts in a jumble of confusion. She saw Billy, and the park, and John, and then — the police station and then finally…, the priest. The priest! "No! I remember now! No! For God's sake, get me out of here! No! No! I have to go NOW! NOW!"

"Ma'am, please," the nurse said. "Don't do that. You will pull your IV out."

Sylvia began thrashing wildly on the bed, her feet kicking the tightly tucked sheets loose from the bottom of her bed. "Damn you! Let me go! I must get to Billy! Billy! BILLY!"

As the nurse bent down to prevent Sylvia from getting up, Sylvia pulled back her fist and with all of her might slammed it hard into the nurse's jaw. The nurse's glasses fell to the floor, along with her clipboard, clattering against the tiles with a great shattering clack.

"Code Grey! Code Grey! Room 312 — Code Grey!" the nurse screamed into the intercom.

*****

"John, you know we will do everything humanly possible to help," Christopher Perry, administrator of New York Presbyterian Hospital, said. "You and Sylvia have been such good friends with Gloria and me over the years. I am just glad I could help out in this crisis. Sylvia can stay here as long as she needs to, so at least you don't need to worry about that."

John sighed as he leaned forward in the overstuffed wingback chair in Christopher's office. He put his head in his hands and said, "this is such a nightmare. Just a nightmare! If you hadn't agreed to let Sylvia stay here, I don't know what I would do. I couldn't have her taken to Bellevue, Chris. I just couldn't." With tears welling up in his eyes, he said, "I really appreciate you allowing her to stay here, especially after what she did to that nurse."

"Our staff is very professional, John," Christopher said. "No doubt, Nurse Johnson has seen much worse. And luckily, it appears the doctors have Sylvia fully sedated now. She will sleep for the rest of the day, and perhaps even tomorrow too. That is what she needs — rest."

"Yes, definitely," John said. "I don't know what I am going to tell her when she wakes up, though. I can't imagine what is going to happen when I have to tell her about—"

"—You don't need to think about any of that now. These panic attacks can look much worse than they really are. But…, it should pass soon, and once she is in her right mind again, it will be all right."

"But what if it doesn't pass?" John said. "What if this is it?"

"It will pass," Christopher said. "After all you two have been through today, it is no wonder she had a breakdown. It is completely understandable. Although I am no psychiatrist, my people in this field assure me her condition is temporary. The brain is a highly complex organ. It sometimes reacts defensively like this to protect itself from pain."

"It has been so horrible — horrible!" John said, his voice trailing off as he choked up. "I, frankly, don't know what I am going to do. I feel like I am at the end of my rope, and that rope is fraying pretty badly, right now. The police are starting their search for Billy, but…"

Christopher got up from behind his desk and walked over to John, putting his hand on his shoulder. "No doubt they will find him. I know a lot of those guys over in the missing persons department of the NYPD, and they are top notch. I am confident they will find Billy."

"I am not," John said. "I was confident until I saw Sylvia's reaction to the police sketch. She clearly recognized the man who took Billy before she…. Since then, she has been unable to make any sense. Your staff has to keep her drugged just so she doesn't get violent. I just…, just…"

"This is a horrible time," Christopher said, "and I am sure the shock of Billy going missing just caused her to…, to…,"

"—Snap?" John said, finishing Christopher's thought. "Yes, but what if she never unsnaps? What then? How am I going to cope with losing my wife and my son on the same day?"

"You aren't going to lose either," Christopher said. "Trust me, this is going to work out."

"And how are the police going to find Billy without knowing who that priest was? I need to find out what Sylvia knows! She knows something! She recognized that face!"

"But, surely the police are—"

"—They are worthless," John barked.

"John," Christopher said, "they are professionals. I am sure they know what they are doing. You must try and stay positive in your—"

"—This is my son we are talking about, Chris!" John said. "This is my little boy, and he is out there, with this…, this priest, or whatever the hell he is, and no one is doing a damn thing about it! I can't stand it! I have to do something myself — something, anything!"

"The sketch must have been of a Priest Sylvia knew in the past," Christopher said. "I know you two aren't very religious, but you told me her parents were. There must be a connection."

"Oh yeah, they were very much so. Sylvia's folks were incredibly strict super Catholics," John said. "You know the type."

"I do," Christopher said. "But…, who knows? Maybe one of the churches up in her old childhood neighborhood might recognize this guy. He might even be working up there right now. After all, like you told me, the police said it is probably someone with a connection to the family. Stranger abductions are extremely rare. You should pay a visit to her old parish."

"That is an excellent idea, Chris," John said as his face brightened a bit. "Frankly, it's the first decent idea I have heard yet."

"And who knows, John," Christopher said. "This may still turn out to be some sort of mammoth misunderstanding. Maybe this priest knew Sylvia's parents or someone else in the family. Does Sylvia have any brothers or sisters? I am sure they could tell you where they went to church as children."

"No," John said. "Sylvia is an only child." He paused before adding, "But…, I do remember something now. Back when Sylvia's parents were still alive, and Sylvia and I were just dating, they dragged us out to Christmas Eve Mass one year. It was in some big old church on the Upper West side…," he said as he closed his eyes. "I can almost see it in my memory. I also remember it was a huge struggle to get Sylvia to go. Eventually, I convinced her it was the right thing to do. Life is too short to always be in battle, especially with your parents."

"Very true," Christopher said. "What else do you remember?"

"It was a long service, but, Sylvia's mom was very happy we went. That is why I remembered it. I just wish I could remember the name of the place." He closed his eyes again and scowled as he concentrated. "The church was somewhere up in the 70s. I can see it in my mind's eye, but..."

"I bet it was the Church of the Holy Sacrament, up on West 71st Street."

"Yes! I think that's it, it sounds right," John said. "How did you—"

"—Confirmation class of 1972," Christopher said as he held up his hand. "My parents lived just around the corner."

"Small world, even here in New York," John said.

"Look..., you need to keep busy," Christopher said. "I understand. It is a terrible situation. I am sure if I were in your shoes I would be crawling the walls."

"I am fighting the urge to leap out that window behind you right now," John said as he pointed over to a large plate glass window with a spectacular view of the Hudson.

"Don't do that," Christopher said. He grinned as he added, "I only have room for one Delaney at a time in here, OK?"

"OK," John said as a faint smile appeared on his face.

"But, you need to go check this church out for yourself. Ask around. Sylvia is in good hands here. There is no reason for you to just sit around and watch her sleep. Trust me, they have her so sedated she will be out for the rest of the day."

"You are a good friend, Chris," John said. "And you will let me know the moment anything changes with Sylvia?"

Christopher nodded and said, "I will leave a message with your service. You still have your pager, right?"

"I do."

"I will call as soon as there is any change in her condition."

*****

John walked the half a block from the subway stop to 152 west 71st street in a daze. He felt as if he were trudging through a sea of syrup, everything around him moving in slow motion. People passed in a swirl of pointless busyness — chatting, yelling, laughing. It took all his strength not to stand in the middle of the street and scream at the top of his lungs.

He had a mission now. Having a task helped tamper the cauldron of rage and panic bubbling up in his gut. When he reached the address, he stopped and looked up at the enormous stained-glass rose window fifty feet above his head. The general appearance of the building, all grey stones, gargoyles, and nouveau-gothic architecture, made him uneasy. It was as he remembered, but, somehow seemed different now. It seemed out of place, like some anachronistic, white elephant jammed unceremoniously between two nondescript, modern, all-glass office buildings. He looked down at his watch — it was 10:30 AM. He had better go inside now. Noonday mass would be starting soon.

When he walked into the church, his eyes were drawn to the large altar in front of him. Various carved statues of saints flanked either side, and numerous stained-glass windows lined the walls of the nave. The church was mostly empty. His ears rang in the silence. Despite the hustle and bustle outside of a busy New York morning, inside this sacred space, everything was quiet. There were a few parishioners praying in the pews, a janitor up to his left running a buffer over the stone floor, but otherwise — silence.

A woman, dressed in blue, passed in front of him. He noticed her name tag indicating she was an employee.

"Excuse me, Miss, but, where do I go to see a priest?"

"We have several priests on staff here, sir," the woman said. "Perhaps if you told me the nature of your visit, I could help direct you."

"It is a rather personal matter," John said. "I am particularly interested in speaking with one of the clergy who has been here for a while. I do not exactly know how this works, but, I assume priests stay put in their parish?"

"Some do," the woman said as her eyes narrowed. "But, it really would help if you told more about your concerns. If this is a counseling issue, we have quite a few—"

"—No, this is not about counseling," John interrupted. "But it is critical. A matter of life or death, actually, and perhaps a priest who has been here for a while can help me. I really do appreciate your assistance in this matter, Miss…" He paused to read her nametag. "Cavalero."

"Father Zimmers has been here for quite some time," she said. "In fact, he had been here for decades when I started, and I have been working here for twenty years."

"Perfect," John said. "So, is he in? Is he available to speak with me? I promise not to take too much of his time."

Miss Cavalero glanced John up and down once more, her eyes darting from his face to his hands. It was apparent he was distressed. His eyes were red and bloodshot and, most telling, he was wringing his hands. She surreptitiously sniffed the air and could not detect any alcohol. Still…

"Please, Miss, I am begging you," John said, his eyes pleading.

"I will see if he is in," she answered. "Follow me. You can wait in our office conference room."

"Thank you so much," John said as he followed Miss Cavalero through a side door.

For the next few minutes, John sat alone in the long, rectangular oak-paneled room. The furnishings were sparse — a simple conference table, a few well-worn green leather chairs and, of course, hanging over the fireplace a large imposing crucifix. He could not help spy signs of disrepair scattered throughout the room. The sight of a chipped wood panel here, a bit of threadbare carpeting there, showed that times were apparently not good at the Church of the Blessed Sacrament. He looked down at his watch and grimaced. It was fast approaching eleven o'clock. He stood up when the woman came back into the room.

"I am so sorry, sir," Miss Cavalero said. "But I am afraid Father Zimmers' calendar is completely booked today. He has mass coming up in a few minutes and confirmation classes to teach this—"

She stopped speaking when John sat down and put his head into his hands and leaned his elbows onto the table. He mumbled, "I am begging, literally begging you. I must speak with Father Zimmers, and I must speak with him today. It is urgent in the extreme. This isn't about me. It is about my wife, who was the only child of two very loyal parishioners who attended here years ago."

"Who? Who did you say you were again?"

John looked up and said, "I didn't say. I am John Delaney, husband of Sylvia Delaney. The Father might know her by her maiden name, Sylvia Padovano. She is the only daughter of the late Vincent and Marie Padovano. Please, I need your help. I am pleading with you with all my heart, please, just go tell him that."

"I will tell him, sir," Miss Cavalero said. "But, I do know when he celebrates mass he always likes to have a moment of private reflection before the service. I cannot promise you that—"

"—Just tell him what I said, please. Sylvia is in real trouble. I promise it won't take too much of his time, but it is crucially important I speak with him today."

She left. A few minutes later the door to the conference room opened. A tiny, stooped, and quite ancient man shuffled inside. John studied the man's face carefully as he entered, desperately hoping it was the man from the sketch. It was not, and this fleeting hope was dashed. The priest in the drawing was in his mid-thirties at best while the man before him looked as if he could have personally participated in the crusades. *But..., perhaps he knows this other priest,* John thought.

"You are Sylvia Padovano's husband?" the priest said as he entered. "It is hard to fathom. It still seems to me like she should be twelve years old." Father Zimmers chuckled and said, "time marches on, I see."

"Yes, it does," John said as he rose from his chair. "I apologize for taking up your time this morning, but, I need your help."

"It seems like only yesterday little Sylvia was preparing for her first communion," Father Zimmers said as he looked wistfully upwards towards the ceiling. "Marie was so proud. I remember blessing her rosary the night before the ceremony."

"Her parents were both very devout, weren't they?" John asked.

"Oh, yes," Father Zimmers said. "It is a shame Sylvia and her parents had a falling out. I prayed with Marie about it many a night before she passed. It was the biggest regret of her life." He shook his head, "Marie was such an exceptional lady."

"Yes, they did not see eye to eye on matters of faith," John said, his legs becoming restless as he shifted back and forth.

"Sadly, they did not," Father Zimmers said. "But..., you said you needed my help with something? Sylvia is in some sort of trouble?"

"Yes," John said. He pulled a copy of the sketch from his sport coat and spread it out on the conference table. "I was hoping you could possibly tell me who this is?"

Father Zimmers put on his reading glasses and picked up the paper from the table. He furrowed his brow and asked, "what is this all about?"

"Do you recognize this man?"

The priest studied the paper before shaking his head and placing it back down on the table. "Cannot say that I do. I have never seen him. Although..., it is only a sketch so I could be mistaken. It isn't the same as a photograph, but this man doesn't look familiar to me at all." He took off his glasses and stared at John. "What exactly is going on here? Who is this supposed to be, and why is his picture only a sketch?"

"You are sure you have never had this man as a priest here before?" John asked. He pushed the paper forward again and said, "please, look again. I need to be sure."

"I am positive," Father Zimmers said. He pointed down at the sketch to the sideburns on the man, and said, "I would certainly remember those. Quite distinctive."

"Is it possible he worked here in the past before you came here?"

"Doubtful," Father Zimmers said. "I have been a priest here nearly forty-five years and have hired all of the priests here personally. I never forget a face, and his I certainly would remember."

John sunk into his chair and sighed.

"Now, I answered your question, so, you need to answer mine," Father Zimmers said. "What is this all about? This looks like a police sketch. Did this priest do something wrong? Miss Cavalero mentioned Sylvia was in some sort of trouble, and in fact, she said it was a matter of life or death. I think you owe me an explanation."

John breathed in deeply and said, "Our little boy was abducted from Central Park yesterday. A witness saw this man talking to our son. This is a copy of the police sketch made of that man."

"Oh, my," Father Zimmers said as he crossed himself. "That is terrible. Just terrible."

"You can see why I came here, then," John said. "The police told me stranger abductions are very rare, so, on a hunch, I was hoping it might have been a priest Sylvia knew from her past."

"I completely understand," Father Zimmers said as he sat down and studied the picture again. "I wish I could help. I really do! Have you checked your own parish?"

"We don't attend a church, Father," John said.

"I see," Father Zimmers said as he shook his head. "Such a shame. I will certainly pray for your little boy at Mass today."

"I am sorry I wasted your time, Father," John said as he stood up and started to leave.

"No, don't leave yet, son," Father Zimmers said. "Please..., Mass will be starting soon. We shall both pray for your son. God is merciful and will provide."

John frowned, and his eyes started to dart around the room. This was uncomfortable. Now that his theory had been disproven, he needed to move on somewhere else. He knew sitting in some pew mumbling nonsense would not help find Billy.

"Oh, how Marie and Vincent would be so distraught right now. Their only grandchild! I am just sick to think of it. They loved children so much. They both loved Sylvia as much as if she had been their own. I cannot imagine what they would be thinking now," Father Zimmers said. "I suppose it is a blessing they have passed."

"Wait a minute," John said. "What did you mean by that?"

"By what?" Father Zimmers said.

"By, *they loved Sylvia as much as if she had been their own*," John said. "What does that mean?"

"Oh..., I am sorry," Father Zimmers said. "I just assumed you knew. You see..., Vincent and Marie never had any biological children of their own. Sylvia was adopted."

"Adopted? How is this possible?"

Father Zimmers shrugged, and said, "I..., I don't know what to say, but, I know for a fact she was adopted."

"You know, Father, this makes me furious! Did you know, they never told Sylvia this?" John said.

"What? I don't understand," Father Zimmers said. "Why would they need to? She was ten when they adopted her. I actually baptized her the first week she came here to New York."

Chapter 15

April 19th, 2017 - Café Del Sol Mexican Restaurant - Mountain View, California - 10:30 PM

"Mmmmm," Sylvia hummed as she finished the bite of Arroz con Pollo on her fork. "You were right, Father. This has to be the best chicken and rice I have ever had!"

"Hector," Father Morales said. "If we are going to have dinner together, you should call me Hector."

"OK, Hector," Sylvia said. "You have a deal."

"So, are you feeling better now?" Hector said. "You were looking quite ill there for a minute."

"Oh, much better," Sylvia said. "A little food on my stomach was just what the doctor ordered." She grinned and said, "and how delicious. This place is fantastic."

"It is one of my favorites. I come here quite often," Hector said. "And it has long been my experience there are few ills in life that cannot be alleviated by some roast chicken, refried beans, and some freshly baked tortillas."

Sylvia laughed.

Hector continued, "I am glad you are feeling better now. It was quite a spell you had back in Alyssa's apartment. I was afraid I was going to have to call an ambulance."

"It looked far more dramatic than it was in reality," Sylvia said. "I just got a bit light headed for a moment, that's all."

"I think it was more than just being light-headed, Sylvia," Hector said. "You fainted away completely."

"I have been having a lot of trouble with my blood sugar lately," Sylvia said. "That is why going out for something to eat was such a good suggestion. But as to my spell, trust me, it was nothing."

"If you say so," Hector said.

"You seem doubtful."

"We both know why you fainted," Hector said. "I don't know why you are embarrassed about it. It was quite startling when we opened the closet and discovered the idol inside. I mean, it shocked me even, and I was kind of expecting it."

"You mean that creepy little skeleton statue? Well, forget it," Sylvia said as she waved her hand dismissively. "That kind of superstitious nonsense has no effect on me. But…, what does concern me is the effect these things might have on Alyssa. From what I gather, she is quite an impressionable and naive young woman."

"She is just confused but hardly naïve," Hector said. "Actually, from the few conversations I had with her, she seems remarkably astute. Definitely astute enough to realize she was on the wrong path and needed to change course before it was too late."

"So, Hector," Sylvia said. "What now? Are you going to now take Alyssa's little sack of macabre knick-knacks back to the rectory and dunk them in holy water, or something? Is this how your whole system works?"

"I will dispose of them properly," Hector said flatly. "As Alyssa and I discussed."

"Well, hopefully taking items out of her house won't cause any problem with the police investigation of her disappearance," Sylvia said. "If asked, I will vouch for you that her spooky collectibles were the only things removed. But…," she added with a grin, "don't ask me to explain why you took them."

"Well, it is most likely a moot point, anyway," Hector said.

"A moot point? I don't understand."

"Nothing is going to come from any police investigation," Hector said. "I can tell they aren't going to do anything."

"Why do you say that?"

"Think about it from their perspective," Hector said. "Think about the call we made to the cops. I could tell they thought the whole thing was farfetched."

"Oh, I don't think it sounded unconvincing," Sylvia said. "Well..., this is quite a switch! Originally, it was me who was opposed to calling the police. Now that we have, *you* seem to be having second thoughts."

"An old priest complains that a young woman fails to show up for a pre-arranged meeting, and the young woman's nosy neighbor breaks in and spies a towel on the floor of an otherwise neat apartment." Hector raised his eyebrow and said, "So, naturally, these two decide to call the police and report a missing person. Frankly, the whole thing sounds like the beginning of a bad joke — you know, a priest, a rabbi and a water buffalo walk into a bar and—"

Sylvia grinned and said, "—hey, who are you calling a water buffalo?"

Hector smiled, pointed at Sylvia and continued, "but think about it. Neither of us is related to Alyssa in any substantial way. You heard what the police said; there have been no other reports filed of her missing from any family or friends. In fact, there is no hard evidence she is even missing!"

"Well, when you put it that way," Sylvia said. "It does all sound kind of flimsy. I still say something happened to her. I wasn't positive before, but after seeing her phone and purse left behind, I am now."

"Me too, but, I think it may be up to us to find Alyssa," Hector said. "No one seems to think anything is wrong. I mean, even your landlord seemed nonchalant about Alyssa's disappearance."

"Yes," Sylvia said. "And this whole incident is a good argument against having your rent on autopay."

"What do you mean?"

"The landlord told me Alyssa has her rent, as well as all of her other bills, on automatic payment. It appears as long as everyone is getting paid, no one really cares what happens to you." She paused and said, "God, I sure hope if I went missing someone would at least check on me. I hate the thought of falling in the shower one morning and then being found dead six months later."

"No doubt your vicious guard dog would let someone know," Hector said as he smiled.

"Ha!" Sylvia laughed. "You are probably right. I am sure she would start howling like a nut the minute she missed her evening treat."

"Well…, the Lord works his will according to his own, hidden purposes. And it appears it's his will that you and I crossed paths seeking Alyssa. This makes us duty-bound to help her. And I also know, with Jesus' divine protection and guidance, we will be successful. He is our, and Alyssa's, only hope. I know tomorrow morning I will pray for her rescue at morning Mass. Perhaps you would care to join me?"

"Sorry, Hector, I don't do the Mass thing anymore," Sylvia said. "And…, to be perfectly honest, I don't know whether I should get further involved in this situation. I do want to help Alyssa, and I feel I did my part by calling the police, but…"

"But?"

"Well…," Sylvia said as she looked down at the chicken cooling on her plate. "You have been very kind to me, Hector. In fact, far kinder than I deserve after I punched you in the head."

"No problem," Hector said as he lifted his shot glass of tequila to his lips and took a swig. He twisted his face in mock pain as the liquid burned a path down his throat. "As I told you, after two of these, I am good as new. I have completely forgotten about it." He smiled and added, "Plus, I know it was an accident."

"It was, and because you have been so nice to me, I don't want to be rude to you."

"Rude?"

"Yeah," Sylvia said as she shifted in her chair. "You see…, all of this religious mumbo-jumbo makes me a bit queasy. Look…, please take this the right way, but…."

"But…" Hector said.

"But, honestly, I think you are not helping her gain clarity on her situation. All of this…, *stuff*, is unhelpful nonsense; from those black candles and conjuring books back in her closet to…, well…, frankly, the Mass you are going to celebrate tomorrow on her behalf. I know that sounds terribly conceited, and I do apologize. But, in my professional opinion, Alyssa needs help — reasonable help, based on logic, science and reality and not based on all of this superstitious nonsense."

"I appreciate your honesty, Sylvia," Hector said. He smirked and added, "I kind of figured it was something like that. I have a sense of these things. You were raised Catholic, right?"

"Yes," Sylvia said.

"I thought so," Hector said. He pointed to his collar and added, "I can detect an Ex-Catholic a mile away. It is an occupational hazard."

"Yeah," Sylvia said as she looked down to the table. "I'm sorry. I know that was harsh."

"No, I get it," Hector said.

"Really?"

"I do. Believe it or not, I do understand. I don't agree, but I do understand."

"Well, I am not intentionally attacking your beliefs," Sylvia said. "I am not a jerk. But, I just—"

"—Look..., no one is *for* believing in superstitious nonsense," Hector said. "But..., let me ask you a question. You seem like a bright woman, and obviously, you are a good-hearted one. Otherwise, why would you take an interest in helping some woman you don't even know?"

"I try to be a good person," Sylvia said. "But, you have to understand — my whole adult life has been a struggle against this sort of magical thinking. I just cannot be a part of it. I have to base my actions on reason and not in some fairy tale world of Gods and Devils, miracles and magic."

"Yes," Hector said as he smiled.

"I am sorry," Sylvia said. "It is just this sort of thing touches a nerve with me. I grew up drowning in my parent's faith. I had it shoved down my throat day and night. My late mother especially was delusional on the subject. She loved me, and I know she meant well, but honestly — the world she lived in is not a world I care to inhabit. It was not a world based on any kind of reality."

"And what world was that?" Hector asked.

"A world in which everything was part of some grand struggle against otherworld forces. A world where demons lurked in every corner. A world of daily mass and nightly rosaries and constantly looking over your shoulder for the Devil to pop out from behind the couch. As a child, I swore to myself that once I grew up, I would never live my life like that again. I swore that as an adult I would never put my trust in blind faith like my parents did. I would put it in something substantial, something real."

"Yes. This is a common problem. You see, there have been two great errors in thought throughout history," Hector said.

"Oh, what are they?"

"The first is the belief that Demons and Angels are responsible for everything."

"Yes," Sylvia said. "My parents were like that."

"Yes," Hector said, "but, equally fallacious, and possibly more delusional, is the belief that Demons and Angels are responsible for nothing. To believe there is no world beyond the material one, or that other intelligent entities beyond us don't exist or have any influence on our world, is not true either. The truth is somewhere in between."

Sylvia said, "Look, Hector, I really don't want to be impolite —"

"—But you think a belief in God, or any part of the supernatural, is all bunk, right? You think those who believe in a supernatural realm are just fooling themselves, operating merely on faith instead of science?"

"Well," Sylvia said as she grinned. "I am glad *you* said it, and not me."

"Oh, I know the drill, Sylvia," Hector said. "I know how it works. But, honestly, I don't have a strong enough faith to be an atheist."

"What does that mean?" Sylvia said. "Atheism is not a faith."

"All worldviews start from a beginning position of faith," Hector said. "All people operate under a basic umbrella of unprovable beliefs. Atheistic materialism is no different."

"I don't agree with that," Sylvia said. "My beliefs are firmly based in reality, not faith."

"Oh?" Hector said. "Are you so sure about that?"

"Completely," Sylvia said.

"Care to test that theory?" Hector said.

"Sure, why not?"

"Well..., how do you know we are actually having this conversation?" Hector asked. "How do you know you are not just some disembodied head, floating in a jar somewhere, imagining this whole conversation?"

"What?" Sylvia said. "That is crazy."

"Is it? And..., speaking of crazy, how do you not know I am not just some psychotic delusion you are having right now? How would you know the difference? You are a psychologist — you tell me."

"It can be hard to determine that, especially for a patient in the midst of a psychotic episode," Sylvia said.

"Ah," Hector said.

"But, I am not a patient, and I am not having an episode," Sylvia said. "So, I don't see what any of this has to do with faith."

"You are proving my point," Hector said. "You see, you wouldn't know if you were having a psychotic episode, if you were *actually* having one."

Sylvia said nothing, but, she had to concede this point.

"Now, it is a reasonable assumption to operate on that you are not," Hector said, "but..., isn't that always the case? Don't mentally ill people always say they are not mentally ill?"

"True," Sylvia said as she nodded.

"You see, some assumptions about the world you just have to take on faith. Like the fact you are not having a psychotic break, right now; or this chicken on your plate is not a hallucination. Trying to prove either of those things empirically would be difficult."

Sylvia smiled. "Well..., this chicken is pretty unbelievable."

Hector laughed. "Exactly, but..., prove to me you are eating it." He passed his hand through the air and added, "and while you are at it, prove that everything around you is not just a grand hallucination in your own mind."

"OK," Sylvia said. "I get your point. But, there is a huge difference between having a few, base-level, common sense assumptions about reality, and a belief in a world ruled by a divine white-haired man, sitting on a golden throne up in heaven, directing the actions of the universe. Surely, you must see that?"

"I wouldn't necessarily phrase it that way," Hector said. "I don't know, Sylvia. There are far bigger questions you are ignoring when you dismiss everything immaterial as being superstitious nonsense. This is too broad a brush you are wielding."

"I don't think so," Sylvia said. "I think the world has moved on from a need for God. Science seems to have answered all of the big questions now."

"Really?" Hector said as he smiled. "I would beg to differ on that."

"Oh? I am pretty confident," Sylvia said.

"Well…," Hector said. "Here's a good question for you then. And it is the best question of all. There is none bigger."

"I'm game," Sylvia said.

"Why is there something rather than nothing?" Hector asked.

Chapter 16

"MAW MAW, I declare, I think that must be the best plate of fried chicken I have ever eaten," Father Ted said as he pushed himself back from the picnic table. He lifted the back of his hand up to his mouth, wiped away a bit of wayward grease and added, "I really could not eat another bite."

"Puh-leeze," Maw Maw said as she gently tapped him on the shoulder. "A big strong man like you, why, you hardly ate a thing. And you certainly need to save room for pie."

"Oh…, Maw Maw," Father Ted said as he winked. "You are going to fatten me up like one of Joe's hogs."

"Hardly, Father Ted," Maw Maw said. "Might do you some good, though. I think you are a bit on the skinny side anyway." She smiled as she asked, "are you sure I can't bring you back a piece of pie? I am heading up to the house for more iced tea."

Father Ted smiled and nodded, "How could I ever pass up on your world-famous pie? You know I can't resist."

"Wonderful," Maw Maw said. "Just wonderful." She turned to walk back up the hill to the house but stopped when Father Ted spoke.

"You really should be very proud of your granddaughter," Father Ted said. "Sylvia was most helpful to me today. Most helpful."

"Oh?" Maw Maw said.

"Yes," Father Ted said. "And…, I wanted to ask her mother, but, I guess I can go ahead and ask you instead. I think Sylvia should lead the procession tonight. Would that be OK with you?"

"Lead the procession!" Maw Maw exclaimed. "Oh, Father Ted, I don't know what to say."

"You could say yes," Father Ted said.

"Of course, I will say yes," Maw Maw said. "Oh my…, this is just too much. To lead the procession, on Beltane even…, what an honor!"

"You don't think Joe and Darlene will object? I know Sylvia is young and has never been to Circle before, but…, I was quite impressed with her. She is a very bright girl. Very bright."

Maw Maw's face brightened as she inhaled deeply, her blue dress inflating like a great balloon. "Object? They will be ecstatic! I cannot wait to tell them. You have honored our family so much. I don't know what to say."

"You have honored me," Father Ted said as he reached out and gently touched Maw Maw's thick wrist.

"I…, there is so much to do…, so much I need to show her—," Maw Maw stammered.

"—There is plenty of time, and don't worry. I will show her exactly what to do. She picks up things quite quickly," Father Ted said. He shielded his eyes with his right hand and glanced over at the setting sun. "It is just getting dark now. We still have plenty of time before the festivities begin."

"Yes…, yes, you are right," Maw Maw said as she fanned herself with her right hand. Her face was flushed bright pink and beamed with pride. "You know, Sylvia helped me form the circle this afternoon. I knew that girl had the touch. I knew she was special from the first moment I set eyes on her. I just knew it."

"Yes…, the spirit flows full in that one," Father Ted said. His eyes darted up the hill and spied Darlene bringing a fresh bowl of potato salad for the party. He pointed at her and said, "as it does in her mother as well."

"Yes," Maw Maw said as she followed his gaze to her daughter. "But…, let's not say anything to Darlene just yet about Sylvia."

"Oh?" Father Ted said. "Are you sure?"

"Yes," Maw Maw said. "She is such a Nervous Nelly about to-night. This being the first Circle she has hosted in a while, I don't want to add to her nerves by telling her about Sylvia's honor."

"You're sure you don't think she will object?"

"Definitely not," Maw Maw said. "I know my daughter and she will pleased as punch. As will Sylvia's father, Joe, but…, in her condition and all, I think she shouldn't get overly anxious. Bad for the baby, you know."

"True," Father Ted said.

Maw Maw closed her eyes and nodded as she said. "I remember her first attendance at Circle. Darlene wasn't nervous at all, but I was a complete wreck. I was so afraid she would mess up something or do something wrong. It is a lot to remember, you know."

"It is," Father Ted said. "But Sylvia is special. I know she will do well." He watched Darlene approach and saw the harried look on her face. It was stricken; worry lines about burned corn bread, overcook potatoes and soggy green beans were etched into her brow. He grinned as he turned to Maw Maw and whispered, "I agree with your assessment about Darlene. I will let this be a secret for a few more hours at least." He pointed at Maw Maw and said, "Perhaps you should let her know right before the ceremony starts. Let it be a nice surprise."

"Oh, it will be a wonderful surprise," Maw Maw said. "And…, about the altar. Have you any ideas yet? You know, all the girls are dying to know. I have never seen them in such a tizzy."

Father Ted smiled and held his index finger up to his puckered lips. "It's a big secret. Of course, with so many lovely candidates to choose from, it will be hard for Spirit to make his selection. We must await his choice."

"Oh, yes, certainly Father," Maw Maw said.

"And who knows," Father Ted said. "Perhaps you will be chosen?"

Maw Maw howled in laughter. "Oh, Father Ted, you are the limit. I know you are joking. My altar days are far behind me. But," she added as she put her hand on her left hip and swiveled. "It is nice to be lied to."

"I'm not lying," Father Ted said. "There is no age limit for being chosen. And a fine woman like yourself would make a wonderful—"

"—Please, stop," Maw Maw said as she put her hand on the back of his head. "You are already making me feel too old." She paused as she luxuriated in the feeling of his thick black hair in her chubby fingers. Her eyes drifted shut and she sighed. "Oh…, if only I were thirty years younger!" She withdrew her hand.

"Father Ted," Darlene said as she walked over to the picnic table and put the bowl down in the center. "We have tons of potato salad left. I do hope you will have some more."

"Honestly," Father Ted said as he shook his head. "You gals are going to kill me. So much good food to eat and in such quantities, I am liable to bust a gut. I know I must have eaten a dozen of your deviled eggs today."

"Oh? I will go get some more," Darlene said. "I am so relieved you liked them."

"Liked them," Father Ted said. "I loved them!" He pointed up the hill to the others enjoying themselves and said, "I must say, Darlene, you put on a fantastic Circle. I think Spirit will be most pleased we had it here this month. The evening has been spectacular!"

"See Darlene," Maw Maw said, "you fretted for nothing." She glanced down at Father Ted and said, "all afternoon she has been as nervous as a turkey the day before thanksgiving. I told her everything was perfect, but, she wouldn't listen."

"Come on, Momma," Darlene said as she lightly blushed.

"Well…, you should listen to your mother, Darlene. Everything has been perfect. So perfect, in fact, I bet this might be the best Beltane celebration yet," Father Ted said.

Darlene started to speak but then winced, grabbing her stomach with her left hand.

"Are you OK, Darlene?" Maw Maw said.

"Oh, yes," Darlene said as she straightened back up. "Just a little kick, that's all."

"Praise be!" Maw Maw said as she threw her arms up in the air. "The quickening! The quickening has come!" She turned to Darlene and asked, "when did this happen?"

"This morning," Darlene said. "About as far into the pregnancy as I was with Sylvia when she first got rowdy."

"You and your sisters were quite feisty when I carried you all," Maw Maw said.

Father Ted closed his eyes and said, "I knew Spirit was pleased today from the second I woke up — and now we have proof! It is a clear sign of approval. As clear as a cool October afternoon!"

He reached over and touched Darlene's belly, his smile growing wide as his fingers ran over her stretched cotton sundress. In a soft voice he said, "all the glows of life a-blurring, through the misty shades of time; the breath of life is stirring as grapes blossom on the vine. As the blood of the young starts flowing, first breaths muffling in their throat; tiny limbs begin a-stirring, as a vigorous newborn goat. The nameless one smiles wide, his cruel mouth yawning full agape, the black bull is shod for the famous ride of Europa's divine rape. To the mountains we cry havoc, to the valleys we cry war, from the golden dawn of wisdom, to a foaming distant shore. A greater treasure giveth no one, a higher prize to man unknown, a glorious new day is dawning, a fresh seed shall soon be sewn!"

Chapter 17

April 19th, 2017 - Café Del Sol Mexican Restaurant - Mountain View California - 11:00 PM

"HONESTLY, HECTOR," Sylvia said, "I haven't really given it much thought."

"You haven't thought about *that* question?" Hector said. "The question of why there is something rather than nothing? How is this possible? This is the ultimate question!"

"Well…, I suppose, but, I guess it just doesn't seem relevant to me," Sylvia said.

Hector shook his head and said, "now you are hedging, and, no offense intended."

"None taken," Sylvia said.

"But frankly, I don't believe it. You are obviously an intelligent person and curious about the world in which we live. For you to claim you are not curious about why all of this," he paused to wave his hand out across the room, "exists is a huge dodge. In fact, it is beyond a dodge and borders on willful blindness. You know there must be some explanation to the question as to why there is something rather than nothing."

"Maybe the universe just always existed," Sylvia said. "Did you think of that? If it did, then, problem solved. There would be no reason to have to create a God to explain something that just *is*."

"All evidence strongly points away from an eternally old universe," Hector said.

"Well, of course, you would say that," Sylvia said. "You are a priest, after all."

"I am not talking about theological evidence, but, scientific evidence, Sylvia."

"Oh? Like what?"

"Like the Big Bang, for example. This event points to an absolute beginning of the universe. In the beginning, there was nothing but complete and total nothingness. Out of which, all matter, energy and even time itself sprung forth, approximately fourteen billion years ago."

"So, no seven days of creation, eh?" Sylvia said.

"You should know better," Hector said with a smile. "Most Christians, like any scientifically literate person, believe in a fourteen billion-year-old universe. The science is pretty much settled on this point. With that in mind, and, to add on to the story of the big bang, the second law of thermodynamics also points to an absolute finite beginning. This law shows that all energy that has ever, or will ever, exist was created at the first moment of the Big Bang. And, since that time, all this energy has been slowly evaporating. Now, surely you see the implications."

"I am afraid I don't," Sylvia said.

Hector said, "the implication is; if the universe is eternally old, we should have run out of usable energy trillions of years ago."

"Well..."

"And this, coupled with the fact Edwin Hubble proved that the universe is expanding, through his observations of the Doppler shift of light, makes any eternal past theory impossible to maintain," Hector said.

"Hubble, as in the Hubble Telescope?" Sylvia asked.

"The very one," Hector said. "His discovery, along with the work of Georges Lemaitre, of an expanding finite universe slammed the lid down hard on any possibility of an eternally old universe. It is just not a feasible option anymore."

"How so?"

"Well..., if the universe is not only expanding, but speeding up, then the galaxies and stars we see today should have expanded far beyond our ability to observe them."

"I don't understand," Sylvia said.

"It is hard to comprehend," Hector said. "But, consider this — scientists tell us the universe is fourteen billion years old. They also tell us the galaxies we are able to observe are over ninety billion light-years away. Pretty crazy, eh? Space is expanding faster than the speed of light!"

"And this means what?"

"It means if the universe were any older than it actually is, everything would have expanded beyond our ability to observe it. We just happen to exist at the *exact* right place and the *exact* right time to be able to observe the universe we inhabit. The fact we can make any sense of the universe at all proves it was created."

"It is interesting," Sylvia said. "I may concede there is a 'force' that created the universe; but, this is a long way from calling this force 'God.'" She grinned as she added, "I am relieved to hear you quoting from scientists and not just theologians, Father — much better evidence, you know."

"Science and religion are not in competition," Hector said. He smiled and added, "and it is ironic you just made that statement."

"Oh?"

"Yes," Hector said. "Because you see, Georges Lemaitre was not only a world-famous scientist, and a discoverer of the Big Bang, and a good friend and colleague of Albert Einstein, but, he was also a priest. Science and religion fit quite well together."

"Perhaps," Sylvia said quietly.

"And since anything that begins to exist must have a cause, and the universe began to exist..., well...."

Sylvia smirked and said, "Yes. I will go out on a limb and accept the beginning of the universe has a cause. I get your point. But..., I know you are going to say the cause is God, but, I reject that. It could just be a force — like gravity, or dark matter or something else. It doesn't have to be an entity with a personality and a will. It doesn't have to be some divine being sitting on a golden throne in the sky. That is pure conjecture."

"Again with the golden throne. Well, I will not comment on God's choices in furniture," Hector said.

"Sorry for the golden throne jibe. It was a bit snarky, I must admit," Sylvia said. "But I apologize only for the tone, not the sentiment."

"No problem," Hector said. "But, if you imagine a force powerful enough to cause the creation of the entire universe; all matter, all energy and even time itself, it would have to be extremely powerful."

"Of course," Sylvia said.

"And if you have this incredible 'force,' or 'entity,' outside of time and space, and it was able to create everything from nothing, well...," Hector said as he paused. "If that isn't a job description for God, I don't know what is."

"But you are projecting your own values on this cause," Sylvia said. "You call it God whereas I might just refer to it as a blind force."

"A blind force did not create the universe," Hector said. "A mind did. This is very clear from the evidence."

"Why do you say that?" Sylvia asked.

"Do you realize just how precarious the universe is?" Hector asked. "Do you understand if just one of the couple of dozen variables governing the laws of nature were altered in just the slightest, infinitesimally tiny way, life would be impossible?"

"I will admit," Sylvia said. "I am not up on astrophysics, so I am no expert."

"Well, I am no expert either, but, here is what I do know. Take the force of gravity, for instance. The value of the force of gravity could have been anything. There is nothing about it that requires it to have the strength, or weakness, it does. But..., if it were altered by just one trillionth of a degree stronger, the universe would have collapsed on itself. And if it were adjusted just one trillionth degree weaker, the universe would have flown apart into smithereens at its birth. Galaxies, suns, and planets would never have been able to form. The fact it is set as *precisely* as it is proves it must have been designed that way. And..., where there is design..., there must be a designer, right? A designer is not a brute force."

"Now hold on a minute, Hector," Sylvia said. "You can't make a statement like that."

"Oh, why not?"

"It could have just been an accident," Sylvia said.

"Quite a lucky accident, I would think," Hector said.

"Stranger things have happened."

"Really?" Hector asked as he cocked his head to the left. "So..., if you are walking in the woods, and you just happen upon the space shuttle sitting out in a clearing — the most complicated machine ever constructed, by the way. Infinitely simpler than the entire known universe. And if you saw this, your reaction would be to just shrug your shoulders and say, 'oh well, I guess a tornado must have blown all this metal together in just the right way. Stranger things have happened'."

"This is kind of an extreme example," Sylvia said. "I think you are exaggerating."

"If anything, my example is not extreme enough." Hector said. "Consider this also, I only talked about gravity having to be finely tuned for a life-permitting universe to exist. The reality is there are dozens of other factors, each just as delicately balanced on a knife's edge that are required for existence. They *all* have to exist in order for the universe to be conducive to life — everything from the weak and strong nuclear force, the expansion rate, as well as the distribution of energy and matter throughout the universe. Each of these constants are staggeringly unlikely to exist at the values they do, and yet, each are crucial for the universe to exist in the form it does. The likelihood of all these things coming together simultaneously, inside a grand, amazing accident, is beyond the realm of rational probabilities." He paused and added, "as Einstein himself said, 'God does not play dice with the universe.'"

"I don't know, Hector," Sylvia said. "I admit, the probabilities are small, but..., it still could have just been an accident. Anyway, isn't this the theory behind the Multiverse? Given enough alternative universes, eventually there will be one that emerges as perfectly balanced. We just happen to live in that universe. After all, we couldn't live in any other one, could we?"

"Ah, yes," Hector said, "the old reliable Multiverse." He laughed as he added, "it never ceases to amuse me how the Multiverse, which itself would have to be finely tuned in order to exist, is more palatable than believing in the most likely scenario — God."

"But…, it is a valid explanation, right?"

"Only if one doesn't understand arithmetic," Hector said. "I am sure the Multiverse would have been very popular back in my old Parish."

"Where was that?" Sylvia asked.

"I was the rector of St. Joan of Arc church in Las Vegas years ago."

"Ah!" Sylvia said. She laughed and added, "I bet you heard some interesting confessions there."

Hector nodded and said, "I certainly did. As you might guess, Las Vegas is the capital city for people who do not understand how arithmetic works. The whole city was founded on the concept of mathematical ignorance."

"So true," Sylvia said. "After all, they don't build billion-dollar casinos paying out, do they?"

"No, they do not. The house always wins," Hector said. "But look…, there are only three distinct possibilities for the universe being like it is: chance, necessity, or design. Science has consistently shown the universe is not the way it is out of necessity, so, it is fine-tuned either by chance or design."

"OK, so?"

"The Multiverse hinges on reality being as it is by sheer chance. This is a major problem. To think the universe is so perfectly aligned, simply as the result of an amazing accident is just too mind-blowingly unrealistic to take seriously as an option. Design is the only feasible option."

"I don't know, Hector," Sylvia said. "I know many scientists believe the multiverse is the explanation to this problem."

"Sadly, they do," Hector said. "But they hold this belief, not because of reason. There is no more proof of the Multiverse than there is of God. In fact, there is considerably less evidence supporting it. And if the Multiverse actually did exist, it too would have to be explained, as it would require an even more fantastical level of fine-tuning than the universe itself. No, this belief in the Multiverse theory to explain away the fine-tuning problem was born out of…, dare I say it…, *faith*."

"Faith?" Sylvia asked.

"Yes," Hector said. "Faith in wanting to maintain a belief in a reality without God. As I said before, I don't have that strong of faith. I need to have statistics and arithmetic on my side."

"Come on now," Sylvia said. "That is rather dismissive."

"It is," Hector said, "but, it is dismissive for a reason. People of science should know better. And..., sticking with the Vegas theme, suppose a person was at the roulette wheel, and the marble landed on Red 32 a thousand times in a row. This would be pretty extraordinary, wouldn't it?"

"It would," Sylvia said.

"And what do you think a reasonable person would surmise by this?"

"I see where this is headed," Sylvia said.

"Yes," Hector said as he smiled. "A reasonable person would wonder if the game is rigged. Now, it is remotely possible it is all legitimate, and the gambler just got very lucky. Possible, but highly unlikely. Now, imagine the same scenario I described, but instead of landing 1,000 times in a row on Red 32, it was a trillion times. Would it still be reasonable to say it is just by chance?"

Sylvia said nothing.

"You know the answer," Hector said. "The answer is clearly no — it is not reasonable. Any rational person would know something is not right. And that, my dear, is the ultimate answer to the big question. This game is not an accident. We didn't just get really, really, *really* lucky. The wheel is rigged. The game is fixed; and, if the game is fixed, there must be someone who fixed it."

"OK, Hector," Sylvia said. "You have made some interesting points and have given me a lot to think about."

"I try," Hector said.

"But..."

Hector raised his eyebrow and said, "I knew there would be a but."

Sylvia reached across the table and pointed at the crucifix hanging around the priest's neck. "I may be able to accept some sort of ultimate force being God as you have described. This may be reasonable. But..., this is not what this is all about, is it? No." She reached over and lifted the cross around his neck into her hand and said, "This is your God, isn't it? Not some ultimate force. This is a bridge too far for me to pass."

"Why is this a bridge too far?" Father Hector asked.

"Come on, Hector," Sylvia said. "You are a very smart man, I can tell. But..., I mean, the virgin birth, and the whole walking on water bit. It's all too much. Doesn't all of that seem far-fetched to you? Look, I concede you have made some good points tonight, and, frankly, some give me pause. But you forget, I grew up Catholic. I know the whole drill about Christianity and I just can't buy any of it. Do you *really* believe all of this..., stuff?"

"I do, Sylvia," Hector said. "I believe all of it."

"I'm sorry, I don't," Sylvia said. "My parents tried to instill their faith in me — God knows they tried. But, as soon as I got out of their house, I got as far away from all of it as I could."

"Well, perhaps they didn't tell you the whole story," Hector said.

"They seemed pretty thorough. I heard the story, and I didn't buy it."

Hector raised his hand and motioned to the waitress. "I don't know about you, but, I could go for some coffee and churros. Are you game?"

"Do those churros come with chocolate?"

"Of course," Hector said. "Do they come any other way?"

"Well, sign me up," Sylvia said with a smile. "I am never one to turn down chocolate."

Hector placed their order with the waitress, and after she left he turned to Sylvia and asked, "And as we wait for our dessert, do you mind if I ask you a question?"

"Of course not," Sylvia said.

"I understand people struggle with faith. Unfortunately, many people have bad experiences with religion during their childhood."

"Yes, I know I did," Sylvia said.

"It is a shame. But, I am curious..., regardless of all your negative experiences with religion, I want you to answer just one fundamental question for me."

"OK, I'll try," Sylvia said.

Father Hector asked, "Who do you think Jesus was?"

Chapter 18

April 28th, 1996 - New York Presbyterian Hospital - Room 312 - New York City - 2:00 PM

JOHN STARED BLANKLY AT HIS wife lying motionless in the hospital bed. His mind was numb with grief, worry and most of all — exhaustion. It was the end of a ten-hour vigil. Soon he would have to return to their apartment. This repetitive pattern of hospital/apartment/police department and back to the hospital was approaching nearly a week and his body was fast reaching its limits of endurance.

Lying prone in her hospital bed, Sylvia had never looked more beautiful, or for that matter, tragic. In her left arm an IV was attached to a drip bag hanging from the chrome rack overhead. Numerous wires hung down from pads adhered to her temples, crisscrossing her chest before finding their home in the EKG monitor to the side. Pings punctuating the moving lines on the monitor revealed her brain was active. She would recover eventually, but not yet. For a week she had not spoken a word or even moved an inch on her own power.

John reached over and took her hand inside his. He closed his eyes and sighed. He needed her, and loved her more than ever, but..., part of him wanted her to stay unconscious. He hoped that Billy could be found before she woke up. The horror was too much for her fragile psyche to take.

He let her hand go and it dropped to the bed. He stood up and stretched, his back creaking and popping like dry twigs on a November afternoon. Hospital guest chairs were not designed for long-term use. His eyes roamed around the room and he sighed. At least here she was well tended. There was some solace in this. Even during the worst week of his life, he could at least take comfort in that. Even pitiful consolation, such as having your comatose wife cared for in a top-notch hospital, was precious to him now. A small flickering candle always burns brightest in the darkest room.

A nurse entered, glanced across at one of the various monitors arrayed on the back wall and dutifully wrote down some numbers into her log. Over the past seven days, John had seen this routine many times. It was simple, efficient, and oddly comforting. Like the changing of the seasons, or the ticking of a grandfather clock, it was at least some pretense at normality in a world gone mad. Somewhere else, at least, life was going on as usual.

Various nurses would enter the room to check Sylvia's intravenous feeding bag a few times a day, update her charts, and roll her over to avoid bed sores. Often, they would make pleasant chit-chat before departing. An hour or so later, another would return to do the same thing again — rinse and repeat, all day long.

"I think your wife is showing some signs of improvement, Mr. Delaney," today's nurse said.

John smiled weakly and nodded.

"Yes," the nurse said as she looked down at the chart. "All of the vitals are close to normal. Nothing unusual is showing in the brain activity." She stopped herself and added, "at least, nothing that can be detected."

John nodded again but said nothing. He was never sure if such a non-report required a response.

"Have the police gotten any leads on your little boy?" she asked.

John shrugged and mumbled, his lips moving and noises emitting from his throat. He didn't know what he said. It didn't matter anymore. He was so tired of lying, both to himself and to others. All his systems were on automatic now. *Keep up a brave front. We are praying for Billy. All will be well. Just have faith. Yada Yada Yada.* He knew this dance well and could motion through the steps better than Gregory Hines. It was all very nice and totally sincere, but he believed none of it. He knew the dark truth. As each day passed, that truth grew gloomier, although none would acknowledge it. To say it, was to make it happen — and no one wanted that. The phone mercifully rang, ending the tiresome forced happy talk, and the nurse answered.

"Room 312..., Yes, sir ..., Yes...," she said. She glanced over at John and added, "Yes, he is here... I will send him right down."

"Who was it?" John asked.

"Mr. Perry, our administrator," the nurse said.

"Oh? What did Chris want?"

"You know him?"

"Yes," John said. "He and his wife are good friends with Sylvia and me."

"That explains it," the nurse said. "Well..., he wanted you to come to his office when you get a chance. He said to tell you he may have made some progress with an issue you asked him to look into."

For the first time in days John smiled. He jumped up from his chair and raced out the door. *Maybe..., just maybe...* His feet flew down the highly polished white linoleum halls to the elevator.

A few minutes later, he was sitting in Christopher Perry's office again.

"I will tell you, John," Christopher said. "This is the damnedest thing I have ever seen."

"So, what do you think?" John said. "When that old priest told me Sylvia was adopted..., and not just adopted as an infant, but as a ten-year-old child, I thought he must be crazy, or maybe I was losing my mind! I immediately ran home and got her birth certificate."

"Yes," Christopher said as he picked up the document from his desk and glanced at it again.

"And as you can see, it says clearly that she was born in this hospital on November 23rd, 1966 to Vincent and Marie Padovana," John said. "Now, I know I must be mad to draw you into this black helicopter conspiracy, but..., were you able to find the doctor listed in your archives? I know it is crazy, but..."

Christopher's brow furrowed as he put the document down on his desk. "You see..., here's the thing—"

"—Jesus! Don't tell me you can't find the doctor!"

"Oh, I found him all right," Christopher said. "Or at least the record he worked here, but..."

"But?" John said as he stood up from his chair.

"But...," Christopher said as he lowered his voice. "You might want to sit down."

"I am tired of sitting," John said. "All I have been doing for the past week is sitting! Sitting and waiting! Waiting for the police to find my son. Waiting for my wife to recover from..., whatever the hell it is that is wrong with her!"

"John," Christopher said in a warm tone. "Please..., please sit down."

John sat gently on the chair, gripping the armrests with both hands, his knuckles now bone white.

"This birth certificate is a forgery," Christopher said. "I've seen forged documents before, but this is the weirdest one I have ever seen."

"I don't get it. Why do you say it is a forgery?" John asked. "It has the official seal on it and..., for Christ sakes, they even have Sylvia's social security number on the form."

"And there is the problem," Christopher said. "The number doesn't add up."

"What do you mean the number doesn't add up?"

"What is your social security number?"

"Mine?"

"Yes, yours," Christopher said.

"050-38—"

Christopher held up his hand. "OK, that is all I need. Now, you were born in New York in..., 1963, right?"

"Yes!" John said. "You got all that just from the first few digits of my social security number?"

"John, I deal with these numbers all day, every day. After a while, you understand how they work and can read them clearly."

"But, what does this have to do with Sylvia's birth certificate?" John said. "Look, I know she didn't get along with her parents, but, they were good people. I know they certainly wouldn't commit a fraud."

"And they didn't, *technically*," Christopher said. "And this is why this was so cartoonishly easy to discover. You see, if you didn't suspect something was wrong, you would never question any of it." He pointed to the first few digits of Sylvia's social security number and said, "her number begins with 400-74."

"Yes," John said.

"Those codes are reserved for Kentucky, John, for a Kentucky birth in 1966." He pointed to the birthdate and said, "Which matches up to her birthdate, but, not the location."

"I don't understand," John said. "What does this mean?"

"This is her real social security number, but, this document was created in 1976."

"How can you tell that?"

"I did some investigation on the physician listed — Doctor Marstens. He only started working here in 1974 and —"

"—What did he say? Did you ask him about this? This could be some sort of break through here!"

"He is dead, John. I talked to his widow," Christopher said. "He died two years ago. But, she told me he was very good friends with Sylvia's father. They used to go to Kentucky every spring to go fishing and rented some sort of cabin down there."

"Where was this cabin? When did they—"

"—Dr. Marstens' wife told me they abruptly stopped going in 1976. She didn't know the reason why, but, Dr. Marstens and Sylvia's father had some sort of big falling out after they got back. So, I put two and two together and—"

"—I don't know what this is all about," John said. "But, by God, I am going to find out! Where in Kentucky did they used to go?"

"Some little town I have never heard of — Pikeville."

"Pikeville Kentucky," John said. "OK. I need to see this thing through. I cannot imagine for the life of me why an obstetrician would forge a birth certificate for some little Kentucky girl to appear like she was born in New York. Why do that? It is just crazy! Crazy!"

"Here is the crazier thing," Christopher said. "Dr. Marstens was not an obstetrician."

"Oh? I just assumed. What kind of doctor was he?"

"He was a psychiatrist and a pretty renowned one at that. I looked up some of his old published articles — quite impressive. He was fairly famous, especially in the treatment of post-traumatic stress disorder, although, it wasn't called that then."

"That is Sylvia's field!"

"Yes, weird, isn't it?" Christopher asked. "Did she ever mention him?"

"Never," John said. "I never heard the man's name until today. But then again, I never knew Sylvia was adopted until all of this happened."

"And, I suspect, neither does she," Christopher said. "It appears this whole document was designed to hide this truth from her. But why? This is the big question. What happened that was so horrific, it required all of this?"

"This is why I must go to Pikeville," John said. "I don't know how, but I know my boy is there. I know that somewhere at the bottom of this twisted rotten barrel, that crazy priest from the police sketch has our boy and he is in Pikeville. Maybe Sylvia recognized him from her past and that is why she collapsed. I know there must be a connection. I just know it!"

"I think you should leave this matter to the police, John," Christopher said. "You could tell them what you know and they can take it from here."

"No!" John erupted. "I must do this myself. I will tell the police what I know, but, I also know they won't do anything. It is too speculative for them to follow up on, but, I will. I will go down to Pikeville and get my boy!"

Chapter 19

April 19th, 2017 - Café Del Sol Mexican Restaurant - Mountain View California - 11:30 PM

"Jesus? You mean *the* Jesus?" Sylvia asked.

"Yes, *the* Jesus," Hector said. "It is a simple, yet not easy to answer question. And it is the one question you and every other person on this planet has to eventually answer. All must take a stand on who they think Jesus is."

"Well...," Sylvia said. "To be frank, I haven't really thought too much about Jesus since I left home for college, so I don't know how to answer. I do take issue with your statement, though. Why do you say every person must answer that question? If you ask me, the way you stated it is very imperialistic, ethnocentric and rather heavy-handed."

Hector smiled. "It is neither imperialistic or ethnocentric. It's a realistic assessment of the way the world is. Regardless of whether someone identifies as a Christian or not, there is no denying Jesus has had more of an impact on history than anyone who has ever lived. There isn't even a close runner-up."

"I suppose you are correct about that," Sylvia said.

"Well..., I am happy to hear you say that," Hector said. "You would not believe how many otherwise intelligent people have fallen under the sway of that idiotic '*Jesus is Horus*' theory these days." He shook his head and added, "the things people believe — sad, really."

"I heard all of that Horus nonsense back when I was a professor at NYU," Sylvia said. "It is quite the rage on campus now."

"Yes," Hector said. "Sadly, sometimes it takes tremendous effort, years of study and an advanced degree in order to learn the most stupid things imaginable."

Sylvia laughed and said, "Hector, you shouldn't slam my old profession! I was in academia for many years, you know."

"Oh, sorry," Hector said. "I meant no offense."

"None taken," Sylvia said. "But, I will admit, there is much truth in what you say. Who was it that said, 'the only Marxists left in the world are in North Korea and in the economics department of Yale'? Your point is well taken, but that doesn't mean one should automatically be a Christian, of course."

"No, of course not," Hector said. "I only meant to say claims Jesus never existed are insane. No rational person should take such theories seriously."

"Look, even though I am not a Christian, I haven't fallen down that rabbit hole," Sylvia said. "I earned a minor in History, and, to say Jesus never existed and is just a completely mythological character, is crazy, just as you state. There is far too much evidence that a rabbi named Jesus of Nazareth existed in the first century. Everything points to it." She smiled as she added, "although, it does not mean the man was the son of God, however. He was just a misunderstood, and highly mythologized, itinerant prophet. You know, back then, you couldn't swing a dead cat without hitting a couple of dozens of those guys."

"True," Hector said. "But no one thinks any of those other prophets are the son of God. Only Jesus has this honor. Did you ever wonder why that is?"

"I suppose it was good PR for Jesus by his early followers," Sylvia said. "But, in all seriousness, I suppose after Jesus died, his followers exaggerated his deeds, and his deification progressed over time. Legends build up gradually, especially in a pre-literate society such as first century Judea. As each subsequent generation heard miraculous tales about Jesus, he slowly evolved into — God."

"Well," Hector said. "That would be a good theory—"

"—See! I told you I would—"

"—It would be a good theory," Hector continued. "Except for the reason every fact you cite is inaccurate."

"How so?" Sylvia asked.

"Well…, first of all, your timeline is all wrong," Hector said. "Legends do crop up over time, but, it takes many years, perhaps hundreds, for a legend to take root. The Gospels were written far too early to have become mythologized."

"How early were they written?"

"Mark, the earliest of the Gospels, appears to have been written in the 50s AD. Luke and Matthew in the 60s, and the latest, John, appears to have been composed in the 90s. Given that Jesus was crucified around 30AD, these accounts are very close to the source of the event. Far too close to have become legendary."

"You are making my point, Hector," Sylvia said. "If Mark, the oldest of the Gospels, was written in the 50s, and Jesus was crucified in 30AD, that is a gap of twenty years. Who knows what kind of crazy stories can crop up in twenty years? I don't know if we can trust those documents as actual *history*."

"Oh?" Hector said as he grinned. "I assume you have no qualms believing the history of Julius Caesar or Alexander the Great, then?"

"What are you getting at?"

"Well, if the passage of twenty years casts doubts on the validity of a document, try hundreds of years! In both the case of Julius Caesar and Alexander the Great, the surviving biographies were written hundreds of years after they died. The Gospels, on the other hand, are incredibly early. And, in addition to being written so close to the actual events described, the ancient copies of the gospels are incredibly numerous. In fact, due to the sheer number of documents we have relating to the Gospels — Jesus' life, death, and resurrection is the best-documented event in ancient history."

"What do you mean?" asked Sylvia.

"If you compare the surviving copies of the Gospels to other ancient documents, such as the Iliad, the quantity of copies outnumbers it by a factor of twenty. There is an embarrassment of riches for scholars to study original ancient Gospel texts."

"Yes…, but…," Sylvia said. "I don't think you can trust the Gospels. I mean, they were written by Christians, and, of course, they are biased."

"Unlike those non-biased biographies of Julius Caesar and Alexander the Great, right?" Hector said. "I think you are showing your biases now."

"Hardly! I am being objective," Sylvia said.

"I am sure you think you are," Hector said. "But, you must know, *everyone* is biased. The idea of there being some sort of neutral, uninterested, unbiased history — or even news for that matter — is a fiction. And it is a fiction now just as much as it was two thousand years ago. Every author, knowingly or not, has a point of view and it influences what they write. In fact, if you think about it, one has to be interested in a subject in order to write about it in the first place. After all, how many biographies are written by authors who do not care about their subject?"

"That is true, I suppose," Sylvia said.

"But that does not make what is written incorrect, however."

"I will concede that," Sylvia said. "But…, you forget something. I grew up on this stuff. I had the full force of Christian dogma jammed down my throat every day, so I know all about it. If you are going to base your core beliefs on the Bible, you are going to be in serious trouble. The whole structure is built on a house of sand. The Bible is far too full of inaccuracies for any thinking person to take it seriously."

"Ah…," Hector said. "It is funny you say that. I always thought some of those…, inaccuracies, as you put it, were proof of the Bible's validity."

"Now you have me curious," Sylvia said. "I must admit, of all of the religious arguments I have heard over the years, inaccuracy as proof of truth is a first."

"Well…, think of it this way," Hector said. "The Gospels were written from eyewitness accounts. At the very least, they were compiled a few dozen years after the events."

"Yes," Sylvia said. "And that is sort of my point. How can we trust them?"

Hector held up his hand and said, "Do you really think they would agree on everything? The fact they disagree on minor points tells me they are true. It would be far more suspicious if they were in complete alignment."

"Why do you say that?"

"If the texts agreed on everything, it would indicate they were created through collusion. It would show they were invented, just like any other type of fiction. Any good detective will tell you that if two witnesses' stories agree too much, they know they have colluded on their testimonies. People always remember events slightly differently from one another."

"But, Hector," Sylvia said, "isn't that a problem? I mean, in one gospel account you have two angels at the tomb. In another, you just have a mysterious man in white. One gospel has the nativity story with the shepherds and the angels. Another has the three wise men and the slaughter of the innocents, while the other two make no mention of either event. With such wildly differing stories, that often contradict one another, how can you know what is true and what is not? Doesn't that make the whole text suspicious? It seems to me the best course of action would be to just chuck the whole mess."

"Hardly," Hector said. "The gospel accounts may disagree on minor details, but, they all agree on a central point."

"And that is?"

"Jesus was crucified, died, and buried — and then three days later, he rose from the dead," Hector said. "And that, my dear, *is* the point! If Jesus rose from the dead, then he is who he says he is — God."

"I don't know, Hector," Sylvia said. "If the accounts disagree on the minor points, I don't know why you have such faith they will agree on the major one."

"Interesting point, but, consider this," Hector said. "A few years ago, I read an account of the survivors of the Titanic disaster. Several hundred people were fished out of the North Atlantic back in 1912, and when they were interviewed, the reports they gave on the sinking of the ship differed greatly."

"How so?" Sylvia asked.

"Roughly half said the ship sank bow first, straight down into the water. The other half said the ship broke in two and then sank, both sections separately. It was not until the wreckage was discovered that the second account was proven to be what happened."

"I don't understand what this has to do with the gospels?" Sylvia asked.

"This," Hector said. "Although the Titanic survivors disagreed greatly on how the ship went down, you will notice, none said the ship did *not* sink. The Gospels are the same. Unimportant details may disagree, but all four gospels document the same amazing event — Jesus rose from the dead. This is the most important event in history."

"Assuming there is no other explanation," Sylvia said.

"Yes," Hector said with a chuckle.

"Why do you laugh?"

"People have been trying to come up with an alternate explanation for the resurrection for centuries. All have failed," Hector said. "What amazes me is, given the supposed intelligence of our age, and the sophistication of our generation, the resistance to facing this basic fact remains very strong."

"I think you are a bit too triumphant, Hector," Sylvia said. "I am sure there are plenty of possible natural explanations for this mythological event. There is no reason to conjure up some imaginary 'God' to make sense of it."

"OK," Hector said. "I am all ears. What do you think happened?"

Sylvia paused, took a sip of her coffee and said, "I accept that Jesus lived — and died. This is beyond dispute. But…, perhaps, after his crucifixion, his followers wanted to keep his movement going. After all, a dead Messiah is not that inspiring, but, a risen Messiah, plus a son of God no less, now *that* is how you get a movement started! It doesn't seem surprising to me at all that his followers would invent stories of his resurrection to give their movement a bit more…, oomph."

"Oomph?" Hector said as he smiled. "So, they lied?"

"Maybe," Sylvia said. "Stranger things have happened — especially in the world of religious zealots."

"Hmmm," Hector said as he scratched his chin. "It is an interesting theory, but, alas, a fairly old one and completely discredited."

"Well, of course, you would say that," Sylvia said. "You are a…"

"Zealot?"

"Well…, no," Sylvia said. "I wouldn't say zealot exactly, but you are obviously a religious person. It makes sense you would not give the 'stolen body' theory any credence. But, you have to admit, it would explain things, would it not?"

"No," Hector said. "And you don't need to be religious to see how that theory is bunk."

"Why?"

"Well, first of all, it would involve a massive conspiracy to hide the body, right? I mean, Jesus died and was buried, but you now have the problem of his tomb. All the evidence points to an empty tomb. Even the original critics of Christianity agree on the reality of an empty tomb. So, for your 'stolen body' theory to be true, Peter and the other apostles would have to steal the body."

"They could have," Sylvia said.

"Yes, but, then they would have *known* Jesus did not rise from the dead," Hector said. "They would have known what they were preaching was a lie."

"People lie all of the time, Hector," Sylvia said.

"Yes, they do…, but, if this was a lie, it does not line up with the other known facts of their lives. Take Peter for instance — he denied Christ at his trial, was embarrassingly absent from the crucifixion, but then later, he is going to steal the body and hide it? And then, after all of that trouble, he is going to go around professing Jesus rose from the dead, ultimately dying himself for preaching that belief? Who knowingly dies for something he knows to be a lie? Who does that?"

"Well…, I….," Sylvia stuttered.

"And another thing," Hector said. "All four of the gospels stated that women were the first witnesses to the empty tomb. Now, if it were not true, why would the fictitious story include this embarrassing detail? It certainly did not help make the case to early converts."

"Embarrassing?"

"Yes," Hector said. "I don't mean to sound sexist here, but, there were certain unpleasant realities in first century Judea. Women's testimony was considered worthless. So, to have the first witnesses of the resurrection be exclusively women would have made the story *less* believable to audiences, not more. And if the whole story was made up, why make that up?"

Sylvia said nothing, pausing to stir her coffee.

"And if Peter was going to be the leader of this emerging movement, which he of course was, why would he intentionally have himself portrayed so poorly? I mean, the guy denied his friend and then abandoned him at the moment of his most extreme need — the crucifixion. Hardly a heroic character, is he?"

"Well…, maybe he and the other apostles hallucinated images of the risen Jesus?" Sylvia asked. "I know with some of my clients back in New York, especially after a tragic loss, they often see their dead loved ones. The mind is a tricky thing, Hector. You would be surprised at the phantasms it can create. Moreover, these hallucinations can seem quite real."

"Oh yes," Hector said. "No doubt they can. But, how many times do multiple people have the same hallucination of the same event at the same time?"

"Well…, given the nature of hallucinations…," Sylvia said as her voice trailed off.

"It doesn't happen, does it?"

"No."

"And yet, in this example, there were multiple sightings of the resurrected Jesus by individuals, groups of three or four, all of the apostles together and even five hundred people simultaneously. This doesn't seem like a hallucination, does it?"

"I will admit, it doesn't meet the classical definition," Sylvia said. "But…, these were all grief-stricken followers. Perhaps one person had a hallucination, and then another, and then through the power of suggestion—"

"—Explain James then?"

"James?"

"Yes, James, the half-brother of Jesus. He was not a follower of Jesus during his lifetime. In fact, the gospels indicate that he, like most of the rest of Jesus' family, were embarrassed by his ministry."

"Why was he embarrassed?"

"Do you have any siblings?"

"No," Sylvia said.

"Well, I do," Hector said, "a younger brother, Pedro. Let me tell you, if Pedro suddenly started preaching he was the Son of God, I would probably try to get him locked up in a mental institution."

Sylvia laughed. "Yes..., I met a few Jesuses at Bellevue during my residency. A couple of Napoleons were there too as well as a smattering of Caesars and one John Wayne to round out the collection."

"John Wayne?" Hector asked.

"Yes," Sylvia said. "A tiny little Italian guy, with a lisp, believe it or not. I bet he wasn't any taller than five two. If his delusion weren't so tragic it would have been comical. I can still see him strutting down the hall, saying 'Howdy Ma'am' to me every morning. Sadly, the world is not short on schizophrenics or bi-polarized individuals."

"And that, no doubt, is what James thought about his half-brother, Jesus. Now..., imagine you did have a little brother who claimed to be God. What would it take for you to suddenly reverse your opinion that he was mentally ill and then ultimately die proclaiming he was God after all?"

"I don't know," Sylvia said. "Probably something big."

"Yes," Hector said. "It was for James too — something very big — such as Jesus returning from the dead to speak to him." Hector sipped his coffee and then added, "Even more remarkable is the case of Saint Paul. How would you explain his conversion? He certainly would not have had any grief-related hallucinations relating to Jesus — he never met him before the resurrection. In fact, Paul was the greatest persecutor of the early church before his conversion on the road to Damascus. Explain that. Paul saw the risen Jesus and had such a life-altering change he became the most important and influential apostle of all?"

"All right, maybe the hallucination theory is invalid, but, that still doesn't prove anything," Sylvia said.

"Oh?" Hector said. "I think it might."

"Look, maybe it is possible Jesus didn't even die on the cross? Perhaps he was just severely wounded and, after he was placed in the tomb, a few days later he revived on his own. When he returned, his followers just thought he had risen from the dead. This would certainly explain the appearances, wouldn't it?"

Hector grinned and said, "Assuming the highly unlikely possibility Jesus revived in the tomb after being nearly scourged to death and hanging on the cross for six hours. Then somehow in his weakened state, he pushed away the stone, and overcame the guards. Then three days later he stumbled into his followers — I doubt they would declare him a God. If they saw a broken, bloody, nearly dead man like that; I am sure they would probably rush him to a doctor! They certainly would not have thought he rose from the dead." Hector paused before adding, "and regardless, if it did happen like you say, you still have a major problem."

"Which is?"

"Well…, eventually, Jesus would have died, right? What finally happened to his body? You see, a revived, but mortal Jesus doesn't solve anything. You still have the same problem as you had before — an empty tomb. No, Sylvia, all of the naturalistic explanations of the empty tomb are unrealistic and do not match up with the other facts we know. Only one explanation remains that fits all of the facts. Jesus rose from the dead. And…, since he did, then Jesus is who he says he is — God! And that is the biggest, and best, news of all time!"

"Maybe," Sylvia said. "But…, it still seems pretty irrelevant."

Hector sighed and shook his head. "If I live to be a hundred, I will never understand how people can remain so…, unmoved by this, either one way or the other. If God exists, and if he sent his son Jesus to die for our sins, well…, what bigger news could there be? What could be more relevant than that? Claim it isn't true, or, say you believe something else, or say you believe with all your heart and soul Jesus rose, but to say it is irrelevant is inexplicable to me."

"I understand your points, Hector, and you make a fine case for your point of view," Sylvia said. "But despite all you have said, I just can't accept the God you profess. The world is too screwed up. If there is a God, and it is a big if, well…, he certainly isn't worthy of worship. This whole planet is a total disaster."

"Ah…," Hector said as he nodded. "I understand. We live in a fallen world, Sylvia. A fallen and evil world, but…, it is all going to be —"

"—Spare me the sermon," Sylvia said as she held up her hand. "I know the drill, the whole snake in the garden and fall of man and the guy in the red suit with the pitchfork and horns." She yawned and looked down at her watch. "It is getting a bit late for all of that." She smiled and said, "I don't mean to be rude. I have enjoyed our dinner, but, I need to get home and go to bed. I am exhausted and I have to go to work in the morning."

"Of course," Hector said. "But..., to the issue at hand, about Alyssa."

"Yes, about Alyssa," Sylvia said. "Look, I want to help, but how can—"

"—You said you got a call at your office, right?" Hector said.

"Yes."

"You don't have to get too involved. When you get to work tomorrow, maybe you can look it up on the caller ID? Let me know the number. It might give me a lead or something."

"You have no faith in our friends in blue?" Sylvia asked.

Hector rolled his eyes.

"Yeah, me either," Sylvia said. She smiled and added, "I do want to help Alyssa, and, after this lovely dinner you bought for me, how can I not help you?"

Hector nodded and said, "see, my evil scheme has been revealed. Churros always make a compelling case."

"That they do!" Sylvia said. "Give me your card and, first thing tomorrow morning, once I get to work, I will call you with the number. Hopefully, you will find out this whole thing turns out to be nothing but a big misunderstanding."

Hector's face darkened as he reached into his sports coat, pulled out his card and handed it to her. "I hope so, but I doubt it. I am quite worried about Alyssa, and I just hope she has not submitted to the forces of evil."

"There you go again," Sylvia said as she took his card and shook her head. "You sound so sensible most of the time and then.... Look, it has been my experience most problems in life are either caused by mental disorders or, just random meaningless accidents. There is no reason to conjure up some sort of dark forces to account for everything. Evil is a human constructed concept."

Hector frowned and said, "You are wrong, Sylvia. Dead wrong. Whether you want to believe it or not, evil exists. You can count on it. Evil is a force and has a name, and most definitely exists."

Chapter 20

THE WHITE BOX WAS THE source of endless fascination for all the children playing in the backyard, especially, Davy Johnson. From the moment Father Ted had directed the men to lower the crate onto the ground, it had been the subject of intense juvenile speculation and debate. *What do you think is inside? Why is it locked? Why such a big deal about a simple box?* The special way the grownups treated it only heightened their curiosity: gently placing it onto the ground, lovingly caressing the sides as it settled onto the earth, mouthing unheard words to the sky as they finished their task. It was all so mysterious. By the end of the afternoon the kids were in an uproar over it; their tiny minds bubbling at the possibilities within.

It had been a long day, too. Full of pent up energy, they were ripe for excitement. The rambunctious and rowdy bunch agreed on little, but they did agree on this — Circle was a bore. It was a monthly slog of complete and utter tedium. This was something their parents dragged them to against their wills, something to be endured. But today, with this mysterious box in their midst, things were different for a change. Something new was happening. Each could not help eyeing the enticing crate all afternoon, just waiting for them like a wrapped present sitting under the Christmas tree. All they needed to do was get someone to crawl under that tree and pull off the bows, ribbons, and paper, and that person was naturally, Davy Johnson.

The adults eventually walked around the house to the front yard, and now the coast was clear. Davy saw his opportunity. For the first time all day, the box was unattended. The other kids mobbed around him as he knelt in front of it. His eyes narrowed as he studied the lid, the hinge, the sides; his mouth growing dry as he felt a dozen curious eyes boring into him.

He reached out with his chubby right hand towards the lid. His hand shook as he felt across the top for the latch. When he found it, he gritted his teeth and clasped his fingers around the metal knob, slowly turning it and releasing the lock. He needed to be quiet. This was a wuppin-worthy offense, but, he was committed now. He was too close to the finish to turn back.

Sweat beaded on his forehead as Davy lifted the small door on top of the crate. A grinding metallic creak groaned from the rusty hinge. He glanced up the hill, afraid one of the parents may have heard. Luckily, they had not, and he turned back to the box. He slowly lowered his hand into the opening. Hot, acidic bile burned in his throat as his fingers sank into the dark interior.

He stopped as an electric tingle danced up his spine. He heard something shift inside. It was a quiet sound, but distinct. Something writhed. In a flash, he ripped his arm out of the opening. In his desperation to free his arm, he hit the side of the crate, and the door on top slammed shut with a loud bang. As the clang echoed through the still, late afternoon air, he winced.

"Chicken!" Bobby Hollister hooted. "I knew you were a chicken! You just talk a big game, little baby Davy. Little Baby Davy! Little Baby Davy!"

"I..., I'll do it. Just give me a second," Davy said as he scanned the crowd of kids surrounding him. He felt their horrified yet judging stares. He would not fail again.

"I was just warming up," Davy said. He paused and then started to lower his hand into the box again.

"Davy Johnson! You stop that right now, or I'll tell!"

He quickly pulled his hand out again and spun around to confront his accuser. He smirked when he saw her.

"Mind your own beeswax, Sylvia," he said. "This is none of your business."

"It is my business," Sylvia said. "Father Ted doesn't want anyone messing around with his stuff. You know that! You should —"

196

"—Why don't you shut up, Buttface!" he said. "You think your Queen of the World just because Father Ted talked to you today!"

"Yeah, Sylvia," Doris McLane said. "I've seen what you been doing. You've been all lovey-dovey with Father Ted all afternoon. Maybe you are going to *marry* him!"

"Shut up, Doris," Sylvia said. "You don't know what you are talking about. You are just a baby!"

"Oh, I know plenty," Doris said. "And I am not a baby! I will be seven next month! And I know all about your *boyfriend*, Father Ted. I hear what my Mommy and my Aunts say about him when they think I am not listening."

"What do they say?"

"Oh, all kinds of things," Doris said. "They LOOOVE Father Ted. They think he is a hooty, and I bet you think he is a hooty, too."

"Hooty?" Sylvia said.

"She means Hottie," Davy said as he shook his head. He turned to Doris and said, "You are such a retard."

"Am not!" Doris said. "I know what they said, and they said Hooty!"

"Well, hooty hottie, it doesn't matter," Sylvia said. "If you guys don't leave Father Ted's box alone, I am going to go tell. He won't like you messing with it."

"Tattle Tale! Tattle Tale!" the others cried in unison.

"I'll do it," Sylvia said. "Don't think I won't!"

"You ain't going to do nothing," Davy said. "I know you want to know what is in this box as much as we do. You aren't fooling anyone."

"I..., I...," Sylvia stuttered as she felt her eyes drawn to the box. Davy's words struck her like a cinderblock slamming into her gut. He was right. She did want to know, and her mind reeled. *What was in there? Was it another..., no, it couldn't be that, could it?*

She inhaled sharply and said, "OK..., but..., hurry up, will you? If you are quick, I promise I won't tell. I can't stay long. I know Maw Maw will be calling everyone in soon. It is almost dark, and she told me to go inside and get ready."

"Get ready for what?"

"Circle, silly," Sylvia said.

"You're too young for Circle," Doris said. "You know it is just for grownups. They never let us kids stay outside for that."

"Well, shows what you know. I guess I am all grown up now," Sylvia crowed. "Father Ted chose me to lead the procession tonight!"

"Well then, maybe you should go get ready for your *wedding* procession to your b-o-y-f-r-i-e-n-d!" Bobby said. He then sang, "Father Ted and Sylvia, sitting in a tree, K-I-S-S-I-N-G. First, comes love, then comes marriage then comes Sylvia with a baby carriage!"

"Shut up, Bobby! You don't understand. You don't know anything about anything!"

The others pointed and laughed and then joined in, singing, "Father Ted and Sylvia, sitting in a tree, K-I-S-S-I-N-G. First, comes love, then comes marriage then comes Sylvia with a baby carriage!"

"I am not staying around for this! Do what you want with the box, I don't care," Sylvia shouted. "I have to go get ready, so go ahead and play your baby games!" She turned and ran back up the hill to the house, leaving Davy Johnson and the other children alone.

Once Sylvia was gone, Davy's face fell as he knelt back down into the dirt again. The moment of truth had arrived. Scanning the circle of his peers, he felt every eye on him. He couldn't back down now.

"Go ahead, big shot," Bobby cackled. "Or are you too *scared?*" he added, dragging out the syllables as his words pounded through the air like buckshot.

"Back up," Davy barked as he ordered everyone to move away. "I need room."

"Don't choke, Davy," Bobby taunted as Davy lowered his hand into the box again.

Davy grimaced as his hand descended and he felt his fingers hit the bottom of the crate. The hairs on his arm were standing up straight, his whole body fighting back a collective shudder rapidly roiling up from his gut. The inside of the box was warm and wet, like a moist, dripping cave. It wasn't at all what he expected. He heard something shift inside again, and he swallowed hard. He heard something move. It was very quiet, just the tiniest of noise. The sound grew clearer now, a gurgle..., a faint, sloppy, wet, gurgle.

*****

"What do you think, Father Ted?" Joe said as he lifted a large wooden cross and steadied it on the ground. "I have been working on it since last week. I sure hope you like it."

"Wow, Joe. It is impressive," Father Ted said. "Very impressive. Is that oak?"

"Yep," Joe said. "Chopped the tree down myself, just as you instructed. You know, my granddaddy planted that tree, so I know how proud he would be to know it finally ended up being put to a good use."

"Oh yes," Father Ted said as he took the cross in his hands and gently caressed the wood. "He would be most proud! This is a real work of art here, Joe. A real masterpiece. No plyboard here, no sir." He studied the grain of the wood carefully, grinning as he observed the finely etched wood carvings on the sides and the fact that it was constructed of one solid piece. He said, "So…, how on earth did you get it so exact? I was expecting you would have to fasten the crossbeam together with rope."

"Oh, Father," Joe said as he looked down at the ground and smiled. "I don't mind telling you, it was a real ordeal. The trunk I selected was enormous — almost a hundred years old. That was why I chose it. It was the only way I could get it built without using any metal. You did say no metal, right?"

Father Ted smiled and nodded. "That's right, no metal. You are a good man, Joe. Everything is all natural, just as Spirit commands. Amazing job, simply amazing!" Father Ted said as he held the cross out straight in front of him. It was tall, well over eight feet, and felt heavy in his grip. Still, a doubt lingered. "Are you sure it will hold her weight?"

"Hold her weight?" Joe said as he laughed. "Shit, Father, this could hold two or three! She ain't that big, you know. It'll get the job done, no problem. I guarantee it. A better question would be will the nails hold firm?"

Father Ted grinned. He reached into his pocket and pulled out four stainless steel spikes. He lifted them up into the air. They glimmered and glinted in the fading sunset. At least eight inches long, and incredibly thick, they were more like railroad spikes than carpenter nails.

Joe laughed and said, "Oh yeah, those'll do. Those'll do just fine!"

*****

Back in the house, Sylvia walked into her bedroom and stopped dead in her tracks. Draped on her bed was a long white gown. She smiled. It was beautiful. In the gathering gloom, a single ray of sunlight streamed in from the window in the hall and lit up the garment spread out on her bedspread. She reached down, lifted the hem into her fingers as her grin grew wider. It was so soft — pure silk. The fabric felt like tiny butterfly wings on her skin. It was thin too; more delicate than any garment she had ever felt in her life. The gown was translucent and glowing as the rays from the fading sunset danced across the fabric.

"Put it on, Sylvia," Maw Maw said.

Sylvia jumped. "Oh, Maw Maw, you scared me!"

"Sorry, dear," Maw Maw said as she stepped forward out of the shadows. "I was up here waiting for you to come up and find your gown. This is a big night for you, you know."

"I do," Sylvia said.

"So…, go ahead and put it on," Maw Maw said. "I want to see how it looks on you. I bet you'll be pretty as a picture."

Sylvia lifted the gown off the bed and started to pull it over her head. Maw Maw reached out and stopped her.

"What are you doing?" Maw Maw said.

"What do you mean?"

"I mean, why are you putting it on over your clothes?"

"Oh…, I thought," Sylvia said as she looked down at her hand. It was clearly visible through the material. "You mean you want me to—"

"—Yes, Sylvia," Maw Maw said. "You have to take off your clothes first."

"All of them?"

"Yes!" Maw Maw said as she shook her head and added, "Don't be such a silly girl. You know how to get dressed properly."

"Uh…, OK, Maw Maw," Sylvia said. "Are you sure it will be OK?"

"Of course! You want to be like the grownups, don't you?"

"Yes!"

"Well…, this is what all of the women wear when they lead the procession for Circle. I wore this very gown myself, when I had the honor, as did your mother when she served."

"OK," Sylvia said as she blushed. Reluctantly kicking off her shoes and pulling off her socks, she sat down on the bed. After a few moments, she had stripped off everything and put the gown on. It felt amazing against her bare skin. So light! The fabric even tickled her stomach as it clung tight against her flesh.

"Oh, Sylvia! You look beautiful!" Maw Maw said. She grinned as she reached down to a paper bag at her feet and pulled something out. Sylvia squealed when she saw it.

"Maw Maw, is that for me?"

"Of course," Maw Maw said as she stepped forward and placed it on her head. "Tonight, you are to be the Princess of Beltane…, and every princess needs a crown."

Sylvia vibrated with excitement as she felt the flowering crown slide over her forehead. It pinched a little, the thorns of some of the roses digging into her skin, but, she didn't care. Once Maw Maw withdrew her hands, Sylvia raced across the room to her mirror and gazed at her reflection. It was perfect. The crown was made of numerous flowers: roses, gardenias, hydrangeas and most perfect of all, five big purple rhododendron blossoms spaced along the rim. All of the flowers were held together by a long strand of ivy interwoven with lady's breath. She really did look like a Princess.

"I am so glad it fits," Maw Maw said as she bent down and kissed Sylvia's forehead. "I made it myself this afternoon. You know, that big brain of yours takes up a lot more space in your head than mine did at your age."

"It is a little tight," Sylvia said as she fiddled with the side.

"That's OK," Maw Maw said. "It just means it won't fly off during the ceremony. So…, do you like it?"

"Like it? I love it! I love it so much!"

"I am so glad," Maw Maw said.

Sylvia glanced back at the mirror again. Her smile disappeared, replaced by a look of horror. The fabric of her gown was so thin, she appeared nearly naked in the mirror. She looked up at Maw Maw and said, "But…, the boys…, Bobby and Davy…., they are going to see my—"

"—Bobby and Davy aren't going to see anything, Sylvia," Maw Maw said. She glanced down at her watch and said, "they are children, and in fact, it is time to bring them inside. So, while they are inside with the other kids, you, the Princess of Beltane will be outside with the rest of the grownups celebrating Circle. They are going to be stuck in the house with the other kids watching the ABC Friday Night Movie."

"Yes," Sylvia said as she self-consciously covered herself with her hands.

"Now…., if you are still too bashful to wear your beautiful gown," Maw Maw said, "I can just go ahead and tell Father Ted you aren't grown up enough for Circle. Then you can stay inside with the other children and—"

"No! I am ready! I am ready!" Sylvia said.

Maw Maw smiled and nodded. "Good girl. I knew you would be."

*****

"What's in there?" Bobby cried. "What do you feel?"

"Just give me a second," Davy said as he squinted his left eye and wriggled his hand further into the box. His heart was pounding hard and fast in his chest, like a thousand drummers performing a riotous march. "I think…, I think I feel something. It feels like something is… Oh, God! What the…? What is it? What is it?" he screamed as he jerked his hand out of the box.

"No! No!" Davy shrieked as he leaped up and down like he was on fire, his light tan khakis turning dark as hot urine flowed down his left leg in a thick gushing stream.

"Davy peed his pants! Davy peed his pants!" Doris sang as she laughed and pointed at his shame.

"What are you boys doing down there?" Maw Maw shouted from the top of the hill. "Are you all messing with Father Ted's box?"

"No Ma'am!" they shouted in unison.

"You better not be," Maw Maw said. "Now..., come on up here this instant. We are about to start Circle."

"Oh...., do we have to?" Bobby said.

"Yes! But hey, I made brownies and y'all can stay up late and watch the movie on TV," Maw Maw said.

"Hooray!" Doris cried as she and the others leapt to their feet and clambered up the hill towards the house. Davy said nothing. He kept his head down and his hands in front of his urine-soaked pants as he trailed after them.

"What was in the box, Davy? What was it?" Bobby said as he walked beside him. "You sure were freaked out!"

"I don't want to talk about it," Davy said. "Not now, not ever."

*****

After the kids were sent to the TV room in the basement, Maw Maw called Sylvia downstairs. Butterflies stirred in Sylvia's stomach as she walked barefoot across the kitchen floor and opened the back door. She still felt nearly naked in her paper-thin gown. A warm blush rained over her body, but..., she knew she had to comply. Closing her eyes tightly, she took a deep breath and stepped out onto the porch.

"Sylvia!" Darlene shouted from the yard. "Just look at you! You are so pretty."

"Isn't she?" Maw Maw said. "As pretty as you were at your first Circle."

Others gathered around and said equally encouraging things. As they spoke, Sylvia's butterflies stilled, her blush disappeared, and her face beamed. Her smile grew even wider when she saw Father Ted approach. Reaching the porch and standing over her, he lightly cupped her chin with his hand and said, "I have never seen such a pretty Princess of Beltane in my life. Never!" He paused before adding, "Our lady will be so proud. So..., Sylvia, are you ready to begin?"

"Yes, Father Ted," Sylvia said. "I am ready."

Father Ted nodded, turned to the crowd and said, "Oh sacred night has fallen. The sun has left the sky. The deer have ceased their running, the birds no longer fly. The dark of night descends, the Spirit is on the rise, let us now prepare ourselves, glorious Beltane has now arrived!"

Sylvia breathed the cool night air deep into her lungs, her entire body electric with anticipation. From her vantage point on the porch, she could see the whole yard at once. Everyone was staring at her. Off in the distance, she watched the glorious sky blaze as the sun finally slipped beneath the horizon, the orange and reds fading into a deep dark purple. To her left, she watched the torches around the circle being lit. To her right she saw…, she saw…., she saw her mother, and Maw Maw, and Father Ted and all the others start to undress. As she watched clothes drop to the grass, her mind reeled. *What is happening? Oh my God, what is happening?*

Click… Click… Click…

Chapter 21

April 21st, 2017 - Floriston, California 5:30 AM

MELODY SUMMERS STRETCHED HER ARMS high over her head. She closed her eyes and took in a long gulp of mountain air into her lungs. Her body was perfectly aligned in the Lotus position, and she felt the Chi surging through her spine. After a brief meditative pause, she released her breath and slowly lowered her arms back into prayer hands in her lap. "Namaste," she said before opening her eyes.

She smiled. Her vantage point, high above the Truckee river, on the upper deck of her three-story, bright pink, clapboard home, enjoyed a spectacular view. From up here, she could see everything in the valley below for miles around, and it was spectacular on a beautiful crystal-clear dawn such as this. In late April, spring still hung fresh in the air, the dismal winter a distant memory. The hellish summer was still a few months off. The peaks of nearby Carpenter Ridge remained capped with snow while the meadows below, fed by the ice-cold Truckee river, was bursting forth in a riot of color - an endless field of purple crocus and yellow daffodils gently swaying in the breeze. Floriston, Melody's hometown since 1968, certainly lived up to its name, *flowers at the place.*

Now that her yoga routine was over, she stood up and walked back inside to her kitchen. It too, like everywhere else in her house, was bright and sunny, the golden rays of dawn just now flooding across the cheerful yellow tiled walls. Above her, innumerable sprays of freshly picked herbs hung from a rack over the big copper kitchen sink. At her feet, newly harvested vegetables overflowed from a dozen hand-woven baskets on the brick floor. The whole room smelled garden fresh —

just as she always insisted. She lifted a cast iron skillet from a hook on the wall, pulled back her long gray hair into a ponytail and began to cook. Breakfast indeed is the most important meal of the day, one of the many lessons she had learned in her 71 years. Her consistent, all-natural healthy diet was one of the many reasons her age was not apparent. She barely looked fifty.

After a few minutes of preparation, breakfast was ready — eggs, freshly baked bread, ripe tomatoes, and kale. She arranged everything on a tray just so before ascending the stairs to the second floor.

"Wakey Wakey," she said when she reached the upstairs hallway. "It's breakfast time!" She opened the guest bedroom door and as she entered, added, "Time to get up and eat, Alyssa. You know you are eating for two now." Her face dropped. The bed was empty and the window open.

Melody slammed the tray down hard onto the dresser with a loud clang. Her face reddened as she screamed, "Damn it, Darryl! Get your ass up here, right now! She ran off again!"

*****

At 9:35 AM Sylvia stumbled into her cubicle at UVid. Her hair was a mess. Her makeup was haphazardly applied and looked like it had been plastered on with a trowel instead of a brush. Topping off her disheveled look, dark circles ringed her blood-shot eyes. She had severely overslept, and it showed, but at least she was here.

"It looks like someone had a rough night last night," Heather said as Sylvia passed by her desk.

"You have no idea," Sylvia muttered. "Sorry I am so late. I slept through my alarm."

Heather shrugged. "Ah yes…, playing snooze bar roulette? I'm an old pro at that game myself, although, I have learned the only winning move is not to play."

Sylvia nodded and smiled.

"But hey, don't apologize to me. It's not like I'm the boss around here," Heather said. "And…" she paused as she pointed over to Steve's office, "it's not like our actual boss gives a shit what time you get here anyway."

"Yet another perk of working here," Sylvia said. "I could easily get used to this."

"In fact, I know that if you have a particularly raucous reason for being late, the more depraved and illegal the better, Steve is liable to recommend you for a promotion. He just loves tales of debauchery and depravity, especially if they are exceptionally spicy and original."

Sylvia laughed. "Well…, I don't know how *debauched* my evening was, but…, I know I did end up slugging a priest." She smirked and added, "would that count?"

"Damn girl!" Heather said. "I always heard you east coast girls were real badasses, but that is especially hardcore!" She laughed as she thumped her fist onto her own chest and added, "respect."

"Well…, I am not ready to join the Crips or the Bloods just yet," Sylvia said, "but I am glad to see you approve." She leaned forward and looked at the display on her desk phone. "Now…, first things first, do you know how the caller ID thing on this system works? I never was very technical, and I don't want to erase anything by accident. I told Father Morales I would—"

"—Wait just a minute on all that!" Heather cried. "You can't just drop a bomb like that and then leave me hanging. I thought you were kidding about the priest. Now…, what happened? You really punched a priest? No joke?"

"No joke. I really did, but it was an accident," Sylvia said. "And I promise I will tell you all about it. But first, I promised I would call him back with a phone number."

"Who?"

"The priest."

"The priest wants a number from your office phone? What is this all about?" Heather asked.

"Remember the crazy call I got about Alyssa?" Sylvia asked.

"Yes."

"It's about that. Apparently, he was Alyssa's priest."

"Wow! I had no idea. I didn't think she was the religious type," Heather said. She leaned over the phone, pointed to the screen and said, "See, if you just hit the back arrow on the display, it will cycle through all of the inbound calls you have received in the last few days. I think it can hold fifty numbers in memory."

"Is this on all of the phones?"

"Yes. UVid installed caller ID on all the phones a couple of years ago. It seems some of the employees were getting harassing calls."

"Well, luckily I haven't gotten many calls so far," Sylvia said, "just a couple, I think, and most of them were telemarketers. In fact, I think the only 'non-wrong number' I got was that one weird call for Alyssa." She hit the button on the display and cycled through a couple of 'name unknowns' before reaching the call in question.

"*Mountain View Antiquarian Books and Supplies*," Sylvia said as she read the name.

"Oh, I know that place," Heather said. "Down on Castro street, I think."

"Well then, the plot thickens," Sylvia said. "An occult bookstore — this just gets weirder and weirder."

"I told you Alyssa was into some whacky shit," Heather said. "And now to know she was hanging out with a priest too, on the side — what the hell? You think you know someone."

Sylvia pulled out Father Morales' card and started to dial the number. Heather reached over and pressed down the release on the cradle, hanging up her phone.

"Hey! I was making a call here," Sylvia said as she furrowed her brow.

After glancing down at the card in Sylvia's hand, Heather said, "You need to stop for a minute and think this out before you make this call." She pointed at the card and said, "so, this number is for the punched Padre?"

"It is," Sylvia said. "I ran into him in Alyssa's apartment."

"You were in Alyssa's apartment last night?"

"Yes. You see, her door was unlocked and..., look..., it's a long story. I promise I will tell you all about it. I really do promise. But..., I also promised Hector I would call him with this number first thing this morning."

"*Oh?*" Heather said as she raised her eyebrow. "So, it is Hector now. I am curious. Did you get up to some ecclesiastical naughty business with Father Hector? I can just see him now, all Latin, and suave, and so very off limits."

"You have been working here at Perve Central too long, Heather," Sylvia said as she shook her head. "It has corrupted your young mind. For one thing, Father Morales is old enough to be my father — which would make him old enough to be your *grandfather*."

"Ewwww," Heather said. "Thanks for bursting my romantic bubble."

"And for another thing, he is really a great guy," Sylvia said, "and seems quite committed to his religious vocation."

"Oh, I see," Heather said as she rolled her eyes. "That must be why you punched him, then."

Sylvia laughed and shook her head. "No, no, it is not like that. Jeesh…, this is just too hard to explain, but, he seems really concerned about Alyssa. Frankly, I am too. It is all so weird. When I went inside her apartment, it looked like it had not been inhabited for weeks. I think something might have—"

"—Look, Sylvia, in all seriousness," Heather interrupted. "If I were you, I wouldn't get any more involved with this situation. You don't know if this whole thing isn't some kind of freaky set up?"

"A setup? What are you talking about?"

"Hey, listen, you got that bizarre note in your mirror, and then that crazy call, and then you find out you are living next door to Alyssa?" Heather asked. "You don't find this odd?"

"I do," Sylvia said.

"I tell you, this whole thing stinks," Heather said. "Who knows, maybe this is all some sort of elaborate prank? Alyssa was a weird chick. Maybe she and the priest are planning some sort of—"

"—A prank? Well, that would be a pretty elaborate prank, don't you think?"

"Well, yeah."

"And for what?" Sylvia asked. "And why?"

"But this priest, I mean, what's his deal? Why did he come to Alyssa's apartment last night, all of a sudden, and just happened to run into you?" Heather asked. "Where did you say he works? Maybe he isn't even a real priest."

Sylvia looked at the card again and said, "He's a real priest." Holding the card out she added, "see…, he works at Saint Sebastian Catholic Church."

"Well, I still would steer clear of him," Heather said. "Who knows what this priest is really up to with Alyssa. It seems too coincidental to me. You can't know what's really going on. I mean, I thought those guys only went for altar boys, but who knows, maybe he is branching out?"

"Heather! My God! You are far too cynical," Sylvia said. "He's not like that."

"So, you say," Heather said.

Sylvia said, "I know what you are hinting at, but, really…, I know what I am doing. I promised the guy I would call him with the number and I will."

"OK," Heather said as she jerked her hands into the air and opened her palms. "Don't let me be accused of interfering."

"I swear, Heather," Sylvia said as she lifted the receiver to her ear and began to dial. "This is the end of my involvement, just a simple phone call. Alyssa is Father Hector's problem now, not mine."

Heather nodded and said, "good thinking."

*****

The rocks dug deep into Alyssa's soles now. The old access road she was running down was built for three-ton logging trucks, not tender bare feet. A few spots of red drizzled behind her, splattering the sharp gravel with splotches of bright red - a rare shock of color in an otherwise green darkness. Pine Trees reached to the sky on either side of her, blocking out almost all light as the massive branches interlaced each other overhead. All was just a long, endless tunnel of green. In the gloom, it could be dawn, or noon, or dusk — she had no way of knowing. But she knew one thing, she had to run faster.

She stopped and gasped. She was out of breath, the ache in her side having ratcheted up from a slight twinge to a now constant throbbing pain. *Damn, I'm out of shape*, she thought. It had been over an hour since she wriggled down the drain pipe to freedom. It might have only been twenty minutes. Who could tell in this dim green hell?

But she did know it was growing late and they would be sure to miss her by now. Then they would come looking for her, and of course, would never relent until she was found. They would never let her go, not after, after…. She closed her eyes and started to run again, now faster than before. Her one tiny window of opportunity for escape was closing, and she knew it was closing soon.

As she stumbled down the road she plunged the depths of her memory. She wished to God she had paid more attention to where Darryl was driving when he brought her up here. *Where the hell is I-80? It has to be close! It just has to be!* She stopped again, bent over and grabbed her knees, nearly bursting into tears from the raging fire in her side. When the pain passed, she glanced up and smiled. There ahead, through the thick canopy of trees, she saw a light. She was at the end of the woods. Best of all, she heard a car and began to run once more.

Her pace quickened now as she tapped her last store of energy. Her face broke into an exhausted smile as she emerged from the forest. Staggering forward, she collapsed to her knees onto the side of the road and flailed her arms towards the lone car approaching. Mercifully, it slowed and pulled over to a full stop. She closed her eyes and whispered, "Thank you, God! Thank you! Thank you!"

When she opened her eyes, she saw the car. It was a 2015, jet black BMW convertible and the top was down. The driver, to her amazement, was as gorgeous as his vehicle, and to her relief, he looked friendly and concerned.

"Are you OK, Ma'am?" the driver asked.

"Please…, you must help me," Alyssa screamed. "I have got to get out of here!"

"Are you hurt? I think you might need to go to a doctor," the driver said. He pointed down and added, "your feet are bleeding."

"I'm OK, but I really need to get out of here, right now!" Alyssa said. "Please, please won't you help me?"

"Is someone after you? Look, I think we need to call the—"

"—There is no time! Please! Please can you not just take me away from here?"

"Of course, of course. Get in," he said.

"Bless you, sir," Alyssa said as she clambered inside. "Bless you! You have saved my life!"

Once she was settled in her seat, the driver started the motor and floored the accelerator, speeding out of the gravel as a giant cloud of dust rose up behind them.

"I can't possibly thank you enough," Alyssa said as she continued taking nervous glances over her shoulder behind them. She sighed in relief once the piney green tunnel faded in the distance.

She exhaled and felt her pulse softening. She was safe. She glanced over at the driver, his eyes were focused firmly on the road. She looked down at noticed her blood-stained feet and ripped clothes. "I am sure this looks very strange to you. You are a good man to have stopped."

"No need to thank me, Ma'am," the driver said. "You obviously are in trouble. But..., you are right. It does look very strange. I have to ask, though. What are you doing way out here in the middle of nowhere? You know it isn't safe, right? Who are you running from? I really do think we need to call the police now."

"It's a long story," Alyssa said as she again reflexively glanced into the rearview mirror. She sighed as she sunk down into the seat, luxuriating in the elegant leather covers. "No need to call the police. Please..., don't involve the police."

"OK, but I should take you to a doctor, at least," the driver said. "You are hurt."

"No, it's all right. I'll be fine. I just need to get some miles behind me," Alyssa said. "I know this is weird and I can explain everything as we drive. Assuming, of course, you aren't stopping anytime soon. Like I said, it's a long story."

"Well, we will have plenty of time for you to tell it — if you want to," the driver said. "I am heading to Seattle, so, I can let you off anywhere you want. Take all the time you need to..., catch your breath."

"That is great, just great," Alyssa said as she sighed in relief.

"So, where to?"

"I..., just let me get my bearings for a minute. It has all been too much to process," Alyssa said as she massaged her right foot with her hand.

"Take your time," the driver said.

Alyssa smiled but then gasped when she pulled her hand into her lap and saw the blood covering her fingers. "Oh..., I am so sorry, I don't want to mess up your—"

"—Don't worry about it, Ma'am," the driver said. "I needed to get the car cleaned anyway. Look, I'll take you wherever you need to go, but I insist we take you to a doctor. Those cuts look pretty deep."

"I was running for quite some time," Alyssa said. "Since just after dawn, and I guess I tore up my feet."

"Running barefoot in the woods?" the driver asked.

"I..., I was running away," Alyssa said.

"Who from? Look..., maybe you should just go ahead tell me what is going on."

"I guess I do owe you that," Alyssa said. "After all, you are a true lifesaver. I..., I really doubt you will believe me..., but..., the short version of my story is, my boyfriend and I are having a major disagreement about my pregnancy, and I had to run."

"Oh? You are pregnant?" the driver said. "Why..., you aren't showing a bit."

"You are kind," Alyssa said. "But, you are obviously a good liar."

"I never lie," the driver said as he turned to her and smiled.

"You are quite the charmer," Alyssa said. "I am definitely pregnant. None of my jeans fit worth a damn anymore. I know in a few weeks I will have to break down and get some maternity clothes."

"So, let me guess," the driver said. "You want to keep the baby, and the boyfriend doesn't, right?"

"Well..., sort of," Alyssa said. "I definitely want to keep it, and he..., I..., I can't really talk about it. It is just too—"

"—Raw," the driver said. "I get it. But, don't you worry about a thing, girl. You are in good hands, now." He reached over and patted her shoulder. Alyssa sighed. She felt safe and for the first time in weeks, she was at peace. He cupped her chin with his palm and a smile formed on her face before it disappeared into a wince.

"That's it!" the driver said. "I'm taking you to a doctor."

"That's all right. I'm OK," Alyssa said. "The baby just started kicking a couple of days ago, and I am still not quite used to it. It catches you off guard, you know."

"I can imagine it would, but, it is wonderful, though," the driver said. "New life is the greatest gift. I haven't had any children, but, if I did, I know I would be thrilled to feel the first stirring of life."

Alyssa sat up straight in the car and looked at the driver again. Nothing about him registered odd or menacing on her internal monitoring system. She was an expert in sniffing out perves…, well, all except for Daryl, but with this guy it was different. It was all clear. There was something sincere, earnest, and warm about him. The fact he looked like a model and had such a great car didn't hurt matters either. Butterflies rustled in her stomach, but these were not from nerves. These were stirring elsewhere. Her eyes flashed, and she felt a warm tingle run up her body from her toes as she gently bit her lower lip. With a sigh coming from her mouth, she lifted his right hand up from the armrest between them and pressed it firmly against the side of her belly.

"Can you feel it kick?" she asked.

The driver smiled and said, "Oh, yes!" He paused and then added, "oh, glorious woman who life bestows, who calms the reaper from ceaseless mow. Like sprig of pine or babbling brook, from the darkest green verdant nook, Spirit come forth and shine upon, this blessed daughter of your golden dawn."

"How beautiful," Alyssa said. "Just beautiful. What is it?"

"A blessing," the driver said. "A blessing for your baby."

"Wow, I am so honored. It is…," Alyssa said. "It is like you are a —"

"—Priest?" the driver interrupted.

"Yes," Alyssa said. "Are you a priest?"

"I am," the driver said. "Just up this way on regular circuit."

Alyssa laughed and shook her head. "Just my fricking luck. I finally meet a nice guy, who is handsome and kind, and he turns out to be a priest! Oh well…, another great idea of mine shot to hell." She pressed her index finger against the crew collar of his black t-shirt and said, "You must be in your civvies, today. You know this is false advertising, sir! You need to announce your…, vows."

"Sorry," the driver said. "We don't always stay in uniform, you know."

"Maybe you should."

"Say…," the driver said, "the next town is still a little way off. I thought we could catch some lunch when we get there."

"Sounds great," Alyssa said. "I am starving."

"Me too. In the meantime, do you mind if I put on some tunes to pass the time?"

"Not a bit," Alyssa said as she stretched her arms up over her head and luxuriated in the feel of the wind rushing through her fingers. "It might keep my mind off my bloody feet."

The driver reached across to the dashboard and turned on his MP3 player. He turned the volume up loud to compensate for the rushing air. He glanced over at Alyssa and winked. He said, "and such a lovely pair of feet, too."

"Oh…," Alyssa said. "I didn't think priests noticed such things."

The driver said nothing but smiled.

Once the first few chords of the music played, Alyssa nodded and said, "Oh, I know this song. It reminds me of back home."

"Me too," the driver said.

The singer's haunting voice began to belt out the mournful tune — *"I…, am a man, of constant sorrow. I've seen trouble all my days…"*

Chapter 22

April 30th, 1996 - Daniel Boone Motor Lodge - Room 214 - Pikeville, Kentucky - 7:45 AM

JOHN STOOD IN FRONT OF the large motel window staring out at the empty, leaf-filled pool in the courtyard. Summer was still a few months away, so he supposed it was possible it would be emptied and re-filled, but the evidence showed otherwise. The faded depth markers, shredded beach umbrellas, and dry rotted lounge chairs encircling the ruin indicated there had not been very many swimmers here lately. What would be the point? Coupled with the rusty brown shag carpeting beneath his feet, and the cheesy wood paneling in his room, everything at the Daniel Boone Motor Lodge, like the pool, was in decline. In fact, the whole town of Pikeville seemed caught in a cycle of perpetual descent. It was as if a neutron bomb exploded twenty years ago and locked everything into a 1970s kitschy hellscape, the people all gone but the buildings remaining. This town was definitely not on the regular tourist circuit. This was no rural haven or rustic vacation spot. This was something else entirely. Someplace John would never want to visit, but it was precisely where he needed to be — and it sickened him.

His mind drifted back on the events of the past few days. The long trip from New York to Pikeville had matched his spirits — one long greasy slide into decay and doom. The darkness grew as each milepost whizzed by his car. Once John turned off I-81 onto route 460, it was as if the fading light became even dimmer. There were more restaurants closed than open, and he witnessed more plywood-covered businesses than he had ever seen before in his life. The sign in front of the local U-Haul rental center said it all — "Sorry, no outbound trucks available

216

until further notice." Hard times had come to Pikeville, and from the looks of things, they had come quite a while ago.

He refocused his thoughts on the present and resumed staring out the window. He sipped the stale coffee from his Styrofoam cup. It was supposed to help shake his headache. It didn't. There had been a dull throb in his skull for three days now, never quite letting up. As the caffeine took root, his synapses loosened, and the blood vessels in his brain began pumping. He sighed. It was a little better. It wasn't perfect, but, it was the best he could hope for under the circumstances.

As he finished his coffee, he ran his hand over his abdomen. The sharp pain there matched the one in his head. His mind, and his gut, were in a riot of dread. It took all his will just to target his scattered thoughts onto something — anything but the horror of the present.

John squeezed his eyes tight. He could not dwell on that right now. He didn't have the luxury for grief. Grief will not save Billy. All he could do was move forward, like a sleepwalker meandering through an endless fog on autopilot. His constant calls to the police for status updates on the search for Billy, all ended with the same answer — *no updates at this time*. Well-meaning social workers repeatedly said, "We are doing all we can do. We will call you if there is any change." It all made him want to scream.

When he was finally able to wrestle his thoughts away from the horror of Billy's kidnapping, his mind flooded with memories of Sylvia. The endless days spent at her hospital bedside — hoping, pleading, cursing at her to wake up. His prayers were all for naught. She had checked out. Perhaps he should do the same. *It would be easier, wouldn't it?* To just slip away into those warm, inviting dark waters of madness — no worries there, only the sane left to clean up the mess. But, he could not. He would not. He had to move. He had to *do* something. He looked down at his watch. It was past eight. They should be open now. Closing his eyes tight, he prayed one last futile prayer — *Please God..., please! Please let me find Billy. Please!*

After a quick unproductive call to his phone service to check for messages, there were none, he got into his car and made the drive to the Pikeville police station. It was a short trip. Traffic, or what counts as traffic in rural Eastern Kentucky, was light. His biggest challenge was avoiding being run off the narrow mountain road by one of the enormous coal trucks frequenting the highway. They were out in great abundance today. After a few close calls, he arrived in the center square of Pikeville and parked his car. Glancing in his mirror, John straightened his tie and double checked the envelope he was carrying — twenty copies, it should be more than enough.

"Can I help you?" the receptionist asked as John walked inside the station. Her accent was thick but pleasant.

"Yes, I was hoping to talk to the detective in charge of old missing person cases?"

"Well…, he's out right now," she said with a smile. "But if you leave your information, I can have him—"

"—Oh…, well, how about regular cases, then," John said as he started to open his envelope. "I need to see if anyone in your department has ever seen the man in this picture."

The receptionist laughed and said, "Well…, they're out too."

"Out? The *whole* department is out?"

"It ain't a big department," the receptionist said. "It's only Buddy. Well, Buddy and me, but I ain't technically official, only part-time."

"Buddy?"

"Buddy Johnson," the receptionist said. "He's our chief of police. And…, well…, you see, he goes fishing at this time of year. Sort of our slack time, you know."

"Your whole department is one guy?" John asked. "What if there is an emergency?"

"I can always get him on the radio. He does stop by to check on things at least once a day," the receptionist said. "He ain't that far away, though. He likes to go fishing up near the Big Tug river out on—"

"—When do you expect him in?" John interrupted.

"I can't say, really," the receptionist said. "Like Buddy always says, there's Eastern Standard time, there's Daylight Savings time, and best of all, there is Fishing time. Rules are a bit different during fishing time. Instead of a leap forward, fall back, it is more like fall way-way back - like eight days back!"

"Has he checked in today?"

"No, not yet," the receptionist said as she glanced up at a large clock on the wall. She pointed at John's envelope in his hand, and said, "But hey, if you leave a copy of the picture, I will leave him a note, and I am sure he will get right back to you. Do you have a number you can be reached?"

"I don't live around here," John said. "Look…, it is critical I speak with him today. I have to get back to New York as soon as possible. My wife is very ill."

"I'm sorry to hear that. But, I can't promise you when he will—"

"—You could radio him, though," John said.

"That is only for emergencies," the receptionist said. "Buddy's real strict on that."

"My little boy has been kidnapped! I think that's a pretty big emergency!"

"Oh, my!" the receptionist said. "I am so sorry. Let me get all of your information!" She paused and added, "But…, I thought you said this was an old case?"

"The picture is connected to my son's disappearance. He was kidnapped in New York, ten days ago."

"New York?"

"Yes, New York, and I have reason to believe my son has been brought to Pikeville," John said.

"I assume you reported this to the New York Police, then?" the receptionist said.

"Of course, I did! What kind of father do you think I—"

"—Please, sir, no need to shout," the receptionist said. "I'm just trying to help."

"Sorry," John said. "As you can imagine, this has been the most hellish few weeks of my life."

"I cannot imagine what you must be going through. You will definitely be in my thoughts," the receptionist said. She pointed at the envelope in John's hand and added, "Are those pictures of your son, then?"

"No," John said. "They are copies of the police sketch made of the man that took my son."

"Can I see them?" she said.

John nodded and passed her one of the pictures.

"He is quite a handsome fellow, isn't he?" the receptionist said. "And a priest? This is very strange. Very strange indeed."

"I don't know if I would call the bastard who kidnapped my son handsome!" John shouted.

"I didn't mean it that way," the receptionist said. "I was just making an observation. And, I think, it may end up being good news."

"I cannot possibly see how," John barked.

"A guy like that is not going to be able to melt away into a crowd. He will definitely be noticed. Someone will recognize his picture. I am sure of it, but..., what exactly is the connection to Pikeville? I would have thought the NYPD would have—"

"—It's a hunch I have," John said. "My wife was adopted from here, but, under very mysterious circumstances."

"Mysterious circumstances?"

"It's a long story, but, I think her birth parents were into some kind of..., I don't know, cult or something. I knew her adopted Mom and Dad very well. I just know there must have been some crucial reason they adopted her with no paperwork or any official records. I think she may have been taken from her birth parents against their will, and I am guessing Sylvia was taken for a good reason."

"That is quite a charge," the receptionist said.

"It is, but, I discovered Sylvia was born here despite her official records showing otherwise. Her father had a vacation home in Pikeville. That can't be a coincidence. I think he may have abducted her on one of those trips and brought her back to New York, and I think this man in the picture was part of that cult. He may have taken our son as revenge. There was no official adoption paperwork for Sylvia, so it is quite a mystery."

"Ah," the receptionist said, "When do you think your wife's abduction would have taken place?"

"Back in 1976," John said.

"Well..., now I understand why you wanted to see the cold case files, then," the receptionist said. "What do the NYPD say about all of this?"

"They aren't that enthused about my hunch," John said.

"I see," the receptionist said flatly. She looked up at the clock and added, "Well, even though I can't use the radio for just a hunch, hopefully, Buddy will check in soon. I am sure he will try to help if he can. I can call you if you—"

"—I'll wait," John said as he turned to his right and spied a plastic orange chair. "If that is OK with you?"

"OK with me," the receptionist said, "but it might be a while. I would look through the files myself, but, I am not authorized."

"I understand," John said.

"You know, Buddy has been in Pikeville forever," the receptionist said. "I am sure if there were any child abductions here twenty years ago, he would remember."

"OK," John said dismissively as he gritted his teeth and picked up a magazine from the table in front of him.

"Would you like a honey bun and coffee while you wait?" the receptionist said. "I just feel terrible you have to sit here."

"Honey bun?"

"Oh yeah, trust me, once you take a bite, you will think you went to heaven. It'll make the wait go by faster. Let me rustle you up one. Buddy loves them and buys them by the case. We have an extra couple of boxes in the back."

*****

Hours passed as John waited for Buddy to return. He ended up eating several honey buns and consumed at least a gallon of coffee during his wait. By the end of the day, his eyes were blurry as he had read, and re-read the three back issues of *US Weekly* magazine in the lobby at least eight times. If nothing else happened today, he knew he was entirely current on every conceivable angle of Mariah Carey's love life and what the Spice Girls wore out to all of the hottest clubs in London. As it neared five o'clock, the receptionist said, "I am so sorry, but, it doesn't look like Buddy is coming in today after all."

John grunted and stood up. "I don't mind telling you, I am underwhelmed by the Pikeville Police so far."

"I am sorry," the receptionist said. "But, my offer still stands. I can take one of your pictures and show it to Buddy when he comes in. There really was no need for you to wait around like this all day."

"I just need to see if he recognizes the man in the sketch. I can't leave Pikeville until I know for sure," John said. "I doubt it would take five seconds of his time."

"You know," the receptionist said as she grinned. "I don't know why I didn't think of this earlier, but I may have a solution for you."

"What?"

"Up on Route 460, there is a diner, Emma Lou's Country Kitchen. The owner has been running it since Moses was still in high school. She knows everybody, and I mean, literally, everybody in town. I bet if you showed her the picture, she would clear this up in two minutes. I know if that man ever lived here, she would recognize him."

"You think?" John said. "I was sort of thinking Buddy would need to check this photo against the computer files."

"Honey…, that ain't happening. Our files aren't that sophisticated," the receptionist said. "I been telling Buddy for years we need to upgrade, but this town is just too cheap. Any check against old case photos would have to be done manually."

"Oh…," John said. "Well…, can you tell me how to get to Emma Lou's?"

"That I can do," the receptionist said. "And, like I said, if you leave a copy of the sketch with me, I can tell Buddy about your situation when he gets in. But, I am telling you, Emma Lou is going to be your best bet. The woman is amazing! Every time I see her she asks about my Mom, and all my brothers, and she knows them all by name. Hell, she even reminded me about some cheerleading award I won back in '86. An award I had forgotten all about! I think she has some kind of photosynthetic memory."

"You mean photographic memory, right?" John said.

"Yeah, that's it," the receptionist said. "She is definitely the woman to talk to about things that have gone on in this town. She knows where all the bones are…," she paused. "Oh, uh, sorry."

"Thanks," John said as he started for the door.

"Be sure and order her ham biscuits," the receptionist said. "You won't ever have any better. I can guarantee it!"

John nodded and left. The drive to Emma Lou's Country Kitchen was quick. Despite not having a map, it was relatively easy to find. When he pulled into the parking lot and saw the considerable number of trucks parked outside, he knew the receptionist must have steered him right. His father always said to eat where the truckers eat, as they knew all the best places. Emma Lou, unmistakably, did quite a brisk business.

He stepped inside the diner, all glistening chrome and glass, and walked to the counter. Fresh pecan pies were displayed on a rotating stand beneath a glass dome. The smell of fried chicken filled the entire restaurant. Every table was taken. This was the first place in Pikeville that seemed to be prospering. He spied an open stool at the counter and took a seat.

"What do you want to eat, honey?" the waitress said as she placed a glass of water down on the counter.

"I don't know yet. Do you have a menu?"

"A menu?" she replied, her eyebrow raising up as a look of astonishment raced across her face.

"Yes, a menu," John said. "I don't know what you have to offer."

"Ah...," the waitress said. "You must not be from around here, then. Hell, it's been so long since I gave out a menu, I will have to go in the back and find one. Everyone tends to know what they like before they get here."

"No need to do that," John said. "I heard the ham biscuits were good."

"Damn straight," the waitress said. "Best in the south. And what would you like with that?"

"What do you recommend?"

"Our pork chops are excellent," the waitress said. "So are our chicken and dumplings."

"Maybe the chicken and dumplings, then," John said. "Pork chops with ham biscuits might be a bit too much pork for one meal."

"Honey, you are hilarious," the waitress said. "Now I know you ain't from around here. Everyone knows you can't be too rich, too pretty or have too much pork on your plate. Hell, our bacon wrapped, deep fried, hot dogs would probably send you right over the edge."

"They might at that. Say...," John said. "Is Emma Lou here?"

"She is," the waitress said.

"I would love to talk to her," John said. "I was told she knows everything there is to know about Pikeville."

"And then some," the waitress said. "But, she's kinda busy right now, you know, with the cooking and all. At this time of year..., well, it is always a madhouse."

"I would really appreciate talking to her," John said. He pulled the police sketch out of the envelope and showed it to the waitress. "I need to know if she has ever seen this man before. It's important."

"Shew-eee!" the waitress said as she held the picture up to her face. "That boy is one 'hunka hunka of burning love'." Her eyes drank in the sketch, studying the chiseled features and movie-star-good-looks of the subject with great intensity. She paused when she saw the Roman collar around his neck, and her face dropped. "Don't it just figure. The hot ones are always either gay, or something else is wrong with them. A man of the cloth, too. Ain't it a shame? Such a waste."

"I bet that wouldn't stop you, Doris," the trucker sitting beside John teased. "But it don't matter. You know, *my* offer still stands. I'd be a much better man for you than some sissy preacher boy."

"In your dreams, Frank," Doris snapped.

After a long belch, Frank said, "I just laid out some new AstroTurf in the back of my El Camino. I would love to have you be the first to break it in."

"Charming, ain't he?" the waitress said as she quickly turned back to John. "Well..., tell you what. I'll go show Emma Lou the picture and see if it rings a bell. Trust me, if he were from around here, she'd know."

John thanked her and sipped his water as Doris took the picture back into the kitchen. A few moments later, Doris and another woman came out. The woman looked to be in her late eighties at least. From the sallow look in her complexion and the extra hundred pounds she was carrying around her waist, she was not in good health. Her face was friendly and inviting, though, so his hopes rose.

"Is this your picture?" the older woman asked.

"Yes, and, are you Emma Lou?" John said.

"I am," she replied. "Where did you get this? I am very curious. I think I know this man."

"I knew it! I just knew it!" John said.

"Yes..., I never forget a face," Emma Lou said. "But..., why the sketch? I am confused."

"He may be related to an old case I am working on. Did you ever hear of any children going missing around here, say, back in '76?"

"Oh dear, yes," Emma Lou said. "Tragic. Just tragic. I heard about it from a friend. She said the girl's parents were beside themselves with grief. Police never did find her."

"I never heard about any of that," Doris said. "And I have lived here all my life."

"Well..., not everything makes the papers, you know," Emma Lou said.

"Oh, thank God," John said. "I can't believe it. I just can't believe it! I was right!"

"Maybe you need to tell me what this is all about," Emma Lou said.

"It is a long story, but, I think my wife is the little girl that went missing."

"And this picture?" Emma Lou said. "What does it have to do with the case?"

"That man kidnapped our son!"

"Mercy! How awful," Doris cried. "And you think—"

"—What is your name, sir?" Emma Lou asked.

"John..., John Delaney."

Emma Lou took off her apron and said, "I think you need to come up to my house, right away. I have something to show you that might help with this situation. This is serious. Very serious indeed."

"Oh, Jesus," John said. "So, you really do know this man? You know what he is capable of, then. Tell me! Tell me what you—"

"—I know of him," Emma Lou said. "But..., I have something up at my house that might help. My late husband always chided me about being a packrat, but, I do keep everything. I know I have a letter that…" She paused before adding, "But shoot…, my ride ain't going to be here until nine. My son-in-law borrowed my truck today."

"I can take you," John said. "We can go right now! If…, if you don't mind. I am desperate here. I…, I…," he added as he choked back a sob.

"Yes. I see we need to go, right now, just like you said. We need to go find your little boy, and we will," Emma Lou said. She turned to Doris and said, "Do you mind taking over in the kitchen for me while I'm gone?"

"No sweat, Emma Lou," Doris said. "I can get Francine to wait tables in my place."

"You're a doll," Emma Lou said. She turned back to John and said, "Now, let's go. I sure hope your car has good traction. I live way out in the sticks."

*****

Forty minutes, and at least forty stories later, John and Emma Lou turned onto yet another narrow and unpaved road. He had long ago lost track of where they were. She had not exaggerated. This was about as rural as it got.

His shocks were taking quite a beating as they bounced over the uneven dirt and gravel path, but he didn't care. Shocks can be fixed. Tires can be patched. To finally have a big break, and possibly find Billy, was beyond value. For the first time in weeks, he felt he was making progress. He turned and looked at Emma Lou and smiled. She was the first person to actually help him in this whole process.

"I can't thank you enough, Emma Lou," John said. "This has been rough. Rougher than I can —"

"—No need to say anymore," she said. "I just can't imagine what I would've done if someone had snatched one of my youngins back when they were little." She paused and added, "And, before we go any farther, you need to do me a favor."

"Oh?"

"Yeah, we've been in this car for a while, and, gotten to know each other quite well."

"We have," John said.

"So, you don't need to call me Emma Lou anymore," she said. "All my family and good friends call me Maw Maw."

"OK, you have a deal," he said. "So…, Maw Maw, how much further to—"

Maw Maw pointed to a turn off into the woods and said, "—Oh, it's right up there. Not much farther now, I swear."

Chapter 23

April 21st, 2017 - Mountain View Antiquarian Books and Supplies - Mountain View, California - 11:30 AM

THE BELL OVER THE DOOR rang as Father Morales walked inside the bookstore. After a quick glance around the interior, he sighed. He knew he was out of his element. To his right, on a small table, a collection of magic crystals were for sale. The sign was hand written — Love crystals, buy 2 get 1 free — this week only!

A thick cloud of patchouli and sandalwood incense assaulted his nostrils and he struggled to hold back his cough. It was an age-old problem. Even back at his church, he had issues with incense. His life-long allergies created a sneezing fit every time he swung the censor for Mass. He cleared his throat and walked further inside the store, taking out his handkerchief and covering his nose to try and filter out some of the scent.

Thankfully, it worked, and he breathed clear as the smoke dissipated a bit. Despite the thin grey haze in the air, the shop was surprisingly bright inside. He looked to his left and saw several rows of book-filled shelves. A quick glance at the titles told him this wasn't the neighborhood Barnes & Noble. A title caught his eye — *A Modern Witches Guide to Love, Life and Attracting Prosperity.* He picked it up. The cheery pastel colors of the binding and the beautiful, half-clad female model on the cover concealed the sinister contents inside. *So many people play with forces they don't comprehend. Fools!* He shook his head and turned to his left.

More shelves were stocked with every conceivable herb and spice imaginable. Some he recognized as being used in benign healing rituals.

Others, like the jar of Mandrake he spied, were for more diabolical purposes. He saw something else, too. It was something he was sadly very familiar with and he sighed. Several rows of jar candles, all emblazoned with the image of a cloaked, female skeletal figure, lined the top of the bookcase. He knew this image well, having seen it not only back in Alyssa's apartment, but in great abundance in his native Mexico. They were icons to the ultimate abomination, Santa Muerte, the patroness "saint" of death. He grimaced in disgust as he turned away from them and walked to the front of the store. *To think the land that venerated Our Lady of Guadalupe could devolve to this atrocity.*

The clerk at the cash register was an attractive young woman, her beauty still apparent despite the enormous dragon-shaped ring protruding from her bottom lip. She exuded cool aloofness beneath her overly pale makeup and jet black dyed hair. She smirked as he approached and said, "Checking out the competition today, eh Father?"

"I was wondering if you could help me?" Hector said.

"Oh, I bet I could help you with a lot of things, Father," she said as she lazily ran her eyes up and down his tall frame. She closed her eyes, opened her mouth, and ran her long, pierced tongue over her face jewelry. Dropping her voice an octave, she mockingly added, "all kinds of things. Things your woman denied mind could never imagine." She laughed as she added, "I was wondering, do you boys in black still wear that cilice around your thigh? Kinky! I bet I could take that thing for a whirl and tie it around your —"

"—I am serious, Miss," Hector interrupted. "I really do need assistance."

The clerk shrugged and stood up straight, "OK, OK, I'll play it straight. No need to get your panties in a bunch. I was just having a little fun with you."

"Does a Darryl Summers work here?" Hector asked. His tone was even. He would not give her the satisfaction of seeing him rattled.

"Yeah, we have a Darryl Summers here," the clerk said. "And he is a real asswipe, too." She sneered as she added, "Why do you want to know? Darryl never was one to hang around with the priestly sort."

"It is a personal matter. I really do need to speak with him."

She shrugged. "So, would I. The little bastard picked a horrible time to run off. I can't imagine what his Mom will say when I tell her. Especially at this time of year."

"Mom?"

"Yeah," the clerk said. "She owns this place, but he 'runs' it," she added with an emphasis on the scare quotes, "and I use that term loosely. Lately, I have been running it by myself."

"Do you have any idea where he went?"

"You sure seem very curious about a little creep like Darryl," the clerk said. She crooked her mouth into a sly grin and added, "Was he an old altar boy of yours, or something? You wanting to restoke an old flame? And here I thought you and I made a connection. I'm very jealous."

Hector fought back his scowl and said, "This is no joke. It is very important. Do you know where he went?"

"He split a couple of weeks ago. I thought it was just another example of his getting his dick stuck in a mousetrap. That boy sure never could keep his zipper closed, and trust me, I should know. But, yesterday he called to check on things and said he would be back after Beltane. You can always come back then."

"Beltane?"

"Yeah, you never heard of Beltane, Padre?" the clerk said. "Oh, you'd love it! All sorts of silly fun, just like your Mass. It's only a few days away now, on the 30th. There is a big ass festival taking place up at his Mom's."

"And where is that?"

"It's all listed on the poster in the back of the store," the clerk said as she pointed. "Hell, we've been swamped with these Wiccan hippie assholes for days now, getting ready for the big day. I'll be glad when it is over." She sighed and said, "I guess I should have been a dental tech just like my Mom said."

"So, I take it you don't buy into any of this, then?" Hector said.

The clerk grinned, picked up a pink crystal from the counter, held it in the air and said, "No. It's all crap, but hey, it pays the bills. If people want to fork over good money for some two-dollar rock they think will bring them true love, more power to them. If they want to buy some stupid candle that looks like a drag queen Skeletor from the old He-Man cartoons, who am I to stop them? It's the American way, right?"

"I don't think so," Hector said. "It is a sin to take advantage of people's primitive superstitions — especially when you are messing around with things that should not be disturbed."

"Well, it's funny you should say that," the clerk said as she laughed. "You boys in the Catholic Church have your own racket going pretty nicely, don't you? What with the holy water and rosaries and such. Don't like the competition, do you?"

Hector cleared his throat and said, "About Darryl — is he a believer in all of this?"

"Yeah...," the clerk said, "I think so. I used to think Darryl thought it was all crap too, but, I was wrong. I suppose when you have a mom like he has, it's going to warp your mind. Or..., who knows, maybe that redneck bimbo he knocked up screwed with his head? He never was that bright."

Hector raised an eyebrow and said, "Oh? So, he *was* the father."

"Wait a minute, Padre," the clerk said as she narrowed her eyes and stared at Hector, "what is this all about, really? Are you some kind of cop? You seem a little too interested in..." She opened her eyes wide before nodding. "Oh..., yeah. I get it now. This isn't about Darryl at all, is it? You must be friends with that crazy-cracker babe, Alyssa! She must have told you about my call." She threw her head back and laughed, "Jesus H. Christ, this is rich! I must have spooked her so badly she needed to sic her priest on me." She scowled as she leaned across the counter. "Well, you can tell that mountain whore that she can keep her man all she wants. I don't give a shit about him. I just want my money. Can you remember that? Can you remember that, Father?"

"I can remember," Hector said.

"Good..., now..., either buy something, or...," the clerk paused as the door opened and a couple of customers entered. She observed their dismissive side glance at the priest. She continued in a whisper, "get the hell out. You are bad for business, you know."

"OK, I'll leave in a moment," Hector said as he turned and walked to the back of the store. He avoided eye contact with the two young women strolling up to the front. He shook his head as he could not help but notice they were both carrying Santa Muerte candles. He considered saying something to them but stopped. He had other business to attend to and knew his discouragement probably would not have made any difference.

When he reached the back of the store, he stopped as his eyes were drawn to a large colorful poster hanging on the wall. The psychedelic letters were large and decorated in the archaic Art Nouveau style. If he didn't know any better, he could have easily mistaken the sign for an old rock festival poster from the sixties. He walked closer to read the details and instantly knew it was no Rock Festival poster. *Beltane Festival 2017 - Floriston California — sundown on April 30th, 2017. A rare treat this year — the Feast of Moloch to be performed by the High Priest himself! Ample parking provided on the grounds — gates close at 6:00 PM.*

Moloch! He thought to himself.

A shudder went up his spine as he wrote down the complicated directions to the festival.

*****

Much later that afternoon, back at UVid headquarters, Sylvia was sitting in the "Eye Bleach" lounge on one of the overstuffed couches. Lying on the floor in front of her, a young woman was just waking up.

"Better?" Sylvia asked.

"Oh, good God, yes!" the woman said as she opened her eyes. "That was amazing! How did you learn to do that?"

"Years of practice at a very underpaid and underappreciated position back east," Sylvia said. "It is far more rewarding here. So…, let's make sure everything worked. Clear your mind."

The woman nodded and closed her eyes.

"Now, let's check the locks. I am going to say some trigger words and I want you to gauge your reactions, OK?"

"OK."

"Stiletto…, Puppy…., Crush…, Laughter…," Sylvia said.

The woman smiled, shook her head and said, "Nothing. I have no idea what you are talking about, and I know that is a good thing. I consciously recognize these things were related to what was upsetting me, but nothing is happening. It is all clear."

"You have no ill feelings? You don't feel sick?"

"Nope, nothing," the woman said as she stood up. "Thank you again, Sylvia. You are a Godsend. I haven't slept for weeks and now…, I finally feel free."

"You don't remember anything?"

"Nothing! It's all just a big blank slate," the woman said. "Locked in a safe, guarded by my late grandfather…, with his shotgun, of course." She winked and added, "Click… Click… Click…!"

"That's the ticket!" Sylvia said, "Click…, Click…, Click…"

After the woman left, Heather, sitting beside Sylvia on the couch, said, "Damn, but that is always impressive to watch. You have a real gift."

"Thanks," Sylvia said. "I have to admit, this whole crush-fetish thing is just about the worst thing I have ever heard of. Frankly, I would have thought I was beyond shocking, but obviously, the parade of internet perverts continues their long, unending march"

"It certainly does," Heather said.

"I mean…, who gets off on watching women in high heels stomp puppies to death?" Sylvia asked. "Jesus! I may have to perform my technique on myself now."

"Yeah, this particular kink is especially heinous," Heather remarked. "But you know the rule."

"Yes," Sylvia said with a sigh. "Rule 34 wins again."

"It always does. And…, it kind of makes me wonder what your old priest friend is into?" Heather said with a laugh. "You know, it has always been my experience those God boys always turn out to be the biggest freaks. The more vanilla the coating, the spicier the center."

Sylvia shook her head and sighed. "You need to lay off Hector. I am a pretty good judge of people, part of my training, you know. I did not detect anything weird about him at all."

"So, it seems you got to know your new boytoy quite well last night," Heather said. "Those sexy Latin guys are hard to resist."

"I did get to know Hector quite well," Sylvia said. "And now I am going to ignore your childish insinuation and stop talking."

"Oh, you are no fun," Heather said as she grinned. "But in all seriousness, it does seem like you two had quite the chat. So, did he lay a lot of religious mumbo jumbo on you?"

"No. In fact, much of what he said last night made a lot of sense. He really got me thinking."

"Oh, brother," Heather said as she rolled her eyes. "Please don't turn into some kind of Holy Roller type. You are the first office buddy I have had that was cool. Don't blow it by turning into a Jesus freak."

"I'm not," Sylvia said. "But..., well..., let me ask you something."

"Ask away," Heather said.

"Why do you think there is something rather than nothing? It is an astonishingly good question if you think about it."

"Shit happens," Heather said.

"This is your cosmological worldview?" Sylvia said. "Shit happens? This is your explanation for the creation of the whole universe and the fact that all sorts of factors had to perfectly align for life to be possible? Shit happens? Really?"

"Sometimes it's a lot of complicated shit," Heather said as she smiled. "Frankly, all I can think about right now is the margarita waiting for us at Fred's place."

Sylvia nodded. "Yes, I am more than ready! It has been one hell of a day, and I can taste the salt already." She glanced down at her watch and said, "well..., it is already past six, I guess we should head out." Heather nodded, and they both walked back to their desks to retrieve their purses. When they arrived, Sylvia's phone rang.

"Sylvia Marstens speaking," she said as she answered the phone. She paused and said, "Oh..., it is good to hear from you, Hector."

Heather, standing to the side, covered her mouth, and suppressed a laugh. Sylvia waved her off.

"Yes..., Yes..., Oh? Well..., I can't tonight," Sylvia said. "That is interesting. Really? That is very interesting — now you have me curious."

Heather really struggled to contain her laughter now, her whole body shaking as she tamped down the giggles.

"But..., how about lunch tomorrow?" Sylvia said into the phone. "Yes..., yes, the same place we went to before, right? OK, I will see you at noon."

"Well, well, well," Heather said as Sylvia hung up the phone. "Seems like someone is trying to slip out of his vow of chastity. Girl..., you still got it."

"Shut up, Heather," Sylvia said with a laugh. "He says he wants to tell me something relating to Alyssa."

"A threesome he has arranged, perhaps?"

"Stop it!" Sylvia said as she blushed and laughed.

"Sorry, I can't help myself," Heather said. "But, in all seriousness, what did he say?"

"He was a bit vague, but, it seems Hector found out something about Alyssa that has him quite upset. He wants to tell me about it."

"What was it?"

"I don't know, he said he couldn't really go into too many details on the phone. But, he did say something about..., Beltone, or Belfame, or something. I couldn't really follow him. His accent gets more pronounced when he is agitated."

"Oh, I bet he is agitated," Heather said. "I can only imagine what kind of crazy kinks something called Belfoam involves. So, where are you meeting him for lunch?"

"The same Mexican place he took me to last night."

"Ah..., how sweet, your second date," Heather said. "Are you going to let him go all the way, or do you save that for the magical third date?"

"Honestly, Heather, you are impossible," Sylvia said. "Now, let's go get that Margarita, although I shudder to think what you are going to be like after the tequila kicks in."

*****

Darryl Summers stood in front of the window looking out over the mountain valley below. His face was expressionless, devoid of any emotion. The setting sun cast a severe glare in his face. His eyes, brown and dull, were slightly glassy and squinting in the harsh light. After a few minutes of silence, he closed his eyes and started to speak.

"I don't know why you wouldn't listen? We had an agreement. You made a commitment and commitments still mean something in this world." He paused and added, "If you had just gone through with your promise, none of this would have been necessary. But..., it doesn't matter now, does it?"

He inhaled deeply and said, "we talked about this! We discussed it! You said you wanted to have an abortion anyway, so what's the big deal? Won't this be the same thing?" He shook his head and said, "If you had just been cool. If you had just done what you said you would do. Such a waste! I told you Mom would take them if you ran away again!" He turned from the window, opened his eyes and faced into the darkened room.

On a bed in front of him was Alyssa. Her hands were chained to the headboard. Her mouth was gagged. A single, golden beam of sunlight shone through the window illuminating the pristine white bedspread pulled up to her chest. It glowed blindingly white in the last rays of daylight. All except the foot of the comforter where the material was dark and wet. There the fabric was stained deep red. Alyssa was awake. Her eyes were wide open and she stared forward unblinking into the room. Drool dribbled out of the side of her gagged mouth. She was silent. She had long stopped screaming. There was no point anymore.

Darryl walked across the room. When he reached the door, he opened it but before he left, he turned back and said, "I guess we won't have to worry about you running away anymore."

Chapter 24

April 30th, 1976 - Pikeville, Kentucky - 9:30 PM

FATHER TED WAS BARELY VISIBLE on the lawn. Only the faintest outline of his glistening physique was perceptible in silhouette, as the circle of torches cast wild and sinister shadows across his body. Everything was now in place for the ceremony to begin. Long awaited Beltane had come.

The new moon above cast no light, ensuring a pitch-black sky. Located so far from town, the house was completely dark, every light having been extinguished before the ritual began. Maw Maw, as always, prepared well. She had seen that the children were well occupied in the basement, loading them up with a good stock of homemade brownies, all the soda they could ever want to drink and a movie on TV. Kid heaven! They would not be coming upstairs anytime soon, but, she still latched the basement door from the outside — just in case.

The whole assembly was gathered around the circle of torches on the back lawn. All were skyclad, like Father Ted, their bare bodies blurred in the dim flickering light. The orange flames illuminated an undulating pink sea of exposed flesh.

Silence ruled the night. Everyone stood in reverential quiet as even the wind fell to a dead calm. Only the crackle and pop of the torches could be heard in the stillness. All were waiting — patiently, insistently, hungrily anticipating Father Ted's call to worship. Five minutes passed, and then ten, and then twenty, the tension mounting as each minute ticked by. Finally, Father Ted, his golden baritone voice smashing the silence into shatters, stretched out his arms wide to his sides and began to chant.

"Oh, glorious night above, your pitch-black wraps the sky, the earth awaits your word, wrapped in its dark disguise; arise ye Gods of old, arise ye Prince of lies, arise ye ancient ones, we wait for words of the wise! Arise! Arise! In glorious triumph, we wait for thee to rip the earth and rise!"

"Arise! Arise! Arise!" the naked and sweating crowd sang in unison.

"Behold!" Father Ted shouted as he pointed up to the dark, moonless sky. Every eye followed his hand, peering into what seemed an infinite void above. Even the stars were obscured tonight, leaving a coal-colored firmament overhead and nothing but endless night — a shrill, shrieking expanse of nothingness. "Before the Gods shall rise, we must remember their descent!"

"Tell us, Father Ted! Tell us of their descent!" the crowd shouted.

"Behold!" he cried. "From Heaven he fell like lightning, his glory was brought below, five ebony torches were lit, from the fires of him brought low. Their eternal flames were kindled, from the brazier forever subsumed, with fire that never extinguishes, from fuel that never consumes." He closed his eyes and added, "Oh, great flames, we bless thee! Bring destruction to your children. Come, come and savor the coming storm soon to envelop the world! Come! Come, my children and savor!"

"Come and savor!" the crowd chanted. "Come and savor!"

Father Ted pulled his hands close to his chest and bowed his head. The crowd followed suit as all voices fell silent once more. After another period of rising silent tension, he began to chant once more, his voice quiet but growing louder with every verse.

"All Hail our Lady of Shadows, profanity is thy name, mother of abominations, cursed is the fruit of thy womb. All hail our Lady of Shadows, profanity is thy name, mother of abominations, cursed is the fruit of thy womb. All hail our Lady of Shadows, profanity is thy name, mother of abominations, cursed is the fruit of thy womb. All hail our..."

At the back of the crowd, swinging and swaying with the rest of the group, her sagging breasts flopping back and forth like two old empty hot water bottles, was Maw Maw. After the ninth verse was chanted, a few in the crowd stopped singing and glanced back in irritation. Something was wrong. The ceremony was not proceeding as planned. Maw Maw too stopped chanting, opened her eyes, and looked over her shoulder. With a whisper, she said, "Sylvia! Sylvia, it is time for you to go up to the front now."

Sylvia was rigid and stone silent, her eyes opened wide as she stared blankly ahead. Her bare feet were rooted to the earth as if frozen in concrete. Her mouth was bone dry, her lips blue and quivering. Bone-chilling terror gripped her spine. Her breathing was short, rapid, and very shallow.

"Sylvia!" Maw Maw said as she stepped forward and tugged on her elbow. "Everyone is waiting. Come on Sweetie, you'll do just fine. Don't be scared."

Sylvia, operating on pure adrenaline, forced her reluctant feet to move and began to walk. On a tray in her hands, she carried the skeleton she had dressed earlier. Its stark white dress shimmered in the crackling torchlight. A silver bowl was placed between its bony fingers, a golden dagger lay at its feet and glistened in the reflected flames. As she walked, the assembly enveloped her, reaching out to the icon as she passed.

"Send your blessings upon us, our Lady!" one cried out.

"Glory! Glory to you and your sons of dread!" came another.

"All Hail our Lady of Shadows, profanity is thy name, mother of all abominations, cursed is the fruit of thy womb!" shouted another.

When Sylvia reached the center of the ring of torches, Father Ted stepped forward and said, "Who is worthy to approach the altar of abominations?"

"None are worthy!" came the response from the crowd.

"What is the law?"

"Do what thou wilt, is the whole of the law!" the crowd cried.

"What is the price to be paid to our glorious Lady?" Father Ted asked.

"Blood!"

"And what shall be done with this blood?"

"Wash us, our Lady! Wash us in the blood, glorious Goddess of Shadows!"

"Yes...! Yes...! Yes...!" Father Ted shouted. "Wash us, wash us in the blood, our glorious Lady of Shadows! Prepare our bodies to be a living and fitting sacrifice to your sons, our Goddess, and redeemer!" He turned towards Joe and a small crowd of men standing off in the shadows and nodded. Seeing the signal, the men walked towards the woods in silence. Father Ted turned back to the crowd, and said, "Let the whole earth be silent before her, the mother of all abominations!" He closed his eyes and held his hands out, palms up to the sky. The crowd followed suit and silence descended upon the lawn like the heavy first snow of December.

After a few minutes passed, the stillness was shattered by an unearthly screech coming from the woods. A great howl of pain echoed through the air, both inhuman and soul-shredding in its ferocity. Hearing this, Father Ted smiled as he opened his eyes and shouted, "Arise! Arise! Arise!"

From behind Father Ted, a large wooden cross was pushed forward into the air. A great shout of joy erupted from the crowd when it came into sight. There, hanging upside down from the cross beam, and still alive, was one of Joe's prize pigs. It was an enormous beast, and it shrieked and struggled to free itself from the vast metal spikes driven into its legs. Sylvia, seeing this infinite horror, began to cry.

Father Ted glanced down at Sylvia and winked. "No tears, little one," he said softly as he bent down close to her face. "I am so proud of you. You are doing just great."

She shuddered as his hot breath passed over her cheek. Everything about this was wrong - more horrific and evil than anything her mind could comprehend. She could not look at the grisly scene enfolding before her, and yet, she could not look away. Time slowed, and her vision filled with sights of writhing naked worshippers shrieking hoots of joy to the suffering, dying hog above her. She closed her eyes tight but found she could not keep them shut. She had to look. She had to see! She fixed her gaze firmly on Father Ted's face. It was the only place she could look without seeing that which she knew her young eyes should not see.

His eyes looked back at her and, to her relief, were calm and serene, warm even. He bent down close to her again and whispered, "do you remember what you say next, Sylvia? Remember what I told you? You have to give Our Lady's instruction."

Sylvia's body shook like leaves in a hailstorm but found she had at least stopped crying. She was too frightened for tears now. There would be plenty of time for tears later. She nodded and robotically said the words he had taught her earlier, "Oh great High Priest, our Lady demands you shepherd her people properly, according to the ancient ways. Wash them, Priest. Wash her people in the blood." She lifted the tiny white clad skeleton into the air and added, "Take this knife and prepare the harvest. Take this bowl and fill it. Make your offering of sin for the people of shadows."

Father Ted's face beamed as he heard her speak the words flawlessly. He winked again and whispered, "Excellent job, Sylvia. Diana Prince could have done no better." He stood up straight and bellowed out to the crowd. "From the mouths of little children, our Lady maketh her will known to all!"

With his left hand, Father Ted reached down and removed the bowl balanced between the idol's fingers. With his right, he picked up the knife lying at its feet. Turning back to the crucified hog, twitching, and screeching out its final death yowls, he paused. In one quick flash he slammed the knife deep into the groin of the beast. He held the bowl beneath the foaming jowls of the pig while simultaneously dragging the blade down the suffering animal's stomach and chest. Blood gushed out of the wound and filled the bowl. Now brimming with the profane offering, he lifted the bowl high and drizzled the gory contents onto his forehead. The crimson baptism flowed down his face and across his bare body. As he coated himself he laughed and shouted, "Glory! Glory! Glory!"

Sylvia was nearly knocked to the ground as others rushed forward to the center of the torches. All around her was a frenzy of scrambling and scratching, all clamoring to find a place at the feet of Father Ted. He smiled as he refilled the bowl and began anointing the supplicants. One by one, all were coated with thick, hot, blood.

Sylvia flinched as she watched the last person anointed and felt all eyes turn and gaze upon her. She alone was unbathed, and she felt dizzy, like she was falling down a well, everything swirling and swaying as she tried not to pass out. Her nostrils were filled with the acrid, coppery stench of death and she coughed back a gag. Her flesh broke out in an icy blanket of goose pimples when she watched Maw Maw and Father Ted approach.

Maw Maw, her thick rolls of belly fat dripping with fresh gore, smiled and said, "Your turn now, Sweetie. Come on. You need to be washed in the blood, too. There are no exceptions."

Sylvia stood rigid. Her mouth was open, but her voice gone. The scream that struggled to erupt from her throat was stuck. Boiling bile rose in her throat and she gagged once more. She choked it back down, and with all her willpower forced herself to nod.

Father Ted grinned and stepped forward. He raised the bowl over her head and tipped it, pouring the still warm blood over her scalp. The wafer-thin robe clinging to her body was splattered with thick red streaks as the blasphemous stew ran down her face.

With the entire Circle now baptized in gore, each began to run their blood-covered hands over their naked bodies, smearing the sanguine mixture into their skin in an increasing frenzy. In a joyful and ecstatic howl, they screamed in unison, "Glory! Glory! Glory!"

Father Ted stepped back into the center of the circle and turned towards the crate set off to the side. With his bare foot, he reached over and kicked open the hatch. He then stretched his legs wide and held his arms out straight on either side. His body stiffened as he stared blankly ahead.

"And they shall take up serpents," he whispered before chanting, "Come Spirit, come. Come Ashtaroth, come Baphomet, wreak vengeance in the name of the burned and tortured. Come Pan, come Bacchus, restore thy temples that hath been destroyed! Come Ishtar, come Marduk, mighty Babylon shall rise again! Come Isis, come Set, the Nile shall flow red with the blood of the children of Joseph! Come Baal, come Moloch, the plains of Megiddo shall be filled with the bones of thy enemies! Come most dazzling one of all, come Angel of the Morning Star! Come forth and make thy choice!"

"Yes! Yes! Yes!" the crowd shouted in response. "Come forth Spirit and make thy choice!"

Sylvia was transfixed. The crate, the object of such juvenile curiosity earlier, was now open and something was emerging from the hatch. At first, in the dim light, she could not see what it was, only that it was moving and appeared to be stark white. Once it fully arose, however, she saw it in full, and a cold rush flowed over her body. It was a snake, only, it was the largest she had ever seen — at least five feet long. Her eyes were transfixed as she watched the serpent slither over the grass, flicking its forked tongue until it found Father Ted's bare calf. Its red eyes glowed like tiny burning coals reflecting the torchlight.

Father Ted remained motionless as the snake licked his leg. He continued his chant as the serpent glided up his body, coiling its tail around his stomach before coming to rest on his shoulders. Once in place, Father Ted began to spin, chanting, "Spirit shall make his choice! Spirit shall make his choice!"

All the women, including Sylvia's mother, Darlene, rushed forward and knelt before Father Ted in a circle. They too were chanting, swaying their bare, blood dripping breasts in time to the beat.

"Spirit shall make his choice! Spirit shall make his choice!"

After five or six revolutions, Father Ted stopped, and the serpent slipped off his outstretched arm and onto the neck of Darlene. Father Ted raised his arms to the sky and shouted, "the choice has been made! It is the almighty Moloch, and he has chosen his Altar!" The women all screamed in unison, "Glory! Glory! Glory!"

Father Ted reached down and took Darlene by the hand, bringing her to her feet. He led her to the table set up in the middle of the torches. She climbed on top and lay down, stretching her legs out wide and exposing her bare womanhood shamelessly to the crowd. Sylvia flinched and looked away. No daughter should see her mother like this!

Father Ted knelt before Darlene, the newly anointed altar of Moloch. He reached towards her, running his hands over every inch of her exposed body before stopping and gently massaging her protruding belly. As he caressed her flesh, he chanted, "Virtus enim estis gloria nostra fiet Kingom vester venturus sit infernum terris!"

Darlene moaned and thrashed as Father Ted ran his hands over her and continued to chant his prayer. Suddenly, she went silent. Her legs stretched out wide as her muscles stiffened. A final ear-piercing shriek exploded out of her lungs as sweat poured off her blood caked skin. The crowd knelt before them chanting, "Glory! Glory! Glory!" Darlene was now limp, her arms and legs dangling lifelessly over the sides of the table. Father Ted slowly stood up and lifted something into the air. In the dim light, and through the flailing arms of the crowd, Sylvia could not make out what it was. She could see it was small, and red and…, *Mommy! Mommy! NO! NO! Mommy!*

"Take! Eat!" Father Ted shouted as the crowd bolted forward in a mindless frenzy. "The Feast of Moloch has been given for you!"

Click… *Click… Click…*

Chapter 25

April 21ˢᵗ, 2017 - St. Sebastian Catholic Church - Mountain View, California - 8:30 PM

FATHER HECTOR MORALES PUSHED HIS chair back from his desk, removed his reading glasses and rubbed his eyes. They were tired and blurry. For five hours, he had not left his office once; his full attention focused laser-like on his studies. There, on his incredibly messy desk, amongst his prized pictures of the 2002 championship Saint Sebastian Boys Boxing team, an old faded photograph of his long-dead parents, and a newly emptied carafe of coffee, were his books. Dozens of them were scattered haphazardly across the surface. All were worn with age. Their pages were yellow and crumbling, their jackets torn and faded. Most he had not looked at since seminary, and that was ages ago. Tonight, however, he was making up for lost time. He sighed as he took out his highlighter and began to mark another significant, and gruesome, passage in the text. It was not his first. Sadly, these obscure long forgotten works were all too relevant now.

They were all written in an earlier age; a pre-Vatican II era when talk of demons and black masses, satanic rituals and blood sacrifices were still subjects to be taken seriously. Now, however, the church was far too sophisticated for such Medieval talk. The modern, enlightened world had advanced well beyond such primitive Dark Age superstitions. But…, perhaps the evolution has been premature. Perhaps the wisdom of the ancients still has something to say. Mankind never truly progresses, it only shifts. The move is not up or down but back and forth. A tidal shift was taking place in the world and Hector could feel it. He could see it and most of all, he could smell it. A roaring tide of evil was rising fast and his gut wrenched at the thought that Alyssa was caught in the undertow — a fresh new face to satisfy the appetite of an age-old horror.

He had been reading one book in particular for quite some time. It was riddled with his post-it notes, highlighting the many passages he found useful, as well as chilling. As he turned each page, some new unspeakable horror was revealed. The current chapter was the most disturbing yet. It filled him with a soul-crushing dread more than any he had read all afternoon. It was entitled — *Dark Rituals used at the Feast of Moloch.* He put his reading glasses back on and resumed his studies. When he heard a soft knock on the door, he jumped.

"Father Morales," an aging female voice said from the other side of the door. "Are you sure you don't want me to make you dinner? It is quite late, and you have been in there all afternoon."

"Sister Margaret," Father Hector said as he sighed before smiling, "You always take such diligent care of me. Let me just finish this chapter, and I will be right down. And maybe, instead of you making dinner for us tonight, I can order pizza. I could really go for a Pepperoni-Lovers right now."

The door swung open wide and Sister Margaret marched inside. "Have you lost your mind, Father?" she exclaimed. "You know you have high blood pressure. In fact, the doctor said you should be having mostly salads now." She shook her head and said, "Pizza is completely out of the question. You know you need to cut back on meat — Pepperoni-Lovers indeed!"

"Salad? Ugh," Hector said. "Is that what you were planning to make?"

"Yes!" Sister Margaret said as she crossed her arms in front of her. "And that is what we are going to have."

"I am a man, Sister, not a goat," Father Hector said. "If the Lord had intended us only to eat vegetables, then why did he make animals so delicious?"

Sister Margaret huffed. She smiled and said, "You are impossible, you know that? Well…, you have many dietary sins to atone for, you know. So not only are you going to have salads for the rest of the week but there will be no dressing."

"No dressing?" Father Hector said. "This seems a rather harsh penance."

"Yes, it is, and you deserve it," she said. "I know where you went out to eat last night, Father. Honestly…, Chalupas? Burritos? Are you trying to have another heart attack?"

"And just how did you know that?"

"The same way I keep track of all my students," she said with a grin. "I have eyes everywhere — including a couple of very observant busboys at Café del Sol."

"Those little Judases," Father Hector said with a chuckle.

"Yes. You see, they may be afraid of you, Father, but they are terrified of me!" she said.

"Smart boys. I always did say we have the brightest kids at our school." He held up his hands and said, "OK, OK, salads it is."

"Good," Sister Margaret replied. "You need to eat right for a while, to make up for your transgressions at Café del Sol."

"Correct," Father Hector said. He grinned and added, "especially since I am eating lunch there tomorrow."

"Father!"

"Sorry, can't be helped, official business," Father Hector said. "And…, while we are on the subject, can you help me with the copy machine? If you can just get me started, I can make the copies I need."

"You do remember you have to lean on it, right?" Sister Margaret said. "The cover always pops open if you don't lean on it."

"I never can do it right."

"What do you want me to copy for you?" she said with a sigh.

Father Hector lifted his book from his desk and Sister Margaret leaned forward to look at the title. He pointed at the post-it notes and said, "Sorry, but there are a lot of passages I need copied."

She read the title of the book and said, "*A treatise on the Black Mass and other Satanic Rituals* — Oh, my!"

"Yes! And, I hope you don't mind, but, I will need it for my lunch tomorrow. Regrettably, I had all of my suspicions confirmed today."

Sister Margaret crossed herself and said, "I will be sure to say the Saint Michael prayer twice tonight at Vespers."

"Always a good idea," Father Hector said.

*****

Fifty minutes later, in the church office, Sister Margaret was finishing the last of the copies while Father Hector struggled with the stapler. They both looked up when the internal alarm bell rang. Since Father Hector lived in the rectory next door and Sister Margaret lived in an efficiency apartment in the church basement, between the two of them, someone was almost always on site. They never locked the doors, wanting the house of God open to all. They did have a motion detector installed in the chapel, however, and this was the alarm that sounded.

Sister Margaret glanced at the clock on the wall and said, "Who on earth could be in the sanctuary at this hour of the night? It is nearly 10 o'clock!" She walked over to a small window that looked out into the nave and pulled back the curtain slightly. The sanctuary was completely dark. At the back of the church, however, she saw light coming from under the door of one of the confessionals. She turned back to Father Hector and whispered, "it appears someone has come in for confession tonight."

Father Hector walked over to a closet and retrieved a purple stole. He placed it around his neck and said, "I wonder if it is one of our students? Well…, if someone needs to make a confession at this hour, my guess is it is pretty important."

She nodded and reached over to the copies Father Hector had been struggling to staple. It was a considerable stack of papers. She picked up the tiny stapler he had been using and said, "you know this is far too small for the job." She pointed over to her desk at a larger model and said, "we usually use 'Big Bertha' for stacks this thick." She shook her head and said, "I will just go ahead and redo all of this while you go hear the confession. Honestly, Father!"

"You're the best, Sister," Father Hector said as he slipped into the hall that led to a side entrance into the church.

When he entered the opposite side of the occupied confessional, he turned on his light. After a few moments of silence, he started to speak. A young female voice interrupted and said, "Bless me, father, for I have sinned." The voice quickly added, "is that right? Is that how you start?"

"Yes, just right. You are doing fine," Father Hector said. "So..., how long has it been since your last confession, my child?"

"I..., I have never been," the voice said. "You see..., I'm not a Catholic."

"Oh? I don't understand. If you are not Catholic, why do you want me to hear your confession?"

"It isn't really about all that, Father Hector."

"You know who I am? How do you know my name?" Father Hector said as he leaned forward and stared at the screen separating the compartments. He squinted as he tried to make out the details of the face through the thin slats of wooden mesh, but he couldn't see clearly. It was too dark. All he could see was a dimly lit figure, obviously female, sitting alone in the darkness. She had turned the light off in her compartment.

"I am a dear friend of Alyssa Brewster," the voice said. "She has spoken very highly of you and told me how you helped her so much in the past. Because of this, I thought it best I come speak with you now, in person."

"Ah, Alyssa is a wonderful girl. But, if this is not a confession, I am not clear on why you are meeting me in this way. Why not just come to my—"

"—You need to know about things that are going on, Father — dark and unspeakable things. Alyssa is in real trouble and really needs your help. I fear you are her only hope. I am very worried about her."

"Yes," Father Hector said as he sighed. "Alyssa is quite troubled, but, apparently she has been fortunate in having a friend like you. I too am quite worried about her."

"You should be," the voice said. "We all are."

"But..., since this isn't a confession, perhaps we should discuss this in my—"

"—No! No, we must do this my way," the voice said. "You see..., *they* are watching. They are always watching."

"They?"

"Yes. They see everything. I read online they can't see inside a church — especially when the sacraments are present, so this should be safe. Are the sacraments present here, Father? I saw the red light was lit on the altar."

"Yes…, but, just exactly who is this *they* you are talking about?"

"You know exactly who they are," the voice said.

Father Hector paused as he felt an icy corkscrew crawl up his back. He said, "Maybe it best you tell me everything that is going on. For example, what do you know about her boyfriend, Darryl? I think he may have taken Alyssa down a path she shouldn't go."

"Definitely! She and Daryl have both been playing around with forces they do not understand, and now the bill is due. Neither seem to understand the fact some doors, once opened, can never be closed."

"You are so right," Father Hector said. "You seem quite knowledgeable about this sort of—"

"—What are you wearing, Father?" the voice interrupted.

"Excuse me? Why are you asking me that?"

"Are you wearing one of those little purple scarves around your neck?"

"You mean my stole?"

"Yes, I guess that is its proper name," the voice said. "I have seen priests wearing them on TV shows, but I didn't know what it was called."

"Uh…, yes…," Hector said. He lifted the edge of his stole up in his hand and looked at it before adding, "I don't know why you want to know about my stole, though."

"I know priests sometimes wear it, right? Like at confession."

"Yes…? But I don't know what this has to do with Alyssa."

"Ah…, perfect." The voice said. "You know, purple is my favorite color and I have a small purple angel my grandmother gave me. I hold it every time I try to pray. I am glad you are wearing purple for me today. It is such a happy color."

"Yes, we priests do wear purple, but, only for solemn occasions, not happy ones. Purple is only used for confession, Lent and other penitential occasions."

"You didn't answer my question, Father," the voice said.

"Oh…, what question?"

"Does your stole have a special significance for you, like my angel does for me?"

"This is a rather personal question."

"It is, but, I really want to know. It is important to me. Surely it is not a difficult question, is it?" The voice paused and then said, "Perhaps I should go, especially if you are not willing to be straight with me."

Father Hector said, "No. Please don't go. It…, well…, as it turns out, yes, it does have a personal significance for me. I have had this particular stole since my ordination."

"When was that?"

"Back in '76."

"1976?"

"Yes…, I know to you that must seem like the dark ages, but it wasn't that long ago. Trust me," Father Hector said. "But…, back to Alyssa…, you seem to have quite a bit of information about what is going on with her. I need to know what you know. You obviously are a good friend and want to help her. I do too, but…, I think it best if we discuss this in my office. I can have Sister Margaret put on some coffee and—"

"—Teach me to pray, Father. I want to pray for Alyssa."

"Oh…, yes, of course," Father Hector said. "Do you know the 'Our Father'?"

"No," the voice said. "Can you teach me? Will it help Alyssa?"

"Prayer always helps," Father Hector said. "Now, I will begin, and you follow along."

"Do you pray with your eyes open or closed?"

"Closed, generally," Father Hector said. "Didn't your grandmother pray with you? How did she do it?"

"Closed," the voice said. "Let me hear the prayer a few times first and then I will join in."

"OK," Father Hector said. He closed his eyes and began to pray. "Our Father, who art in heaven, hallowed be thy name. Thy kingdom come, thy will be done, on earth as it is in…" His eyes flew open as the door to his confessional swung wide. He yelled, "Hey! What are you doing?" All was a blur for the next five seconds — a screech, a dark figure, a black hoodie, a pair of hands reaching towards his face, a sharp scratch on his cheek and then — silence. The sudden burst of violence passed quickly. Now that it was over, he heard nothing but the sound of sneaker-clad feet running out of the church.

Temporarily stunned, Father Hector sat up and caught his breath. His face burned, and he felt a trickle of blood on his cheek. Shaking his head clear, he scrambled to his feet and charged into the nave, searching for his assailant. It was too late. The mysterious attacker was long gone.

"Father Morales, are you OK?" Sister Margaret shouted as she rushed inside and turned on the lights. "I thought I heard a scream."

"Yes, I'm all right," Father Hector said. "I'll be OK."

"What happened?"

"I have no idea, but I fear, nothing good," Father Hector said.

Her eyes grew wide as she pointed at him and said, "What happened to your face? You are bleeding."

"I'll be fine," he said. He felt the side of his cheek and added, "it appears to be just a scratch."

"And your shirt! It is all messed up and torn. Look, you even dropped your stole," Sister Margaret said.

"What!" Father Hector shouted as his hands shot up to his chest and he began feeling for his vestment. It was gone. He quickly turned and glanced back into the confessional. It wasn't there. His face dropped. The girl must have taken it.

"I am calling the police, right now!" Sister Margaret said. "Imagine, attacking a priest! In his own church, and in the confessional, of all things! What is this world coming to?"

"There is no need for that," Father Hector said. "I fear we are well past the point where the police would do any good."

Chapter 26

April 30th, 1996 - Route 119 - 10 miles west of Pikeville, Kentucky - 10:45 PM

"ARE YOU SURE THIS is the right way, Maw Maw," John asked as he turned off the narrow road and onto another dirt-covered path. This had been the pattern for the last hour. Maw Maw had continuously been directing him up various unpaved mountain roads before suddenly pointing to another turn he had to make. It seemed to go on all night. "I could swear we have been by that last turn before."

"It's the right way. I'm sure of it," Maw Maw said. She turned to him and smiled as she added, "A grown woman certainly should know where she lives I would think! I may be old, but I ain't got Alzheimer's, you know."

"I'm sorry. Of course, but…, it is so dark out here," John said. "Frankly, I don't know how any of you are able to navigate these back roads — especially at night."

"It's a skill."

"And here I thought driving in New York was bad! Everything here seems to look the same to me. It would be very easy to get lost on these old mountain roads."

"Yeah," Maw Maw said. "They can be crookeder than a hound dog's leg. But, you get used to it." She laughed as she added, "my daughter keeps pushing me to move into one of them fancy old folks' homes down in Florida. She says these old mountain roads are too much for me to drive, especially in winter. Can you imagine that?"

"She may have a point. I can't imagine driving here in the snow," John said.

"It can be a real challenge," Maw Maw said. "But…, once these hills get in your blood, it's hard to let them go. There's just no place like home."

"Of course," John said. "But, still…, with all these twists and turns, it sure is confusing. Do you make this drive yourself, every day?"

"I do," Maw Maw said. "And trust me, when you have to swerve into a ditch to avoid one of them coal trucks smashing into you head on, it gets pretty exciting. That sure gets the old heart valves pumping." She laughed as she added, "better than getting a hot Folger's enema!"

"Oh my God," John said as he laughed.

"And hell…, I bet if I moved into one of them fancy places down south, my brain would rot away into jelly in three months."

John nodded and said, "you may just be right."

"But…, no worries now," she said as she pointed up the road. "My driveway is just up ahead. We're almost there."

John squinted as he looked towards the small opening in the trees on the right side of the road. If she hadn't pointed it out, he would easily have missed it. With not another house in sight for miles and the moon dark, it was pitch black outside the car. He smiled at Maw Maw and sighed. He was glad they were almost there. His hands ached from gripping the steering wheel so tightly. Driving these unfamiliar back roads was a physical as well as mental challenge, and his eyes were weary along with his hands. He kept his high beams on full blast to help him perpetually scout the edge of the woods for suicidal deer.

He turned onto the path and headed through what looked like yet another dark tunnel into the forest. The branches hung low over the road, making the dark night even darker. They drove for about two minutes, and after emerging from the tree-shrouded path, he stopped the car. Up on the hill in front of them, he saw the silhouette of a large farm house come into view. All the lights were turned off inside, but, it wasn't entirely dark. A faint orange glow emanated from behind the house. As he started driving up the long driveway his headlights spotlighted multiple cars parked on the front lawn.

"Are you having company?" John asked.

"Oh, yes — a big to-do, tonight."

"I hope I'm not intruding."

"Not at all!" Maw Maw said. "In fact, it is most fortunate you are coming. I know several of my guests are going to be most helpful in your search."

"You think?"

"Oh, I am quite sure."

"I hope you are right. I really don't want to intrude, especially since you have been so helpful to me," John said.

Maw Maw reached across the front seat and gently patted John's hand. "You aren't intruding at all, dear. In fact, I think having you here tonight is going to make the party extra special."

As they continued up the hill, his car bounced and lurched over the rough driveway. It was very narrow, essentially just two deep tire ruts in the dirt, dotted with numerous potholes and shallow gullies. He had to slow his car to a crawl just to avoid destroying the struts entirely. At five miles an hour, it was a slow slog up the muddy drive. *Land must be cheap here,* he thought. When they approached the house, and passed even more parked cars, he noticed a Pikeville Police car among them. "Is Buddy Johnson going to be here?"

"Oh yes," Maw Maw said. "You know him? He is an old family friend."

"The clerk sure wasn't kidding when she said you were the woman in the know," John said. "I don't know Buddy, but, I was looking for him earlier. Frankly, if I had known about you this morning, I could have saved a lot of time and come to your diner first."

"All roads lead to Maw Maw," she said with a laugh.

John spied an open patch of grass, parked the car, and the two of them walked up to the house.

"Let's go around back," Maw Maw said. "I think the party is probably in full swing now. I want to introduce you around."

"OK," John said.

They walked around the side of the house. The backyard was enormous, a giant open field gently sloping towards the forest fifty yards away. He squinted as he spied figures standing around a circle of torches at the edge of the woods. They were too far away to see clearly, but, he could hear singing. Maw Maw gently took his elbow and directed him down the hill towards the light. When they were close enough for him to see clearly, he froze.

"What! What the hell is all this?" John shouted as he turned to Maw Maw. "Everyone is…, are they…, naked? What sort of freak show is this?"

"Ah…, the guest of honor has finally arrived," a voice bellowed from the darkness on his right. "We've been expecting you."

John snapped his head around to face the voice. He watched a man saunter out of the gloom. When the stranger came into focus, and they locked eyes, John's skin crawled. It was the man from the sketch!

"You! You!" John shouted as rage gripped his gut and he lunged forward. His body was working on pure reptilian response now. He pulled his fist back to attack but stopped cold. Something flashed before his eyes. Now that his vision was adjusted to the darkness, he could clearly see the whole scene around the torchlit circle. His muscles froze as his eyes widened. He staggered backward, nearly falling. "What! What! What in God's name is happening here?" he shrieked. "This can't be real! This can't be happening!"

"And they have built the high places of Topheth, which is in the Valley of the Son of Hinnom," Father Ted said. "And thou shalt consecrate to me all the firstborn. Whatever is the first to open the womb among the people, both of man and of the beast, is mine."

"What…, what in the hell are you doing? No! No! For the love of God, NO!" John screamed.

Father Ted continued, "And the offering was made for Moloch, and turning to his people, he said, take…, eat."

"—Oh my God! Oh my God! Oh my GOD!" John wailed, his voice pitching into an animal-like yowl. He raised his arm and pointed into the center of the circle, his face frozen in a silent scream. The ring was filled with dozens of naked, writhing, blood-soaked men and women. All were kneeling and desperately scratching at something on the table before them. White teeth flashed as licking lips gurgled in orgiastic pleasure. One of the crowd looked up from the feast and glanced back at John. As their gaze met, the man smiled and a thick stream of blood drooled from his busily chewing mouth.

"What are they doing? JESUS CHRIST! What are they doing? It can't be! This can't be real! I have to wake up! For God's sake I have to wake up!" he screeched.

John spun back towards Maw Maw, his mind shattering. She nodded and smiled. In a lightning quick movement, she slashed her hand through the air at his neck. John opened his mouth to yell, but nothing but a wet gasping gurgle emerged from his lips. He fell to his knees. After crumpling to the ground, he gripped his throat as a hot, thick torrent of red poured out over his fingers. His body went still.

Maw Maw wiped the dripping razor blade on her apron and said, "I always say, there ain't nothing better than having family home for the holidays."

Chapter 27

April 22nd, 2017 - Stevens Creek Trail - Mountain View, California - 6:15 AM

DERREK PITMAN GLANCED DOWN AT the Fitbit on his wrist and grinned. He was already up to 8,000 steps, and it wasn't even 7:00 AM. It was a good start. He took his right hand and clasped it around his left wrist, counting out his heartbeat manually as he continued to jog in place. He still liked to double check it, old school. His smile grew wider. Target heart rate achieved! *Top that, Steve! The lazy bastard is probably still in bed.*

At his feet, wagging his tail wildly, was Rex, Derrek's Golden Retriever. There were few things Derrek loved more than running, but when able to do so with his dog, on a beautiful spring Saturday morning, and on a surprisingly empty Stevens Creek Trail, it was heaven. Making this perfect day even more glorious would be, of course, his winning of the weekly fitness challenge against his older brother Steve. Based on this latest Fitbit data, he appeared to be well on the way to achieving the trifecta.

After a brief pause to take a swig from his water bottle, one he gladly shared with Rex by squirting a stream into the dog's mouth, Derrek bolted into a full run. Today, since it was so early, and the weather was flawless, he thought it would be nice to run "off trail" for a bit. He glanced down at Rex galloping beside him. The dog was in a complete state of bliss, his fully extended tongue flopping loosely in his jowls. Derrek knew his four-legged jogging partner would like some off-trail time too. To run free and open, with nature in full bloom around them would be sheer perfection. He turned to his right onto a rarely used dirt path and jogged through an opening into the forest. Rex barked loudly and leapt in the air as they entered the woods. Apparently, he approved of the detour.

As Derrek and Rex ran deeper into the forest, the undergrowth around them grew tighter. Low hanging branches began to scratch Derrek's arms and face. He ignored it at first, a few scrapes and nicks are a small price to pay for communing with nature, but, after one particularly sharp pine branch smacked him in the eye, he stopped. The 'forest run' was a better idea in theory than practice. It was time to turn back.

"OK, boy, back to the main trail," Derrek said as he called out to Rex who had run ahead of him by about twenty feet. The dog, ordinarily obedient, did not return, though. He just stood motionless, staring intensely at something up ahead on the path.

"Come on, boy, we have to go. Come on, boy. Come on," Derrek said as he walked up to the dog. His pace was slow since he was quite winded. It had been a vigorous run. When he was around six feet away from Rex, Derrek looked at his dog and immediately froze. Something was wrong with Rex. The dog's hind leg muscles were tense, as if ready to pounce, and the hackles on his back were fully raised. The fur on his tail, as well as that around his neck, was standing out straight. Most alarmingly, he was emitting a low, menacing growl.

"What is it, boy?" Derrek said. "Do you see a coyote or something?"

As he came alongside Rex, Derrek grimaced, covered his mouth and gagged. The stench was horrific as his nostrils were assaulted with the rank odor of rotting meat. He glanced down at the ground for the source. He saw something a few feet ahead of them in the middle of a clearing. It was a small round object, less than a foot long, and was covered entirely in blowflies. Even more disturbing, it was evident this strange object had been deliberately placed here for some unimaginable reason. This was no dead squirrel or half-eaten raccoon. This thing had been used for some sort of ritual.

The fly covered mass was positioned in the center of a pentagram. The symbol, a five-pointed star inside a circle, had been traced onto the ground with a trail of black ash. At each of the five points of the star, individual jar candles had been placed. While covering his mouth with his shirt, to attempt to block the stench, Derrek leaned in to get a closer look. Each jar was emblazoned with a skeleton-like figure on the front, clad in an elaborate white wedding dress. One glance inside one of the candles showed the burned wick was still intact and the sides remained blackened. These candles had not been outside long, perhaps just a few hours. Any longer exposed to the elements and the jars would have been filled with rainwater, as it had rained the day before. This also would certainly have washed away the ash circle.

"What kind of freaky shit is this?" he said.

Derrek looked over to his right. He saw a small, fallen branch and he reached down and picked it up. He needed to see what was under that swarming blanket of green iridescent flies and he certainly did not want to touch it with his bare skin. Stick in hand, he gently pushed the sharp tip into the revolting glob. He also simultaneously pulled his T-Shirt up tightly over his nose to block out the overpowering reek of rotting meat. Rex wanted no part of this adventure, and now wisely started to back up, his threatening growls now replaced by high pitched whines.

"What the hell?" Derrek said as he poked the stick further into the mass and it collapsed, like a punctured soufflé, dissolving into a pool of putrid black blood. The flies swarmed away and revealed what was beneath. It was a beef heart, like one would buy at a butcher shop. Something else was also here. A piece of fabric was coiled around the disembodied organ. Derrek gingerly worked the point of the stick beneath the wrapping and lifted it into the air. It was a long, narrow purple cloth resembling a scarf. When the excess blood dripped off the silk fabric, and he spied the golden embroidered cross on the front, his stomach sank. He recognized it immediately from his days as an altar boy. It was a priest's stole!

"Let's get the hell out of here, boy!" Derrek said as he dropped the stick and backed away. Rex needed no further encouragement and they both raced back towards the main trail.

*****

"I am going to the Farmer's market this afternoon, so, if there is anything special you want me to pick up, let me know," Sister Margaret said as she walked into Father Hector's office in the rectory.

"Well, I guess ribs are out of the question," Father Hector said. "I was kind of hoping you would make pork carnitas again."

"Oh, no, Father," Sister Margaret said. "And since you have no *healthy* suggestions, I'll just double up on the spinach and strawberries then."

"You are very harsh," Father Hector replied.

"You'll thank me," Sister Margaret said. "And…, it could've been worse. The strawberries were a treat."

"What time will you be back?" Father Hector asked.

"Before noon, unless of course, they have a fresh delivery from those specialty organic farmers in the valley. Then, I may go crazy, and who knows? Regardless, I will be back no later than 3:00 PM."

"Let's hope it's before noon then," Father Hector said.

Sister Margaret smirked, ignoring the comment. "How about you? When do you expect your lunch to be over?"

"I'll be back before 2:00," Father Hector said. "I have to get back early as I still must finish up tomorrow's sermon."

"You need to get some rest, too. You were up far too late last night with those books of yours. And after that assault in the church, and all, you need to take it easy," Sister Margaret said. She shook her head and added, "I still say we should have called the police. You aren't a young man anymore. You could have been seriously hurt."

"Bye Bye, Sister," Father Hector said.

"OK, OK, I can take a hint, but, today, do me a favor."

"For you, anything," Father Hector said.

"Good. So, today, try and go easy on the Chalupas, all right? They do come without pork, you know. You can order them with just cheese and salsa."

"I am shocked at you, Sister," Father Hector said as he winked. "From where I come from, what you are suggesting is the gravest heresy imaginable."

Sister Margaret just shook her head and said, "Honestly!"

*****

A few hours later, Father Hector looked down at his watch and winced. It was already 11:30 AM and time to leave for the restaurant. If he didn't hurry now, he would be late. It was so typical of him to lose track of time in his office, especially with so many distractions. He glanced over at the books he had been reviewing the night before and sighed. *So much to do and so little time to prepare.*

He grabbed the package Sister Margaret had prepared for him and headed out the side door to the driveway. The bundle was thick and heavy, there had been a lot of pages to copy, and this was yet more evidence that Sister Margaret was the best. She always was doing more than he could ever ask. He glanced across the rectory driveway to the adjoining church and noticed her car was still gone. Obviously, the organic farmers from the valley had shown up — God help him. He could only imagine the pounds of rutabagas and endless bags of kale she was loading into her cart at that very moment. It was going to be a long, crunchy week, but, of course, she means well. He certainly could stand to eat better.

He climbed into the front seat of his car and placed the package on the passenger's seat. After pulling down his seatbelt and fastening it, he placed his key in the ignition. Before starting the engine, he stopped. He heard a noise coming from the back seat. It barely registered in his ear, but it was … *something*. He turned around to look. Nothing was there. He waited a few more seconds, cupping his ear and listening intently to see if he could hear the sound again. He did. He couldn't place the noise, but it sounded a little like paper rustling. He took the key out of the ignition.

Father Hector kept a messy car, always had, so he wasn't too surprised at the rustling noise. Sister Margaret was always joking about his *rolling trash bin*, as she called it, and he just hoped a mouse had not gotten inside his car somehow. He had heard of such things. No doubt a clever rodent could make a veritable feast on the scores of candy wrappers, dropped French fries and various and assorted other snack debris that had fallen to the floor. It would be a veritable vermin paradise, and he was sure he would never hear the end of it from Sister Margaret if his car ended up mouse-infested. It would confirm every complaint she had ever made.

After thirty seconds of silent listening, he chalked the whole incident up to his imagination. His ears were aging, too, and, maybe this was a symptom of early onset tinnitus? *Who knows?* He put his key back into the ignition.

The sound returned. It was just the tiniest of rustling coming from behind him. A low, barely audible swish, gaining strength and a bit louder than before. Now he knew it wasn't his imagination. It was real. Something was sliding over one of the empty plastic coffee cups, or stray Taco Bell bags littering the floor. He sighed, took out the key, unfastened his seatbelt, and got out of the car.

He opened the back door and, for several minutes, ran his hands through the trash on the floor, feeling around for anything warm and furry burrowing in the sea of paper and plastic. *If Sister Margaret could see this, she would have a fit.* Throughout his search, his body was tense as he expected a rat to lurch out of the garbage pile at any moment. After rifling through the contents for a few more minutes, and finding nothing, he knew his car was rodent free. It wasn't *that* big of a car, after all. He looked down at his watch and sighed. Now he knew he would be cutting it close, but, he would still make it.

He returned to the driver's seat, fastened his seatbelt, and put the key in the ignition. He turned the motor over and the engine roared to life. He put the car in drive. *I definitely need to clean out the car this afternoon when I get home.* As he reached the end of the driveway and started to turn out into the street, he felt something brush against his leg. He looked down with a start and jerked back in shock as his eyes grew wide.

"Oh my God!" he screamed. "Oh my God!"

There, slithering out from beneath his seat, a white snake emerged. It was enormous, easily taking up the entire floorboard. It quickly coiled itself fully around his leg and lurched upward into his lap, extending its upper body towards Father Hector's chest. Its large diamond-shaped head, with dull, red eyes, now hovered just inches away from his face. With his right hand clutching his chest, and his left foot stomping on the brake, Father Hector's eyes rolled back in his head, and he slumped over into the passenger's seat.

*****

"Are you *still* waiting for your party to arrive?" the waitress asked as she glared down at Sylvia. It was 1:30 and she wasn't making any money from a table hogged by a single woman drinking water all day.

"I guess not, but…, let me check one more time," Sylvia said as she looked down at her phone. She started to press redial, but then stopped herself. Five messages were more than enough. He wasn't coming. *Stood up by a priest! A new personal low.*

"So, can I get you anything, or…, do you need more time?" the waitress asked as she visibly rolled her eyes.

"You can start us out with a big plate of nachos and a full pitcher of margaritas, Senorita!" Heather said as she suddenly appeared from around the corner and sat down at the table. The waitress nodded and headed off to the kitchen, happy to finally have something other than water to bring to table six.

"What are you doing here?" Sylvia said once the waitress was out of earshot.

"Snooping," Heather said as she winked.

"On me?"

"Of course," Heather said. "I just had to check out this Father McHottie myself!" She looked to the left and then to the right, and said, "Sadly, it appears he is Father McNottie. No show?"

"Yeah, he's a big no-show," Sylvia said. "Stood up twice in two days."

"What are you talking about?" Heather asked.

"You, last night," Sylvia said. "We were supposed to get a drink, remember?"

"Sorry about that. I had a headache and needed to turn in early," Heather said. "And who knows, maybe I was so jealous of your big date today I had to go home and cry into my pillow? It is such a shame he didn't show. I was really looking forward to meeting Father McHottie."

"First of all, remember? I told you he is probably old enough to be your grandfather."

"You mentioned his age before, and, I have reconsidered my position. There is nothing wrong with GPILFs at all," Heather said.

"You will have to explain that reference to me later, but, second of all, you do remember he is a priest?"

"I have seen some pretty sexy Padres in my day. I wouldn't let that stop me."

"At the very least," Sylvia said, "get the pet name right. He is from Mexico, not Scotland. He would never permit himself being called Father McHottie, on principal."

"OK," Heather said, "how about Father Elhotto? Or would it be Lahotta? I never could remember the masculine/feminine rules for nouns." She grinned as she added, "This is exactly why I flunked third year Spanish in college."

"Heather, you always make me laugh," Sylvia said. "Even though you are a horrible eavesdropper."

"Guilty as charged," Heather said.

"And you have no respect for personal boundaries."

"None," Heather said as she nodded.

"But, you are a true friend," Sylvia said. "I am glad you ended up having lunch with me today."

"Great!" Heather said as she turned to her left and spied the waitress approaching the table with a pitcher of Margaritas. "And now, let us put a hurting on the fresh lime crop."

Sylvia smiled and said, "You have a deal."

*****

The sun drooped low in the sky as Sister Margaret turned into the parking lot of Saint Sebastian Catholic Church. Her eyes glanced over to the clock on the dashboard of her 1992 Honda Civic. She saw the time — 4:30 PM and winced. Time had completely gotten away from her, and she hoped Father Hector hadn't started to worry. Perhaps she would make some flan to make it up to him. He always did have a sweet tooth. Besides, how could she be blamed? How could she have known the Northern California Natural Herbs and Spices convention would be meeting at the farmer's market today?

The passenger seat of her car was loaded with at least six crates of strawberries and arugula, with her trunk and back seat equally loaded down with a whole host of other fresh vegetables and herbs. She stepped out of her car and grabbed a few boxes off the front seat before something caught her attention. It was Father Morales' car. It was sitting at the end of the rectory driveway which was very strange and out of place. Father Hector always parked under the carport by the rectory — always. She looked over to the rectory again and then back to the car, and wondered if his emergency brake failed. There was a slight slope to the driveway, after all, and the same thing had happened to her before. Ten years earlier her parking brakes had failed and her beloved Civic had drifted down the same slope. Luckily, it hit the mailbox and did not go into the street. She put down her boxes and strolled over to investigate.

When she got near the car, a shudder shot up her spine. The motor was running. Something was wrong — very, very wrong. She dashed to the car. When she arrived at the driver's side door, her eyes grew wide. Through the window, she saw Father Morales slumped over in the passenger side seat.

"Father Morales! Father Morales!" she cried.

*****

Sylvia yawned as she put the paperback book down into her lap. She stretched as she glanced over at the clock on the wall. It was 11:30PM. The afternoon of margaritas with Heather had taken their toll. Both had wisely decided to Uber home. Neither she nor Heather were in any condition to drive. Snowy, snoozing on Sylvia's lap, raised her head and yawned too. Pommes always enjoy a group nap and when Sylvia began to stir Snowy growled. She was not ready to be moved.

"Hey, now!" Sylvia said. "None of that nonsense."

Snowy, properly chastised, stood up and stretched before leaping up on Sylvia's chest and licking her face.

"Now, I think it is about time for us to go to bed," Sylvia said. "But first, I think a nice hot bath is calling my name." She shook her head and added, "Just look at me! Living the wild life out here in California, all alone on a Saturday night and ending it with a hot bath." Snowy barked, and Sylvia scratched behind the dog's ears. She turned to Snowy and said, "It is a good thing you aren't a cat. Then the stereotype would be complete."

Sylvia walked into the bathroom and turned the faucet hard to the left — extra hot, just like she liked it. Large, billowing clouds of steam rose from the rapidly filling tub. The water began to foam after she tossed in her favorite jasmine bath bomb. She dropped her robe, grabbed her Lady Catherfield romance, and eased down into the hot water. "Ahhhhhhh!" she said as the hot water enveloped her body.

She tried to read, but, it wasn't five minutes before the combination of tequila and the hot, soothing water had Sylvia drifting off to sleep. She didn't wake, though, as she had her head propped up perfectly on her bath pillow. She was an old pro at tub napping. Her book did not fare so well and had slipped underwater with her. Now it was destined to plump up to twice its normal size.

Snowy, however, was not asleep. Her back fur was standing up straight, and she was in a full attack stance, staring at the mirror. Her growls turned to whimpers as the temperature in the bathroom started to drop. Snowy shivered and cried as she watched something being written on the fogged-up mirror. It said, *WON REH EVAS NAC UOY YLNO.*

Chapter 28

THE WOODS WERE LITTERED WITH sharp rocks and sticks. As Sylvia ran, dead branches and thorns shredded her exposed, young flesh. Blood poured off cuts on her feet. She was so tired, every muscle in her body aching. Her breathing was rapid and short, and her side felt if it would tear apart at any moment. She scrambled forward to find a way out of the pitch-black forest.

She could see nothing; blind to all but the endless expanse of nothingness before her. The trees were thick above her, most rising thirty feet into the darkened sky, their intertwining branches shrouding an already moonless night into complete black. She always feared the dark. She had long been taught that horrors unknown lurked in the inky night; but now, this view was upside down. The light chilled her more. She slowed down as pain ratcheted up her left side and she started to crumble to the ground, her overworked thighs collapsing. She did not stop running, though.

Her heart raced in her chest, and despite the pain radiating through her gut, growing more agonizing by the second, she pushed on. A blood-stained terror had her in a death grip. It blindly shoved her forward. Pine branches, bristling hard as diamond needles, continuously scratched her arms and face. The thin white gown she had been wearing was long gone, having been reduced to shreds by the thicket and leaving her naked and even more vulnerable.

Her thoughts were a jumbled mix of horrifying images, playing in her mind in a continuous loop. Mouths dripping with blood. Her mother shrieking in agony. A rabid, frenzied, naked mob — ripping, shredding, chewing, laughing, eating. Eating! Eating!

Click... Click... Click...

She squeezed her eyes tight. *It will all be right! It will all be right! It will all be right!* It was only a few yards more. She must keep running. Running. Running.

Her hands were clasped tightly to her chest, clutching something in her palms. It squished and oozed in her death-like grip. Suddenly, she stopped. She heard something. She heard a noise behind her, something other than the sound of her own heartbeat in her ears. It was far off and muffled, but the sound was getting louder, and thus closer. Her blood froze. Voices! They were calling her name! She began running again, only faster and more reckless now. Her body operated on raw reptilian power, flinging her forward into the darkness.

Click... Click... Click...

One hundred feet behind her, a single bluish beam shone haphazardly through the trees. Another beam soon joined it, and then another. Within seconds, a dozen lights blazed through the branches. Soon the forest was ablaze with flashlight beams, accompanied by a chorus of voices shouting in the night. Their calls were strange, an odd mixture of anger and sweetness.

"Sweetie! Sweetie! Come back home now," one voice called out. "We have to finish the feast!"

"Sylvia, honey, Maw Maw made you a special batch of brownies!" another said. "With extra walnuts too, your favorite! Come back to Circle and you can have some."

"It's OK to be scared, Sylvia. We understand," a third said. "But, you must come home now."

"Your mother is crying, Sylvia," Maw Maw said. "She is crying for you to return home!"

"Sylvia! Sylvia! SYLVIA!" shouted Joe.

Sylvia's legs flew beneath her. She choked back a sob. They hadn't seen her yet. She had to be quiet. The sound of her running through the brush was leading them to her, like a wild animal pursued in the hunt. She willed her wails down deep into her stomach and rushed forward into the dark, trying hard to run in silence.

After a few more minutes of stumbling quietly through the undergrowth, she stopped. Her heart soared. Through the dim woods, she saw it. The forest was ending, and in the distance, through a clearing, she saw a lighted porch lamp. The friendly yellow light seemed to beckon her, opening its arms in a golden warm glow, calling her forward. She had to hurry. She had to get to that light!

Click... Click... Click...

*****

"If you think this country is going to elect some redneck, peanut farmer, nobody from Georgia as President of the United States, you are going to need to go into therapy yourself! Perhaps..., you can cut yourself a discount rate on your own head shrinker's couch," Vincent Padovana said. He shivered before walking over to the fireplace and stoking the dying embers. April nights in Kentucky were still chilly. Summer was still far away, but, it was at least warmer than New York.

"You are fooling yourself," Dr. Tom Marstens, said. He laughed as he popped open another Schlitz, their fifth of the evening, and added, "and you still think Mo Udall is going to be nominated, right?"

"I do."

"Then, it is you, pal, who needs therapy. Possibly, even shock therapy if you still think that is going to happen."

"Look...," Vincent said, "this is Udall's year. And if he is nominated, he's President. I mean, if the Democratic party doesn't win in '76, with that hopeless Ford in office, and after the disaster that was Nixon, well..., they might as well fold up their tent and go into another line of work."

"Ah...., this assumes Ford is nominated," Dr. Marstens said. "I think Reagan is giving him a real run for his money."

"How many of those have you had today?" Vincent said as he pointed at the freshly opened can of Schlitz in Dr. Marstens hand.

"This is only my third."

"Obviously psychiatry doesn't require a lot of math. It's your fifth, buddy," Vincent replied as he smirked. "And, of course, that isn't counting any of the beers we drank out on the boat."

"Now, Vincent, you know we don't count *fishing* beers. They are an integral part of the process!"

Vincent threw his head back and laughed. "Very true, but, I still think all the hops are catching up with you."

"You are wrong about Carter," Dr. Marstens said. "And for God's sake, you must know this country will never elect a guy named Mo to the presidency. Larry or Curly, yes. Mo…, out of the question."

"Asshole," Vincent said with a chuckle. "But…, I can guarantee there will be a Mo in the White House before some washed up former B-movie Actor like Reagan any day."

"I wouldn't bet on that," Dr. Marstens said. He sighed as he sank back into the shabby, brown, Naugahyde Barcalounger. He popped up the footrest and said, "God, I have missed this."

"Me too," Vincent said. "We should really come down here more than a couple of times a year."

"We should," Dr. Marstens said. "Maybe we should invite the girls to join us in the fall?"

"I don't know about that, Tom," Vincent said. "That might change things too much."

"If we asked them to come, they wouldn't give us such a hard time about our 'boys' trips," Dr. Marstens said. "I don't know if it would change things that much."

"Damn right it would," Vincent said. He held up his cigar and said, "like no more of these in the house. Marie can't stand it when I fire up my stogie."

"Yeah, Gladys hates them, too. That would not be good," Dr. Marstens said.

"No. As much as I love my wife, if we made this a couple's weekend, it would be ruined. It is great to have a refuge out here in the middle of nowhere," Vincent said. "With no phone, no honey-do lists. A place where you and I can fish, smoke, and just drink beer all day.

And then, for the rest of the night, we can just sit around and yell about—"

"—Politics?"

"I was going to say, yell about nothing, but, you are right. It does usually end with politics."

"Well…," Dr. Marstens said, "for a guy who thinks Mo Udall is going to win the nomination, politics means nothing!"

"You really don't know what you are talking about, Tom," Vincent said. "I'm telling you. Mo is going to go all the—"

Bam Bam Bam Bam Bam Bam Bam

Vincent stopped speaking in mid-sentence and spun towards the kitchen at the rear of the cabin. Someone was pounding on the back door, and, from the ferocity of the pounding, they wanted inside — now.

"What the hell?" Dr. Marstens said.

"My thoughts exactly," Vincent said.

Bam Bam Bam Bam Bam Bam Bam Bam Bam

"I guess I should go see who it is," Vincent said.

"We both should, but, we should be careful," Dr. Marstens said. "It is very late, and, I don't want some sort of *Deliverance*-moment tonight."

"Jesus! You had to bring that movie up again. I wish to God we had never seen it," Vincent said as the two of them walked into the dimly lit kitchen and opened the back door. There, standing on the back porch — quivering, naked, and covered in blood, was Sylvia.

"Holy God!" Vincent cried. "What happened to you, little girl?"

"Where are your parents? What happened? You can tell us," Dr. Marstens said.

"Take, eat…," Sylvia said, her tone robotic, her eyes glassy.

"I think she is in shock," Dr. Marstens said. "We need to get her inside and get her warm."

"You are right, of course," Vincent said. "You are the doctor."

The two of them led Sylvia into the living room. Vincent grabbed an NYU blanket off the back of the broken-down couch. Dr. Marstens took it and wrapped Sylvia in the blanket before starting to wipe the blood off her face. He said, "Vincent, go into the kitchen and bring me a fresh towel and some warm water."

"Absolutely," Vincent said as he rushed back into the kitchen. Once inside, and as he started to run the water over his hand, he called back, "what in the hell do you think happened to her? Does she have a cut? That is a lot of blood!"

"It is!" Dr. Marstens said as he checked Sylvia's pupils for shock. They were fully dilated. Her quivering had not ceased. She even seemed to be getting worse, despite it being warm inside. She was covered in blood from head to foot. The blood, however, was not her own. He turned to the kitchen and said, "It doesn't appear she is seriously injured. Just some cuts and scratches, but..., this is very strange. I don't know where all this blood came from. Scratches don't bleed this much." He looked into Sylvia's eyes again and his heart sank.

They had a bleak, lifeless look in them that chilled him to the bone. In his psychiatric practice, working with veterans returning from Korea, and then later, Vietnam, he had seen that same look. A distant, detached, and petrified gaze, dead eyes staring off into space at something too awful to articulate. Eyes that had seen too much, too soon. Eyes that wanted to block out something — terrifying, horrific and beyond human description. Not all wounds are on the surface. Not all injuries can be seen with the naked eye. He, as a psychiatrist, knew better than most. Some things seen, could never be unseen.

"What on *earth* happened to you, little girl?" he whispered. "You can tell me. I'm a friend. I promise I will never, ever hurt you. You are safe here."

"Take, eat...," Sylvia whispered, clutching her hands tighter to her chest.

"How is the water coming?" Dr. Marstens said as he called out to Vincent.

"Still warming up," Vincent answered as he continued to hold his hand under the running water. "I'm afraid the water heater is on the fritz. I think I will have to...," He paused as something caught his eye outside the kitchen window. It was a movement out in the woods. He spied a flash of light coming from just past the tree line. "Hey..., I think I see something out back."

"Let me see what you have there," Dr. Marstens said as he resumed talking to Sylvia. He pulled her small hands away from her chest and gently prodded her fingers open. When she released her grip, he smiled and looked down into her palms. His eyes widened now, and he lurched backward as if burned by a flaming cinder.

"Oh my God! What the hell is this?" Dr. Marstens exclaimed, his throat suddenly going bone dry. He started to speak again, but barely a whisper could emit from his mouth. He looked down into Sylvia's palm again, just to make sure he was not imagining things. He was not. He fought back his gag reflex. There, in the pit of her hands, was a tiny leg. It was obviously the limb of a premature baby, and..., there were teeth marks on the thigh. The leg had been partially... eaten!

"Did you say something?" Vincent called from the kitchen. He noticed something else moving at the tree line again. Now it was a bit clearer than before. It was several flashlights beams moving back and forth, coming from deep in the woods. "Hey," he called out to Dr. Marstens, "I think someone might be coming for her. Maybe it's her parents? I bet they must be worried—"

"—Vincent! Turn off the lights!" Dr. Marstens shouted.

"What? What are you talking about?" Vincent said. "What is wrong, why are you—"

"—For God's sake, Vincent," Dr. Marstens cried. "Turn off all of the lights — NOW!"

Chapter 29

April 27th, 2017 - UVid Headquarters - Mountain View, California - 4:45 PM

"Is HE STILL out?" Heather whispered as she looked down at Steve, lying prone on the floor of the Eye Bleach Lounge.

"He is," Sylvia said. "But, he should be coming out soon. He had a pretty nasty ride this afternoon. I had to take him down pretty deep."

"What was his issue?" Heather asked.

"You know I can't tell you," Sylvia said.

"And you know I will pester you until you do," Heather said. "Must we go through this dance?"

"Forget it. And anyway, it was something far too disgusting to discuss in public," Sylvia said. "And now…, I really need to get back to —"

"—I know Steve told us he was squeamish about bodily fluids," Heather said. "I bet he reviewed one of those awful 'shower' videos. I know I had a slew of them in my queue today." She shook her head and said, "It must be the time of year, you know. April showers bring May flowers, and in this case, I bet those showers were golden!" She laughed as she added, "disgusting!"

"It had nothing to do with golden showers," Sylvia said. "Sheesh! We need to talk about something else."

"Brown showers, then?"

"Ugh, please," Sylvia said. "Nancy just gave me a Kit Kat bar earlier. I would like to not taste it on the way back up, if you don't mind."

"But, I am getting warm, aren't I?" Heather said. "I can tell. You would be a lousy poker player."

"Yes..., sadly, you are getting warm. I have to admit, you have an amazing sense about these horrific things."

"What can I say?" Heather said. "I am a regular Perve whisperer."

"Well, it is way worse than... *that.*"

"Come on, Sylvia," Heather whispered. "What is it? Just tell me. What could possibly be worse than a brown shower?"

"You really don't understand the concept of personal boundaries, do you?"

"You know I don't," Heather said with a grin.

"Well, you'd be surprised," Sylvia said as she shook her head. "But, shhhh," she added as she placed her forefinger over her lips. "You really do need to be quiet, so I can finish up with Steve. I need to bring him out now."

"Just give me a little hint," Heather whispered. "You know I hate being out of the dirt loop."

"Honestly, Heather, you must be the nosiest person I have ever met."

"No doubt."

"OK..., well..., have you ever heard of a ruby shower?"

"That's a new one," Heather said. "No, I have never heard of it. What is it?"

Sylvia leaned over and whispered something into Heather's ear.

"Oh, dear God!" Heather shouted. "The things people get off on!"

Sylvia said, "I think that shatters Rule 34 into smithereens. In fact, it may require a whole new rule, maybe numbered 39!"

"It just might," Heather said.

Sylvia smiled and said, "I am pleased, though, to finally find something to shock the likes of you. It's a high achievement. So, now that your curiosity has been quenched, can I get on with this? I must really finish things up here."

"Hey, before you do that," Heather whispered as she pointed down to Steve, still lying on the floor. "While he is still under, maybe you can plant a few clever ideas in that freshly tilled subconscious of his, eh? Like…, maybe, oh, I don't know, maybe he is going to feel a little extra generous with our bonus evaluations next month?"

"You do know I can hear you?" Steve said as he opened his eyes.

"What? I thought you were under," Heather said.

"I told you he was coming out," Sylvia said. "We were just finishing up when you barged in here."

"Yeah," Steve said as he sat up fully. "And you are seriously harshing on my buzz, Heather. Cameron Diaz and Emma Stone had just finished locking up my secret vault when you started yapping. And, of course, they did get a bit dirty and sweaty in the process, so… I was helping them fill up the tub with extra bubbles for their hose down. Scrubby scrubby scrubby."

"Jesus, Steve," Heather said. "Even when you are under, you are still a perve."

"Hey," Steve said, "you conjured up your dead Grandma to lock away your traumatic memories." He grinned as he added, "I just happen to find that other, curvier guardians are more effective in locking up mine."

Sylvia laughed and shook her head. "Well, Steve, I guess it doesn't really matter who you pick to act as your guardian, as long as it works. So, did it work? Are you able to clear your mind now?"

Steve stood up and stretched. "Oh, yes! Wow! You are amazing, Sylvia. Simply amazing! It really worked! And, I don't mind telling you, I had my doubts." He turned to her, winked, and said, "Click… Click… Click…!"

"Click…, Click…, Click…," Sylvia said.

Sylvia and Heather walked back to their desks. Once there, Sylvia's phone rang, and she picked up the receiver.

"Sylvia Marstens speaking."

"Sylvia…, you don't know me, but…., I really felt I should give you a call," came the voice on the other line. It was an older woman speaking, and, from her tone, it was obvious she was quite upset.

"Who is this?"

"My name is Sister Margaret Rose," the caller said. "I worked with Father Hector Morales at Saint Sebastian."

"Ah…, well…, look, there is no need to reschedule the lunch, Sister," Sylvia snapped. "I really don't appreciate being stood up. Especially by a priest who then has his assistant call—"

"—Father Morales is dead," Sister Margaret said.

"Dead?"

"Yes, dead. He passed away on Tuesday. I have been meaning to give you a call, but…, I have been so busy with the arrangements and all. I had to contact his sister in Mexico City and, it…. It has been very difficult."

"Oh, my," Sylvia said. "I am so sorry. What…, what happened? I was supposed to meet him for lunch just this past Saturday."

"I know," Sister Margaret said. "He was just leaving to go meet you when he had a massive heart attack in his car. He never made it out of the driveway."

"How terrible!"

"It is," Sister Margaret said. "But, of course, we both know where he is now, and that is comforting. I was with him at the hospital the entire time he was in his coma before the end."

"Is there anything I can do?"

"Actually…, there is something you can do," Sister Margaret said. "He briefly regained consciousness in the hospital, right before he passed away. In his delusional state, he thought he had overslept and was late for his lunch meeting with you."

"Oh?" Sylvia said.

"Yes. He was very insistent I get a package, as well as a message, to you. He had the package beside him in the car when I found him. I know he would want you to have it. His service is tomorrow afternoon at 2:00 PM at the church. If you could come, I would be most appreciative. I know this was one of his final wishes."

"Yes, of course," Sylvia said. "I didn't know Father Morales very well, but, from what I did know, he seemed like a fine person. I would be honored to attend his funeral."

"He was," Sister Margaret said. "He was one of the finest men I have ever known. I will see you tomorrow after the service? I will give you the package then."

"Yes, you can count on me," Sylvia said. "But..., you said there was a message?"

"Oh, yes," Sister Margaret said. "I am so sorry. I am so rattled. Things just aren't the same without Father Morales."

"I understand."

"Yes..., in that brief moment of consciousness, he told me to tell you he was positive that they were going to use Alyssa's unborn child at the Feast of Moloch on Beltane."

"What does that mean? And who is this they? And what is Beltane?" Sylvia said.

"I'm sorry. I really don't know the answers to any of that," Sister Margaret said. "But, Father Morales was very agitated at the end. He may even have been delirious. I..., I think he knew he wasn't going to make it, because, right after he said all this he slipped back into his coma. He never woke up again."

"Oh, this is terrible. I am so sorry. I will be there, tomorrow."

"Thank you, Sylvia," Sister Margaret said. "God Bless."

Sylvia hung up the phone.

"So, what's this Beltane business all about?" Heather asked as she poked her head above the divider. "And..., did I hear right, did Father ElHottie die?"

"Heather! My God, you are such a snoop," Sylvia said.

"Guilty as charged," Heather said as she smiled. "I know, I'm sorry. It is one of the hazards of working in cubicle-hell."

"Well, don't be disrespectful," Sylvia said. "Yes, Father Morales passed away. He had a heart attack on the way to meet me for lunch last Saturday."

"Oh, that is awful," Heather said. "I'm sorry I made a joke. I have a sick sense of humor sometimes. It is a classic deflection technique. So, who called you?"

"A nun that works at his church. She has a package he wanted me to have."

"And all of this Beltane stuff?" Heather asked. "What's with that?"

"You have amazing hearing, girl," Sylvia said. "I don't know what that was all about, but, it was in his message. The nun asked me to come to Father Morales' funeral tomorrow at 2:00 PM and she would give me the package after the service."

"So, are you going?" Heather asked.

"Of course," Sylvia said.

"Steve!" Heather called out. "Sylvia and I are taking off tomorrow afternoon to go to a funeral. So, don't be charging us vacation or anything."

"No problem, I assume the other Quarts can handle the load," Steve called back from his office. "Plus, I'm off tomorrow, anyway, so, you could have probably skipped out early and I would have been none the wiser. But, now that I know—"

"—You little bastard," Heather snapped.

"What are you doing?" Sylvia asked as she glared at Heather.

"I'm going with you, of course. This kind of thing is right in my wheelhouse."

"Well…, you can come if you want. I am sure I would enjoy your company, as always, but…, can you behave? You know this is a funeral, right? It is not a joke."

"Sylvia!" Heather cried in mock indignation. "I'm an adult. I know how to behave at funerals, and besides," she added as she passed her hand over her customary long black dress. "You certainly know I have the right outfit to wear. I am funeral ready 24/7/365."

Sylvia chuckled and shook her head. "OK, but, please don't embarrass me."

"I promise I won't. I'll be good as gold. But, the thing is, I have to go now. I am very intrigued about all of this. Far too intrigued to miss out."

Chapter 30

May 7th, 1996 - Pikeville Police Department - Pikeville, Kentucky - 9:45 AM

"PIKEVILLE POLICE DEPARTMENT, may I help you?" the receptionist answered.

"Yes," the voice on the other line said. "This is Captain Dave Karpinski of the New York City Police department. I was hoping to speak with a..., Captain Buddy Johnson?"

"Oh, certainly," the receptionist said. "He is in a meeting right now, but, I can go get him."

"Thanks, I would appreciate it."

The receptionist covered the receiver of the phone with her hand and mouthed. "It's the New York City Police on the line."

Buddy Johnson, standing by the coffee pot, nodded, pointed to his office, and went inside. The receptionist prepared to transfer the call.

"OK, sir, I am putting you through," the receptionist said.

"Thanks."

"Captain Johnson speaking," Buddy said.

"Yes, Captain Johnson, this is Captain Dave Karpinski of the New York City Police Department."

"Glad to speak with you," Buddy said.

"I was wondering if you could help us out up here."

"I'll try, although, I don't know what some Podunk police captain can do to assist the greatest police force in the world. But, I will certainly give it my best shot."

"We are tracking down leads on a missing person case up here. We have some information that leads us to believe the person in question may be in your area."

"Oh? Ok, give me the rundown."

"The missing person is a John Delaney. He is a resident of New York City and is a Junior partner at the law firm of Fitzgerald, Cameron, and Duncan. He is married and is six feet three inches tall and—"

"—Is this guy looking for his son, by any chance?"

"Yes! So, you know where he is?"

"Well…, to be honest, I am looking for him too."

"I don't understand."

"The guy came into town about a week or so ago, and checked into the Daniel Boone Motor Lodge, room…, 214."

"Well, you seem to know all about Mr. Delaney. He must have made an impression on you."

"Oh, yes," Buddy said. "He made quite an impression around here. Quite an impression indeed. I know for a fact he pissed off every merchant and waitress in Pikeville in the brief time he was here. Ran all over town making all sorts of wild accusations. He even came in here, talking about some wacky, dark conspiracy to kidnap his son. Frankly, I think the guy has a screw loose."

"Well, Captain Johnson, his son, Billy Delaney, was kidnapped and there is an open investigation on his case. But…, your information about the Daniel Boone Motor Lodge checks out with the credit card records we subpoenaed. I called the motel and they referred me over to you."

"Oh, no doubt they did," Buddy said. "Look…, I'm sorry the guy's son was kidnapped. I really am. And…, that may explain some of his behavior. Hell, if someone snatched my little boy, I would probably go nuts too."

"So, what happened to him, Captain?"

"The guy totally trashed his room at the Motor Lodge. He ripped fixtures out of the wall, peed on the carpet, kicked in the TV. Real lowlife vandal kind of behavior. He also came in here and said all kinds of crazy things to my receptionist. Kept saying that voices told him that aliens, or some such thing, took his son out west somewhere. I think I heard her say it was Oregon, but, I wouldn't swear to it."

"Aliens?"

"Yeah…, crazy, isn't it? Look, I don't really care what folks believe, it's a free country and all. But, I got involved after Raj Patel, the owner of the Daniel Boone Motor Lodge, filed a complaint for the damages."

"I see."

"No one has seen hide nor hair of him in over a week," Buddy said. "Hey…, you said the guy was married, right?"

"Yes."

"Would it be possible for me to speak with his wife? I know this must be trying for her, but, there are the damages at the—"

"—Mrs. Delaney is in a deep coma. Has been for a few weeks now."

"Oh, I am sorry to hear that. Well, shoot. I don't really have much more to add about Mr. Delaney. I really wish I could have been more helpful to you, Captain."

"No, you have been very helpful, Captain Johnson. Very helpful indeed."

"How so? You don't know any more about where John Delaney is than when you first called me."

"Oh, I know plenty," Captain Karpinski said. "Now I know at least one place in America where John Delaney is not. He is not in Pikeville, Kentucky. That's something, at least."

Buddy smiled and said, "Yep. I reckon you are right. My guess is he might be out in Oregon by now."

"I'll put out something on the wire," Captain Karpinski said.

"And hey, if you find that guy, tell him he owes Raj Patel, owner of the Daniel Boone Motor Lodge, $384.76 for damages."

"I…," Captain Karpinski said before he paused. "It was good speaking with you, Captain Johnson."

"Same to you, Captain Karpinski," Buddy said as he hung up the phone. A few seconds passed before the receptionist entered the office and broke the silence.

"Do you think he will buy it?" the receptionist said.

"Oh yeah," Buddy said as a greasy smile crept across his face. "Hook, line, and sinker. You heard the Captain. He knows Pikeville is the *one* place in America where John Delaney ain't."

The receptionist grinned and nodded as she ran her tongue slowly over her lips. "Yeah…, well, sort of."

Chapter 31

April 28th, 2017 - Café Del Sol Mexican Restaurant - Mountain View California - 6:30 PM

"IT WAS A REALLY nice service, don't you think?" Sylvia said. "Really nice."

"It was OK, I guess," Heather said. "But, there seemed to be a lot of getting up and down."

"You must mean the kneeling and the standing," Sylvia said.

"Yeah, halfway through the service I was about to stand up and ask; is this a funeral or a jazzercise class?"

"My God, Heather," Sylvia said. "The things that come out of your mouth."

"I had to fight the urge to yell out to the priest conducting the show to not hog the bong. I mean, it is only good manners to pass that thing around every once in a while. Give someone else a toke. It isn't polite not to share."

Sylvia slapped her hand to her forehead and said, "First of all, it's not a show, it's a service. And second of all, do you mean the thurible?"

"Hey, I don't care what you call it. My old roommate called hers Betty, and, I had a boyfriend in college that made one out of a plastic toy dinosaur. He named it Bongzilla."

Sylvia laughed. "You aren't serious, are you? This is too much, even for you."

"No," Heather said as she chuckled. "I'm not serious. I'm not stupid, Sylvia. I know it was incense. I was just trying to lighten the mood a bit. Funerals are a big downer, you know."

"Yes, it was a somber occasion," Sylvia said. "Even though I haven't been to church in years, it was nice to be back in the pews, even under such dark circumstances. Being at Saint Sebastian brought back a lot of good memories with my Mom and Dad at the Church of the Blessed Sacrament in New York. They were both the staunchest of Catholics, you know."

"I think you mentioned it."

"Once inside, it all came back to me. It really felt like coming home," Sylvia said.

"And you were worried about me acting up and ruining everything," Heather said. "See, I behaved, right?"

"You did," Sylvia said. "You surprised me and rose to the occasion."

"I clean up nice, occasionally. I thought the eulogy was very moving."

"It was," Sylvia said. "Although I didn't really know Father Morales very well, it appeared to be an accurate tribute. He seemed like a very nice man. And obviously he was very well loved and appreciated by the congregation and his many former students. There was not a dry eye in the place."

"Well, I do know one good thing," Heather said. "Thank God those Catholics don't have open caskets at the wake. I was glad to avoid the 'Oh, doesn't he look good' conversation I am used to having at other funerals I've attended. Those talks are both creepy and insincere. The dead always look dead."

"Yes, they do," Sylvia said. "I saw my fair share during my residency back in New York. You never really get used to it, though. Everybody is so..., grey."

"But, I will give Father Morales...," Heather said as she smiled. "See..., I didn't call him Father McHottie."

"You are making progress."

"I will give him credit, though," Heather continued. "He sure had good taste in restaurants. Damn, these burritos are to die for." She paused and added, "figuratively, of course."

"Yes," Sylvia said as she smiled.

"And it sure seems appropriate to have dinner here after his service," Heather continued.

Sylvia nodded and said, "It does, and plus, the margaritas aren't half bad either." She raised her glass and added, "To Father Morales."

"To Father Morales," Heather said as they clinked their glasses. She paused after they took their sips. She pointed at the stack of papers next to them on the table and asked, "So…, what are you going to do about all of this now? Pretty creepy, eh?"

"Yes, pretty creepy is a massive understatement," Sylvia said. "I don't quite buy into all of the supernatural elements Father Hector alludes to in his notes."

"No, that is all obvious bullshit," Heather said.

"But…, it doesn't mean there is not something to be genuinely concerned about here. There don't have to be literal demons in order for people to commit some pretty heinous crimes in their name. I mean…, the description of the Feast of Moloch is chilling…, just chilling." She turned to Heather and asked, "What kind of person was Alyssa, really? Did she seem like the type to be involved in something like, like a…"

"Like a Satanic cannibalistic cult?" Heather asked. She smirked and added, "I would not have thought Alyssa the type, but, hey, you learn something new about a person every day, right? Ironically enough, knowing about all this now only makes her seem more interesting to me. She was always a bit too vanillish for my taste. Now, she seems almost cool."

"Cool? Are you joking? I was planning on calling the police about all of this. I mean, you saw the flyer Father Hector took from that bookstore. Beltane is the thirtieth. That's this Sunday! And, the flyer specifically mentions the high priest coming in for a special Feast of Moloch. I think the police need to know about this."

"Yeah, well, I want to hear how that call goes," Heather said. "Be sure to let me listen in." In a mocking tone, she said, "Yes officer, you see, this priest friend of mine died recently, and he was convinced there is a cannibalistic Satanic cult that kidnapped my neighbor. Where? Oh, up near those fancy vineyards near Floriston. Yes, that's right, right off exit four. Oh, no officer. No one has reported her missing. Why, yes officer, I know this 'so-called' crime is being advertised in broad daylight, in some kind of hippy bookstore, but I am certain it is going to happen. Yes, you agree? Wonderful. I think you are right, twelve Blackhawk assault helicopters should do the trick." She rolled her eyes and said, "Sheesh. They will laugh you right off the phone."

"Well…," Sylvia said. "I feel we should do something. I mean, Alyssa is missing."

"Is she?" Heather asked. "I am still not so sure. I think she was just pulling a prank, and you and Father Hector just got caught up in it. I mean, those crazy messages, and the phantom ice cream, and what not? How do you explain all of that? I would not be a bit surprised if Alyssa and her boyfriend, Dickweed—"

"—Darryl," Sylvia corrected.

"*Whatever*," Heather continued. "She and Darryl are up there in Floriston right now, dropping acid out on that big ashram and having a big old laugh about all of this. Frankly, she seemed more of that type."

"I don't know," Sylvia said. "You do make a good point, but, I still think I should call the police. I feel I owe it to Father Hector."

"I tell you what," Heather said. "It's the weekend and I don't have any plans. Do you?"

"My schedule is open."

"I say Sunday, I pick you up early. We drive on up to Beelzebub Lake, or whatever the hell they call it, and make a day of it."

Sylvia laughed and said, "Beelzebub Lake! You crack me up, sometimes."

"We will have our cell phones," Heather said. "So, if we see anything weird, we can call the police. Otherwise, when *nothing* happens, we can just sit back and enjoy the crazy show. I bet there is some freaky shit that goes on up there, and hey, who knows, maybe there will be some sexy Satanists to hook up with? You know, those devil boys are always so hot. I dated this guy in a Death Metal band a few years ago and let me tell you something, that guy was smoking!"

"—You want us to go up there by ourselves?" Sylvia interrupted.

"Why not?" Heather said. "Look, now I kind of want to go. It seems pretty exciting and, well, my Netflix queue is empty."

"I don't know Heather, this seems like a bad idea," Sylvia said.

"It's only three hours away," Heather said.

"Still..., I think—"

"—And how about this, there are a bunch of wineries up there. We can hit the road early and stop at a few on the way up."

"So, you are proposing we have a combo winery trip / satanic cult-busting weekend? You are crazy!" Sylvia said as she laughed. "I think I'll pass — although, the winery option is tempting. But no. I am going to do what I originally said I was going to do, and just call the police and tell them what I know. That's my good deed for the—"

"—You're no fun," Heather said as she pouted. "Well..., you can do what you want. I can't stop you. But, as for me, I am going to go check out this devil festival for myself. It sounds like a fricking riot."

"It sounds dangerous, Heather," Sylvia said. "I really think you should think this through."

"You know I won't," Heather said. She smiled and added, "you know I have an impulse control problem."

Sylvia laughed and nodded. "Yes, I know."

"And this is all about nothing anyway. It's all just a bunch of nonsense. So, when you see me back in the office on Monday, with a deep tan and a sunny disposition from having a nice relaxing day in wine country, you can eat your heart out."

"That'll never happen," Sylvia said.

"Oh? Just try me," Heather said.

"You *never* have a sunny disposition," Sylvia said. "There isn't enough wine in California."

"Touché," Heather said. "But..., I bet my disposition would get a lot brighter if you went with me. Please! It will be so much more fun if you came along. I hate traveling alone, but, I will."

"Heather," Sylvia said. "I don't want to sound like your mother, even though I am old enough to be her. I really don't like the idea of you going up there alone."

"Don't be so melodramatic, Sylvia," Heather said. "I am telling you, this whole thing is nothing but a big hoax."

"A woman has gone missing!"

"Please, stop with that," Heather said. "I doubt very seriously anything is going to happen at some Hippie festival, right out in the open. Do you realize how crazy this sounds?"

"I don't care. I think it is way too dangerous."

"The only danger I envision encountering is the danger of seeing some unfortunate fashion choices. No doubt there will be nothing but a sea of tie-dyed peasant skirts and Birkenstocks up there."

"But still…, Heather, in all seriousness, it isn't safe. You don't have to believe in some sort of Satanist conspiracy to realize it is dangerous for a woman alone to go to some bizarre event like this. Who knows what these people are capable of?"

Heather reached into her purse and pulled a taser up to the top edge, just revealing the intimidating looking metal prongs over the lip of her bag. "Don't worry about me. Any Satanic Cannibals that try and make a snack out of me will find their asses shocked into next week. This thing can drop a moose in one jolt." She winked and said, "and plus, nobody puts any teeth on my body without my express invitation! And even then, only after plying me with a half a dozen jello shots at least."

"Holy crap, where did you get that thing?" Sylvia said.

"I had an old boyfriend who was a cop," Heather said. "He may have been a total doofus, but, he did fix me up with some pretty killer swag. So…, if you aren't going to join me, do me one favor at least. Don't call the police. If they show up, I could get in real trouble for having this taser on me. It is not legal for the public to carry these and Todd could get fired if they find out he gave it to me."

Sylvia paused and after a long sigh said, "Is there no way I can talk you out of going?"

"None," Heather said.

"Well…," Sylvia said. "I know I am going to regret this…., but, I guess I am going to have to go with you. You need adult supervision!"

Heather smiled and said, "Wonderful! You won't regret it, I promise. And you are so right, I do need adult supervision. Thanks, Mom!"

Chapter 32

August 4th, 1976 - 115 West 73rd Street, Suite D - New York City, New York - 2:30 PM

THE WINDOW AIR CONDITIONER IN Dr. Thomas Marstens' office was running hard. The compressor was working overtime with a high whine and a steady hum. The temperature outside was brutal. The heatwave that had gripped the Northeast by the throat since early July was relentless and showed no signs of stopping anytime soon. With the temperature topping the upper 90s every day, it was if New York, still recovering from the extravagant Bicentennial festivities on July 4th, had caught a fever and it had yet to break. Waiting patiently, as well as nervously, in the chilly waiting room, were Vincent and Marie Padovana.

"Vinny, are you sure we are doing the right thing? I mean…, this is so, I don't know, unorthodox," Marie said as she clutched her husband's arm. "It doesn't seem right. What if something goes wrong? What if it doesn't work?"

"Tom knows what he is doing," Vincent said. "You know he is the best psychiatrist in New York. Hell…, he is probably one of the best in the world. If anyone can help our little Sylvia, he can."

"Well…, yes, I suppose you are right," Marie said. "But, I don't know about these methods he is using. It seems so…, unnatural. I mean, she doesn't remember anything now."

"That is a blessing," Vincent said. "We should thank God every night she can't remember what happened."

"But, what are we going to tell her? She is ten years old. She is going to eventually ask questions — about her childhood, about where she was born, about her baby pictures. How are we going to—"

"—It's all been arranged, Marie," Vincent said. "I have a few friends in the courthouse, and, with Tom's signature on the birth certificate, for all practical purposes it will look like she was our natural born child, a healthy baby girl born to Vincent and Marie Padovano at New York Presbyterian. We kept everything we could the same, where practicable, so, it is all set." He turned to her and held her hands in his. "You always wanted a child of our own, right?"

"Of course, I did! You know I have prayed and prayed for this."

"Well, God has provided."

"Of course, but…, there is no shame in being adopted, Vincent. Lots of children are adopted. Even President Ford is adopted! I don't understand why you and Tom insist on all this cloak and dagger business. It's not right. It makes us seem like criminals."

"Marie, we can't take the chance. We can't risk her birth parents ever finding her."

"I know you said they were bad people," Marie said.

"Oh, they were bad people, all right. You weren't there, Marie. You didn't see what we saw."

"If they were as bad as you say, I still don't know why you didn't call the police? I wish you would just tell me what really happened. I am your wife, and now, Sylvia's mom and you and Tom are hiding things from me! I won't stand for it. I have a right to know!"

"You do have a right to know, I know that. But, Marie, this is for your own protection," Vincent said. He looked into her eyes and added, "You just have to trust me on this. We couldn't call the police. We couldn't do this straight. Tom suggested, and I agreed, that we go about things this way, and I think he is right. I believe it's God's will that we found Sylvia like we did."

"But why can't I just know what happened? I am her mother! I need to know what happened to her!"

Vincent cupped her face and said, "there are some things, Marie, you don't want to know. Some things are best left unheard, unknown, and unseen. One day, I am certain, you will understand, and you will thank me when you do. We owe it to Sylvia to give her as normal a childhood as we can. She deserves that."

"Yes, yes," Marie said. "Every child deserves a happy childhood."

"And I love her, as much, or maybe even more, than if she were our biological child."

"I feel the same way," Marie said.

"And I feel that, in some way, God brought her to us. We are in the perfect situation to take care of that terrified little girl."

"Yes, you are right," Marie said.

"So, if you love Sylvia as I do, and you want to protect her; after today, we will never discuss this again. After we bring her back home this afternoon, everything will be set. You know, I already obtained a spot for her at St. Catherine's Catholic school up on Riverside Drive."

"Oh, Vincent," Marie said. "How wonderful! St. Catherine's is a wonderful school."

"I have already talked to the Headmistress and it is all arranged for her to start in September."

"Aren't they going to need to have her transcripts, or records, or something?"

"Luckily," Vincent said as he winked. "The Chairman of their Board of Visitors is a client of mine. There will be no questions asked — none. It has all been nicely arranged. You see, she was *always* a student there. Her records had just been…, *misplaced* until recently."

"Will that hold water? It seems too…, sketchy."

"Who at the school is going to question a direct intervention from their Chairman? And after this year…, well, there will be ample actual records to deal with, right?"

"I suppose so," Marie said. "Still…"

"And Marie," Vincent said as he smiled. "Her newly 'found' transcripts show she has performed very well in math, just like her Dad."

Marie reached up and stroked Vincent's cheek. "You just arranged everything, didn't you? Sylvia is lucky to have you as a father. You are a very clever man."

Vincent kissed his wife's hand and said, "And she is lucky to have you as a mother. In fact, she must have gotten her love for English class from your side of the family." He grinned and added, "it seems she got all As last semester."

"I hope you aren't being too clever here. I hope this all works out," Marie said. "I hate living a lie. When Father Zimmers baptized her, I made a promise to—"

"—It is absolutely necessary," Vincent said. "Remember, we need to never speak of it again after today. Father Zimmers is the only one to know about the adoption, and, he is going to be the last. Agreed?"

Marie sighed and said, "agreed."

"We need to do it for Sylvia."

"Yes, for Sylvia."

"Vincent, Marie, can I get anything for you?" Dr. Marstens said as he entered the room.

Marie stood up. "How is she, Tom? Is she going to be all right?"

"Oh, yes! I am glad to announce she is not only going to be all right but, her progress has been phenomenal. You have a very bright little girl there. Very bright. She is a quick study."

"But…, what does she remember, Tom?" Marie asked.

"She remembers she has a Mom and Dad, named Vincent and Marie, who both love her. She remembers she is a good student at St. Catherine's, and she loves English and Math," Dr. Marstens said.

"You told Tom about the arrangements you made at St. Catherine's before you told me?" Marie said.

"I had to," Vincent said.

"And Sylvia also remembers the stomachache you brought her in to see me about is now gone," Dr. Marstens said.

"Stomachache?" Marie asked.

"I thought it best to keep the cover story simple," Dr. Marstens said. "So, did you bring the doll I told you about? She had such an affection for it, things can move much more effectively if we can build on something already present in her subconscious."

Marie reached down into her purse and pulled out a Wonder Woman doll. "Yes, I got this at Macy's, just as you said."

"Perfect, just perfect," Dr. Marstens said.

"Tom," Marie said. "I need to know something. I…, I need to ask what she can remember from…, before?"

"She doesn't remember anything, Marie. It has been..., erased. CLICK..., CLICK..., CLICK..."

"Click, click, click? What does that mean?" Marie asked.

"Oh, it's just a technique I employ. It's not important. What is important is Sylvia is ready to come home."

"But these..., implanted memories you put in her mind, aren't they all fake? Isn't it possible she will figure it out?" Marie asked.

"What is your favorite Christmas memory, Marie?" Dr. Marstens asked.

"What?"

"Your favorite memory. Everyone has one. I just chose Christmas, because a lot of people have very warm feelings around this holiday."

"I don't know where you are going with this."

"Humor me," Dr. Marstens said. "It will help you understand the technique I used on Sylvia."

"OK," Marie said as she furrowed her brow. "Well..., I guess it would be of my Grandmother. After Midnight Mass we would all come home from church and she would stay up with me after everyone went to bed. We would drink a glass of boiled custard and watch the Pope on TV. It was great, just Nonny and me."

Dr. Marstens smiled. "That is a beautiful memory. Now, what would you say if I told you it isn't true?"

"What? I remember it perfectly. I can see the tree and my Grandmother. I can even taste the nutmeg and vanilla from the custard."

"The mind is a powerful organ. In fact, one of the reasons I became a psychiatrist is my fascination with the human brain. It is far more complicated and complex than we can possibly understand. And..., it is highly subjectable to suggestion. The line between fantasy and reality is very thin, Marie. Very thin indeed. How do we know what we *think* we know? How can one be sure that what happened, really happened? You see..., you can't, really. Everything that happens to us in life is all just stored in a series of biochemical reactions in a two-pound slab of meat in your skull. These memories can be changed and manipulated to be anything you need it to be. Reality is not as concrete as you might think."

"I don't know about that, Tom," Marie said.

"Now, close your eyes, and focus on that memory," Tom said as he turned to Marie.

"All right, I am," Marie said as she closed her eyes.

"Do you see the TV?"

"Yes."

"And a commercial is coming on, right?"

"It is! How did you—"

"—And in the commercial, a woman is coming on the screen, and it is— who? Who is on the screen now?"

"It…, I…, I don't understand. It is…"

"Wonder Woman, right?"

"My God!" Marie said as she popped open her eyes. "It is! But…, how? That show wasn't on back when I was a kid. That is a modern show and…, it is in color. We didn't get color TV until I was in High School."

"Click…, Click…, Click…," Dr. Marstens said as he smiled.

"*You* did this?" Vincent asked.

"I did, last week when Marie came in for a background consultation about Sylvia. I anticipated she would have some objections."

"I remember you talking to me, but…, how did you do this without my knowledge?" Marie asked.

Dr. Marstens smiled and said nothing.

"I may have some objections about this myself, Tom," Vincent said. "This is unethical! You shouldn't mess around with people's —"

"—Objections noted. Look, I am sorry, but, I had to do it," Dr. Marstens said. "I only want what's best for Sylvia. I have grown quite fond of her. You two have been given a gift of a beautiful daughter. I know if I had a daughter, I would want her to be exactly like Sylvia."

"Well…, I am touched you are so committed to Sylvia's well-being, but you should not have experimented on Marie without her knowledge," Vincent said. "This is not right, Tom. It is not right at all!"

Dr. Marstens stood up and said, "Sometimes the ends justify the means. I am sure you will feel differently about my methods once you see the results, which will be right now." He pressed the intercom button on his desk and said, "Phyllis, please send Sylvia in."

The door opened, and Sylvia rushed inside. "Mommy, Daddy, I feel so much better! Dr. Marstens fixed me all up."

Tears welled up in Marie's eyes as she saw Sylvia's face. Outwardly, she appeared to be a bright, happy, smiling child, just like nothing was wrong. And it is true— nothing was wrong. With she and Vincent, they all are a family now.

"Are you ready to go home, Sylvia?" Vincent said.

"You bet, Daddy," Sylvia said. "Oh…, Dr. Marstens said you would get me some ice cream on the way home if I was good." She turned to Dr. Marstens and said, "I was good, wasn't I?"

"You were very good," Dr. Marstens said. "You did everything I asked."

Vincent choked back a sob as he said, "I…, I would be thrilled to buy you ice cream, Sylvia."

"I love you, Daddy," Sylvia said. "And Mommy, too!" As she turned to Marie, Sylvia caught sight of the Wonder Woman doll and squealed. "You remembered to bring it! Dr. Marstens said you would."

"Yes, Sylvia," Marie said. "I remembered. Now, let's go home. I look forward to playing together in your room."

"You're the best, Mommy. I love you so much."

Marie began to cry. "I love you, too, Sylvia. More than you can ever know."

Chapter 33

"I WILL SAY THIS, for a bunch of Satanists, they sure have a topnotch selection of specialty goat cheeses," Heather said before she laughed and chomped down on a cheese-laden cracker. "Yummy! It tastes so deliciously evil!"

"Heather, you really are too much," Sylvia said as she took a sip of her Chardonnay.

"So…., do you feel stupid yet?" Heather asked.

"Not yet," Sylvia said. "Although, I think I am on the road to it."

"And you were all worried about there being some kind of Satanic cult up here," Heather said. She spread her arms wide to highlight the festival and added, "this is about as diabolical as a Renaissance Fair. In fact, I half expect to hear someone crank up some old Joan Baez tunes any minute."

"God, I sure hope not. Then we would definitely know the devil was at work," Sylvia said with a laugh. "So, have you seen Alyssa anywhere? Remember, I haven't ever met her. I just saw her picture once. I doubt I could place her in a crowd."

"I've been looking," Heather said. "Frankly, it's probably a lost cause. Alyssa has that generic blonde-girl look about her. God knows, California is filled with that type. Out here, in this Hipster-Doofus Wonderland, forget about spotting her in this crowd. She would blend right in quite easily with these tie-dyed, Wiccan whack-jobs." Heather paused as something caught her attention. She pointed down the hill and said, "Hey, will you lookey there. They are giving away free samples of Riesling!"

"Don't you think you've had enough?" Sylvia said. "We hit four wineries on the way up here."

"I know, wasn't it great?" Heather said. "After all, if I am going to sell my soul to the devil, shouldn't I at least get a free souvenir glass? You know, something stamped with - *I went to Beltane 2017 to sell my soul to Satan and all I got was this stupid mug* - on the front."

Sylvia laughed and shook her head as she followed Heather down the hill to the wine vendor. She was feeling much better now, the tension that had been building in her gut for days was fading away. She also felt, she had to admit, very foolish. Heather was right. The place was about as benign as a local Farmer's Market. And, to make the devil-baked conspiratorial plot seem even more preposterous, the day was gorgeous. Somehow it is hard to think about dark occultic practices when standing in a flower-laden meadow. The whole earth seemed to be bursting into bloom simultaneously. It hardly seemed a proper setting for some demon infested, human sacrificial festival.

The crowd in attendance was small, perhaps forty people, and hardly appeared diabolical. There was not a black hood or necklace of human skulls in sight. More Simon and Garfunkel than Marilyn Manson. The sparse attendance was not surprising either. The location was far off the grid. Overall the atmosphere was quite upbeat. Children played in the yard and there was an interesting and eclectic mix of people milling about. If one did not know different, the event could have easily passed as just another hipsterish, upscale, vegan, folk event, so common in California.

Sylvia was always fascinated by people watching and was especially curious to see what kind of vendors show up for such an unorthodox event. She smiled as she approached one of the card tables manned by an older woman hawking her wares. It was just what she expected. How could she have gotten so swept up in Father Hector's craziness? *I don't think they would sell handcraft soaps at a real Satanic Black Mass.*

"Beautiful day, isn't it?" Sylvia asked the vendor.

"Oh, it is. I can't remember a prettier Beltane in years," the woman replied. "Can I interest you in any handcrafted soap? I make these myself. Personally, I think the lavender/honey is my best."

"They are lovely, but no thanks," Sylvia said. "But..., say, maybe you can tell me something? This is my first time here and I was kind of wondering what goes on during the ceremony?"

"First time?" the vendor asked. "Wow! You are in for a real treat. This year, the High Priest is coming. I know everyone is just vibrating in pure excitement. My aura has been pegging all week in anticipation, so, I am sure this year's Circle will be the most fantastic ever."

"Circle?"

Click..., *Click...,* *Click...*

Sylvia closed her eyes as she wavered on her feet. She was suddenly unsteady. A wave of nausea and dizziness flowed over her body like an icy shower. Mercifully, it passed.

"Are you OK?" the woman asked. "You look ill."

"Yeah..., I, uh, I just got a little light-headed there for a second," Sylvia said. She lifted her empty glass and added, "perhaps my friend and I made one too many winery stops on the way up here."

The woman threw her head back and laughed. "Oh, mercy, it's easy to do. We are so blessed here in Northern California. So much wine and never enough time."

"Amen to that," Sylvia said. "But..., back to today's festivities, I am curious. What exactly happens tonight?"

"Well, usually Melody starts the ball rolling around sunset," the woman said. She looked down at her watch and added, "just a little over an hour from now."

"Who is Melody?"

"Melody Summers," the woman said as she pointed up to an enormous house on the side of the mountain. "That's her place. She owns all of this."

"Impressive."

"Oh, she is very impressive and quite an amazing woman. Came out here from back east quite a while ago."

"Another refugee from the east coast, I suppose," Sylvia said. "Just like me."

"Me too," the woman said as she nodded.

"What happens at Circle?" Sylvia asked.

"Well, Melody starts the procession with Our Lady, and several of the other women dance before it as she takes the icon inside the sacred circle." The woman pointed and said, "see, they are marking it out right now."

Sylvia turned to look. A few women were tracing out a design on the ground with black dust. She squinted and tried to see what they were drawing on the grass but couldn't make it out. They were too far away.

"A pentagram, I suppose?" Sylvia asked.

"Yes. The pentagram is the great symbol of Spirit. The five points of the star pleases him greatly. This year Spirit should be especially delighted since the High Priest will be performing the Feast of Moloch for the first time in many decades."

"What exactly goes on during that ceremony?"

"I really don't know," the woman said. "It is an exceptionally rare event, as only the High Priest can officiate. In fact, it is so rare, I have been in the craft for forty years and never been to one myself." Her eyes sparkled as she added, "and that is why this is such a special treat today. I envy you. To have your first Circle also be the Feast of Moloch is incredible, just incredible."

"Who is the High Priest?" Sylvia asked as she glanced around at the crowd. "Can you point him out to me? I would love to ask him a few questions."

"I don't think he is here yet," the woman answered. "I have never met him, but, I hear he is an old friend of Melody's from back east. I am very excited to meet him myself, though, and I am probably just as curious about the ceremony as you are. Sorry, I wish I could be more helpful."

"You have been quite helpful. Thanks," Sylvia said.

"Oh, one thing, I hope you aren't shy, dear," the woman said. "I thought it worth mentioning since this is your first time."

"Shy? What do you mean?"

"Melody is quite traditional. She always requires our ceremonies to be skyclad. It is the old way, you know."

Sylvia glanced down at herself and gulped. "You mean?"

"Yes…, everything."

Sylvia thanked the woman again and turned to look for Heather. Fun time was over now. It was one thing to hang out at a hippie fair and enjoy some arugula tarts, but quite another to strip down naked in front of a bunch of strangers. There was a limit to her curiosity, and this was it.

"Hey, you know what I just found out?" Heather said as she walked up the hill toward Sylvia. "In an hour, everyone here gets starkers. Can you believe it?"

"Yeah, I just heard that too," Sylvia said. "And..., I think that might be our cue to go."

"Oh, come on, Mom," Heather said. "You're no fun." Heather raised her eyebrow and said, "I think I have spied a couple of hottie Devil worshippers I wouldn't mind seeing flopping their wizard wands around."

"Yeah, but, that also means you get to see some dried up old wands too. I don't think it is worth it."

"Mmmmm," Heather said as she stared over Sylvia's shoulder. "Now there is someone whose wand I would definitely want to see. Yowzah!"

Sylvia turned to look at the object of Heather's desire. She instantly halted, rooting her feet to the ground. There, sauntering down the hill towards them, with a knowing grin on his face, was an extremely attractive man. A hint of recognition flickered across her eyes, sparking her memory like a long dead fire springing to life. She didn't know how she knew him, but, somewhere deep in her psyche, this handsome face was burned onto the floor of her soul. His smile widened as he stepped forward.

"Look at little Sylvia all grown up," Father Ted said. "Shall you help me with our Lady again, tonight? It will be just like old times."

"I..., I..., I don't understand," Sylvia stuttered as her face flushed and she became dizzy. She lurched backwards and started to turn away to run.

Click..., *Click...*, *Click...*

Father Ted reached out and grabbed her shoulder. He said, "Still running, Sylvia? Shouldn't you stop running now?"

"How! How are you here?" Sylvia asked. "This can't be real! It can't! It's not possible!"

"You still don't understand, do you, Sylvia?" His smile curled into a soul-chilling grin as he added, "our Lady won't wait forever."

Sylvia pulled away from him and spun towards Heather. She cried, "we have to go, right now, this instant!"

"Go? You just got here," Father Ted said. "If you leave now, you will miss all the fun..., just like last time."

"Heather, we have to go NOW!" Sylvia screamed. "We have to call the..." Sylvia froze. Everything went black. Her body convulsed into violent shudders before dropping to the ground in a lifeless heap.

Heather smiled as she returned the taser to her purse.

Father Ted cupped Heather's chin and said, "Well done, Heather. I always knew you were my special girl."

*****

Hours later Sylvia's eyes fluttered open. In the dark, with her face pressed to the ground, she saw nothing. Her head throbbed as if it had been crushed in a two-ton press. Her gut churned and every one of her muscles ached. To her horror, as she tried to move, she discovered she was not only bound but naked. Her hands and feet were tied behind her back, trussing her up like a turkey. She could hear, though, and her blood chilled as the voices around her became intelligible. She heard Father Ted's voice, booming through the night, as clear and seductive as it had been forty years earlier.

"Oh, glorious night above, your pitch-black wraps the sky, the earth awaits your word, wrapped in its dark disguise; arise ye Gods of old, arise ye Prince of lies, arise ye ancient ones, we hunger for words of the wise! Arise! Arise! In glorious triumph, we wait for thee to rip the earth and rise!"

Countless voices joined in and sang, "Arise! Arise! Arise!"

Sylvia struggled to lift her head. Sweat poured off her bare back as she thrashed against the ropes. The bonds wouldn't budge. She continued to flail. She had to see what was happening. She had to face this ultimate terror. Her painful exertions made minutes seemed like hours, but she started to make progress. The ropes started to loosen.

With heroic effort, and using up the last of her remaining strength, she managed to raise her face a few inches up off the ground.

Having adjusted to the gloom, her vision was clearer, and she peered into the darkness. She turned towards the voices. They were coming from a circle of torches twenty feet away. A figure was elevated on a table inside the circle. It was a woman. She too was bound and struggling to get loose. Because the woman also was naked, Sylvia could easily see she was pregnant.

"Oh My God! No! No! NO!" Sylvia shouted as her eyes were drawn to the end of the table. The woman's feet were gone. They had been hacked off, leaving only two bloody, tourniquet-wrapped stumps behind. Sylvia gasped and collapsed, darkness falling over her like a blanket of ice.

Click..., *Click...*, *Click...*

Chapter 34

June 11, 1996 - New York Presbyterian Hospital - 3rd-floor nurses station - New York City - 10:15 AM

"EXCUSE ME, MISS," the older man asked as he approached the hectic nursing station. No one looked up. There was no time. The station was only partially covered today. Every available eye was fully engaged in monitoring a floor full of patients and their various charts located along the back wall. A half-dozen phones were ringing and, worst of all, the pharmaceutical cart had just arrived. It was time to dispense all the patients' medications before lunch. With so many of the staff out today, it was going to be a real ordeal. The din of orders being shouted over the constant ringing phones ensured an atmosphere of pure pandemonium.

"Excuse me, Miss," the man asked again. Nothing changed. No one noticed. The reason was not surprising. A lone 86-year-old man, wearing baggy chinos, a loud Hawaiian shirt and sporting a deeply tanned and wrinkled face, was a common enough sight in New York Presbyterian — especially at this time of year. The snowbirds had returned from Florida weeks earlier. Another of their flock wandering the busy halls was not a particularly noteworthy event. So many fly in, and often, never fly back out the hospital doors.

Today it was especially out of control. There had been a Code Blue earlier in room 301, and room 316 was occupied by an unusually belligerent patient who refused to take his medication. But it was the "special case" in room 314 that was making this unfortunate situation even worse.

Room 314 was a problem. For weeks, the patient had lingered in her coma and was manageable. Now that she was awake, however, the truth was harder to hide. She did not belong at New York Presbyterian. She belonged at Bellevue. But being close friends with the director has its privileges and one of those included scoring a private room on this floor.

The old man smiled and shouted at the top of his lungs, "My name is Dr. Thomas Marstens —M-a-r-s-t-e-n-s— and I am here to see Sylvia Delaney — D-e-l-a-n-e-y! She is a patient in room 314 - 3-1-4!"

That seemed to do the trick as every head turned.

"Oh…, I'm sorry sir," Nurse Jones said, "I didn't see you there."

"I gathered that," Dr. Marstens said. He smiled and added, "It seems just as busy now as it was back when I did my residency here."

"Yes…, it is quite busy today," Nurse Jones said. "Uh…, you said you were here to see Sylvia Delaney?"

"Yes," Dr. Marstens said. "The information desk told me she was in room 314." He paused as he sensed the nurse's hesitation and added, "has she been moved?"

"No…, it is just, well, her doctor has strictly limited any visitors. I'm afraid she is unavailable to be seen at this—"

"—Well, I would think a visit from an old family friend shouldn't do any harm," Dr. Marstens interrupted. "And, of course, I was her doctor once. Although, that was many years ago. Perhaps that status could buy me a little professional courtesy?"

"I'm sorry, sir, but the order is pretty explicit."

Dr. Marstens sighed, and said, "I flew all the way up here from Boca last night to see her and I'm flying back tomorrow. I would hate to have to go back to Florida without at least paying her one visit."

"I wish I could help you sir, but, there is no wiggle room here. No visitors, other than immediate family. You aren't immediate family, are you?"

"No, but, I was great friends with her late parents as well as her uncle, Milo. I wonder if he can help me? He has been on New York Presbyterian's Board of Directors for decades now." Dr. Marstens leaned in to study her name badge and added, "I am certain he will be most interested in learning how helpful the staff is here, Nurse... Jones."

Nurse Jones' face tightened. She said, "Well..., let me see what I can do. Let me make a call."

"Wonderful," Dr. Marstens said as he watched her dial. As she whispered into the phone, her eyes kept darting up to study his face. Putting the receiver to her chest, she said, "Uh..., I know this is inconvenient, but, for security reasons, may I see your ID?"

"Certainly," Dr. Marstens said as he retrieved his wallet from his back pocket. He handed his ID to Nurse Jones.

She glanced at it and said into the phone, "Yes, it seems to check out, sir. Sure. It is a Florida driver's license. Yes, the picture is definitely him. OK, the name on the license is Dr. Thomas Marstens, 3582 West Palmetto Drive, Apt C, Boca Raton, Florida, 33431. Yes... OK."

She put the phone down and said, "Our Executive Director would like to speak with you in person."

"Certainly," Dr. Marstens said.

Nurse Jones picked the phone back up and said, "I'm sending him right down, sir."

*****

Ten minutes later, Dr. Marstens was directed into the administrator's office. He smiled as he looked around the room before sitting down into an overstuffed chair. It was just like his office back when he still had his practice. All the dark wood and the obligatory bookcase filled with aging leather-bound journals — it was so familiar and comfortable, like an old friend. He breathed in deeply and savored the smell of old medical books, a scent he knew so well. He turned his head to the door just as it opened. The director entered.

"Dr. Marstens, sorry to keep you waiting," the man said. "My name is Christopher Perry. I am the Executive Director of the hospital."

"Pleased to meet you, sir," Dr. Marstens said as he stood up.

"Please sit," Christopher said. "The nurse says you are an old family friend of Sylvia's?"

"Yes, we go way back."

"How nice…," Christopher said as he continued to study the man's face.

"Is there a problem?" Dr. Marstens said. "I really do want to see Sylvia before I have to go back to Florida."

"Well, you see, uh…, well….," Christopher stammered.

"Please, I need to know what is going on with Sylvia. I read about the tragedy in the paper."

"You get the Times in Florida?"

"Of course, I do. What else would I read?" Dr. Marstens said. "I was a life-long New Yorker before I retired to Boca. I still subscribe to the Times. I read all about her case in the paper. Tragic. Just tragic. For both her son and husband to go missing without a trace. I am sure it was a horrific blow." He paused and added, "you may not know this, but, I had Sylvia as a patient when she was just a child."

"What kind of medicine do you practice, Dr. Marstens?"

"I practice Psychiatry, or, I did until a few years ago when I re-tired," Dr. Marstens paused as his face dropped. He glanced down at his watch and said, "Look, I don't mean to be rude here, but, this seems like an awfully extravagant procedure to go through just to visit a patient. What is this really all about?"

"Well, there is no way to ask this politely."

"Ask impolitely, then," Dr. Marstens said as he smiled.

"I…, I thought you were dead? Your wife said you—"

"—You must mean my ex-wife."

"Ex-wife?"

"Yes, Gladys and I divorced a few years ago," Dr. Marstens said. "Frankly, I'm not terribly surprised she said I passed away. She told me it would have been easier if I had died." He smirked and added, "I know we spoke a lot about that before our divorce was finalized. I guess, in her mind, somehow she thinks I did."

"Oh, I am sorry," Christopher said.

"Yes, divorce is always difficult, especially after so many years together, but, I think Gladys is far happier," Dr. Marstens said. "Especially now that she has 'killed' me off, so to speak. In all honesty, once I retired, things went downhill." He paused and said, "we got along so much better when I was a workaholic and never home!"

Christopher laughed. "I know what you mean."

"It is a shame, too, but...," Dr. Marstens said, "it isn't that uncommon — particularly among members of my profession."

"Oh?"

"Yes," Dr. Marstens said. "The divorce rate among psychiatrists is double the national average."

"I didn't know that," Christopher said. "I would have thought differently."

"Oh no, not at all," Dr. Marstens said. "In fact, having a background in psychiatric therapy, and even conducting marriage seminars, is no guarantee of marital success. In fact, I think the reason the rate is so high is like that old proverb. You know, the one about how the village cobbler's children never have any shoes."

Christopher laughed.

"But..., I have to ask," Dr. Marstens said. "Why were you talking to my ex-wife?"

"It is a complicated story," Christopher said. "You see, I am very good friends with Sylvia and John."

"Is John her husband? Is he the one who is missing?" Dr. Marstens asked.

"Yes," Christopher said as he frowned. "I hope the police can find him. It has just been a horrible time for everyone. With so much time passing, however, I am beginning to lose hope."

"I am so sorry."

"Thanks..., but, did you know your name is on Sylvia's birth certificate?" Christopher asked. "It came up a few weeks ago when John was trying to figure out what happened to their son."

"Yes," Dr. Marstens said. "I was very close to Sylvia's father. In fact, we were best friends for many years. I..., I helped him out with Sylvia's adoption. It was a challenging case."

"Oh?"

"Yes," Dr. Marstens said. "We kept it very private."

"If you don't mind, can you tell me why?"

"Well..., I would prefer not to go into too many details," Dr. Marstens said. "But, I can share this. Sylvia was originally from Kentucky. Her situation there was pretty horrific. A terrible abuse case, alcoholic family, beatings, the whole gambit of horrors. I think you can get my drift."

"Yes. But, why didn't you call the police?"

"Times were different back then," Dr. Marstens said. "They are better now, I don't mind saying. Back then, the courts, and especially the courts down in Kentucky, were not particularly open to the idea of parents being abusers. It all worked out in the end, though. Vincent and Marie were wonderful parents to Sylvia. We all thought it best for her own welfare that she be shielded as much as possible from the terrible realities of her past."

"I see," Christopher said. "How did she recover from all of that trauma?"

"Oh, I worked with her for a long time," Dr. Marstens said. "And, I was hoping to help Sylvia again. What is her current condition?"

"It is beyond our capabilities to treat here, Dr. Marstens," Christopher said. "This is not a Psychiatric Hospital, but, I promised John, and…"

"No, I get it," Dr. Marstens said. "You have been a good and loyal friend to keep her here, but, you are right. This is no place for a psychiatric patient. What are her symptoms? Has anyone made a psychological diagnosis of her condition yet? No doubt, a shock like losing your son and husband at the same time can trigger psychosis — especially for someone who has a history of prior trauma."

"Yes," Christopher said. "She was brought in originally after her son went missing. Total collapse. Catatonic. When she finally started to come out of it, unfortunately, John went missing. After learning of his disappearance, she had a complete breakdown and since has shown acute psychosis."

"What does she do?"

"Well…, night and day, she just sits on her bed, rocking back and forth, staring at the wall. I will tell you, Dr. Marstens, the look on her face is unnerving, to say the least. It is almost as if she sees something we cannot. Something out there — beyond the walls of her room. Eerie."

"Does she say anything? Has she spoken?"

"She doesn't respond to questions. She is talking, though. But..., the thing is, she only says one thing, over and over."

"What?"

"It doesn't make much sense, Dr. Marstens," Christopher said.

"I wouldn't expect it to. The rantings of the mentally ill often do not, but sometimes, they can lead to certain insights. What does she say?"

"Well, she has her hands clutched very close to her chest, and she just keeps mumbling, 'Take..., Eat, Take..., Eat...,' all day and all night long. I know the staff up on Three have filed several complaints with me already. This is not something they are trained to address. She probably will have to be transferred to Bellevue soon. We just cannot manage a patient with her condition in this facility. I am trying to forestall this as long as possible. I..., I owe it to John."

Dr. Marstens' stomach dropped, and his eyes welled up. He cleared his throat and said, "You know, Sylvia is almost like a daughter to me. Gladys and I often remarked that, if we had a child, we would have wanted it to be Sylvia. Such a lovely girl. I must see her now. I know I can help her. I must help her! Not just for her late parents, but also for me."

Christopher nodded.

A few minutes later, Dr. Marstens stepped out of the elevator onto the third floor and walked down the hall, past the nursing station. The nurses waved him through. He reached room 314 and opened the door, bracing himself for what he might find. It was just as he was anticipating.

Sitting on the bed, her eyes glazed and wide open, her mouth drooling and her hands tightly clutched against her chest, was Sylvia. It had been many years since he had seen her, but, in many ways, right now, she looked exactly like that terrified girl from so many decades ago. She was rocking and mumbling and showed no reaction to a visitor coming into her room.

"Sylvia, this is Dr. Marstens speaking," he said. "Can you hear me?"

The doctor smiled as she turned slightly, and their eyes met. He did not detect a look of recognition, but, at least he had her attention.

He grinned when he saw a small spark kindle in her eyes and she stopped mumbling. He closed the door behind him, turned back to Sylvia and said, "Listen to me very carefully, Sylvia. I want you to clear your mind. I know you have been through a horrible shock, but, just like before, I will make it all better. Do you remember? Do you remember me helping you in my office when you were a little girl?"

Sylvia nodded and mumbled, "Take..., Eat...."

"Good! Now, all will be made well. Sylvia, you are going to have a new life along with a new name now. We are going to lock these fresh horrors away, just like we did before." He choked back a sob and added, "Best of all..., at last, you will be just like the daughter I always wanted."

Sylvia said nothing but continued to rock.

"Now, close your eyes, Sylvia. Close your eyes and remember. I want you to remember how we locked all the bad memories away — click..., click..., click..."

Chapter 35

May 1st, 2017 - 2:11 AM

SYLVIA'S EYES POPPED OPEN. She immediately re-shut them due to the blazing bluish-white glare blinding her. She paused for a few seconds before reopening them. Thankfully, the glare was gone, and everything now came into sharp focus. She gasped as she took in the view and blinked twice. *This has to be a dream. There is no way this is real.*

She was standing alone in a forest. It seemed to go on forever in all directions. Located on a gently sloping mountainside, the ancient trees around her reached upwards of fifty feet into the sky. Their enormous heavy branches created a natural cavern-like enclosure with their interlocking limbs. Instead of the bright green of spring filling her vision, all around her was covered in a blanket of pure white snow.

Sylvia looked down. She was wearing a long white, silken robe. It fit perfectly on her body. Loose and comfortable, she had never felt anything this luxurious on her skin. The garment was flawless. As she lifted her sleeve up to inspect it, she peered at the details in the fabric. Sunlight, breaking through the canopy overhead, danced over the silken threads and cast a rainbow of colors across her arm.

What is this place?

Sylvia glanced up at a patch of blue peeking through the treetops. The sky was a bright, brilliant cobalt blue. Large pink clouds floated by, changing colors as they traversed the heavens. She gasped once more. Nothing in her experience could have ever prepared her for such a vision of utter beauty and peace.

After inhaling deeply, she sighed. An unexpected warm breeze brushed across her nose. A smile crept onto her face as she recognized a familiar scent. She knew that smell. It was so familiar, and yet, so hard to place. She giggled as it came to her. It was the subtle perfume of freshly falling snow, the scent of the first blush of winter. It was the sweet bouquet of snow days home from school and hot chocolate, with extra soft marshmallows. It was the delicious aroma of getting wet and cold while making a snowman all afternoon before coming inside and warming by a blazing fire. It was snow! Snow!

She looked up again as enormous, soft white snowflakes, each the size of her hand, began floating gently to earth. Sylvia held her arms straight out at her side, turning her palms upward. Her skin tickled as the huge flakes burst onto her flesh. They were neither cold or wet, but warm and soft, like the feel of sand under her feet on a glorious June day at the beach.

She reflexively wiggled her toes and laughed as she glanced down. She was standing ankle deep in snow. *How is this possible?* She was not cold but warm. The warmth did not come from outside her body, but from somewhere deep inside her soul. It was a cozy, safe feeling of complete peace and acceptance. Joy, both indescribable and inexplicable, surged through her body and she burst into giddy laughter.

Everything was so strange and wondrous, and yet, at the same time, oddly familiar. Her mind flooded with images of a long-ago Christmas spent in Vermont. Other memories rushed in of a glorious summer she and her parents spent on the Jersey shore. These memories joined together with others in a swirl of nostalgic recollections. She felt the warm, wet sand oozing through her toes. She began to twirl, just like she did as a little girl. It was all so disorienting, but also, familiar and safe. She tried to make sense of the contradictory images pouring over her, but, could not. She knew one thing for certain, though. She never wanted to leave.

In mid-spin, she stopped. Off in the distance, she noticed a lone figure walking towards her through the feathery snowdrifts. She leaned forward to see better and laughed when a perfectly formed flake burst over her nose. It rang like melodious wind chimes when it dissolved on her skin. *Incredible!* She shook her head clear and refocused her attention. She wanted to meet this other person, to share this joy with someone else. Although entirely alone in a patch of strange woods, she had no fear. Her heart was bursting with nothing but love and affection.

When the newcomer was a few yards away, an electric jolt charged through her spine and she dropped to her knees. She knew that walk. She recognized that gait. She could not see or recognize the stranger's face yet, his form shrouded in a swirling mist of glowing snow, but something deep inside her sparked. She knew him. She did not know how, or from where, but, it didn't matter. She knew him. As the figure drew closer the mist dissipated. He was now clearly visible. It was a little boy, and...., she inhaled sharply. He was wearing a Spiderman costume.

"I brought you your ice cream, Mommy," the boy said as he lifted the Dove bar up to Sylvia. "I'm sorry it is so late."

"Billy! Oh! Billy! I..., I remember! I REMEMBER!"

"I'm sorry you had to wait so long," Billy said. "But..., all has been made right. You did it, Mommy! You got my messages in the mirror. You helped save Alyssa! I knew you would."

"Billy! Billy! But..., I..., I don't understand! I don't understand any of this!" Sylvia cried.

"I know," Billy said as he smiled. "It is not for you to understand."

"I must! I must understand, Billy!"

"You will understand everything in time," Billy said. He turned and pointed to his right. Sylvia followed his direction. He was pointing at something on the ground. It was a large iron strong-box, laying half buried in the snow.

A rusted chain encircled the box. Protruding up from the ivory drifts, Sylvia spied several locks cast off to the side. She glanced back at the strong-box and saw only one lock remaining. She turned back to Billy who held a key in his hand.

"It is time, Mommy," Billy said. "We are not meant to bury our pain forever. Pain must be redeemed. It must be used for its ultimate purpose."

"I'm afraid, Billy. I'm afraid of that box," she said. She reached out and caressed his face. Waves of affection and maternal love flowed over her. "I know I should be sad, but..., for some reason, I am not. I know you were taken from me, and..., JOHN! Oh! Oh!"

Billy said, "Daddy said it best I come here to meet you alone."

"John is here? I…, I remember! I remember everything, now!"

"Not everything, Mommy," Billy said. "You do not remember everything yet. There is still more pain to redeem."

"I want to weep, Billy, but, I cannot. I want to cry! I must! It is so…"

"There are no tears here, Mommy," Billy said, "they belong to another place. Here, they have been banished forever." He pointed behind him, into the woods, towards a bright blue glow pulsing at the end of a long, snowy path. "Wisdom comes from remembrance, Mommy. For it was written, *He shall wipe every tear from their eyes, and there will be no more death or sorrow or crying or pain. All these things are gone forever."*

"Who? Who will wipe away the tears?"

Billy smiled, and said, "Jesus will. Just as He promised He would."

"But…, but Billy, you were taken from me," Sylvia said. "You were…., you were so young — nearly a baby. My baby! My only baby boy!" Her eyes grew large as she added, "where was Jesus then? Who wiped my tears when my only baby was taken from me and murdered?"

Billy nodded and reached up to touch Sylvia's face. "Jesus was with you, Mommy. He shared every tear you shed. He sobbed right along with you on those countless dark nights. He was always there, standing right beside you."

"But why? Why? Why does God allow this?"

Billy smiled. "You cannot know. No mortal man can know. The mind of man is clouded when he is bound to the earth. His vision is obscured."

"Speak clearly, Billy," Sylvia said. "If God is just, there must be an answer! There must be! Why was my baby taken from me? Why were you killed? Why did you have to die?"

Billy nodded and said, "There is an answer, but your ears cannot hear. There is a plan, but your eyes cannot see. There is a design, but your mind cannot grasp it."

"I don't understand," Sylvia said. "I don't understand what you are saying. This was a senseless tragedy! You were killed! You…, my only son!"

"Oh?" Billy said. "And you think God doesn't understand that? Do you think the Lord of the universe doesn't share your pain? Do you imagine He does not understand the suffering of his people?"

"Can He?" Sylvia asked.

"God watched his only son die too," Billy said. "For, it was written, *For God so loved the world that he gave his only begotten son, that, whosoever shall believe in him shall not die, but have everlasting life.*"

"But Billy," Sylvia said. "Why did you have to die? Of all the billions of people in the world, why you?"

"My work on earth was done."

"I needed you with me, Billy! I miss you so much. Since you died, I..., I...," Sylvia cried.

"Mommy, you do not understand," Billy said. "I am not dead. I live, and, you shall too."

Sylvia shook her head and stared down at the ground.

Billy reached forward and brought her chin up to meet his gaze, bringing them eye to eye. "We are all created for eternity, Mommy. Our time in the fallen world is short, just the briefest flitter, like dandelion seeds dancing on a soft summer breeze. Puff, pfffft..., and we are gone, blown away by the wind. But, even then, it is not over. It is not the end. It is not even the beginning of the end. It is but the end of the beginning! When we pass, the truth is revealed. We who are saved do not perish. We continue — forever. And like those drifting dandelion seeds, when all is restored, at the end of time, we shall burst forth in glory in a beautiful, flawless bloom. But, until then, we wait here in paradise."

"Paradise? Are you happy here, Billy? I must know that you are happy."

"Mommy, listen. I suppose you cannot truly know. Eventually, you will. Once you have glanced into a blooming rose and seen the universe open wide. When you have gazed into the setting sun and heard whispers in the tide. When eternal bliss greets every day, and joy fills up your soul. When you have heard Angelic choirs sing out and know thy saintly role; only then when all death is gone, and love and joy reigns supreme, can your mind begin to understand eternal heavenly things."

"I…, I…, but there is so much pain. There is so much suffering in the world. How can we make sense of it? How can God allow it?"

Billy said, "Remember, Mommy. *For our light affliction, which is but for a moment, worketh for us a far more exceeding and eternal weight of glory.*" He grinned and added, "But…, I can see you are struggling to comprehend. It is not easy."

"I will try to understand, Billy," Sylvia said. "I will try."

"You will, Mommy. You will," Billy said. "One day, when you come back, you will join me, Daddy, Father Morales, and your baby brother. Then all will be revealed."

"My baby brother? What do you mean? I don't have a brother!"

Billy smiled and pointed to the box. He said, "You don't remember. He was taken before he was born. He too is here, as are the dear parents who raised you, Granma Marie and Grandpa Vincent."

"I…, I…, I…," Sylvia stuttered.

"There is so much more for you to remember. Our time grows short. You need to return. Your earthly work is not yet done."

"Return? No! I can't lose you again! I can't!"

"You must go back. It will only be for the briefest of moments. Just the blink of an eye from the standpoint of eternity," Billy said. "But before you go, there is something you must take care of first. There is one final lock you must remove. Our pain serves a purpose, Mommy. Our suffering is not in vain. God does not waste our grief. Our anguish will be transformed into our greatest joy. I know what I am saying to you cannot be fully understood, but, it is still true. Offer your pain to God." He held up the key and said, "And remove the final lock."

"Oh…, oh Billy, I…, I…," Sylvia said as she shook her head. He pressed the key into her hand.

"You have hidden from your pain for too long, Mommy. You must do it. You must remove the final lock."

Sylvia nodded and knelt onto the ground. She placed the key into the lock, turned it to the right and heard the tumbler release — click… click… click… The lock fell into the snow with a light thud, and the chain slipped off, disappearing into a fluffy white snowdrift.

"I love you so much, Mommy," Billy said as he rose and began to drift backward, into the bluish white tunnel of snow-covered trees. Behind him, a brilliant bright light radiated deep in the woods. "I love you more than you will ever know," he said. "But..., we will be together again. I promise! Goodbye, Mommy. Goodbye!"

"Billy! Billy! Don't go! Not yet, please not yet! I remember! I remember everything! You can't go! Not now!" Sylvia cried as she raced after him.

Billy just smiled, floating just above the ground out of her reach. He waved to her as he floated towards the light.

Sylvia followed and found it too difficult to keep up. As she trudged through the drifts, her momentum decreased as she slogged forward. The snow grew deeper, reaching up to her knee at first, and then her thigh before finally topping out at her waist. She soon was stuck fast and began to thrash wildly.

She glanced around for something she could use to free herself from the snowdrift — a branch, a log, anything. There was nothing. The trees were too high to reach. She did see something, though. Like a forest decked out for Christmas, tiny blue lights formed on the branches. They blinked and flashed brightly against the white backdrop of snow, growing in intensity as each second passed. As Sylvia continued to struggle, the flickering grew faster, and the blue brighter before eventually crashing over her in a blinding sapphire wave.

Chapter 36

May 1st, 2017 - Floriston California - 2:12 AM

"Pratt! Did the smelling salts work?" Officer Pete Hanson shouted.

"I'm not sure," Officer Joshua Pratt answered, "She started to come around, but then passed out again. I think it's OK. It looks like she just has gone back to sleep. There for a minute, though, I thought she was a goner. I couldn't find a pulse."

"What about now?"

"I took her vitals. They seem normal. Well…, as normal as can be expected in this situation."

"How do those rope burns on her wrists and ankles look?"

"I think she'll be all right. I can't be positive until she wakes up, though. It's possible she sustained some permanent nerve damage."

"I hope the other ambulance gets here soon," Pete said. "Notice anything else? It seems like that medical training class you took really has paid off."

"I don't see any excess swelling," Joshua said.

"How about that taser burn on her neck?" Pete asked.

"I bet that was a real kick in the head," Joshua said. "I don't think it will cause any lasting damage." He paused and looked back at Pete and said, "God knows what these bastards were planning to do to her."

"Who the hell knows? At least we got here in time," Pete said.

Joshua looked down at the woman and said, "Yeah, just barely, though. She's lucky. It could've all been much worse."

"True," Pete said. "Well…, the Floriston rescue squad is on its way. I called for another ambulance after they took that poor girl to the hospital. They just radioed and said they would be here in fifteen minutes. We'll have them take her to Tahoe Forest, too."

"I think the police and EMT resources of Floriston are going to be stretched mighty thin tonight," Joshua said. "I bet they haven't seen this much action in a decade."

"Yeah…," Pete said. "And I doubt they have enough space in their jail to handle thirty shrieking, naked, blood-spattered, devil worshipers. I am sure it's pure mayhem up there."

"Did you get a good look at that pregnant girl we sent off in the ambulance?" Joshua asked. "That poor girl. They hacked her up like a side of roast beef." He pointed down to the unconscious woman at his feet and added, "Jesus! I hate to think what they would have done to this lady here had we not come when we did."

"The girl will survive," Pete said. "I am confident. She seems tough. The EMT told me she was in shock. He did say she should make a full recovery, though. Well, as full as can be expected."

"Those bastards!"

"At least her baby is OK. Hopefully, she can be helped. You know, they can do wonders now with modern prosthetics. It's not like the old days."

"No…, but, I know it isn't professional to say this," Joshua said. "I wish I could have five minutes alone with the bastard that chopped that young woman's feet off! I swear to God, I would pummel his ass into the dirt. I would make damn sure he wouldn't even think about hurting any women in the future, I can tell you that! What kind of person does something like that?"

"Animals, no doubt — complete and deranged monsters," Pete said. "You are new to the force. Sadly, in time, you will become quite accustomed to monsters. Do me a favor, though. Keep that kind of talk just between us. I don't want the Captain hearing you say stuff like that."

"No…, but still…"

"Look, I get it," Pete said. "I feel the same way. But, we, as police officers, cannot allow our personal feelings to get in the way of our duty. Justice has to take its lawful course."

"Yeah, but just look at all of this!" Joshua said as he pointed out over the field. "This whole thing is crazy! What kind of justice system can handle nutjobs like this?"

Pete nodded. In silence, they stood and gazed out over the macabre scene, absorbing the full horror. The torches around the pentagram continued to burn. In the center of the flaming circle, the altar was still in place, saturated and dripping in a thorough coating of fresh gore and blood. Above it, a stark-white, bloodless pig dangled upside down from a makeshift cross. It was completely drained of life. The thick open slash in its throat almost appeared to move as the severed wound caught the light from the flickering flames below.

Out in the meadow, the scene was made even more surreal by the reflection of the continuous flash of blue police lights. The glare caught the sight of a few handcuffed, blood splattered stragglers, naked but for the police blankets wrapped around their shivering bodies, being pushed into the back of several squad cars. It had been a long and bizarre night for the tiny Floriston police department, every officer available pressed into service by the late-night emergency State Police request for backup. On the ground at Pete and Joshua's feet, pools of still warm hog blood covered everything, and, in the cold mountain night air, a light trail of steam rose from several red, shimmering puddles.

"I tell you, Pete, this is just about the most fucked up thing I have ever seen," Joshua said. "I mean, have you ever seen anything crazier than this?"

"Nope..., never," Pete answered. "Not in all my years. Not even from my time in Afghanistan and Iraq, and trust me, I saw my share of twisted shit there. This is definitely one for the archives." He pointed above them to the unholy and blasphemous mockery of the crucifix and said, "and holy crap, just look what they did to that pig!"

"Yes," Joshua said as he shook his head. "I wouldn't even know how to begin to describe it. I don't envy you filling out the report on all this!"

Pete sighed and said, "yeah, I have no idea how I am going to even begin writing the AAR. I mean, if we didn't have the pictures you took, I am sure the captain would say I was lying — or drunk. But this? No way. He would think I was making it up. It is beyond belief! Who would do such things?"

"Assholes," Joshua said. "Sick, perverted assholes. But, I guess this does finally explain all those complaints we have been getting from the farmers about their missing livestock. It turns out, old Sister Margaret was right again — as usual."

"Good thing she was, too," Pete said. "I would have gotten my ass in a real sling if I had staked this out, without permission, and it had turned out to be nothing."

"Well..., what could you do? 'Ours is not to question why'"

"'Ours is but to do or die', right?" Pete said. "Yeah..., see..., I remember. Those years at St. Sebastian High School were not wasted on me."

"Well, Sister Margaret beat those lessons into us both," Joshua said. "As you remember, if she tells you to do something, you DO it!"

"And you don't ask questions," Pete said. "It's funny, I graduated twenty years ago, but, she still commands my instant compliance."

"I bet if she hadn't become a Nun, she would have been a very good drill sergeant."

"She was much scarier than my actual drill sergeant," Pete said as he laughed. "And I was in the marines, if you remember!"

"Yeah," Joshua said as he smirked. "I think you have mentioned that..., a few bazillion times."

"Shut up, asshole," Pete said with a grin. "But..., those were the good old days back at St. Sebastian High, weren't they?"

"They sure were," Joshua said. "It was good seeing Sister Margaret again on Friday, even though it was under such sad circumstances. I will really miss Father Morales. He was a good man."

"He certainly was," Pete said. "I can only imagine what he would say about all of this!" he added as he pointed out over the scene.

"Did Sister Margaret explain how she knew something was going on up here?"

"No," Pete said. "And, of course, I didn't ask."

Joshua laughed. "You were a good student."

"Actually, I was a bad student," Pete said. "But, I remember her yardstick," he added with a chuckle.

They both looked down when they heard a small moan coming from near their feet. Joshua pointed at the woman on the ground, naked underneath the sizeable gray blanket they had placed over her body. Her face was covered in blood. She coughed loudly.

"That's a good sign," Joshua said. "She's coming out of it now. I will say this again. She got really lucky tonight. Really, really lucky. I bet if we had been five minutes later we might have had a 187 on our hands."

"Easily," Pete said as he leaned down over the woman and spoke. His tone was low and friendly, and he said his words slowly and deliberately. "Are you OK, Ma'am? Can you hear me? If you are unable to speak, please raise your right arm."

Sylvia opened her eyes. The blue flashing lights temporarily caused her to wince and close them again.

"Ma'am, can you feel your fingers and toes?"

"Who…, who are you?" she said as she re-opened her eyes.

"She can speak," Joshua said. "That's good."

"I need you to try and move your fingers and toes for me, Ma'am," Pete said. "You were tied up pretty tightly. You also had a severe electrical shock from a taser. We need to check your extremities for nerve damage."

Sylvia nodded and complied. She was relieved when everything seemed to move properly. When she tried to speak again she found she couldn't. Only a grunt emerged from her mouth. Her tongue was thick, and her throat was dry as sand. It hurt to swallow.

Her mental fog began to lift, and pain began searing through her body. She felt hot bile in the back of her throat and started to feel sick. She sat up. She blushed when she realized she was naked, covered only by a police blanket. She wrapped the coarse woolen covering tightly around her shoulders.

She rubbed her wrists and ankles as her fingers explored the deep cuts in her flesh from the ropes. The wounds were raw and burned as if on fire. The only pain worse was the one in her skull. Her head was pounding. She opened her eyes fully to allow them to adjust to the semi-darkness. The flashing blue lights continued to cause her to squint and her head to throb.

"That's great, Ma'am," Pete said. "I think you are going to be all right! You were very lucky. I've seen injuries like yours cause permanent damage. Now, just sit back and relax. The ambulance should be here any minute."

She opened her eyes wide and cried, "I remember! I remember!"

"What Ma'am?" Joshua said. "What do you remember?"

"Do you think she is having a stroke?" Pete whispered. "She did take quite a jolt from that taser."

"I'm not having a stroke, officer," Sylvia said. "I am telling you, I remember. I remember... everything!" Her hand flew up to her mouth as she gasped. "EVERYTHING! Oh, God! Billy!"

"Who's Billy?"

"My son."

"Was he here? We will find him, I—"

"—No..., he...., he died. A long, long time ago."

"I'm sorry," Pete said.

Sylvia smiled and added, "But, I know where he is. I will see him again one day, and he is happy."

Pete smiled back and said, "Yes! *'No eye has seen, nor ear has heard, nor mind has conceived what God has prepared for those who love him'.*"

"But..., I do remember," Sylvia said. "I remember everything! *Everything!*"

Pete said, "I..., I didn't want to subject you to any questions before your recovery, but, we will need to get a statement from you soon. If you are up to it, please tell us what you know about what went on here."

Sylvia dropped her head into her hands and sobbed. "I... I should have called the police. I knew I should have called the police before Heather and I came...," She stopped herself and cried, "Heather! She... Oh my God!"

"Are you referring to a Heather Stringer, aged 24, from Mountain View, California?" Pete said as he looked down at his notepad.

"Yes..., she..., she attacked me! She..."

"We know. We retrieved the taser and have her in custody, Ma'am," Pete said. "Along with quite a few others."

"Alyssa! Oh, dear God, did they—"

"—Is that the girl who was maimed?" Joshua whispered.

"I assume, so," Pete whispered back.

"Is she all right? Her baby! They didn't get her baby, did they?"

"No, Ma'am," Pete said. "The EMT said her unborn baby will be fine and she should make a full recovery. We got here just in time."

"How did you know Alyssa?" Joshua asked.

"Father Morales was right," Sylvia said as she stared out into the field. "He was right about everything!"

"Father Morales?" Joshua said. "You knew Father Morales? How do you...hey, wait a minute," he said as he paused and studied her face. "You were at his funeral service on Friday, right? I recognize you now, once I knew the context."

"I was there," Sylvia said. "And so was Heather."

"That's right, I remember her too," Joshua said as he wrote something down in his notebook. "This is very interesting. I don't know where this case is headed, but, it certainly is an interesting development."

"You were at Father Morales' funeral, too?" Sylvia asked.

"Yes, we both were," Pete said as he pointed to Joshua. "We were both very close to Father Morales. We were students of his back in High School, and we both still attend St. Sebastian Catholic church. Father Morales was a fine teacher, a wonderful priest, and an overall great man. I will really miss him. But, how did you know him? Better yet, how did Heather? There has to be a connection."

"It's a long story..., but, Heather was only there because of me," Sylvia said. "In fact, I wouldn't have even known Father Morales had passed away had his assistant not asked me to come to the funeral. You know, Father Morales was going to have lunch with me the day he had his heart attack. I learned from papers his assistant gave me that he wanted to warn me about all of this," Sylvia added as she pointed over to the bloody altar. "Father Morales was so worried about Alyssa. I know he was planning on coming here himself today to help her. He was absolutely convinced she was in danger, and, by God, he was right!"

"He was right," Pete said. "As he was about most things."

"I knew I made a mistake. I swear I was going to call the police, but, Heather said they wouldn't believe me."

"Obviously, she had planned on bringing you up here and didn't want any police involved. For what purpose, or how all of this relates, I cannot say…, yet. But, I will figure it out. I will," Joshua said. "In a way, Heather was right about one thing. If you had called the police, we probably wouldn't have believed you."

"So, who called you then? What made you believe them?" Sylvia said.

Pete and Joshua looked at each other and smiled. Simultaneously they said, "Sister Margaret."

"Sister Margaret called you?" Sylvia said. "SHE is the one who gave me Father Morales' notes about all of this. She was the assistant I was talking about and is the whole reason I came up here!"

"Well, that explains how Sister Margaret knew about this," Pete said. "My God, that woman still has eyes in the back of her head — twenty years later."

"Just like the old days," Joshua said.

"This isn't too much for you, is it, Ma'am?" Pete said. "I hadn't intended on questioning you until after you were checked out by the hospital."

"No, I'm feeling a bit better," Sylvia said. "But…, I could use a cup of coffee." She shivered as she wrapped the blanket tighter around her body. "And…, my clothes."

"Sorry, I can't help you with the clothes, Ma'am," Pete said. "We found some in the field, but, they were shredded. I am sure we can get you something to wear at the hospital. Now, about the coffee," he added as he turned to Joshua. "That we can do something about."

"Going to get it right now, Boss," Joshua said.

"We always carry a thermos," Pete said as he turned to Sylvia and winked. "And we have donuts, too. You know, we have a stereotype to maintain."

Sylvia smiled and shivered again.

"It is a bit chilly tonight," Joshua said as he returned with the thermos and a Styrofoam cup of steaming hot coffee. He handed it to Sylvia and said, "this should warm you up."

"Thank you," she said before taking a long sip. The warm coffee rushing down her throat helped. Her shivers subsided, and she said, "I really want to help as best I can. I owe it to Father Morales."

"Ma'am, I feel sure you can. Now, I know we have a thousand questions to ask, so if it is too much, just let me know."

"OK."

"Good," Pete said. "But first things first, can I have your name?"

"My name is Sylvia Mars—," she paused. "My name is Sylvia Delaney!"

"OK, got that," Pete said as he wrote down the information. "Now, we have a Darryl Summers in custody, along with his mother, Melody Summers. What can you tell us about them? They seem to be the central figures here."

"I don't know much, but, I do know Darryl was the boyfriend of Alyssa. I can't explain what this is all about, though, but...," she stopped cold. After clearing her throat, she said, "they aren't the ones orchestrating all this. It was the high priest. Did you get Father Ted?"

"Who?" Joshua asked.

"Father Ted, the high priest," Sylvia said. "Surely you captured him. He is the ringleader."

"I..., I don't know," Pete said. "I thought we had everyone we arrested identified, but..., I don't have a Father Ted in my notes. Is it possible he goes by another name?"

"It's possible, I guess," Sylvia said. "If you saw him, he would be hard to miss."

"What does he look like?"

"He is tall, probably around 6 foot 3, and maybe 185 lbs. He is quite handsome, dark longish hair, very striking — almost like a young Elvis. I am sure you would remember him. He is pretty hard to forget."

"How old is he?"

"That is an amazingly good question," Sylvia said as her eyes grew wide. "I don't know how it is possible, but, he looks to be maybe 30? Not much older than that."

"What do you mean by 'that is an amazingly good question'?" Pete said.

"He can't possibly still be 30...," Sylvia muttered. "That was forty years ago! It just can't be possible?"

Joshua looked at Pete and shrugged. Pete returned the shrug, and turned to Sylvia and said, "are you sure you are OK, Ma'am? I got your description. It is very distinctive. I am certain we didn't arrest anyone who matches that description."

"Oh, you have to be kidding," Sylvia cried. "He must have gotten away. But how? He was leading the ceremony. You must have come after it was over."

"No, we saw the ceremony, Ma'am. There was no Father Ted, or whatever his name is, here. I think you might be confused."

"I think not," Sylvia said as her face fell. "He must have escaped."

"That would have been hard to do," Joshua said. "We called the Floriston PD once we saw what was happening and had the whole place surrounded. I can assure you. No one got off this mountain. No one!"

Sylvia shivered. "No. He slipped away somehow. He is still out there!"

"If anyone got away, Ma'am, we'll get them," Pete said. "This sort of crime will not go unpunished."

"I wish I had your faith, Officer," Sylvia said. "It seems to me like evil always wins in the end."

"Oh, you can't believe that," Pete said.

"Trust me, I do," Sylvia said. "Evil reigns. My son, my husband and my brother were all taken from me and savagely murdered. Now that my mind is clear, and I can remember everything, it appears my entire life has been hostage to evil. There may be a God, I see that now, but it sure seems like Satan is running the show down here. How do we make sense of all of this? How can a good God allow such evil and suffering? How can we live with the horrors of our past?"

"It is hard, Ma'am. I know it is hard," Pete said. "I saw many things on my tours in Iraq and Afghanistan I never want to see, or think about, again. Some things seen that can never be unseen. It is a struggle, but, I am a Christian and I trust God. We cannot begin to comprehend the providence of God or try and understand his grand design. We only need to trust him. There is an answer, but our ears cannot hear. There is a plan, but our eyes cannot see. There is a design, but our mind cannot grasp it."

Sylvia's eyes widened, and she said, "What did you say?"

"All things happen for purposes we can never truly know. But this does not mean we suffer in vain. Our troubles are not forgotten by God, he shares in our grief."

"It all seems so senseless. There cannot be a reason for such evil. Maybe God doesn't care what happens to us?"

"We may not know the reason," Pete said. "But we do know the reason isn't because God doesn't care. He sent his only son to die for all of us, after all. An uncaring God would not do that."

"But how will this be made right? How could it ever be made right?"

"I know when I get to Heaven," Pete said. "I will learn more in the first five seconds than I would in a thousand lifetimes on earth. After all, once you have glanced into a blooming rose and seen the universe open wide. When you have gazed into the setting sun and heard whispers in the tide. When eternal bliss greets every day, and joy fills up your soul. When you have heard Angelic choirs sing out and know thy saintly role; only then when all death is gone, and love and joy reigns supreme, can your mind begin to understand eternal heavenly things."

Sylvia stood up and cried, "WHAT? Where did you hear that? Who told that to you? I must know where you heard—"

Pete smiled and said, "—Back in High School, Father Morales told me an interesting story when I had the same questions you are asking now. I too was troubled by the overwhelming amount of evil in the world. Trust me, being a combat marine, and then a cop, has not given me any rose-colored glasses about the ways of the world since."

"I would guess not," Sylvia said.

"It's pretty messed up. But, Father Morales said we cannot ever know how everything fits together. Only the all-knowing God sees the whole picture. Have you ever heard the Chinese parable 'We'll See'?"

"No, I haven't," Sylvia said.

"It's good, you'll like it," Pete said. "Once upon a time, there was an old farmer who had worked his crops for many years. One day his horse ran away. Upon hearing the news, his neighbors came to visit. 'Such bad luck,' they said sympathetically, 'you must be so sad. '"

"'We'll see,' the farmer replied."

"The next morning the horse returned, bringing with it two other wild horses. 'How wonderful,' the neighbors exclaimed! 'Not only did your horse return, but you received two more. What great fortune you have!'"

"'We'll see,' answered the farmer."

"The following day, his son tried to ride one of the untamed horses, was thrown, and broke his leg. The neighbors again came to offer their sympathy on his misfortune. 'Now your son cannot help you with your farming,' they said. 'What terrible luck you have!'"

"'We'll see,' replied the old farmer."

"The following week, military officials came to the village to conscript young men into the army. Seeing that the son's leg was broken, they passed him by. The neighbors congratulated the farmer on how well things had turned out. 'Such great news. You must be so happy!'"

"The man smiled to himself and said once again. 'We'll see,'"

Pete paused and said, "We cannot always see the ending of the story from our perspective. But God, who sees all, and knows how everything that exists in the universe affects everything else, does. To presume we can even begin to fathom this infinite complexity is above our paygrade."

"But what about Satan?" Sylvia said. "It sure seems like he is triumphant over the world."

"Satan has already been defeated," Pete said. "The first strike against the nail in the palm of Christ's hand, on Good Friday, sealed Satan's doom forever. He is finished. And in the spirit of eternal spite that infects his diabolical being, Satan tries to hurt God the only way he can, by tormenting those whom God loves — us. It is for naught. Every evil inflicted on us on earth will be redeemed a thousand-fold, in glorious joy, in Heaven."

"But what can we do about it here? How can we fight back against Satan on this side of eternity?"

"Ah, that is the question, isn't it?" Pete said. "Here, Sister Margaret was most instructive. An exceptional woman, she certainly takes no guff from anyone. Not from a bunch of rowdy, misbehaving, hormonally-charged boys, like I was, and certainly not from some defeated, pitiful Devil."

Pete unbuttoned his top shirt button and pulled out a small silver medallion hanging from a chain. "Sister Margaret gave this to me when I graduated from the Police Academy. She made me promise to always wear it and pray the prayer daily."

Joshua, standing nearby, pulled out a similar medallion and said, "She gave me one too."

"What is it?" Sylvia asked.

"It's a Saint Michael's Medallion. He is the patron saint of police officers."

"What is the prayer?"

Saint Michael the Archangel, defend us in battle, be our protection against the wickedness and snares of the devil; may God rebuke him, we humbly pray; and do thou, O Prince of the heavenly host, by the power of God, cast into hell Satan and all the evil spirits who prowl through the world seeking the ruin of souls.

"So, you see," Pete said. "Satan may cause all sorts of troubles in this world, but his days are numbered. Soon, he will be sent into Hell where he belongs, along with the rest of the evil spirits who prowl the world seeking the ruin of souls."

Sylvia was quiet. She finished her coffee and looked down.

Pete opened his thermos and refilled her cup. He said, "Why don't you come with me to St. Sebastian's for Mass this coming Sunday? After the service, you can join my wife and me for breakfast at Millie's Diner. It'll be great, and we'd love to have you. What do you say?"

"Will you be having donuts for breakfast?"

"Of course!" Pete said with a laugh.

"Thank you. I think I would like that," Sylvia said. "I think I would like that very much."

Chapter 37

IN 1956 AMERICA WAS AT war, albeit, a cold one. Communism was on the march in Europe, the Warsaw Pact had just been established, and the fledgling Hungarian Revolution had recently been crushed by Khrushchev. In those fevered days, with the Red Bear on the loose, President Dwight D. Eisenhower, the savior of Western Europe, the author of the miraculous D-Day landings, and overall national hero of the country, proposed to build a true Interstate Highway System to enhance the defense of a nuclear-war frightened nation. It was built, and a big part of that system was Interstate Highway I-80.

Covering nearly 3,000 miles, and spanning the entire country, I-80 is a true modern marvel. Starting on the Pacific coast in San Francisco, it winds its way east, over soaring mountains and across scorching deserts, before coming to its final destination in Teaneck New Jersey.

For much of its continent-wide trek, there isn't much to see, and there sure is a lot of it. Countless indistinct towns rush by the endless repetitive landscape. A never-ending parade of artery-clogging fast food restaurants, along with a cavalcade of motels, hotels, and no-tells for every conceivable desire and budget lay just off every exit ramp. A giant slog traversed by an army of long-range truckers, from sea to shining sea.

Fifty miles east of Floriston, California, just outside the town of Fernley Nevada, I-80 crosses into a patch of pure desolation — the Great Basin Desert. For one hundred miles, it is a drive of absolute, nothingness. Just miles and miles of brown desert with no sign of human life to be found — a total and complete blank on the map. No doubt, if the moon had a highway on it, it would look like this.

Driving into this void is for the adventurous only. In the summer, it's a nightmarish hellscape in the day, where temperatures easily top 115. At night, it may be cooler, but, those headlights better be working. It is dark with the kind of darkness rarely seen elsewhere in the country. The complete black that only can come from the lack of any artificial light. There can, of course, be beauty in the desolation, a serene sense of awe emanating from the void. On some nights, if the clouds are light, the glories of the milky way can be seen in the big open sky. On others, when the moon is full, the highway itself can be breathtaking. The lunar rays dance over the specks of reflective material in the asphalt, looking like a great shimmering river of silver flowing through an ebony slash of nothing. But tonight, there was none of that. There was a new moon. Tonight, it was just miles and miles of utter gloom.

There are no other vehicles on the road. Not surprising, actually, as even road-hardened truckers avoid driving this stretch of I-80 on a moonless night. No, there is only one car on the road this early morning, a 2015 jet black BMW convertible, heading east, with a sole occupant. The driver is a handsome man, as attractive as his car. As he passes mile marker 77, and the last 'Check your gauges' billboard fades into the distance behind him, and nothing but inky darkness stretches out in front of him, he smiles. On a beautiful chilly spring night like this, he is driving with the top down. His longish black hair whips backward in the fury of the wind. It is silent inside the BMW, a deathly quiet except for the lion's roar of air from the drive.

He reaches over to the dashboard, all glowing green from the lights on the display panel and turns on his MP3 player. Over the howling wind, the first strums of the guitar riff rings out, followed by the soulful sound of the singer's voice.

"I..., am a man of constant sorrow. I've seen trouble..., all my days."

About the Author

Paul Creasy was born in Radford, Virginia, the only child of Victor (Gene) and Marla Creasy. He grew up in the small town of Bluefield, West Virginia before moving to Richmond, Virginia where he graduated from Virginia Commonwealth University.

He continues to reside in Richmond today, with his lovely wife Mary and their rambunctious puppy Truffle. Apart from writing, Paul enjoys old horror movies, obscure documentaries, new books, Christian apologetics, ballroom dancing with his wife, and traveling extensively.

Further information can be found at www.paulcreasy.com